Mother's Gold

Lacey Cook

Copy and line edits by J. J. Fischer

ISBN: 978-1-7638474-0-8

Author's notes:

Written under the pen name **Lacey Cook**, this captivating novel marks an exciting new chapter for a seasoned storyteller. Known for crafting unforgettable narratives, the author brings a fresh voice to **literary and historical fiction** weaving a tale of family, redemption, and the timeless search for something greater. After enchanting readers with supernatural stories, the author now ventures into a genre rich with history and profound human experiences, showcasing versatility and depth as a writer.

The author's book is set in Australia and primarily follows Australian conventions of grammar, punctuation, and spelling.

Edithburra and Willward are fictional Australian towns.

That's all drugs and alcohol do,
they cut off your emotions in the end.
Ringo Starr

Prologue

My mother told me stories, half-truths disguised by smiles that never quite reached her eyes. She claimed they found me in a cabbage patch. There was no love in that revelation, no understanding that seeds of abandonment could take root in the fertile soil of my young mind, their tangled vines slowly choking any fragile self-worth I possessed.

Then came the stars. Those twinkling points of light, she said, were loved ones who had died. My dad, she claimed, was now just another star in the vast expanse. So, I looked to the dark, starry sky and spoke to my dad. He did not speak back. Self-doubt and emotional withdrawal set in, creating a pattern that would take me years to undo.

What she should have told me was this: that life is a battle, waged on countless fronts where wounds are inevitable, and the wounded need tending; that scars linger as reminders, casualties are an unfortunate certainty; that hearts will be broken, and secrets will weigh heavily on the soul.

But I suppose if I had been told such things, I would've wanted to retreat to the safety of my mother's womb. Seeing as that was impossible, I followed her into the fray, where the battlefield of life awaited.

In this battle, my mother found solace in writing letters. Young and innocent as I was, I never thought to inquire about their recipients. It later became clear these letters were her way of dealing with the hardships of life.

The letters held a secret—a revelation that would only come to light at the end of her journey. The weight of this secret saddened me, for it spoke of burdens borne in silence for far too long.

And thus, my story begins with a letter.

November 1959
South Australia

My dearest Martha,

How I wish you were here. Grieving is so hard. Many kind words were spoken at Harold's funeral. It's so sad that we're so far apart. I miss you so much more now with Harold gone.

I cannot remember if I told you about the wee town we ended up in. After leaving the army, Harold got a job working on the railways. The town—really a village—has a history as a goldfield. It is in the middle of nowhere, and is hot, very hot. Not a lot of mining takes place anymore but there is still some prospecting.

The heat gets to you. You drink a lot. In some ways, I think the drink had a lot to do with Harold's death. I'm sure it did.

At Harold's funeral, one man kindly gave me a nugget of gold as a memorial gift. Its shape was heart like. He just came up to me and asked me to open my hand. I did so hesitantly, and he dropped the nugget onto my palm and told me it may not be worth a lot but would help if needed. I found this such a kind gesture and hold the nugget close to my heart when thinking of Harold.

The funeral was a small affair. I couldn't expect family and friends to travel to this far-off land. It took us long enough to get here; many, many weeks that seemed like years. I know my loved ones were all with me in thought.

The war and alcohol killed Harold. He had not been himself for many years. At times, I felt something else was bothering him, but I'll never know. It's something unknown that I'll take to my grave.

My heart longs to return home, but the children seem settled in this country. Although boredom is getting them into trouble. Quinn, my youngest, is good at keeping himself occupied, but his older siblings are ready to move on and escape the boredom.

We'll all be moving to a place in Victoria soon. The army has helped us find some temporary accommodation. I'm not sure how long we'll live there. It's only a short-term solution.

I'm feeling overwhelmed with thoughts of you and home.

I'm sorry this letter is only brief. I'll write again soon once we settle in Victoria.

All my love,
Elizabeth

Part 1 – The Young Boy

Victoria, Australia
1964 Autumn
Five years post funeral

1 The Pickup

The train groaned as it entered the station, the faint smell of metal and old leather hanging in the air. Mum sat forward, clutching the straps of her handbag on her lap. Her eyes darted outside the window, jumping from one thing to the next, searching for something—or someone. A sign passed by: WILLWARD.

"I think this is the stop, Quinn." She stood and waved me on. "Come, let's go." She looked behind me. "Don't forget your comic books."

That wouldn't have been good, leaving Archie and the Phantom abandoned on a train. The Phantom would've survived. Not so sure about Archie.

We stepped out of the train and onto a bitumen platform. The air was fresh and full of screeching cockatoos. I spotted the birds just behind a boundary fence, swarming around a large gum tree, arguing amongst themselves as they searched for seeds.

Mum smiled. "Our welcoming party."

I turned to see who was coming, but no one headed in our direction. People were moving in the opposite direction, towards a building further down the platform. A few more screeches echoed across the sky. Ah, Mum meant the birds. I grinned and shrugged, taking in the scene around me. The gum tree's leaves glistened from an earlier rainfall, and the breeze held a slight chill.

Mum gestured to a vacant seat on the platform, and we made our way over. With her gloved hand, she wiped the moisture from the seat before we sat down. The chill of the cold steel seeped through my pants, a sharp reminder of the warmth we'd left behind at the hotel in Melbourne—not really a home, but a warm place with radiator heating while we looked for a home.

"Give me your comics and I'll put them in the carry bag," Mum said.

I handed the comics to mum. She appeared jittery, unable to sit still. A few minutes later, a tall man headed towards us. He wore jeans and a checkered blue shirt you could play draughts on. As he neared us, he raised a cowboy-like hat in greeting.

"Mrs Davies?"

Mum sat up straight and then stood. "Yes, hello."

"I'm Tom Molloy, a neighbour of the Warhursts. They asked if I might pick you up since I was in town today."

His name, like his hat, was cowboy-like.

"That's nice of you," Mum said. "I'm Elizabeth and this is my youngest son, Quinn."

He paused, giving me a nod and a warm smile before turning back to Mum. "That's the way we country folk are—we help each other out. Nice to meet you both." With a wink in my direction, he added, "The Warhurst property is about thirty, maybe forty minutes away. A nice drive. You'll enjoy it. Should arrive in time for a late morning tea." He nodded towards the building I'd spied earlier. "We'll exit the platform down there, through the passenger terminal."

We stood and followed him in the direction he'd indicated. Passing through the terminal, we moved among people waiting for the next train. Above the ticket counter, a strip heater glowed, radiating warmth. A man stood beneath it, hands raised to soak in the heat. Some feel the cold more than others.

I tugged on Mum's dress and pointed to the restroom sign. She nodded. "We might just make our way to the restroom before our trip.

"Good idea," the cowboy said.

I pushed open a creaky door and hurried inside, grateful for a moment of relief.

Outside the terminal, the cowboy paused. "It's unusually cold today—more like a winter's day than autumn. But with any luck, the weather will fine up for your visit." He pointed to a blue car—well, half a car, at least. The roof was missing from the back half, with a black cover stretched across the gap. "That's my ute. We'll have to squeeze into the front seat, but we'll manage."

He looked at me. I must have had a puzzled look on my face, for he quickly added, "You'll see lots of utes in the country. Ute is short for utility. We use them to carry things like hay bales and rocks and children." He winked at me, then lifted the black cover. "You can sneak under here if you want but it might be a bit cold."

He was just teasing.

Mum shook her head and gestured towards the front of the vehicle.

As I slid onto the cold leather seat of the man's car, a wave of annoyance came over me. The people we were here to see couldn't find the time to come and meet us?

Mum and the cowboy sat on either side of me, providing some body heat. He gave us both a smile and looked at Mum. "Not too squashy, hey. If we were travelling a shorter distance, the boy could've sat in the back for a bit of fun."

That did sound like fun.

"Oh, I think he's best with us."

If Mum wasn't around, I surely would've been in the back.

As the cowboy drove, I watched the scenery pass and thought of my dog. I missed him already. I pictured the last time I saw him, tossing his head from side to side with a tennis ball in his mouth. That was only a few days ago, and I'd promised him I'd come back to visit him soon. I think he understood—his tail wagged in response. Doggie was with relatives while Mum and I stayed in a hotel in the city. Their house was too cramped for us to stay, and since dogs weren't allowed at the hotel, I'd sneak over to visit him whenever I could.

Mum and Tom, the cowboy, chatted as we continued the drive to the place we'd come to visit. I squished back into the seat to give them a better view of each other. Mum told him that I was the only child still with her, the others having either married or joined the armed services. Tom told us about the town of Edithburra. He said kookaburras were everywhere around Edithburra, and the name must be tied to them somehow. Mum and Tom smiled at each other. They seemed to be getting along well.

The thought of Mum marrying someone other than Dad suddenly popped into my head. Lately, there was a lot of stuff going on around me that I didn't understand. Everybody said that I just had to go with the flow and see where Mum took us next. We were nomads—a word I'd learned at school that stuck in my head. We were people who moved a lot. This man seemed okay. Apparently, he lived nearby, within walking distance of the house we were visiting.

Mum said, "The autumn colours are beautiful."

"They are," Tom said. "Need to thank the early settlers for all the European trees they planted."

"Yes, some people have a vision for the future."

"They do. They did." Tom gave me a smile. It seemed genuine.

Mum nodded as she continued looking out the window. Her shoulders seemed slumped.

"Lance mentioned you've applied for a housekeeping job at the property," Tom inquired.

"Lance…oh, yes, Mr Warhurst." Mum sounded nervous. "I need some work to support the boy. He lost his dad not too long ago, and we're trying to find our footing again."

Yep, there was a lot of stuff going on. A lot of confusing stuff.

"Sorry to hear about the boy's father."

Mum pursed her lips and nodded. "We're getting there…slowly."

I'd still look at the stars at night and speak to Dad. Mum told me I'll see him again at some point. I hadn't quite worked that one out. To be honest, I didn't think much about not having a dad. He was up in the sky watching me, so I tried to be a good boy. In a sense, it was nice having a dad in the sky. No actual person here to report to, just Mum, and she was a softy who let me go on long walks. I was an explorer—a ten-year-old Captain James Cook.

Thoughts sometimes crept into my head that maybe dad hadn't been a nice person and therefore wouldn't be in a good place. But I didn't want to think of him in that way. I only have fuzzy memories of him. Mum tells me he was a good man who made lovely toffee. My siblings don't talk about him—not that I see them much. They're all grown up with their own lives, cruising the ocean on big warships, policing the city streets, and being happily married with kids of their own.

"Well, I hope it all goes well for you," Tom was saying. "As I mentioned, I live not far from the Warhursts. If you end up getting the job, drop in for a cuppa. I see a bit of Mrs Warhurst, but mostly the old man keeps to himself."

Outside the car, the blue sky had turned to gloomy clouds. I sat up straighter when I spotted something barrel-shaped lying on the side of the road up ahead, surrounded by a few big black birds. I leaned forward for a better look as the birds scattered and flew off when we got closer.

"Just a dead wombat," Tom said. "Do a bit of damage to cars, those things. Don't see them as often as the roos. But you'll often spot ravens—the large black birds—feeding on animals hit by cars."

I turned to track the dead wombat through the rear window. It lay on its back, paws to the sky. The black birds had returned to their feast. My shoulders drooped. Was there a place for dead wombats in the sky?

Mum and Tom kept chatting. Bored, I counted dead animals. By the time the car slowed, and I thought we must be close to where we were going, I'd counted seven dead roos, two squashed possums, and one flattened, dead fox. Tom had identified the possums and the fox for me. There were no more dead wombats but lots of ravens.

"That's my house on the right there," Tom said. "The Warhurst property is just behind those big trees up ahead." He pointed to the deep-green, towering trees, maybe ten of them. Arrow-shaped, they were thick at the bottom but narrowed as they shot to the sky.

"They look like rockets," I said.

Tom laughed. "I suppose they do. They're pine trees. Planted by pioneers maybe fifty or more years ago."

I took a peek at Tom's house. It seemed stranded in the middle of nowhere, sitting alone in a grassy field. Trees surrounded it, but it still looked lonely. I've never seen a house so alone before. I wondered if the trees watched over it, keeping it company. It was nothing like the suburbs, where houses crowded together with barely a tree in sight.

We passed Tom's property, slowed down even more, and turned into a dirt driveway where a huge sign hung between two large posts: WARHURST FARM. Mum had drilled the name Warhurst into me. "*Remember Quinn, it's Mr and Mrs Warhurst.*" I had lost count of the number of times she'd told me this.

"Our driveway entrances are pretty far apart, but the houses are close," Tom said. "The Warhursts have a lot more farming land that I do."

"What sort of farm is it?" I asked.

"Kind of a hobby farm at this stage," Tom said. "But they've got bigger goals."

The only hobby I could think of was saving stamps. And goals were what people scored in football. I might enjoy this place after all.

2 The Welcome

We passed the big rocket trees. No house appeared, just more big trees. As the car continued, I caught a glimpse of steel between a gap in the trees. A huge shed. We rounded another large tree, and the house came into view. A boy stood on the grass at the front of the house. He looked at us, turned towards the house, and gestured for others to come out. They did. Now there was a line of people standing in front of the house. My stomach churned.

"Well, here we are," Tom said, pointing to the right. "My house is just over the paddock there. The driveways almost meet, but there's still plenty of space."

Mum made her little throat-clearing noise. "Thank you, Tom, for a most enjoyable trip." She turned towards me.

I got the hint. "Yes…thanks, Tom…I enjoyed the animals." I didn't remember his last name, and the animal comment was dumb. But I was nervous.

Tom opened his door; Mum opened hers. They stepped out of the vehicle. Although I felt secure in the cabin, I knew I had to leave. I slid along the seat and climbed out after Mum. If she could be brave, so could I.

Tom walked around to the front of his ute. "Here's your guests, Lance, delivered safe and sound."

A tall, lanky man, who must've been Lance, gave a small smile and nod. The woman next to him spoke. "Thank you, Tom. Much appreciated. Hope you accomplished what you needed to do."

"I did, thank you, Evie." He turned to my mum with a warm smile. "And nice to meet you, Lizzie. Oops, sorry—, Elizabeth. We country folk shorten everyone's name. And by the way, I love your Scottish accent."

Mum smiled, nodded, and spoke in a soft voice. "Migrated here in the early 1950s. Quinn's the only Australian-born."

Did he call my mum a lizard? I tapped my head. Surely not. Lizzie must be short for Elizabeth. I'd never heard Mum called that before. Funny how people say Mum has an accent—she sounds normal to me. But these country folk talk funny.

One of the welcoming party, a girl about my age, looked at me strangely. My head tapping must've caught her attention. But then her expression softened into a friendly grin.

"Well, they're all yours." Tom gave Mum a reassuring nod and flashed me a thumbs up, then stepped back into his ute.

He wasn't staying? Somehow, I'd gotten used to him, and he felt more familiar than these new people.

Mum nudged me towards the welcoming party. "Come on, love, let's go meet our new friends." The words sounded fake.

I followed Mum towards the line of people. Lance, the tall man, had a drooping moustache that reminded me of a cowboy. He must be Mr Warhurst. His hat was tilted just enough to make me nervous—in movies, bad guys always wore hats like that, hiding their scary eyes. Next to him stood Mrs

Warhurst, a small woman with short, curly brown hair. Her light-blue polka dot dress ended just above her knees. They both looked sad and thin.

I took a quick look at Mum. She wore a similar dress, though hers was a darker blue. She was about the same size as Mrs Warhurst but had more meat on her body. Mum's hair seemed thicker too, though it was cut short like Mrs Warhurst and had the same brownish colour.

Three children hung off Mrs Warhurst—two boys and the girl who had given me the strange look. They all seemed about my age. My eyes stayed too long on the girl. Her hair was shiny, and she gave me a little smile. I felt a tug in my chest.

"Welcome, Mrs Davies," Mr Warhurst said. "And you also, little boy."

I frowned. My footy mates didn't think I was 'little'. I edged closer to my mother.

Mum responded, "Thank you, Mr and Mrs Warhurst. Nice to be here." Her words sounded flaky.

Mum's hand rested on my shoulder. "This is Quinn," she said, nudging me forward. I gave a small nod to the group as a knot tightened in my stomach. Mum had taught me to call adults 'Mr' or 'Mrs' until they gave me permission to use their first name. I was too nervous to say anything at all.

My eyes wandered over the Warhurst family. The girl smiled at me again, but the other children didn't seem to care. Mrs Warhurst's wrinkly face crinkled into a smile as she looked down at me. "Hello, Quinn," she said. "Welcome to our little farm." Then she turned towards her husband and gave him a funny sort of smile. He smiled back, but it looked like a pretend smile to me.

Mrs Warhurst continued, "And these are our children: Jamie is twelve, Katrina is ten, and Steven is eight." She looked at me. "And how old are you?"

"Tt-ten," I stuttered.

"That's nice. Same age as Katrina. You are a tall boy for your age."

I gave her my best smile for telling me I was tall but I avoided Katrina's eyes. Eye contact wasn't my thing. I snuck a look to the left of the group and saw some funny animals, their heads showing above and below timber fence rails. They looked like sheep, but I knew they weren't.

"They're called Angora goats."

"Huh?"

Katrina had moved closer. "Those animals you were looking at. They're called Angora goats."

I took another peek at them. "I…they look a bit like sheep."

"They do a bit. Dad shears them. The wool is called mohair."

This girl's clever and I'm confused. Wool came from goats too? I had suddenly become self-conscious of my own sheared head. Mum liked me having crew cuts.

"You want to go look at them?"

"Later, Katrina," Mrs Warhurst interrupted. "Let's go inside." She shifted her shoulders and headed towards the house. "It's getting chilly." The family followed.

I looked up at Mum. Her eyebrows were furrowed with lines running along her forehead that I hadn't noticed before. She squeezed my shoulder and nodded, signalling that I should follow them. I hitched up my jeans and obeyed. Katrina smiled at me again, but it was different from my mum's smile. It made me feel all funny inside. It was hard to explain, but her smile made me feel kinda special. At the same time, it also made me feel scared—not bad scary, but rollercoaster scary.

We entered the house. A short passageway opened up into a large room. A warm, buttery smell, like something baking, filled the air. The other children hurried towards a black thing in the corner of the room, with a big black pipe running up to the ceiling. It looked like a fat man's belly balanced on skinny legs. They gathered around the belly-like thing, then turned towards us.

The old man, Mr Warhurst, spoke. "You kids are weak. It's not cold."

I wasn't sure if he was being funny. He looked older than his wife, with a craggy, wrinkled face and rough hands. But I figured I had best keep such thoughts to myself.

"It is, Dad," the youngest one said, rubbing his hands together.

"They like the potbelly," Mrs Warhurst told my mum.

Mum gave a gentle smile and a slight nod, like she didn't want to give her uncertainty away. She stood there, statue like.

"Move closer," Mrs Warhurst suggested.

Mum hesitated. But, encouraged by Mrs Warhurst, she moved a few steps closer to the potbelly. I shuffled along with her, then looked up at her face.

"That has a nice, cozy feel about it." Mum relaxed a bit.

"It does," Mrs Warhurst agreed.

I was looking at Mr Warhurst, trying to figure out if he was a nice person or not, when Katrina waved me over. I hesitated, then felt a nudge from my mum's hand. Katrina pushed her younger brother aside to make room for me.

The older brother moved towards a basket full of timber and grabbed what looked like an iron stick. I tensed, thinking he was going to poke me, but instead he opened a door on the potbelly. I stared at the flames flickering in front of me. They were bright red and moved like they were dancing. He poked the stick into the fire, stirred up the flames, and then grabbed more wood and threw it in.

The boy was only two years older than me yet seemed so much older than that. I felt like I was from another planet and had just arrived in a more grown-up world.

3 The Nugget

The coziness of the house had slowed the thumping in my chest. I let my eyes explore the room. The wall behind the potbelly was made of bricks. I longed to touch the bricks, which would probably be earthly warm. Further to the right, against a white wall and near a window, stood a glass cabinet.

"We collect stones." Katrina had followed my gaze. "Come have a look."

She tucked her arm in mine and pulled me towards the cabinet. A fuzzy feeling ran through my body. I looked back towards Mum. What was I meant to do? She just smiled and raised her eyebrows.

"Our Katrina's a friendly one," Mrs Warhurst said, looking at her daughter. "Now, don't scare Quinn away, Kitty."

Kitty? Funny name. She wasn't scary at all—too pretty for that. I looked at the rocks. One shiny rock that looked like a chewed-up piece of gum caught my attention.

"Is that gold?"

"Yep, a gold nugget." Mr Warhurst wandered over to stand beside us. "Found it out here in the bush."

"Must be worth a bit of money." I had heard stories of the gold rush days. "Aren't you meant to melt it down or something?" I looked up at Mr Warhurst.

"Yes, can do but I don't want to. Has character, don't you think?"

This man spooked me. His eyes were like black marbles. I was almost too scared to reply.

Katrina jumped in. "Dad means he wants it to stay the way it is. Keep it in its natural form."

How does a piece of rock have character? "What are the other rocks?" I squeezed out.

"Rocks and minerals, to be correct," said Mr Warhurst. "I'll leave that to Katrina to explain. I've taught her many things about rocks and minerals."

My confidence took another hit. The old man left the room, which immediately felt lighter. I couldn't imagine this man referring to his daughter as 'Kitty'. Though, it was a cute name.

Mum continued speaking with Mrs Warhurst.

"Excuse my dad's rudeness," Katrina said in a soft voice. "His rocks are his world. He can stand here looking at them for hours."

The man has rocks in his head. The thought made me feel better. Katrina swept a stray strand of hair from her forehead and continued to look at the rock display. I was stuck on her face. A smallish nose and long eyelashes. She turned and caught me staring. My cheeks burned. But then she smiled at me like she knew something I didn't.

She pointed to the cabinet. "The coloured stones are gemstones. There's lots of different types. A diamond is a gemstone, but we've never found one of those. Opal is another type."

For a moment I wondered if I could pinch one to make her something—maybe something to hang around her neck. But that was a silly thought.

Above the cabinet, on a narrow shelf, sat a collection of photo frames.

"That's a photo of my dad when he found the gold nugget. Made the front page of the local paper. Not the largest nugget, but rare for around here and good publicity for the area. There was an increase in visitors to the town for a while." She smiled. "A mini gold rush."

She turned to look at her brothers. "Jamie's picked up the rock collecting bug from Dad."

"Huh?" Hearing his name, Jamie looked in our direction.

"Just said that you're also into rocks."

"Yep. What ya want to know?"

I gulped but was again saved by Katrina.

"Nothing. Just telling Quinn about the collection."

She remembered my name. I straightened, warmth flooding through me.

"You want to go see a really big rock, Quinn?" Jamie asked.

The younger brother perked up. "Yep, let's go show him the big rock." Steven stood by the front door, eyes keen. "Should we bring the rifles?"

Rifles? My desire to see the big rock cooled. *Who or what will we be shooting?* But then a brief spurt of excitement rushed through me. Carrying and firing a rifle had an adventurous feel about it. More silly thoughts of showing off to Katrina entered my head. I wasn't sure why, as I'd never held a rifle before, let alone seen one. I might well end up shooting myself by accident.

"Nah, let's skip the guns," Jamie said. "Save them for another time."

"Good idea." Katrina turned her attention to Mrs Warhurst. "Okay if we go up the hill, Mum?"

Mrs Warhurst thought for a moment. "That could be a good idea. We need to chat about a few things with Mrs Davies over a cuppa and scones, so it would be nice if you could show Quinn around. Have some lunch when you come back." She turned in my mum's direction. "Would you like a cuppa, Mrs Davies?"

"Yes, that would be nice. And please call me Elizabeth."

"Elizabeth it is, and I'm Evie, short for Evette."

Mum was gaining some confidence. Maybe the old man had spooked her too, and now that he was out of the room, she had relaxed somewhat. But no sooner had I thought this, he returned carrying a big rifle.

A vision of a stagecoach came to mind. A person sitting with a rifle next to the driver, who held the horse reins. The old man only needed a brown leather vest to fit the part. He already had a cowboy moustache.

The old man spotted me staring at the rifle. "You not seen one of these before, boy?"

"Ah…only in cowboy movies." I'd learnt a lot from those movies. But the way he referred to me as 'boy' bugged me. *It's not like I'm five or something.*

He walked closer and held the rifle up before my eyes. "This is a shotgun. It's good for shooting things close up and things in the sky, like birds." He pulled something out from his trouser pocket and held it between his thumb and finger. "This is called a cartridge, and it's filled with lots of small, metal bullets that explode out when you pull the—"

I felt an arm tuck into mine. "Sorry for interrupting, Dad," Katrina said, "but we want to take Quinn up to the big rock."

The old man lifted the rifle and aimed at the ceiling. He pretended to pull the trigger. "Boom, boom." He lowered the rifle. "Off you go, then. Watch out for snakes."

Mum looked concerned. Maybe she wanted to escape, too.

"Lance, stop trying to scare our visitors." Mrs Warhurst shook her head. "They're city folk and not used to guns and snakes. And Mrs…Elizabeth, we've had very few snake encounters. Snakes prefer to go the opposite direction from us, anyway, and it's a bit cold for them."

Mrs Warhurst gave her husband another stern look. "I've suggested to Lance on many occasions that he should join the local theatre group. He's so much into dramatics."

Lance coughed. "Okay, melodramatics over. I'll leave you be."

"You not joining our chat, then?"

"Nope. I trust your judgement."

"But I think Mrs Davies would like to get to know you."

He gave my mum a strange look, then glanced at his wife. "Okay, you kick off the proceedings. I just need to put the rifle away and check on the goats. I'll be back soon."

A toilet flushed, and Jamie walked back into the room.

"You want to use the toilet before you go, Quinn?" Mrs Warhurst asked. "It's just down the passageway."

Mum nodded at me. "I think that's a good idea."

I gulped and headed to the toilet. Nerves were making me want to wee.

When I returned, I joined the others, and we followed Mr Warhurst, rifle tucked under his arm, out the door. I tapped my sides, imagining six-shooters nestled in their holsters. Large white birds flew overhead. He lifted his rifle.

"Bang, bang. Got ya." The old man gave me a sideways glance.

Show-off. I drew my pistols and shot the shotgun out of the old man's hand. Katrina ran up and hugged me as I holstered the imaginary pistols with a smile. Oh yes, I was dreaming. I watched the old man wander off towards the goats with the shotgun returned to his side.

"My dad fought in the Second World War," said Katrina. "Sometimes, I think he's still there…." Her voice trailed off. "On the battlefields."

Katrina's words hung heavy in the air. *My dad fought too.* But details were scarce, like Mum had a secret she didn't want me to know about, buried like gold, deep underground. I'd seen photos here and there. He'd looked good in his army uniform. But they were just pictures, a moment frozen in time that I could not step into.

I caught another glance of Mr Warhurst near the goats. Was it safe to be around this gun-toting man?

4 Birds and Bees and Yowies

Katrina's voice cut through my thoughts. "Where's your dad, Quinn?"

A question I hadn't worked out an answer to yet. "He died when I was young. Don't remember much. Don't really think about it."

"I'm sorry to hear that."

"That's okay. I've got older siblings. Much older. My brothers sort of act like a dad to me."

"That's nice."

"Mum found me in a cabbage patch later in her life."

"You believe that?"

I laughed. "Of course not." Except I sort of did.

"A stork delivered me."

"A stork delivered you?" I grinned. "Just like in those cartoons. Big white bird with long legs, carrying a huge sack in its beak. Did it drop you down the chimney or place you at the front door?" At once, I regretted my words. I was trying too hard to make an impression.

"Neither." She smiled. "Mum told me all about the birds and the bees. So, I don't believe the stork story anymore."

Maaah, maah.

I turned to see where the sound was coming from.

"Just the goats, happy to see Dad."

"Well, are you two coming or what?" Jamie asked, unlatching a gate.

We charged towards it, and I was happy to be off the subject of the birds and bees. I'd been told nothing. But Katrina had other ideas.

"I worked out the connection, you know?"

"Huh?"

"How we're like animals. I've seen the goats do it." She paused and looked at me. "Are you okay?"

I nodded. "Yeah…I'm fine. Just a bit hot."

She smiled.

I was blushing and I didn't know how to control it.

Jamie chimed in, "And sometimes—"

"Think we best get off the subject, Jamie," Katrina interrupted, tilting her head towards me.

They both laughed. I wanted to be back on the train.

"Okay, sorry," Jamie said. "Should we tell him about the yowie, then?"

"No, not yet." She gave her brother a curious look and pointed ahead. "Lead the way."

What was a yowie? We walked single file along a narrow track. Now and then, I heard movement in the thick shrubbery lining our path.

"Just rabbits or roos, maybe," Jamie advised me. "Should've brought the rifles…could be a yowie following us."

"Stop trying to scare us, Jamie," Steven said, moving closer to his sister.

Jamie *was* scaring me. I focused on the steep climb, taking in big gulps of the cool air. Up ahead, giant boulders the size of sleeping elephants filled the landscape. Smaller boulders surrounded them like they wanted to be friends with the giants. I'd never seen boulders that big before. My mind raced with images of monsters, yowie-like, hiding behind those massive rocks. I really wanted to be back on the train.

Jamie suggested we take a rest. The smaller boulders worked as stools for us to sit on. I peeked behind one of the big boulders before sitting down—nothing but dirt and things that looked like black peas.

"Rabbit poo," Katrina advised.

As we caught our breath, Jamie pointed towards a slope. "Down that way is a creek bed. We go fossicking—looking for gold—when the bed is dry. It was on one of the creek banks that Dad found the nugget."

I wanted to go down there and find a nugget to help my mum. And some extra pocket money would be nice.

"We always take the rifles with us when we go down there."

"Lots of rabbits?" I asked.

"Nope. One day, I was down there with Dad, looking for rocks. I noticed he'd stopped and was staring towards some tall shrubs along the creek bed. I turned to look too. There was a dark shape moving in the greenery. Then came a guttural growl and a grunting sound, human-like. The shrubbery shook as whatever it was started making its way through towards us. Dad raised his rifle just as an ape-like face appeared through the shrubs! It saw us, shrieked, turned, and bolted. I reckon it had to be at least ten feet tall and completely covered in hair. Dad and I just looked at each other and hurried up the hill as fast as we could, just in case the yowie went to get some friends."

"I've never seen a yowie," Steven said to me. "He's just trying to scare you."

"Me neither," Katrina said, joining the conversation.

Jamie had done his job—I was scared. Actually, trembling, but it was cold.

Jamie cupped his hand around his mouth and yelled, "Cooee."

Suddenly, the branches of the shrubs nearest us shook, followed by a howling noise. Steven, Katrina, and I were on our feet and about to take off running when a boy burst out of the bushes, laughing.

Steven charged towards the boy and started thumping him on the chest. "I hate you, Gavin Toohey!"

Jamie grabbed his brother and pulled him away. "Calm down, Stevie."

"About time you got here," Gavin said. "I've been waiting for ages."

"You boys had this planned, didn't you?" Katrina said. "Poor Quinn will never want to come back here now."

My tongue was glued to the roof of my mouth.

The yowie impostor walked over to Katrina and tried to put his arm around her. She pushed him away, and I felt a flicker of satisfaction.

"Ah, Kitty, the scaredy-cat."

"You're an idiot, Gavin." She started laughing. We all joined in. I tried to make my laugh sound natural.

We walked on with our new companion. How good it would've been if a real yowie jumped out and squashed him. Some bushes moved in the wind. I immediately changed my mind about seeing a real yowie and moved closer to the group.

Nothing had prepared me for the size of the big rock. It was the size of the moon. The rock sat perched on top of smaller ones, with a cave-like space underneath where you could easily sleep. Gavin walked over and crawled into the space. I hoped the rock would fall and crush him. Not a nice thought, but he rubbed me the wrong way and I didn't like the way he looked at Katrina.

I watched Katrina climb the rock. She used indents in the boulder as steps and encouraged me to follow. I hadn't climbed a massive rock before. I did it with just a few grazes, but my heart still thudded in my chest. The view from the top was amazing. I scanned the surrounding area and couldn't see any yowies.

After a while, we started our hike back. Gavin walked ahead acting the fool, trying to impress Katrina. She just shook her head and whispered in my ear, "He's an idiot."

That felt good.

"You know, the gully back there, where they encountered the so-called yowie, was where Dad found the gold nugget."

"Yeah, Jamie told us. Must be worth a lot of money?" I had it in my head that gold equalled a fortune.

"Worth zillions," Stevie said.

"Don't think so," Katrina said, ruffling Stevie's hair.

"Dad says that's how we're going on our big holiday. It's like money in the bank, he reckons."

Katrina continued to ruffle Stevie's hair.

"Holiday? You're going on a holiday?" My heart sank.

"Yep, for six months. Why do you think you're here?"

"So Mum can help out with the house?" I asked.

"Yep, and to help out our old man. Feed him, things like that."

"I'm confused."

"We're going overseas to visit one of Mum's relatives who's not well and to have a bit of a holiday. Dad can't come. He's got to look after the goats and the farm." Katrina smiled. "Also, I think he's scared of flying." Her smile seemed to be hiding something.

I looked down at the dirt, shuffling my feet. I thought of Doggie.

"You got any dogs on the farm?" I asked.

"Just the one. With the vet at the moment."

"Ya reckon I'd be able to bring my dog?"

"Nope. Who knows what diseases city dogs carry," Jamie said.

"Jamie's right, Quinn," Katrina said. "Dad's a bit strict like that."

I hoped Mum didn't get the job, but then I looked at Katrina.

She gave me a smile, as if reading my thoughts. "You gonna be okay without me for six months?"

A lost feeling came over me. I tried to shake it off.

"What's your dog's name?" Katrina asked.

"Doggie."

They all laughed. I didn't like that, so I walked ahead of them, wanting to disappear.

"Don't be a sook," Jamie said.

"He's not a sook," Katrina said. "He just misses his dog."

I wondered if I could kidnap Katrina.

5 Hedgehogs and Eagles

Mr Warhurst settled me and Mum in the back seat while he slid into the driver's seat. He rolled down the window, and a cool breeze filtered in. I craned my neck for one last look at Katrina. She stood with her brothers while Gavin hovered in the background. Her mum huddled beside them, waving us off as Mr Warhurst started the car. My eyes watered. It wasn't because of the breeze; it was because I felt I was losing something.

"Lance, wait," his wife called out.

The old man turned to look back. Mrs Warhurst had changed her wave to a halt sign. She ran up to the window.

"I baked some cookies and want Mrs Davies to have some. Give me a sec."

A grunt came from the old man as he watched his wife run back to the house.

Katrina walked up to the car. "Dad, can I come along for a drive?"

With that pleading look on her face, how could he say no? But he hesitated before replying, "Oh, okay then. Suppose company would be nice on the way back." He didn't sound overly convincing.

Katrina ran around the front of the car and climbed in the front seat next to her dad. She turned to us. "You'll love the cookies."

"Oh, I'm sure we will," Mum said.

Mrs Warhurst hurried towards the car, carrying a brown paper bag. Katrina rolled her window down.

Mrs Warhurst handed the bag to Katrina and stuck her head in the window. "Hedgehog slices. My favourite. Enjoy. Bye!"

I thought of the dead animals I'd seen on the road and must have made a face. Once again, Katrina seemed to read my mind. "They're not made from animals, Quinn. No hedgehogs in this country, but they're like the echidnas we know. Only our echidnas are bigger." She shook the bag. "Just a biscuit slice. Yummy."

"Why's it called a hedgehog slice?"

"I've no idea," Katrina said.

"Because it looks like a hedgehog. The colour tones, at least." Katrina's dad started to drive off. His tone matched the sound of the engine.

I wasn't sure if I would eat a hedgehog slice.

Soon after turning onto the main road, we saw Tom's house in the distance. He was close to the road, trimming some bushes. Mum straightened up and waved enthusiastically. He waved back.

Mr Warhurst just stared ahead. Maybe he drove past Tom's place a lot and they got sick of waving to each other. But I didn't think so. I liked Tom but wasn't sure about Mr Warhurst. Maybe they weren't mates, not good friends.

Katrina stared at the road ahead. I missed her already, and she wasn't even gone. I looked forward to the day she would return from her holiday. She glanced at me out the corner of her eye and smiled, as if she knew I'd been watching her.

Earlier, Mum had confirmed that the family were going on a trip to the United Kingdom. That's why we were there: today was the interview. She told me the Warhursts had offered her the job, to look after the house while Mrs Warhurst and the children were away. The old man was staying. I shivered.

A few dead roos dotted the side of the road on our return trip, and on one bend, we disturbed two large eagles feeding on one. The car slowed.

"Yuck."

I looked at Katrina. Her nose was screwed up, but her hazel eyes were shining. I glanced at the eagles. Their eyes, in contrast to Katrina's, were dark brown, almost black, and menacing. The eagles stared at us before taking a few steps back and flapping their huge wings, as if ready for take-off.

"Wow!" I said. "They're massive."

"They are. You'll get to see lots of them," Katrina said.

Crunch.

"Oops, been a few weeks since I've driven. Bit rusty with the gear changes." Mr Warhurst looked at Katrina. "Don't tell Mum. She may never let me drive again." He gave a short laugh.

Katrina stared at her dad. She didn't laugh or smile. Something wasn't right, but I wasn't sure what.

I watched Mr Warhurst as he sped up. The stick he moved next to the steering wheel looked hard to manoeuvre. At least he was taking us to the train station himself and not leaving it to his neighbour.

"You ever driven anything, Quinn?" Mr Warhurst asked.

I fixated on one thing: I had to impress Katrina here.

Katrina turned and looked at me. Her eyebrows lifted.

"Dodgem cars."

"That's funny, Quinn," Katrina said. "Bumping and thumping other cars is fun."

"It is. Did it at the Melbourne Show." If the mention of dodgem cars didn't impress Katrina, maybe the fact that I'd gone to the Melbourne Show would.

"Always wanted to go to the Melbourne Show. Is it fun?"

I straightened. "It is! Though the Mad Mouse was a bit scary."

"Mad Mouse?"

"The Mad Mouse is a wooden rollercoaster," Mum advised. "Quinn enjoyed his time at the show."

What was I doing, telling Katrina I was scared? *She'll think I'm a scaredy-cat.*

"I've never been on a rollercoaster."

"It's fun. Sort of." Be nice to have fun with Katrina. I stared out the window at the rolling hills. They were rollercoaster like. My life was a bit rollercoaster like too.

6 Return to City Life

The return train journey stretched before me like forever. Mum and I sat across from each other. The comics that had kept me busy on the way there lay forgotten beside me. My mind was full of thoughts about our recent adventure, playing over and over like a movie I couldn't stop.

"Are we going back, Mum?"

"I think so." Mum had been mostly quiet, dozing off for a while. She turned to stare out the window.

Mum's voice sounded tired and sad. Maybe grown-up stuff was going on in her head, things that I didn't understand. My thoughts drifted to Katrina, but I knew I should try to forget her, since she was going away.

The train's rattling reminded me of the wooden roller-coaster. I drifted off to sleep, and soon my dreams were filled with rollercoaster moments—Katrina and I seated together, arms waving and laughter echoing, and nervous smiles as we approached each dip and turn.

A loud screech woke me. Mum smiled. "Just stopping at a station. You looked like you were dreaming."

I nodded. My eyelids felt heavy, but I didn't want to fall back to sleep. Not to the rollercoaster—though I wouldn't have minded seeing Katrina again.

The train started moving again. I stared out the window at the ever-changing scenery. I saw loads of rabbits hopping around. About an hour into the trip, a man walking with a boy alongside the railway tracks caught my attention. They carried rifles and waved as the train passed. The man had a rope slung over his shoulder with a bunch of dead rabbits hanging from it.

That may soon be me with the old man. I had mixed feelings about rabbit hunting—it seemed like something all the country folk did. The idea of carrying a rifle was cool, but being stuck with the old man? Not so much.

Countryside and rabbits gave way to houses and cars. After snaking its way through the suburbs, the train finally ground to a halt at Flinders Street Station. Home—a little walk to our home for now at the hotel.

"We just need to collect something, Quinn, here at the station."

Fine by me. The station had a wonderful and strange feel to it. Iron pillars and a galvanised iron roof high above my head made the space feel big and a little scary.

We paused at a counter. The sign said Visitors Help Booth. The lady behind the counter gave Mum a warm smile.

"Hello," said Mum. "I've come to pick up a suitcase left for me by a friend. They said it would be in the cloakroom."

The lady gave Mum directions to the cloakroom.

As we walked away, Mum filled me in on the mysterious suitcase. "It's some of your dad's stuff. We've been carrying it around since he passed away. A friend was keeping it for me but now they're moving house, so I need to find somewhere else to put it."

"Does it have things from the war inside it?"

Mum gave me a funny look. "Nothing of interest to you, Quinn. Just memories."

At least she had memories of Dad, especially as a soldier. I had none.

We followed the lady's directions. At one point, Mum stopped and looked at a poster. The poster said something about a dance on the third floor. A thin smile curved Mum's lips. I think she liked to dance.

A short while later, with the suitcase now in tow, we stopped again and Mum bought scones for us. We nibbled on the scones as we exited the station.

We came out of the concourse, the spacious area covered by the dome, and stood on the steps under the clocks. It felt like we had stepped out of a tunnel filled with mystery.

I watched a man with a long pole changing the time on one of the many clocks. He stuck the pole in the base of the clock, and the clock hands moved. How many times did he do that in a day? Maybe hundreds of times? His arms must get tired.

"He's just updating departure times, Quinn." Mum looked out into the street. "Bit different to the country life, isn't it?" She lifted her eyebrows and tilted her head towards the street.

Yes, it was a lot different. Stepping out of Flinders Street Station shocked me. My head almost exploded with all the sounds. Trams thudded past. Footsteps pounded the footpath. People everywhere.

No trees. No rabbits. No yowies.

Paperboys, dressed in oversized drab coats and about my age, stood on the station steps yelling, "Getcha 'erald!" Over and over, they'd cry out, a chorus that replaced the screeching of cockatoos.

Mum used the brass railing on the far-left side of the steps as support as she carried the suitcase down the steps.

"It was a really old suitcase that looked like it had been in a war. The brown leather was all scratchy, with shiny brass bits on the corners. Mum held onto the handle really tight. I saw that one of the metal snaps wasn't closed properly.

"Mum, one of the snaps is open."

Mum looked at the suitcase and nodded. When we reached the footpath, Mum laid the suitcase down and pressed the snap in. It took a couple of tries before it finally locked. She let out a sigh and then looked down the busy street.

"Well, let's go." The words sounded strained.

Mum and I were staying in a palace. The People's Palace on King Street, a few blocks from the station. I picked up the pace. My head filled with images of food. The scone had made me realise how hungry I was. The ground floor at the Palace had a large dining room with white linen tablecloths and napkins. My favourite food was the cold toast, but I'd have to wait until tomorrow for that. Someone would cook the toast and pile it high on a plate for breakfast. I liked it cold.

Mum always dressed nicely whenever we went to the dining room. Attendants in black and white gave the place a posh feel. I felt special staying there, though I'd heard a few people say otherwise. Housing for the poor, they called it.

Mum loved the food served in the dining room. She'd say it reminded her of the old country—roasts, stews, and pies. I could almost taste the shepherd's pie, my mouth watering just thinking about it. Mum liked me having big servings because she reckoned I needed to put weight on.

As I raced down the street towards the Palace, I suddenly realised Mum wasn't beside me. I looked back to see her settling onto a bench. I tracked back to mum.

"Come on, Mum, I'm starving."

"I know, Quinn, but the suitcase is heavy. They should put wheels on these things."

"Come off it, Mum, who's going to drag a suitcase with wheels? Here, let me help."

She let out a sigh. "King Street is further than I thought. Here you go."

She gave me the suitcase. I lasted a few steps. It *was* heavy.

"Here, let me help you with that, son."

A well-dressed man had reached down to grab the suitcase handle. "Where you heading, son?"

"We're going to the People's Palace," Mum said.

The man turned and looked at Mum. A surprised look passed over his face. Maybe he'd thought I was by myself.

A truck pulled up, and a man threw a bundle of newspapers onto the pavement. By the thud it made, it was heavy. A boy in a grey coat and bare feet headed towards the bundle. Then the boy stopped and looked at the well-dressed man whose hands were still on Mum's suitcase. The man placed the suitcase back on the ground and rushed off.

The boy turned to Mum and me. "You don't want his type hanging around you."

I wasn't sure what he meant. The man didn't seem bad, did he?

Mum stood and grabbed the suitcase. "All good, Quinn. I've got a new burst of energy." She nodded to the boy.

"Where ya heading?" the boy asked.

"People's Palace," I replied.

"Hey, Angelo!" the boy yelled.

A head appeared from the other side of the truck. "What ya want, Jimmy?"

He was either very tall or standing on something.

"You doing a drop at the Palace?"

"Yep."

"You want to throw this suitcase on the back of the truck and give the lady a lift?"

Angelo gave Mum a quick look-over and then smiled. "Sure."

Angelo opened the truck's passenger door and pushed some papers and stuff aside to make room for Mum. He grabbed the suitcase and placed it on the truck's flatbed. He looked at me. "Jump on the back, boy." He ushered Mum to the front seat like a gentleman. I sat on the flatbed, legs dangling over the side.

The paperboy gave me a smile. "Have fun. See ya around." He bent to pick up papers from the bundle on the pavement. As we drove off, I heard him cry, "Getcha 'erald!"

7 End of City Life

I lay in bed, looking up at the ceiling. Light filtered in from the street, projecting dancing images. Mum was sound asleep in the other bed.

My eyelids closed, and I drifted into a dream. I saw a deep cave under a large boulder. Katrina stood there, waving me towards the dark inside. Something waited in the darkness. A pair of yellow eyes appeared, glowing like two flashlights. The boy, Gavin, strolled out of the cave, twirling two torches in the air and grinning. He walked over to Katrina and placed his arm around her waist. She did the same. They turned to me, laughing.

My eyelids shot up and I let out a loud groan.

"You okay, Quinn?"

I sat up and shook my head to clear the dream away. "Yeah, Mum, I'm fine. Just a dream." *Nightmare, more like it.*

I rested my head back on the pillow. I didn't want to close my eyes. But sleep overtook me until someone yelling outside our door jolted me awake. It was still dark.

Mum stood near the door, a silhouetted figure. Filtered light caught her face. She looked scared.

I sat up. "What is it?"

A thud came from outside the door. Mum braced herself against the door. "Not sure. Sounds like people arguing."

I could hear a man's voice. Close and loud. He was saying nasty things to someone.

"Go away!" Mum yelled through the door.

Silence, and then someone thumped the door. "Ain't got nothing to do with you, snooper, so mind your own—"

Mum turned to me. "Cover your ears, Quinn. This man's drunk. Doesn't know what he's doing and saying."

Too late. His dirty words had hit my ears.

A scream, then more crude language.

Mum opened the door and grabbed the umbrella near the door. She entered the passageway with her weapon. "Get off her, you pig!" Mum yelled.

I moved to the door, then stuck my head out the doorway. A lady lay sprawled on the floor, pushing her nightgown down over her legs. A man knelt over her, his fist raised, and his head turned towards my mum.

Doors creaked open. Others appeared in the passageway. The man's head wobbled as he assessed the situation. He stood, uneasy on his feet, then staggered off towards the stairwell. The lady on the floor raised herself up off the ground and started crawling after the man.

Mum hurried towards her. "Leave him. Let him go." Mum grabbed the lady's arms and helped her up. Blood trickled from the woman's nose. Mum wrapped her arms around her.

I went after Mum, wanting to protect her. I stood next to her, but she ushered me behind her.

"It's the grog," the lady said.

"I know."

"He doesn't mean to hurt me."

"Yes, I know. But he has."

One by one, doors closed on the passageway. The drama was over, and no one had offered their help. Mum and the lady stood there. The lady pointed to a door not far from our room. "I'm staying there."

Mum assisted her to the door. The lady opened it. Two young children sat huddled together on a single bed. They stood up, ran to their mum, and wrapped their arms around her legs. She patted their heads.

"You don't have to put up with it," my mum said.

"It's the grog. He changes. Becomes a different person."

"It's not a good change."

The lady lowered her head. She hugged the kids and ushered them towards the bed again. They all sat down, one child on either side of her.

"We're staying here…to get away from him. But he found us." The lady swallowed hard. "We'll be okay. I shouldn't have answered the door."

"Did we do something wrong, Mummy?" one of the children asked.

The mother drew the child closer to her.

"Why does Daddy drink, Mum?" the other child asked.

"I'm not sure, love. I'll talk to him about it."

The mother was trying hard to stay calm. My mum must have sensed this because she walked over and picked up a doll. "And who does this belong to?" she asked.

The smaller girl raised her arm. Mum placed the doll in the girl's arms, and she quickly gave the doll a tight hug.

"Mine's under the blanket, hiding," the older girl said. Mum retrieved the hidden doll and handed it to her. She gave it a big hug.

"Now you girls look after Mum," my mum encouraged them, her words tender.

"Mummy needs a doll, too," the younger girl said.

Their mum gazed at them with a mixture of love and amusement. "You two are my precious dolls."

They giggled in delight.

We stayed for a little longer and then said our goodbyes.

Looking at the mother and her children sitting on a single bed had made me feel sad. But I couldn't figure out why. All these feelings were spinning around inside my head that I didn't know what to do with.

Mum tucked me back into bed, her touch warm and comforting. "You okay?"

"I feel sad."

"Just make sure you never treat a lady like that."

"Why would a man do that?"

"Mostly, it's the drink," she explained, her voice thick. "Some men can't handle the drink. Does crazy things to their heads."

"Was Dad like that?"

Mum's eyes closed briefly. "A little," she admitted, her words barely a whisper.

"Maybe good that he died, then?" I blurted out, instantly regretting my words.

Mum's hands rose to her face. She rubbed her forehead, swallowed hard, then took a deep breath.

My brain felt muddled. That wasn't what I'd meant to say at all. I just wanted Mum to be safe and happy. That's what I had meant to say.

"Your dad was a lovely man, Quinn." She swallowed again. "You have to remember that many of these men who trudged off to war came back as different men. They're trying to escape the cruelty of war and the things they saw. Many still have nightmares."

With a kiss on my cheek, she whispered, "Now back to sleep you go." Tears glistened in her eyes. I thought of the yellow eyes in the cave. I couldn't imagine what kind of nightmares soldiers had. My dad must have had nightmares too and came back a different man.

As I drifted off, I noticed blue lights flashing across the ceiling. The police must be busy rounding up the drunks. Then I was asleep.

May 1964
Melbourne

My dearest Martha,

I'm sorry that it has taken me so long to write. So few letters over the years. I'm sorry. My grieving has not been easy and I'm still struggling to settle down. To be honest, I think I'm running away from things. It's hard to explain.

I can't remember when I last wrote but I know it has been a long time. The children have all left home now except for Quinn. Two have joined the navy, another a policeman. Some married with children.

I've struggled to find work and will soon be moving to another country town in Victoria. I hope things will go better there. It's a small town, very small. The carefree and simple life seems to be vanishing. I think it best to escape to the country, where the simple life remains.

Quinn is a lovely boy. He never asks about his dad but does talk to the stars at night time. In his mind, his dad is a big star. With his siblings gone, he does get lonely, but he's good at seeking out friends.

Harold's later years were an enormous embarrassment to the family. I know I'm still struggling with many things and I'm sure it's affected the children, but I've little energy for them. I think they were happy to leave home but I fear they carry scars with them. Life is hard.

I'd love to save money and come back home for a visit. This is what I'll try and do.

We're staying—

8 Letter Writing

In the morning, before I raced down for my cold toast, there came a gentle knock on the door.

Mum sat at a small desk, holding a pen in her hand. "Hello, who is it?" she called out.

"It's Missy. From last night," came the soft reply.

Mum stood up, setting aside the letter she'd been writing, the ink still fresh on the white paper. She crossed the room and opened the door. Missy stood in the doorway, dressed in a brightly coloured, long-sleeved dress, dark rings shadowing her eyes.

"Just wanted to thank you for your help last night," Missy said.

Mum reached out and gently touched Missy's arm. "That's perfectly okay."

"He fell down the stairs."

"Sorry?"

"My husband, Eric. He fell down the stairs. They needed to get an ambulance for him. He's in a bad way. I'm off to the hospital now."

"Oh dear, that's the last thing you needed." Mum rubbed Missy's arm. "Are you taking the kids?"

"My sister will be here soon. She's picking us up and will help with the kids. She'll drop us back here later."

Mum nodded. "I'm sorry to hear about your husband."

"He'll be okay. He's tough. It may even keep him off the grog for a while. Maybe he'll come to his senses." She gave Mum a hug. "You here for long?"

"Maybe another week. I found a job in the country. Perhaps it'll be nice to escape the city."

Missy smiled and then looked at her watch. "Well, I best be off. Maybe catch up with you later for a cuppa."

"That'd be nice."

Missy left and Mum closed the door. She looked at me and then towards the desk.

"I need to write some letters, Quinn."

"That's okay. I might go for a walk."

Mum let out a deep sigh. "Okay then but remember the rules. Stay on the main streets where there are lots of people. Don't talk to strangers. And be back by noon sharp, okay?"

"I know, Mum. I'll be careful."

She grabbed her purse. "Here's some change for a phone call, just in case."

After gobbling down some toast and juice, I headed up King Street and turned right onto Bourke Street, where leafy trees lined the road and lots of people walked by. A man sat on a building's front steps, holding a newspaper wide open, with smoke drifting from a cigarette in his hand. He lowered the paper, revealing a tartan jacket.

He noticed me looking at him. I shuddered. He reminded me of the man from last night. Both men had scratchy-looking faces, like they hadn't shaved in days.

Walking faster, I peeked back to see he had returned to his newspaper. I turned and nearly crashed into a lady with a shopping basket made of cane tucked under her arm.

"Sorry," I said quickly, feeling my face get hot.

She grunted.

The shops were opening, and the streets were getting busier. I needed to pay attention. After a few minutes of walking, I reached the Southern Cross Hotel, a tall building with a classy look. I'd seen the Prime Minister opening the building on television—some time ago when we visited someone who had just bought a TV. We'd never had one, so I'd stood there watching like I was in a trance. Mum said famous people would stay at the hotel. When the Beatles come to Melbourne—I think they're coming soon—that's probably where they'll stay.

Would I be living in the city when they came? Nope, I'd be at Edithburra. I would have to wag school and jump on a train to go see them.

I walked a few blocks and found myself standing on the corner of Elizabeth Street and Collins Street, staring at a very tall building. A skyscraper. With my head tilted back, I understood why they were called skyscrapers, for they looked like they scraped the sky. I counted the floors. Nineteen. The People's Palace was a tall building with eight floors, but it wasn't a skyscraper.

I sensed something looking at me. A watchful owl perched on top of a fake tree made of bronze in front of the building. Around the bottom of the tree, two bronze statues of kids my size looked as if they were playing and had been frozen mid-game forever. I wondered if they came to life at night when the city was asleep. The sculpture had a magical feel about it, but it seemed weird next to all the busy streets and tall buildings. It made me think of the quietness of the farm and, of course, Katrina.

I passed a store with TVs on display. I stopped and watched a chase scene on one of the TVs involving a fat man and a skinny man. It was funny.

I moved on and headed towards Flinders Street Station. The clocks had a magical pull about them.

As I headed down Swanston Street, I saw a crowd of people, mums holding the hands of their children, whose eyes were glued to a shop window. A gap opened up, so I squeezed in to see what they were all excited about.

A shiny steel maze. Blobs of gold-coloured, ring-shaped sludge dropped from a big steel bowl into sizzling oil, then were carried along on the steel maze like rubber tubes on a river and dropped into another large bowl at the end of the track.

"Mum, can we buy some doughnuts?" a boy asked. The mother smiled and nodded. They headed towards the entrance of the shop.

I might have to bring Mum here. I patted my pockets, even though I knew I had no money, only telephone money.

I caught a glimpse of a man standing behind me in the window. I'd seen him before—the tartan jacket man. His jacket reminded me of something a presenter had worn on a TV show.

He moved closer to me. "Would you like some doughnuts?" the man asked.

"Could you get me some, too?" It was the paperboy from yesterday.

The man turned and hurried away.

"Phew, saved you again." The boy nodded at the departing man. "Need to be careful, mate. There's a number of men who are on the lookout for stray kids."

"What, are they lonely or something?" I asked, confused.

"Nah, not right in the head. They do nasty things to children."

A mother with her child gave us a look and moved away. Maybe she didn't want her child to hear the words coming out of the paperboy's mouth. I wasn't sure if I did either.

We stepped away from the window.

"Perverts?" I asked, not fully understanding what I meant by that. Mum called them dirty men.

"Yes, sort of like that."

"I've met one of them before. In a lane near where I lived. Showed me rude pictures and flashed his thing and then ran off. Told my mum and the police got involved."

"Did they get him?"

"Wouldn't know."

"It's a wonder your mum lets you roam the streets after that."

He was right. "I've heard Mum say that she doesn't want me thinking there are bogeymen behind every corner." But maybe Mum did worry about me when I was out exploring.

The boy gave a knowing nod. "Where are you going now?"

"I was thinking of heading towards the station."

"Me too. I'll keep you company."

I liked that idea. Two were better than one. Felt safer. We started walking. The paperboy had shoes on now—no longer barefooted, but just old tennis shoes with no laces.

"How long you staying at the Palace?" he asked.

"I'm not sure. Maybe another week or so."

"Well, you just be careful if out roaming the streets. There are a few perverts out here also roaming. The city attracts them, and more so during school holidays. And boys like yourself wandering around without a parent are a perfect target."

"But you're not much older than me and I don't see your mum or dad around."

A tram thundered past.

"I live not far from here. They're knocking down the houses on our street. Moving people into housing towers. They call it slum clearance." The paperboy watched some people walk past. "I come into the city to get away from the noise. There's a few of us, so we feel safe in a group, and we're streetwise."

I laughed at his mention of noise.

"What's so funny?"

I jabbed my thumb towards the road. "Pretty noisy around here."

"Different sort of noise. No bulldozers."

"Sounds like fun."

"It was for a little while. We would rummage through the houses that had been knocked down. I found some interesting things."

"Like what?"

"Old photos. Some taken at the goldfields. Really old."

"You mean like Ballarat?"

"Yeah, I think so. One was a picture of a man sitting in front of a timber hut. I sometimes think I'd like to escape to the bush and build a timber hut like in the picture. Chop down some trees. Build a hut."

"I could be moving to the bush soon."

"Well, that sounds like fun."

"I'll probably get to shoot a rifle."

"Wow."

"And I've seen some gold."

"In the bush?"

"No, in a house. The owner collects rocks."

"Well, maybe you might strike it rich."

The paperboy had a sense of humour.

"What's your name?" the boy asked.

"Quinn."

He tilted his head. "Haven't come across that name before. You a foreigner or something?"

"Nope, but my parents are from Scotland. Mum tells me my name means 'wise, intelligent' but I think she makes these things up."

"Well, my name is Jimmy, and I'm not sure what it means."

We neared the station and paused at the pedestrian crossing. Jimmy waved to three boys standing under the clocks. "They're my mates. You want to hang around with us for a little bit?"

The big clock above the departure clocks showed it was 11:15. Mum had said I had to be back by lunchtime, so I had some time. "Yeah, sure." Besides, Mum was busy writing letters.

A letter to Martha (continued)

—at a place called the People's Palace. It's a budget hotel run by the Salvation Army. For some, it's a refuge.

I encountered a lady last night being abused by her husband, who was drunk, of course. We helped her. This morning, in the middle of writing this letter, there was a knock on the door, and it was the lady from last night. She had come to thank me for helping her. She also told me her husband fell down a flight of stairs and is now in hospital. She was off to the hospital to visit him. His drinking causes all sorts of issues.

Quinn is off walking the streets of Melbourne. I sometimes wonder if I should let him wander the streets, but he loves exploring. The way society is heading, though, I may have to keep him with me more.

The siblings do not talk about Harold's death. Have I told you? I cannot remember. It is hard for me to say, but he took his own life. I am angry that he did such a thing. My life is now a mess, and the children have no father. I do feel an unbearable loss and much pain, though. Was I not worth living for? I fight such thoughts, but it is hard. I also believe what he did does not please God.

I am sorry, though words put to paper help me. I suppose he believed he was doing the right thing, maybe believed he was a burden to us. But his death is shrouded in shame and silence. The older children keeping quiet about it. My heart tells me this is not the right thing to do. Though when talking to others, I do not tell them the truth either. Shame grows inside me.

Harold has brought shame to the family. It comes to light when the siblings drink. The tongues get loose and the blame game starts. But then bringing it to light may be a good thing.

Surely there was something I could have done to prevent it. I want to know why he did it. But I am rambling.

Quinn is too young to understand, so we haven't told him how his dad died. I think he believes it was a heart attack. I will tell him in due course, or do you think I should tell him now? I want so much to protect him from the shame. He asks very little about his dad, so I think I'll let it be for now. In my grief, I lie and I am angry that I do this.

I am tearing up as I write these things so I will finish this letter now and write again soon.

All my love,
Elizabeth

9 The Boys

The lights at the pedestrian crossing changed. I was distracted by my surroundings, so Jimmy nudged me to walk on. We headed towards Jimmy's mates. I felt nervous.

"Is this little boy lost, Jimmy?" asked a boy with a black left eye.

"Careful what you say, Ginger. He ain't really little and he lives in a palace."

They all bowed.

This was getting too much. I wanted to leave.

Jimmy placed his hand on my shoulder, which relaxed me a little. "Quinn, this is Jack, Eric, and Ginger."

"Quinn? What kind of name is that?" Ginger's carrot-like eyebrows dived towards his nose as he frowned.

Sometimes I wished I had a different name. But then again, Ginger isn't exactly the coolest name either.

"What happened to you, Ginger? Your dad onto you again?" Jimmy asked.

Ginger lowered his head. "Hate the man."

"It's the grog, mate."

Jimmy's statement reminded me of the lady from last night.

"Your dad drink, Quinn?"

I jumped back to the present. "Don't have a dad."

"Well, you're lucky then," Eric said. "We come to the city to escape our dads."

The world made less and less sense. I thought dads were meant to look after their kids, not scare them away.

"Quinn drew the attention of the tartan jacket man."

"He's a real weirdo, that one," Eric said. "Not sure why the cops haven't rounded him up."

"Yeah, him and a few others," Ginger said.

"Anyone want a smoke?" Jack said. "Grabbed a few out of Dad's packet last night. He was drunk, so he won't miss them."

Only Ginger took up Jack on the offer of a smoke. A mechanical sound came from behind us. We all turned and watched the man with the pole changing the departing times on the clocks.

"Lucky he's sober," Eric said. "Imagine the chaos he would cause, changing times while drunk. People would be standing under the clocks, scratching their heads."

They all laughed. Mine was a nervous laugh. I started to feel edgy about the city. Perverts, drunks. I wanted to be home with Mum.

"How old are you, Quinn?" Eric asked.

"Going on eleven." I didn't want to say ten.

"We're all going on thirteen and we're paperboys," Eric said in a triumphant tone, pumping his arm.

"In a few years, you could get a city newsboys' license and join us," Ginger said.

"Yep, you're a bit young at the moment," Jack said. "It can get a bit hairy out here on the streets. You have to deal with drunks and fights, and sometimes the perverts get a bit too close for comfort."

"Saturday nights are great though," Ginger said. "You get good tips from the blokes coming home from the footy and after the pubs close."

"We all fend for ourselves," Jimmy said. "My dad's not a drinker compared to my mates' dads, so I've had to learn how to look after myself out here. My mates learn at home—how to dodge fists and stay out of the way when things get ugly. Me, I've had to figure it out on my own."

"Yeah, you should've seen him after his first time selling papers at the pub," Ginger said.

Jimmy shook his head. "I remember it well. Scared the living daylights out of me. Like entering hell. So much pushing and shoving. Drunk men saying things you don't want to hear. Some of the better men pushing you away from talk too dirty for young ears."

"And it's where we learnt to swear. My parents aren't too pleased about that," Jack said. "I've been clobbered around the ears a few times for letting slip some of those pub words."

"And you ain't seen nothing till you experience closing time. The men become like animals," Ginger said.

"Closing time?" I knew nothing about pubs.

"The pubs close at six," Jack said. "On working days, the men charge straight to the pub after work. They'll gather with their mates and guzzle down as much grog as they can in a short time and then fall out into the streets and stagger home drunk to their families."

"Sometimes my dad won't even make it home," Ginger said. "Since he's discovered places where you can get sly grog after closing time, we've hardly seen him."

"That could be good, safer," Eric said. "Not having him home."

"I know what you mean," Ginger said. "Sometimes Mum pushes me out the front door to go look for him. That's a scary thing to do. But best I do it and not Mum."

These stories killed any desire I might have had to become a paperboy.

"I reckon something's happening to the world. I'm seeing more and more fights on the trains and trams now. More perverts walking the streets. More drunks." Jimmy pointed to me. "And Quinn here has only been in the city for a short time, and he's had a couple of perverts sniffing around him."

"And I saw a drunk hitting his wife last night in the Palace." I wanted to impress the boys with how tough I was, but I wasn't sure if I wanted to live in the city anymore.

Jimmy looked at me. "You're seeing it all. Drunks and perverts. The man yesterday with your suitcase. Seen him before. He's one of those who likes the boys. Angelo told me to be careful around him."

"Angelo?" I queried.

"He gave you and your mum a lift to the Palace."

"The Palace?" Eric asked.

"People's Palace."

"Oh, I thought you meant he lived in a proper palace, like a big house with a pool," Eric said.

"Nope, it's the place run by the Salvos."

"Thank God for the Salvos," Ginger said.

Eric and Jimmy both looked at Ginger.

He shrugged. "Just something my mum says."

We sat on the steps watching the city life. Cars tooted and trams rattled by. Cigarette smoke drifted past my nostrils, and I wanted to sneeze.

"Why don't we jump on a tram and head to St Kilda tomorrow? Go for a swim?" Jimmy suggested. "You want to come, Quinn?"

"That sounded like fun. I'll ask my mum." Still, I couldn't help thinking it might be a bit cold for a swim.

"Okay. Say we meet here tomorrow at ten."

"Why don't we do something more adventurous, like explore a tunnel?" Ginger suggested.

"That's a big word, Ginger. I'm happy for an adventure," Jimmy said. "Why don't we decide tomorrow when we meet up?"

"A tunnel? What tunnel?" Eric asked.

"There's stories of huge amounts of gold once stored in tunnels under the roads, and some may still be there," Ginger said.

"Maybe you won't have to go to the bush to strike it rich, Quinn," Jimmy said. "Sounds like there may be gold under our feet."

They all looked towards their feet. Cigarette butts and gum littered the pavement.

A tinge of excitement filled me at the mention of gold.

It was time to head back to the Palace. I might see the boys again, but I wasn't sure.

***

On entering the Palace, I saw Mum sitting in the dining room with the lady from last night. I wandered over.

She saw me coming. "My son's returned from his adventure."

Missy's girls sat at another table, drawing with crayons.

"Hello, young man," Missy said. "What did you discover?"

"Doughnuts."

Missy chuckled. "You must be referring to the doughnut place with the machine in the window."

"Yes, I could stand there for hours watching the doughnuts being made. Maybe we can go there this arvo, Mum?"

"This afternoon? Maybe." Mum turned to Missy. "He has an adventurous spirit. Always wants to explore. I just tell him to be careful on his walkabouts."

"It's getting a bit scary out there now," Missy said. "The kidnapping of that boy in Sydney a few years ago has made parents more nervous about letting their kids play in the streets. People are starting to say, 'stranger danger'."

Mum looked at me. She probably preferred that I didn't hear such things. If only she knew of the stories I'd heard under the clocks.

"I think the TV makes people more aware of things," Mum said, her voice close to a whisper. "The world's getting bigger, more fast-paced. When I was younger, the world was a safe place. My world, at least. The last place we stayed at, we slept with our doors unlocked and the windows open. I'm not sure I'd do that in the city."

I wandered over to the girls to look at their drawings, remaining within hearing distance of my mum.

"At another place we lived, Quinn used to walk to the beach by himself, maybe two miles. He was just nine years old and used to love watching the people fishing on St Kilda's pier. He'd also wander the back alleys, although an encounter with a dirty man brought an end to the alleyway wandering."

Missy looked over at me. She looked tired but forced a smile. "Life adventures shape them. We try our best to give them the best life possible. It's hard, though."

Mum placed her hand on Missy's. "We can only try."

"I think we're losing our way. War's done a lot of damage. Why do we want to kill each other so badly? I don't understand."

"There's a mystery behind it all. Even kids at a young age show aggression and selfishness. Once they're adults, it's even more alarming."

"That's mine!" The angry voice interrupted my eavesdropping. I turned to see the girls fighting over a red crayon.

We could have a war on our hands right here.

"Just like what we're talking about." Missy huffed and turned to her daughter. "Camilla, share." Missy stood and walked over to her girls. "You want to go get some lollies?"

The girls nodded, once again smiling.

Missy turned back to my mum. "We must do this again while we're both staying here. Although, I'm not sure how much longer we'll be around. With Eric injured, it might be safe to go home."

"I'd love to," Mum said. "And I do hope things work out for you. Just be careful, though."

I looked at the kids' drawings. One was bright and cheerful—a sun and flowers. The other had a darker feel: a bottle and a rock. The bottle was broken with puddles of red surrounding the rock.

I wasn't sure how safe home would be.

10 The Phone Call

Just after 7:00 am the next day, a gentle tap echoed through the room, followed by a note slipping under our door. Mum, seated at the small desk, gazing out the window, turned at the sound and walked over to retrieve the note.

After reading it, she turned to me. "It's a message to ring the Warhursts." She seemed nervous. "I hope it's not bad news. I really need the work." With a swallow, she folded the note and tucked it into a pocket in her dress.

"Let's get ready and go have some breakfast. I'll return the call afterwards." Mum's voice was croaky.

Downstairs, we sat at a table overlooking the busy street. The clock on the wall showed a quarter past eight. I hadn't asked Mum about going to see the boys.

People came and went. We drank juice and ate cereal while I eyed the toast piling up near the toaster.

Mum followed my gaze. "Go grab some toast. I'll make the call to Mrs Warhurst."

Mum stood and pulled out a small notebook from her handbag. She flipped through the notebook and found the piece of paper from this morning tucked inside. With a puzzled expression, she gripped the note.

"What's the matter, Mum?"

"It looks like a local number. No trunk code." She referred to her notebook. "It's different from the number I used when I first called them. Oh, well." She shrugged. "I'll give the number a call."

I watched Mum wander over to the phone near the entrance to the dining room. As she passed people, she nodded at them. She was always friendly.

Phones were strange to me. We'd never had one in any of our houses. Talking over the wire was weird because you couldn't see the person you were talking with. Watching people's mouths move helped me understand them better.

Maybe with practice, I would get used to phones.

I grabbed some toast, spread thick layers of butter on two slices, and was biting into one slice when Mum got off the phone. She started back towards the table. She didn't look unhappy.

"Lizzie!" Missy called from behind mum

Mum turned. Missy came and gave her a hug.

"So nice to see you again," Missy said. "You have time for a cuppa?"

Mum looked back at me. She smiled.

"I'm good, Mum. Okay if I go exploring?"

Mum nodded. "As long as you're careful. Be back in an hour and remember the rules."

I leaned forward, my eyes pleading.

"Okay, an hour and a half."

I rushed out of the Palace, grinning. Things had fallen into place nicely. I looked back towards the dining room. I should've asked Mum about her telephone call. But she seemed happy, so everything must be okay. I headed towards the station, eager to explore the city with the boys.

Out in the streets, the city seemed darker. Thick clouds covered the sky. The rumbling of thunder matched the rumbling on the streets.

***

I sat with the boys under the clocks, watching the rain pelt down. Water swirled in the drains, putting an end to our plan to explore the tunnels, and the lack of sun made a swim at St Kilda seem less appealing. That was probably for the best—I'd have needed Mum's permission, and time was already a problem. Plus, I wasn't too keen on swimming in the cold water. A brief shiver ran through me.

"I heard a story once," Jimmy said, "about one city street flooding in a massive downpour, and hundreds and hundreds of rats stampeded out of the drains."

Another shiver ran through me. Any desire to explore the tunnels in the future vanished. I looked at Jimmy. Despite his story, he felt warm, like a big brother.

Boredom set in. Rain had a way of doing that.

Sitting on the sheltered steps of the station, I watched a tram screech to a stop. A number of people stepped down out of the tram. Umbrellas popped up, while some without umbrellas ran towards the cover of the station. A lady with a girl hurried past. At first, I thought the girl was Katrina.

I laughed. I couldn't get her out of my head.

"You still here tomorrow, Quinn?"

"Yep."

"You want to hit the park? The luny park?"

"Sure." A roller coaster flashed in my head—the rattling, the screaming. I figured he meant Luna Park. It had a luny vibe about it. My focus went back to the lady and girl walking down Flinders Street. They had some kind of pull about them. The rain had eased. "I might head back to the Palace now."

"Why you staring at that lady and girl, Quinn?" Ginger asked. "You know them?"

"Just reminded me of someone, that's all."

"I think they're country folk," Ginger said.

"Why do you say that?" I asked.

"The clothes they're wearing?"

"Yeah, sure, Ginger," Jimmy said.

"Bright dresses. I reckon most city people wear dark clothes. And that's what the stores sell. My mum tells me this stuff. She works in a department store."

I watched the country folk wander off. Was there any truth in what Ginger was telling us?

"Mum also says country stores only sell old fashion clothes. Whenever her sister visits from the country, Mum drags her out shopping. She goes home a new woman."

"Bet ya she doesn't even wear the new clothes when she gets back to her town," Jimmy said. "She'd stand out like a sore thumb."

Ginger nodded. "Maybe."

I wanted to follow the country folk. "Okay, I'm off. Pity about the rain. Maybe catch up tomorrow?"

"Same place, same time," Jimmy said.

I headed down Flinders Street. Maybe there was truth in what Ginger said, because the lady and girl did stand out. They paused at an intersection. The lady pointed to the King

Street sign, and they crossed the road. Their timing with the traffic lights was good. Mine wasn't so good. I stood waiting for the lights to change as the brightly dressed people walked down King Street.

Soon, I found myself trailing behind the lady and girl, yet I couldn't get a clear look at them as people wove in and out between us. The People's Palace loomed ahead. It looked like Mum was standing on the pavement outside. She waved—not to me, but to the lady and the girl. Noticing me, she gave another wave. The lady and girl turned to see who Mum was waving at.

I froze. It couldn't be…but it was. They *were* country folk—Katrina and her mum.

I stepped towards them, trying to handle the strange feeling swirling inside me. Mum rested her arm on my shoulder. "I'm sorry, Quinn. I didn't get the chance to tell you Katrina and her mum were in town to do some shopping before their trip."

Katrina's warm smile made my legs feel like jelly. I tried not to wobble as Mum guided us all towards a café, and I sneaked a peek at Katrina. She looked amazed by the bustling city. Then she caught my eye, her lips quirked into a playful smile, a glint of mischief in her expression.

"Bet ya didn't think you'd see me again so soon?"

I was still coming to grips with her presence here. I felt like I was in a dream.

Katrina continued. "I begged Mum to take me with her. I wanted to see the Big Smoke."

And me, I hoped.

"Maybe you can take me on a tour of the city."

"I'm not so sure about that, Katrina," said Katrina's mum.

"I'll look after her," I said.

"I'm sure you would, Quinn, but the last thing I want is for my daughter to get lost in this big city."

"Nah, it wouldn't happen. I know my way around."

"Maybe we'll come with you on the tour," Mum said. "But first, let's have a cuppa. You can grab a milkshake if you want, Quinn."

Inside the café, I sat next to Katrina. My tummy was fluttering. "Have you been to Luna Park?"

Katrina shook her head. "Not yet. I think my auntie is taking us to St Kilda tomorrow. That's where Luna Park is, isn't it?"

"Yep."

"Maybe you can come with us." Katrina looked at her mum. "Could Quinn come with us tomorrow?"

"Maybe we could meet there," Mrs Warhurst said.

"I think we could do that. Hope the rain stays away," Mum said.

I caught a glimpse of blue sky through the café window. My dream was getting better by the minute.

After the café, Katrina and I were let off the leash when our mums entered a large department store and told us not to venture far. We needed to be back at the front of the store in twenty minutes. Katrina wanted to ride the escalator. We did this a few times until a security guard told us to move on.

I took Katrina to the tree trunk sculpture. After that, we sat on a bench and talked.

The man with the tartan jacket walked past. He looked at me. A shiver ran up my spine.

"The city can be a bit scary." I pointed to the man who'd passed us. "He's a pervert of some kind."

Katrina's eyes narrowed. "Pervert?"

"Not a nice person."

Katrina moved closer to me. "Maybe we better go back."

"Okay."

Katrina touched my arm. "Quinn?"

I looked at her. She wore a serious expression. "You be careful when you come and stay at our house."

"I will." I replied, my voice tinged with uncertainty. Why had she said that?

***

After Katrina and her mum left us, I felt kind of lost, like something was missing. So before dinner, I went looking for the paperboys. It wasn't long before the familiar shout echoed from under the clocks: *Getcha 'erald!*

I sat on a concrete step near Jimmy and watched him in action. Between his shouts, handing out papers, and collecting money, he asked, "What ya up to?"

"It's weird. You remember the lady and girl I was watching this morning?"

"The brightly dressed ones?"

"G'day, Jimmy boy."' A man grabbed a paper from him.

"Getcha 'erald!"

"They were the people I visited in the country the other day."

"Yep, sounds weird. They following you or something?" A smirk crossed his face.

"Nope, just came to the city to do some shopping."

"Yeah, country folk do that."

"Looks like I'll be spending tomorrow with them."

"That's okay. You can catch up with us another day." He paused and looked at me. "You look a bit excited. You like the girl or something?'

Warmth crept into my face. "We may be going to Luna Park."

"Well, we may see you then."

I wasn't sure if I wanted that. The thought of Katrina finding Jimmy and his friends cooler bugged me.

"Maybe. I'm not sure what time we'll be there."

"Getcha 'erald!" A man handed Jimmy some money and grabbed a paper.

Jimmy gave me a quick look. "No worries. We may or may not see ya."

I felt guilty.

"Getcha 'erald!"

I stepped back as the crowd heading up the stairs to the station had grown and a line had formed to get the paper.

"I'll be off, Jimmy."

Jimmy's hands received money and handed out papers with rapid speed, reminding me of an octopus.

He gave me a quick nod and winked. "See ya."

I turned to go.

"Hey!" Jimmy yelled. "Give us your address so we can come see ya in the bush."

Address? I had no idea what Katrina's address was. "Uh…I'll have to get it from my mum."

"No problem." Jimmy tore a strip of paper with no ink on it. He rested the paper against the wall and scribbled some words. "Here ya go, my address and phone number. Just in case we don't cross paths before you go."

Another wink.

"Getcha 'erald!"

11 The New Home

My adventure in the big, big city was over. Now it was on to the big town and then the little town, each stop bringing me closer to the old man and the secrets I sensed lingered around him.

The houses were less close to each other now, and the train's rhythmic motion made me sleepy. I rested my head against the window. Mum handed me her cardigan to use as a pillow.

In the end, we didn't get to the park. I didn't get the chance to show off my dodgem car driving skills. Sadly, I didn't even get a chance to say bye to Katrina on her Melbourne visit. It was pouring rain the day they were going to go to St Kilda. Mum spoke to Katrina's mum on the phone, and she told Mum her sister was going to take them for a drive down the coast. It only seemed to be raining in Melbourne.

But as it turned out, we needed to catch up with my oldest brother and his family and say our goodbyes before Mum started the new job. I even got to see Doggie. At first he attacked me with doggy affection, but soon he was off chasing the neighbour's kids and their playful pup. I felt good knowing Doggie would be well taken care of while I was away.

I wasn't sure how long we'd be gone. Mum hinted it could be at least six months. We moved around a lot. Maybe she'd find another job in Edithburra after this one, and we could end up staying there. That would be cool—finding a house near Katrina's. I could even bring Doggie to live with us.

I lifted my head and looked at Mum. "Will all the Warhursts be there when we arrive at the farm, Mum?"

"Not sure. I think so."

"Who's picking us up?"

"Mr Warhurst has organised a taxi."

A taxi. Wow. But I had hoped Katrina and her mum would pick us up. Even Tom and his ute. Still, a taxi felt like a bit of a treat.

Mum continued. "Mr Warhurst is busy. Something to do with the animals."

I nodded and smiled, remembering the animals peering through the fence. The thought of seeing Katrina again and going back to the farm made me feel both excited and nervous. I really hoped Katrina was still there. She couldn't have left yet. Still, nagging doubts lingered.

The train trip couldn't go quickly enough.

***

When we exited the station, I spied a man leaning on the bonnet of a taxi.

"Mrs Davies?" He had a thick country accent.

Mum nodded. The driver loaded our suitcases into the boot, then opened the rear door for us and gestured for us to climb in.

Mum sat in the back seat with me. Apparently, that's what you did in taxis. The driver said we'd get to our destination in around forty-five minutes.

A mechanical device had been mounted on the dashboard. I watched the numbers click over as the car travelled. I caught the taxi driver's eyes in the mirror.

"It's called a meter," the taxi driver said. "It clicks over every mile, so we know how far we've travelled."

Each click told me we were closer to our new home. Should I call it a home?

There weren't a lot of dead animals on the road today, or maybe I missed them as my eyes were on the meter. We passed Mr Molloy's house, then turned into the Warhursts' driveway. I was a bundle of nerves, feeling uneasy about seeing the family again. The taxi finally came to a stop and the driver flicked a handle on the meter. He bent forward, squinting at it, and then turned to Mum. "Three pounds should do the trick."

Mum sat up straight and fumbled with her purse. "Sorry, I didn't realise I had to pay."

The driver's lips pressed into a firm line. "I'd love to give you a free trip, lady, but I need to make a livin'."

"Oh, of course, I understand that."

He looked towards the house. "I'm sure the man will give you the money back, as he booked the ride."

"Oh yes, of course he will." Mum had found the money. "Sorry, how much was it again?"

"Three pounds."

I didn't know if the driver was trying to rob us or not. He rolled down his window, and fresh country air rushed in. I could hear the taxi's engine, a crow cawing—or maybe it was a raven—and some goats bleating.

I looked towards the house. There was no movement, except for a curtain falling back into place. Someone had peeked out the window but had not come to the door.

We stood on the gravel driveway and watched the taxi drive off.

"Maybe we got here too early, Quinn."

I hoped Mum was right, but I didn't have a good feeling. The closing of a door echoed over the driveway and the tall, lanky figure of Mr Warhurst appeared.

"Hello there, welcome back." He looked in the direction of the settling dust as the taxi turned onto the main road. "I take it you fixed up the cab driver?"

Mum gave a slight cough. "I did."

"Thanks for that."

"It was three pounds." Mum's words were hesitant.

"Hmm. Getting expensive these days."

Mum looked at me and raised her brows.

"Beats riding a bicycle, doesn't it, boy?"

Oh, no, here we go. "It does. Mum doesn't have much money, though."

"Yes, I understand that. That's why she's here. Come inside. I'll get you both settled."

As we headed in, I looked around. The silence bothered me.

Mr Warhurst's eyes were on me. He seemed to notice my unease. "No one else here, boy. The family's all gone. They'll be on a big plane in the sky soon." He pointed upward.

My heart sank.

He looked at me. "You had hoped to see them? That's nice." I didn't like his grin. "They had to go earlier as our overseas relative has taken a turn for the worse."

"I'm sorry to hear that," Mum said.

Mr Warhurst nodded. "Yes, sadly, I don't think death is far away." He didn't look too sad. He ushered us towards the front door and, as an afterthought, he helped Mum with our suitcases.

"Welcome to your new home." There was a strange tone to that welcome.

12 Rooms with Character

The place was a mess. A newspaper lay sprawled over a coffee table, its pages littered with empty Foster's beer cans. The kitchen bench was equally messy, with more discarded cans and a mountain of dirty dishes threatening to topple over. *Did he throw a party when they left?*

Mum eyed the mess. Mr Warhurst followed her gaze and smirked. "I'll do a quick tidy up once I get you both settled. Now, let me show you to your rooms."

I ended up in Steven's room. The walls were a deep, inky blue, giving it an outer space feel. A rocket-shaped lamp rested on a small bedside table. Plastic toy soldiers guarded the rocket. A rug on the floor had differently coloured and sized circles—maybe the planets. Under the bed, a toy tank aimed its large gun barrel at the doorway. A *boom* sounded in my head while I watched an imaginary shell shooting towards Mr Warhurst. I smiled, and he tilted his head to the side and stared at me. His eyes asked questions.

A dresser stood against the wall with a model airplane sitting on top and some comics scattered around. I resisted the urge to have the plane fly over and drop bombs on Mr Warhurst. A transistor radio sat on top of one comic. A box with 'Monopoly' printed in large letters on the lid lay on the floor next to the dresser. I hadn't played that game before.

Above the dresser, a comic-like poster hung, showing a large, alien-like robot with a girl collapsed in the robot's arms. The title was *Forbidden Planet.* It was my favourite movie, but I was also eagerly waiting for a Beatles movie that was being talked about. Though that would have to be good to beat *Forbidden Planet.*

The silly thoughts lightened my mood. The realisation that I had my own bedroom—an outer-space war zone—also raised my spirits.

"My youngest son believed he saw a flying saucer in the hills near here," said Mr Warhurst. "Since then, he's crazy about space things. The soldiers protect him."

I thought of the yowie. It must be an alien that Mr Warhurst and his son Jamie had seen.

"You get a feel for your new room, mate. Grab a comic while I show your mum her room."

"I'm sure Quinn would like to see where my room is, too." I detected fear in Mum's tone. Why? Was she afraid of this man or just feeling out of place?

Mr Warhurst's bottom lip came up over his top lip. He thought for a moment. "Sure, he needs to know where his mummy sleeps. Follow me."

Mum gestured me forward with her hand and placed her arm on my shoulder. She raised her eyebrow at me and picked up her suitcase.

We left Stevie's space room and returned to Earth. Mr Warhurst opened the door to the room next to Stevie's. I hadn't noticed a smell in Stevie's room, but as soon as this door opened, I knew it was Katrina's room. A sweet smell filled the air.

The pink walls were bare except for a corkboard with bits and pieces pinned onto it. I'd take a peek when I could. There might be some photos of her pinned there. Her bed was the same as Stevie's, with an iron bedhead.

She also had a dresser with a mirror, some raggy dolls sitting on top, and what looked like a record player. I couldn't see any records. Maybe they were in the drawers. Hopefully, she had some Beatles singles.

A colourful lamp sat on the bedside table surrounded by coloured rocks. Just like in Stevie's room, Katrina had a rug covered with different coloured and sized circles—only hers were sunflowers, not planets. Her bed did not have a tank stationed underneath.

"If the bed is too small for you, we may need to find an alternative arrangement."

A small cough came from Mum. She glanced around the room nervously.

I was sure the bed would be okay. Mum wasn't tall. This man was creeping me out more by the minute. I might move the tank into this room.

"Okay, you can unpack, and I'll be in the lounge area if you need me."

"Thank you, Mr Warhurst. I look forward to our time here. Can I call you Lance?"

That didn't sound like Mum. Something felt off. Maybe asking to use his first name would help whatever was going on.

"You certainly can." His spirits seemed to lift. He looked at me. "But still Mr Warhurst to you, young man."

Slight improvement. I'm now a young man. Maybe things were going to get better.

A large box with metal edges sat tucked away in the corner of Mum's new room. Mum pointed to the box. "I'd guess that most of Katrina's belongings have been packed away in that tea chest."

I reckoned it was a treasure chest.

Mum opened and checked the dresser drawers and then walked over to a timber wardrobe. She opened the wardrobe door. The inside was bare except for a few wire coat hangers. "I'll unpack later. Let's go freshen up and I'll tidy up the kitchen for Mr Warhurst."

We stopped at Stevie's room. I had another peek inside my new room.

"Your own room, Quinn. You excited about that?"

"You bet." I gave Mum my best smile.

Where had Stevie packed his stuff? He could have moved his stuff into Jamie's room. A chair sat in a darkened corner of the room. I hadn't noticed that before. It was an old timber chair, with a rifle leaning on the chair's arm. Was it loaded?

"Come on, Quinn. Best not keep the man waiting."

The rifle drew me, but I followed Mum. We strolled into the kitchen area. The beer cans had been picked up and the newspaper neatly folded. Mr Warhurst sat at the dining room table, sipping from a cup.

"The kettle has just boiled," Mr Warhurst said. "There's cordial in the cupboard, if Quinn wants some."

It was the first time he'd called me by my name.

***

Mum served up lamb chops with mashed potatoes and veggies for dinner. Mr Warhurst seemed pleased; he let out a few hmm-hmms. He kept to himself for the rest of the evening.

Mum sat on the bed beside me. "Are you okay, Quinn?"

"Yep, fine, Mum." I lied because I wanted her to be happy. Mr Warhurst was a strange man and although I liked the room, something about our present situation disturbed me.

Mum studied my face. "I watched a movie one night at the Palace with those funny men in it. People called them Fat and Skinny, but they're also known as Abbot and Costello."

Was this a bedtime story? I remembered those men—I'd seen glimpses of them on TV, like on that one in the shop window back in Melbourne.

Mum continued, "The movie was about Dr Jekyll and Mr Hyde. A horror-comedy." She rubbed my head. "Well, the doctor developed a drink that turned him into a bad person when he drank it. He became Mr Hyde. I think Mr Warhurst may be a Dr Jekyll and Mr Hyde type of person. We just need to be careful when he drinks."

I heard movement in the passageway. Had the old man been listening? Mum looked towards the passageway and shrugged. "Old houses make noises."

Sylvester and Tweety jumped into my head. "I know what you mean by the Dr Jekyll and Mr Hyde stuff, Mum, I saw a cartoon with Sylvester and Tweety."

Mum smiled.

"Tweety drank something that a mad scientist had made, and the drink turned Tweety into a giant monster bird. The monster bird chased after Sylvester."

"Poor Sylvester," Mum said.

"Yes, poor Sylvester. But he was only dreaming, so it had a good ending."

"And this will be a good-ending adventure for us, too," Mum said. "Now, off to sleep you go."

The sloppy, lispy voice of Sylvester the Cat whispered sweet things into my head. My first night next to Katrina's room, surrounded by soldiers and aliens. I knew I'd sleep well.

Something woke me. I sensed a presence in the room. My hand reached over for the rocket light, knocking over some soldiers in the darkness as I grappled for the light switch. I flicked it on.

It wasn't strong but gave enough light to see Old Man Warhurst sitting in the chair in the corner. A rifle rested on his lap.

I sat up.

"You're not going to cause me any trouble, are you, boy?" the old man asked.

I fought off the heaviness of sleep. "Sorry?"

"I said, you're not going to cause me any trouble, are you, boy?"

Panic rose in my chest. I shook my head. "No, sir, I am not going to cause you any trouble."

He nodded slowly and stood up. "Good."

He walked out of the room.

My head was back on my pillow. Was I dreaming? I sat up and looked at the rifle. It was now on the floor, and not resting on the chair as it had when I'd first noticed it.

It had been moved.

13 The Schoolhouse

Mr Warhurst appeared pleasant as he drove Mum and me down the narrow road, deeply shadowed by massive trees and giant tree ferns.

Dr Jekyll came to mind. His name had a bad ring to it, but it was really Mr Hyde who was the villain. There was a lesson in that, though I couldn't quite grasp it. I wasn't sure which side Mr Warhurst was showing this morning. Maybe he was leaning towards Dr Jekyll.

Some dark figures were jumping around up ahead on the road, so Mr Warhurst slowed the car.

"Lyrebirds." He stopped the car and wound down the window. "Mating." He leaned forward and watched.

A wonderful sound entered the car.

"They can mimic just about anything. I once heard one barking like a dog."

Mimic? I hadn't heard that word before. Ah, so they're copycats. "What are they doing?"

"The dancing bird with its tail raised is trying to attract the other. Boy-girl type of thing."

Quinn-and-Katrina type of thing, I couldn't help thinking.

A car pulled up behind us. I heard a door shut and footsteps approaching our car. It was Mr Molloy.

"Hello, Lance," he greeted Mr Warhurst, leaning down to peer into the car. "And hello to you too, Lizzie and Quinn."

We returned the greeting.

"Not often you experience the lyrebird mating dance. Nature's put on a show for you." Mr Molloy looked around at the scenery. "I suppose you've never seen trees this big either?"

"Never," Mum said. "Enormous, almost frightening."

"They're known as mountain ash. Can grow to over 300 feet. They like our cool mountain ranges. I find them spellbinding."

"Yes, amazing trees," Mr Warhurst said, "but it looks like the dance has finished. Best get this boy to school."

"Good then, enjoy school, Quinn. I imagine it's going to be quite different for you."

I didn't get a chance to respond, but I wondered what he meant by that.

We continued along the winding, narrow road, then turned into an even narrower road. I pressed my nose against the window, looking everywhere for the school building and sports ground. The car slowed and stopped. Mr Warhurst pointed towards a house. "That's the school."

I blinked. A house? Where's the sports ground?

I shook off my shock and took another look. It was different from what I was used to. Perched on a grassy hill, the 'schoolhouse' had a welcoming feel. A brick pathway wound its way up the slope, leading to the side of the house—

probably where the entrance was. The missing front door gave the place an air of mystery.

A large balcony extended from the front of the house, floating in the air except for the large timber posts supporting it. A man stood there, his hands resting on the rail, looking down at us. He reminded me of the captain of a ship. A pirate ship? The captain waved and gestured with his hands, inviting us up.

Aye aye, captain.

"Well, off you go," said Mr Warhurst. "Don't be too long, Elizabeth."

No "Lizzie" from this man.

Mum and I started our gentle climb up the twisty path. As we passed under the balcony, the captain leant over. "Hi there, you must be Quinn?"

Mum gave me a nudge.

"Yes, sir…that's right." I resisted saying, 'Aye, captain'.

"Well, just head up to the first door. It's open, and you can come on in."

Mum tucked her arm in mine, and we did as instructed. "He seems a friendly fellow," Mum said.

My throat tightened, making it difficult to speak. I felt trapped behind a wall of tangled nerves. Thoughts of pirates and ships were replaced by faces of strangers staring at me. It seemed awfully quiet for a school. I wondered how many kids were in my class.

We paused at the doorway. I looked up the path towards another doorway. Another classroom? Then I looked back to the large room filled with sunlight and stepped inside. I pictured being forced to walk the plank; the pirate world made me feel better.

A picture of the Queen hung on one wall. The familiar smell of chalk filled the air. A large blackboard stood at the front of the room covered with half-erased scribbles. There were maybe ten wooden desks with textbooks and pencil cases on top and shoeboxes scattered on the floor. The desks and empty seats faced the blackboard.

The captain headed towards us. A short man with a mop of dark curly hair, his eyes almost hidden by dark bushy eyebrows. He wore a brown waistcoat over a dark blue shirt and brown trousers. He looked just like a pirate.

"Welcome to our crowded school," said the captain. He chuckled. "No kids today. Sick. Others are away in Willward with their parents, but back tomorrow."

What? *The entire school is sick or away?*

He came over to Mum. "You must be Mrs Davies."

"I am."

"Nice to meet you. My name is Trevor Hecat, the one and only teacher here at Edithburra State School."

Only teacher? No students? Had I just stepped into another world?

Mum placed a hand on my shoulder. "Quinn's just come from a state school near Melbourne."

"Well, he's in for a shock, then. This school has a total of six students. Seven now with Quinn." The captain moved towards me and ruffled my hair. "And three of the six students are from the one family." He gave a short, quiet laugh. "We had hoped for more students this year, but some families moved away."

Mum coughed. "I think Quinn's class size was just under forty, so it's going to be a real shock for him, but hopefully a good one."

"And all forty would've been in the same grade. Here it's all primary school grades together."

"That must be a challenge for you," Mum said.

"Yes, it is, but I enjoy it. It'll be a good experience for your son. Small classes allow more individual attention, though I'm not sure if the small student numbers will help keep the school afloat."

Mr Hecat often raised his eyebrows, showing his dark, mysterious eyes. I looked around the room. School stuff dangled from the ceiling. A colourful mobile of the planets, swayed gently in the breeze. It made me think of Stevie's room. The walls were covered with student artworks, maps, and posters. At the bottom of the blackboard, the captain's name was written in big capital letters. TREVOR HECAT.

A funny name.

"Do the Warhursts come to this school?" Mum asked.

The teacher replied, "Warhurst? I know the family, pass their property daily, but none come to the school. Some of the locals send their kids off to private schools. Thirty minutes or more by bus." He ruffled my hair again. "But you've made a good choice. This is the best school you'll ever go to."

I tried to believe him. I looked around, wondering if this school could become a hideaway for me.

"Come sit out on the balcony and I'll give you a history lesson on the school."

"Oh, I'd love that." Mum pointed towards the road. "But I have someone waiting for me, so I was just planning to drop Quinn off."

"That's alright. I was notified he was starting today. So all good. Where do you live?"

"At the Warhursts."

"Tell you what, I'll drop Quinn off as I drive past the property on my way home. I don't think it will be a full school day today. I only have to focus on one student."

Mum hesitated and then nodded.

I didn't like being the only person the teacher had to give his attention to, but there was no choice. And I'd prefer the attention of the captain over Mr Warhurst. Would Mum be okay?

I was sure she would be. She always tells me that God watches over us.

"That should be okay, Mum. Saves Mr Warhurst coming to pick me up." I'd prefer to be in another car than Mr Warhurst's, but I wasn't going to tell Mum that.

"Well, with term 2 just starting, could I just clarify, how long will Quinn be staying?" the teacher asked.

"Rest of the school year, at least. We'll find somewhere to rent at some point."

"Okay, that's good. So, you're staying with the Warhursts at the moment? Are you relatives?"

"We're staying there to help Mr Warhurst while his family travel overseas. He had to stay and look after the farm. We're not related. It's a paid position, a housekeeper's role, for six months."

"And after that, you'll settle down in the village?"

"That's what I hope to do. Get us settled down away from the city."

"I miss the Big Smoke," the teacher said.

"Really, how come you're here, then?"

"That's a long story."

A car horn sounded.

Mr Hecat pointed towards the road. "That'd be Mr Warhurst. He's not exactly known for his patience."

In this small town, I guess everybody knows each other.

Mum looked like she wanted to talk more with my new teacher, but the car horn blared again, a warning that she needed to hurry down the hill.

I let my mind wander again. I moved the cannon on the pirate's deck to be aimed at Mr Warhurst's car. *Boom.*

"I'll see you later, Quinn. You be good for Mr Hecat."

I came back from the world of pirate ships and nodded.

Mr Hecat raised his eyebrows. I wasn't sure what that meant. Maybe the pirate ship was real. Maybe I'd entered a magical world.

I watched Mum hurry off.

"Come out to the deck, Quinn." The teacher walked in that direction. I followed.

I felt uneasy. I wanted to turn and run after Mum but walking onto the deck calmed me. No walls. Open space. There were no cannons, just a long desk and lots of chairs. Trees and ferns surrounded the deck, except at the front where you could look down the grassy hill. I saw Mum getting into the car. They drove off.

"We have lessons out here sometimes, depending on the weather. Nice, hey?"

"It is."

"I love nature. Do you, Quinn?"

"I think so?"

"Well, after a few months here, you'll know so."

"I really like birds. I don't know why."

"You probably want to fly above everything. Birds give you a feeling of power and freedom."

I nodded. I hadn't really thought about why I liked birds. Maybe I did want to fly. Fly away.

"Come back inside and I'll show you the classroom and our radio room."

I thought of music, but harmony was not what I detected in the radio room. The room had a heaviness about it. Branches on the trees outside filtered the sunlight, casting pockets of the room in shadows. There was a sense that the room was holding its breath, waiting for something to happen.

14 They Shoot Birds

Mr Hecat's car needed cleaning. Dust covered most surfaces inside and out, with a splattering of dead leaves on the roof and bonnet. The vehicle blended in well with the bush surroundings. On opening the door, I detected a metal smell, like the scent of a penny. I moved rubbish on the floor to find a place for my feet and uncovered a tennis racket. I pushed the racket to the side.

As I climbed into the car, I noticed a rifle spread across the backseat. While fighting off the fear of why he had a rifle in the car, I figured that could be where the smell was coming from.

My thoughts wandered. "Yowie."

"Did you say something?"

"Huh?"

"You just spoke."

"What did I say?"

"Not sure. That's why I'm asking."

I sensed anger brewing. I grabbed for my last thoughts. I hadn't realized I'd spoken aloud.

"Yowie. I said yowie. That's what the rifle must be for."

Mr Hecat chuckled. "Have you seen one?"

"Yes," I lied.

"Where?"

"Down near a creek bed. Where people used to go looking for gold."

Mr Hecat started the car and began reversing out of the bushy driveway. "I think you'd have more chance of finding gold than seeing a yowie. And finding gold would be very rare. You probably saw a shadow formed by shrubbery."

"It was ape-like. It saw me and ran off."

"Well, you were lucky it ran off, then." He snickered.

"Yes, I was." Fighting guilty feelings, I looked out the window as we passed what looked like a store. I thought I saw someone run inside.

Mr Hecat chuckled. "Did you see that person zip into the shop?"

I didn't respond.

"It was Charlie, my grade six student. He didn't look too sick to me," Mr Hecat continued, his tone casual.

As he slowed the car down, he mused, "Should I grab the rifle and go after him?"

A surge of fear gripped me. *These country people are strange.* I was speechless and scared, having never been with a teacher by myself before. My head spun, and the rifle in the back seat didn't help things.

"You know I'm joking, don't you, Quinn? Don't want you to think teachers run around the village shooting students."

"I knew…I knew you were just kidding." Sort of. I hoped so.

"The building's a grocery store come lolly shop. My students spend a lot of time there. You should see their teeth." He laughed. "Just joking again, but then I've not had a good look at their teeth. Leave that to their mums."

How long to get home? I hadn't been paying attention on the way here. I hope it's not too far. The teacher seemed weird. I wondered if he was crazy. Maybe he'd gotten kicked out of the city schools and ended up here. That thought didn't give me a good feeling.

The tennis racket fell on my feet.

He noticed. "Just throw that in the back. You play tennis?"

"Nope."

"I can teach you if you want. I'm pretty good."

"I prefer playing footy."

"That's a bit weak; you should try other sports."

"I do. Just haven't ever played tennis."

"We'll have a game one day."

I nodded but inwardly resolved to avoid that at all costs.

We left the narrow road and travelled along a wider main road, then turned back onto another narrow road. This was the road we'd travelled to school on. The massive trees up ahead swayed, as if in welcome.

"That house on the corner is where the Olsen family live. They're the bulk of my students. Their dad's not around much. He's a shearer. Travels a lot to find work. Mum's a lovely lady."

I saw a lady at the side of the house, throwing scraps at the chooks. A large goose walked beside her. She waved to us.

"The kids are most probably hiding, waiting for me to pass." Another laugh. He tooted the horn.

"We saw lyrebirds this morning on our way to school. They were dancing on the road."

"That would've been nice."

We entered the shadowy tunnel formed by the towering trees and large ferns. After we passed through the thickest part of the forest, sunlight flooded the road ahead. Mr Hecat suddenly sat forward and slowed the car. I sat up and looked to see what had caught his attention. A plump bird, but not as big as a crow, was searching for food on the ground along the side of the road.

Mr Hecat stopped and turned off the car. He wound down his window. The bird continued its search for food. Mr Hecat, moving slowly, reached over and grabbed his rifle from the back seat. I moved my head as the rifle barrel passed me.

He's not going to shoot it!

"Block your ears," he said quietly.

I pressed my hands against my ears and noticed I was shaking.

He stepped out of the car, leaned on the open door, took aim, and shot the bird.

I turned away, unable to watch.

The back door opened and he threw the bird on the floor and placed the rifle down on the back seat.

"Pigeons taste like duck. Very tasty. You ever had one?" He climbed back into the car.

I shook my head. I'd never eaten duck and the thought of eating birds brought yucky feelings to my tummy and throat.

"You notice the copper smell in the car? That comes from the blood dripping from the pigeon. I've had a good run of shooting pigeons this week. No time to clean the car, although I've got paper on the floor to let the blood soak in."

He paused and looked at me.

"Are you okay? You look a little pale."

I gave a weak nod. "No, I'm okay. Never seen a rifle go off before. But I've seen dead birds before. Someone was killing them in a street I lived in. They said whoever did it used an air rifle." I was rambling. Nervous.

"Most probably. Air rifles are beginner guns for kids." He pointed to his rifle in the back. "That's the real thing."

I had no doubt about that. He started the car and drove off. Another pigeon searched for food on the roadside. He slowed the car, then sped up again. "Best get you home." He looked out his side window. "I'll let that pigeon live."

I was sure I'd told him I liked birds. How could he kill one in front of me? We drove on in silence. I could smell the rifle and the dead bird.

"The driveway to where you live is coming up. You'll be okay to walk up the driveway? It's not far."

"Yep, no worries." I couldn't wait to bolt from the car.

"Did you want me to save some of the bird for you and your mum to taste?" he said with a smirk.

I wasn't sure how to respond. "I'll ask Mum."

"Okay, see you at school tomorrow. Hopefully, we'll have a full class."

I wondered if the other students existed. Maybe he had shot them.

15 Just Follow the Track

I closed the door and watched the car drive off, spurting out black exhaust fumes. Towards the bottom of the dusty rear window, someone had written CLEAN ME. I turned and looked down the dirt road towards the house, which was hidden by the huge pine trees and tall shrubs. I started walking and noticed the large shed between the trees.

Sudden movement stirred in the shrubbery. I jumped. A yowie?

"You wagging school, boy?" Mr Warhurst stepped out from the shrubbery. "That's not a good start."

He didn't look like a yowie, more like Elmer Fudd with his cap and the rifle tucked under his arm. At least these humorous images were helping me deal with the strange world Mum had thrust us into.

"No, sir. Not wagging. No students at school today, all sick. Teacher called an early mark and dropped me off."

"That's awfully nice of him. He has a reputation for being slack."

"He shot a pigeon."

"Thought I heard a rifle go off."

"The teacher said they're nice to eat."

"Maybe. I only shoot them because they make so much noise. Their *whoop, whoop* call drives me crazy. They can do it for hours. So, I shoot them."

I'd best not tell him I liked birds. He might shoot me.

"You see that track over there?" He pointed to a track just past the shed.

I looked. "Yep."

"That's a shortcut to the main road. You walk that way tomorrow and you'll get to school okay."

I nodded. Walking didn't bother me, and it would be a long walk. A mini-adventure I looked forward to.

"Best go help your mum then. Off you go."

I did as I was told.

After I passed another large pine tree, the house came into view. Mum sat on a chair near the front door, a tea towel resting on her shoulder. She stood up when she saw me, tossed the towel onto the chair and rushed towards me.

"What's happened, Quinn?"

"Nothing, Mum. Just school finished early. Teacher drove me home." She must have forgotten.

"Well, that's nice of him." She smiled. "Oh, that's right! He said he was going to drop you off. Silly me. I think you'll enjoy the school. It's so different."

I nodded, not sure what to say. Mum wanted so much for me to enjoy school.

"Have you eaten pigeon before?"

She screwed up her face. I took that to mean no.

Things were indeed different.

***

I lay in bed, the soldiers on guard. The tank watching over the entrance to the room. I heard footsteps and then the door handle turning. There was a big key in the door, but I didn't lock the door; didn't want to lock Mum out. It opened.

"Are you awake?" Mum whispered.

"Yes, Mum." I raised my head from the pillow. "What is it?"

She came and sat on the side of the bed. "Just wanted to check you're okay." Her voice was soft and warm.

"I'm fine." I sat up. "Living in the country is a lot different from the city. I was thinking I might write a letter to my friend, the newspaper boy, to see if he wants to come visit. He said he'd like to escape to the bush."

"That sounds like a good idea." Moonlight gave the room a soft glow as Mum brushed hair from my forehead. She'd been letting me grow it—crew cuts were going out of fashion, thanks to Elvis and The Beatles. "You'll have to walk to school tomorrow as Mr Warhurst has business to attend to in Willward. He'll be leaving early, and we'll have to get up early, too."

The getting up early bit worried me but I felt better hearing that he wouldn't be around. "That's okay, Mum. He's already shown me the track to follow. I'm just not sure how long it will take."

"Me neither. I'll walk with you a wee bit of the way."

"No need, Mum."

"Just a little."

"Okay. Just don't want a yowie to get you."

"I'll carry a rifle," she said. I could see her smirk in the dim light.

"Good idea." I knew she was joking. Well, I hoped she was joking, as I was sure she wouldn't know how to shoot a rifle.

I slept well and dreamed of birds and rifles. The laugh of a kookaburra woke me.

After breakfast, Mum walked me to the start of the track. She'd found a school bag used by one of the Warhursts and packed me a sandwich and apple. I positioned the bag straps over my shoulders and I was off. I could tell she wanted to walk me, but I'd talked her out of it.

"Pick up a big stick in case you encounter any wildlife. There are no yowies," she reminded me.

"I know, Mum. I'll see you when I get home. Maybe the teacher will drop me off again." I hadn't made up my mind if yowies were real or not. My hope was that they were, but also that they weren't. I laughed to myself.

She nodded and smiled.

The track was covered with pine needles and leaf litter and soft on my feet. I wasn't long into the track when I encountered my first animal. I had entered a clearing with lots of holes and short grass. Rabbits dived headfirst into the nearest holes, vanishing from sight in an instant. One rabbit seemed confused, hopping around, bumping into rocks and logs, unable to find a hole to dive into. I walked right up to it. It had swollen and glassy eyes with white goo dripping out of its eyes.

Not a pleasant sight. I walked on.

After walking through a damp and mossy area, the track connected to the bitumen road. I paused to catch my breath and stood there, taking in the sounds of nature—bird calls, rustling leaves, and the trickling of running water from a nearby creek. A slight gust of wind ran across my face and I felt something on my neck. Just a slight sensation, barely noticeable, like a gentle touch of a dead leaf falling to the ground.

I trudged on. It was a long walk, and with each passing minute, I could picture my disappointed classmates and my teacher staring at me as I walked in late, churning my stomach. My pace quickened.

The forest thickened and the trees grew larger, towering over me. The breeze was no longer gentle, now carrying earthly smells from the massive eucalyptus trees. Wildflowers and shrubs replaced the scent of pine needles. Even with all this beauty around me, the fear of being late kept growing. The frightening sounds of falling branches, trees creaking, and unknown movements in the bushes made me more nervous. The shadows from the trees stretched out like claws, making everything feel creepier.

I was wanting to turn and run back when a car horn broke through all those earthly sounds. I turned to see the dirty car from yesterday. Mr Hecat stuck his head out of the window. "You want a lift?"

Happiness swept away fatigue. Mr Hecat looked at my neck as I got in the car. "You've got a leech clinging to your neck."

"A leech?"

"Yep, slimy, blood-sucking leech. Here, let me get rid of it for you." He leaned towards me. "You have a hanky? There may be a bit of blood."

Mum always made me carry a hanky. I pulled it out of my shorts pocket.

Mr Hecat grabbed a sharp, flat stone from the dash. He pressed it against my neck and pulled off the sucker. He gave me a quick look at the slimy black creature, then threw it out the window.

He tapped his neck. "Put your hanky on the bite area. It may bleed for a little."

I'd live. I wasn't going to have all my blood sucked out of me and I wasn't going to be late for school.

As we drove past the lolly shop, I noticed it was also a post office. I'd write my letter to Jimmy and post it from there.

Mr Hecat parked his car. We climbed out and walked up the grassy hill. Heads appeared above and below the balcony rail.

"Hello, Mr Hecat!" they all screamed together.

Mr Hecat paused and looked up towards the kids.

"Hello to all my favourite children." He placed his hand on my shoulder. "And here is our new student. Say hello to Quinn."

While they all yelled their greeting, I felt the blood rushing to my head. Swallowing hard, I managed to muster a feeble wave. Taking a deep breath, I braced myself for whatever lay ahead.

16 The Class

At the doorway to the classroom, the class all stood there, as if to offer another welcoming.

"Just take your seats. We don't want to overwhelm Quinn with our kindness."

The students sat down, some at desks, some on the floor. Mr Hecat pointed out a desk for me to sit at. He grabbed a chair from a larger desk and sat down.

"Quinn has moved here from Melbourne and is living on the Warhurst property. Now he would love to get to know you all, so I reckon we should tell him a little about ourselves. You know, things about your family, how long you've lived here, pets you may have, and things you like doing."

"Hey, Finn, can I call you Huckleberry?" The tallest member of the class interrupted proceedings.

"It's Quinn, Charlie, not Finn," Mr Hecat said.

Charlie blushed and looked at me. "Oops, sorry."

"That's okay. You can call me Huckleberry if you want." I was trying hard to be seen as nice.

"Nah, Quinn's shorter. It's a funny name, though."

"Charlie likes to read and can also be a bit rude." Mr Hecat gave Charlie a stare.

"I'm named after some Irish relo. Some war hero or something. Mum tells me the name can mean chief, or wise." My voice was shaky. Should I have said "relative"? Maybe they didn't know what relo meant. "That's good…that you like reading. I like reading comics."

"Which ones?" Charlie asked.

"The Phantom…um…is my favourite." My voice was steadying, but I was fidgeting with the buckle on my backpack.

"What about you others? What are your favourite comics?" Mr Hecat asked. "Tell the class as part of your introduction." He looked over the class.

"Okay, let's start with the twins." Mr Hecat pointed to two boys sitting on the floor. They sort of looked alike. "This is Greg and Daniel. They are twins but not identical. As you get to know them, you'll see they're quite different."

Both boys had whitish-blond hair and brown eyes. I didn't think I'd ever seen a person with blond hair that didn't have blue eyes. Their faces were similar.

"I'm Daniel," said one, "and I'm the oldest."

"By seconds," Greg said, tapping his head. "But I'm smarter."

Daniel laughed. "I don't think so."

"Okay, okay. Tell Quinn about yourselves."

Daniel pointed to the tall boy who had called me Finn. "He's our older brother and gets us into lots of trouble. We live just off the main road. Our dad is a shearer. We don't see him much, but when he does come home, he brings lots of good things like comics and lollies."

A cricket chirped outside or so I thought. Greg wore a huge grin on his face.

Mr Hecat raised his brows. "Okay, Greg, show Quinn what you've got."

Greg pulled out a colourful metal gadget from his pocket. He moved his thumb a few times, making a clicking sound. "It's a clicker. Dad brought a few of them home. I'll bring one in for you, Quinn."

"New rule. No clickers in the classroom," Mr Hecat said. "You can click outside."

Greg handed the gadget to one of the girls sitting on the floor to look at. It had a colourful clown on the front. I didn't find clowns friendly; they always seemed kind of creepy to me.

"Dad told us they used to use them in the war to figure out if someone was a friend or an enemy," Daniel said, his voice dropping like he was sharing a secret. "Soldiers would click once and if they heard two clicks back, they knew it was a friendly soldier mate."

Mr Hecat looked at Daniel, then nodded. "That's a good bit of history, Daniel."

It was interesting, but I was trying to work out what we could use the clickers for. It would probably drive Mum crazy, me running around clicking. As for Mr Warhurst, he would probably shoot me.

Greg and Daniel were both staring out the window like they were thinking really hard about what else to say.

"We like Spider-Man and Batman comics!" Greg blurted out.

Maybe a spider web outside made him think of the comics.

A click came from the background. The two girls on the floor were giggling.

"Oops, sorry, Mr Hecat," a girl with short hair said.

Mr Hecat walked over to the girl and snatched the clicker out of her hand. "What did I say?" he asked harshly.

A heaviness came over the room. But then Mr Hecat smiled. I thought of Dr Jekyll and Mr Hyde.

"So, Rosemary, the focus is on you now. Tell Quinn about yourself."

I felt bad for Rosemary. Her eyes looked a little watery, and she was messing with her skirt. She and the girl next to her had the bluest eyes I'd ever seen.

"Rosemary and Jill live at the post office," Daniel said.

"Thank you, Daniel, but I was hoping Rosemary would tell us that."

"Yeah, me and my sister Jill live down the road at the post office. It's also the grocery store. Our house is out the back. We've always lived there."

I liked Rosemary. Even though she was fidgeting, she talked like she wasn't scared. I had a feeling she'd had some trouble with Mr Hecat before.

"You go to the city much?" I asked.

"We've been a few times to visit relatives. My favourite auntie lives in Melbourne."

"Yes, Auntie Bev spoils us." Jill giggled.

"Okay, let's move on to Bruce."

"Can I tell Quinn what comics we read?" Rosemary asked.

Mr Hecat took a deep breath. His bottom lip tucked in. "Hmm…okay, do that."

"I like reading Archies." She pointed to Jill. "She likes reading Daisy and Donald Duck comics."

"There you go. Nice. Okay, over to you, Bruce."

All eyes turned to a red-haired boy sitting at a desk. He reminded me of Jimmy's mate, Ginger. He held a clicker in his hand. He lifted it and pretended to click it. Mr Hecat bit his lip but didn't say a word in response to Bruce's challenge.

"I live not far from where you're living, Quinn. We have a similar farm to the one you're living at. My dad's the local fire chief."

"His dad's a big man, Quinn. Bigger and more frightening than a yowie." Daniel lowered his voice to add, "I reckon even Mr Hecat is scared of him."

Had Daniel seen a yowie? I'll ask him later.

"That's enough, Daniel." Mr Hecat gave him a stern look. "Maybe we should bring this chat to a close."

Bruce tensed up his body, trying to look tough. "I like Superman comics."

"Well, I think we got all comic characters covered."

"What about Quinn?" Rosemary asked. 'How come he's here?"

"Quinn, just remember yowies aren't real. Daniel has a good imagination." Mr Hecat gestured for me to speak.

"Um. Right. I'll remember that." I paused and took a breath. "My mum's got a job at the Warhurst place. She's going to look after the house while Mr Warhurst's family go and visit a sick relative overseas and have a holiday."

"Bet your poor mum has to look after Mr Warhurst too. I know Mrs Warhurst ran around like a chook with its head chopped off, looking after him," Charlie said. "He probably wouldn't even know how to cook a rabbit."

What did these people eat: pigeons, rabbits, yowies?

"Take it easy, Charlie, don't scare Quinn."

Why would I be scared? I wanted to get off the subject. "I saw lots of rabbits on my way to school this morning. One was running around in circles like it was blind."

"It's mix…omat…to—"

"Charlie is trying to say myxomatosis," Mr Hecat advised. "It's a virus used to kill off the rabbits. It worked for a while, but the bunnies got used to it."

"So, some still get the virus?" I asked.

"Yeah, some, not a lot. The one you saw was probably a weak one, maybe already sick," Bruce said. "Rabbits are a big problem here." His face lit up. "You can come rabbiting with us. We use nets and ferrets."

"Ferrets?"

"Remember, we're talking to a city boy here, Bruce," Charlie said.

Bruce gave Charlie a look.

"We place nets over the rabbit holes and use the ferret to chase the rabbit out," Bruce said. "And we catch them in the net when they come charging out of the hole."

"And we make money on the skins," Daniel said.

The thought of skinning a rabbit and eating one, especially with that strange virus lurking around, didn't sit well with me. I was on the verge of mentioning Mr Warhurst's gold nugget to change the subject again, but Mr Hecat interrupted and told us all to stand and take a recess break while he showed me around the school. I wondered why he wanted to show me around again.

I caught a glimpse of Rosemary's eyes as she left the room. Her expression confused me. Was it fear or sadness I saw in her gaze?

17 The Radio Room

As Mr Hecat led me out of the classroom, I felt both curious and nervous. We approached what he called the 'radio room'. I had only briefly stepped into this room once before. We stood at the doorway, and I peeked inside the room. A big tree outside blocked most of the daylight. In the dimness, Mr Hecat pointed out the radio and seating arrangements, his voice a mixture of excitement and authority.

"Let's step inside, Quinn, and I'll give you a demo on how it all works."

The air in the room again felt thick. Something about the room made me feel uneasy—I wasn't sure why. Maybe it was the dim light or the shadows. A tall wardrobe stood in the room, looking dark and creepy.

Mr Hecat turned on the light.

The radio was huge, the biggest I'd ever seen. It was shaped like a tall rectangle, with a giant speaker at the bottom covered by cloth that looked a bit like a net. Above the speaker, there was a row of shiny numbers and knobs.

"We use the radio for our music lessons and some other things."

Mr Hecat walked over to the radio and flipped a switch, then twisted a knob. Scratchy noises came out—bits of music and voices, all jumbled up. He kept turning the knob. Then a song on the radio got clearer. It was loud. The song was *Little Boy Lost.*

Mr Hecat moved his head to the beat, then turned the volume down. "My favourite song," he said.

It was one of my favourites too. I often thought about that little lost boy and how scary it must have been for him.

Mr Hecat turned the knob again. This time, a voice spoke. He looked at me and smiled.

The voice was clear and it was English, but I could only understand a few words. Panic started to build inside me. Why wasn't I able to understand?

"Well, I think we're going to hear a lot more about those warships colliding. Will be talked about for years." Mr Hecat, said looking right at me. "Don't you agree?" His stare grew more intense. "Don't you agree?" He seemed to be getting angry.

My chest was getting tighter. Like something was growing inside me, ready to explode. I took some deep breaths.

He moved closer to me, inches from my face, eyebrows raised. "Don't you agree?" His eyes frightened me.

"Yes," I stuttered.

He shook his head and slapped me hard across the face.

***

At the end of the day, Mr Hecat drove me home. I sat frozen in the car, my mind replaying the slap.

He had told the class that the redness on my face was from falling off a chair while listening to the radio. He laughed, and the class sort of chuckled—except for Rosemary.

As I was about to get out of the car, Mr Hecat leant over and put his hand on my leg. "Sorry about losing my temper. I want so much for you kids to learn and I get annoyed at times. Best not tell anyone. It could cause problems for you and your mum. They may blame you for getting the school closed down. It won't happen again."

I stepped out of the car and watched him drive off. Tears welled up in my eyes. *What was that all about?* I stood there for what felt like hours, numb, unsure what to do.

I jumped at a clatter behind me and whirled around. Bruce skidded to a halt on his bike, kicking up plumes of dust and debris, some of which landed on my shoes.

"You okay, Quinn?"

I quickly wiped my eyes. "Yep. How did you get here so fast?"

"I know a few shortcuts." He got off the bike, placed it on the ground, and walked over to me. He tilted his head to look at the side of my face. "You didn't fall off the chair, did you?"

"I did." I swallowed hard.

"You didn't. Look, I want to be your friend, so you can be honest with me."

I remained silent.

Bruce went back and picked up his bike. He sent me a hard look. "What's with the watery eyes?"

"I sneezed a few times."

"Sure, I believe ya. Listen, Quinn, I know what happened. He's not a nice man. He's got a few of the kids scared, but none will speak up."

Bruce rested his foot on a pedal. "He doesn't come after me or the other boys because our dads would deal with him.

The girls don't have a dad. And I'm guessing that's the same for you because you haven't mentioned him."

My tongue was glued to the roof of my mouth.

"It's okay, Quinn, I'm going to look after you." He looked towards the house. "There'll be bikes around here, ones the family or visitors use. Find one, and we can ride together to school. Saves you getting in a car with him. Okay?"

I nodded.

He rode off.

I walked back and into the house. Bruce could be a good friend. I felt better knowing that he'd be looking out for me.

In the kitchen, Mum reached out with her hand and tilted my head to the side. "What happened to your face, Quinn?"

"A branch slapped me. One of the kids at school held back a branch and then let it fling at me."

"That's not nice." Mum tied an apron around her waist.

"It was sort of funny at the time."

I didn't like lying, but I preferred that to getting myself or others in trouble. And I didn't want to upset Mum. She said lying was a sin. So, God did not like me lying, and in a funny sort of way, I thought it was bad too. *I'll tell Him I'm sorry when I go to bed—if I remember.*

"Mum, I think we'll be sometimes using the radio in class. That scares me a little. I panicked today when Mr Hecat showed me how they use the radio. He got annoyed with me when I couldn't tell what I was hearing. I think it was about those warships colliding."

"Yes, that collision is generating a lot of interest. But try not to worry about the radio. You'll get used to it." She gave me a warm look. "It's hard work being a teacher. They do get annoyed with kids sometimes, so just do your best. Try and stay out of trouble."

Except sometimes trouble came looking for you, and it had certainly found me. I felt sick in the tummy thinking about the radio and Mr Hecat.

"I find it hard to understand people too, Quinn, unless I see them," Mum said. "I need to see their faces, their lips, their expressions. Telephones scare me. Radios are helpful, but I don't know how I'd go if I had to answer questions from someone on the radio. I think I'd panic too."

I shared Mum's dislike of phones. "I can hear music okay," I told her.

"Maybe it's because you don't have to say anything. You don't have to think, just sing along," Mum said. "I prefer to write letters because I can take my time, think about what I want to say."

Mum walked over to the fridge and retrieved some mince. "I'd best start making dinner. Why don't you go and write that letter to your new friend in Melbourne?"

"Good idea, but I might go see if I can find a bike that I can ride to school. That will save me walking or the teacher having to drive me."

I noticed a bruise on Mum's arm. She saw me looking at it and smiled weakly. "Bumped against the doorway."

She was lying, too.

18 The Bike Ride

It was Wednesday. My third day at the bush school, my one-teacher school. I was nervous and worried about Mum, but the thought of my bike ride calmed me.

I found some bikes last night. There were a few in the Warhursts' big shed, which also had bunks. I figured that's where farm helpers stayed, and the bikes were for them to use. I picked one that looked good and pumped up the tyres. By morning, they were still full of air. A good sign.

I followed the track I had walked the day before. Suddenly, I thought I ran over a black snake and flung my legs in the air. But when I stopped and looked back, I realised it was only a stick. I laughed—a nervous laugh.

There was no sign of Bruce on my bike ride, but I'd talk to him at school about his shortcuts and ride home with him.

I arrived early, so I rested my bike against a tree and sat on a large rock near the school. The birdsong was soothing. In the distance, I could see the tops of the large trees swaying in the breeze. On the bike, I'd pedalled fast to escape their large, dark shadows. I'd nearly run over a pigeon, which made me think of the man that shot them. He scared me. My tummy churned.

Two figures walked up towards the school, and I guessed them to be Rosemary and Jill. As they got closer, they greeted me. Rosemary sat down on the rock next to me and Jill headed over to the small playground. Rosemary gave me a smile. "So, you rode a bike here today?"

"Yep. I enjoyed it. Bit cool at times, though." I was glad I wore my jeans, but I noticed some chain grease on them. Mum would not be happy.

"It's a long ride from Katrina's place," Rosemary said.

A surge of excitement hit me. "You know Katrina?"

"She's my best friend." She looked over at her sister climbing the steps to the slide. "Did you get to meet Katrina before she left?"

My heart fluttered. "I did. She seemed nice."

"Oh, she is. I'm already missing her." Rosemary straightened her skirt and settled more comfortably on the rock. "I've already written two letters to her. I stamped airmail stickers on them and sent them off."

As she spoke, I considered writing to Katrina. I was sure she wouldn't mind.

Rosemary continued, "Mum said she'd get me some aerograms; she reckons they'd be better."

What was an aerogram? Something that flew?

"I miss her a lot because I could talk to her about things."

Curiosity got the better of me, and I asked, "What would you talk to her about?"

"School, home, the shop. And now I can tell her about you."

Heat rose to my cheeks. I hoped it wasn't obvious. "That would be nice. I also spent some time with Katrina in Melbourne. She came to the city to do some shopping with her mum before she left. The weather wasn't nice so we didn't do much."

"Oh, that's sad. I remember her telling me about that trip. And that's right, she mentioned a boy. That must have been you." She smiled. "But I didn't get a chance to see her, to say goodbye, before she left for overseas. The family left in a bit of a rush, but she had given me the address of a relative, so that was good."

"They had to go earlier as their sick relative was getting worse." My mind was all over the place with thoughts of Katrina. "Have you heard from her?"

"Not yet. Letters can take up to two weeks to get here from the UK."

"Imagine how slow it would be if we didn't have planes."

"Yeah, years maybe."

We laughed. Voices sounded nearby, and a car was coming up the road.

Rosemary stood. "Well, time for school." She gave me a nervous smile. "Be careful, Quinn. The teacher's not a very nice person."

I gulped. I missed my old school. My big class. My school friends. My old teacher. He was a nice man, and he wore a leather glove on his left hand, because he'd lost his hand in the war. He was a hero, but Mr Hecat seems to be a villain.

The day was uneventful, although I feared having to go to the radio room. I eventually did have to go, but it was with all the class. We sat around the radio and listened to a story.

Mum was right. I could hear if I didn't have to do something. I wondered why I panicked when I was asked to do something by a voice I could not see.

Tomorrow was Show and Tell day. A knot tightened in my stomach. What could I bring? I didn't want to bore the other students.

I ended up enjoying my third day at school. Charlie was the leader, Greg and Daniel kept me amused, the girls were genuinely sweet, and Bruce seemed to be our guardian angel.

There was no Mr Hyde today, only Mr Hecat.

When school finished, I looked down towards where I had parked my bike. There were a number of bikes resting on the trunk of the large tree that stood guard over the school. Only Rosemary and Jill didn't have bikes, as they lived close by.

We rode past the girls as they walked home.

"Why don't you all stop at the shop and grab some lollies?" Rosemary yelled.

Good idea, but I had no money. The boys stopped at the shop and rested their bikes on a metal guard-rail. I stopped but didn't get off my bike.

"Come on, Quinn. Come check out the shop," Bruce said.

I hesitated and wasn't sure what to say. I didn't want them to think I had no money.

"I'll lend you some money," Bruce said.

"No need to do that. I'll have a look inside and bring some money tomorrow."

I stepped through a creaky door into the shop. A bell jingled. It smelled like a lolly shop, a sweet, sugary smell. Shelves were lined with jars filled with colourful treats.

Rosemary was already behind the counter, wearing the hugest smile. An older lady stood beside her—her mum, I guessed.

"Why so many lollies?" I asked.

"City folk visit the national park on the weekends. Mum has a reputation for making the best lollies in the world. We sell lots of lollies on the weekends." She looked at the lady beside her. "This is my mum." She pointed to me. "This is Quinn."

"Well, hello, Quinn. Welcome to the best lolly shop in the world and welcome to Edithburra. You'll have to bring your parents in for a treat. I like to meet new folk."

"I just have a mum."

She nodded, as if understanding something that I didn't.

Rosemary grabbed a jar sitting on the counter. She twisted and lifted the top. A sweet aroma flooded my senses.

"Here, try this." She dropped a black-and-white lolly in my hand and pointed to her mouth. "Suck."

I did as I was told. Soon, a liquorice taste flooded my mouth. Her eyes widened, and she looked like she was waiting for me to say something.

"Hmmm, nice." I should've said something with a bit more oomph.

She grabbed some of the lollies and threw them in a bag, then handed it to me. She looked at her mum, who nodded. "Pay us tomorrow," she said with a wink.

I looked around and saw the others collecting different lollies and putting them into brown paper bags. They all had the widest grins as they strolled up to the counter.

On my bike ride home, my mouth filled with sweetness, I thought of getting some pocket money from Mum. I also thought about Rosemary.

Not another crush.

19 Mr Hyde Returns

I was awoken by Mum's voice, loud and urgent. She was yelling at someone. I scrambled out of bed, heart banging against my chest as I cracked open my door.

Dawn was breaking through, and in the dim light, I saw Mr Warhurst stagger out of Mum's room. He had hold of his trousers like they were about to fall off.

He saw me. "Get back in your room!" he yelled. He used bad language, words I'd hardly heard before. He calmed down a little. "Your mother was having a nightmare, and her screams woke me."

I stepped back into my room and shut the door, trembling. After a few moments, I opened the door ever so slightly and peeked out. He was nowhere to be seen, so I tiptoed out into the passageway. A low, whimpering sound sent a wave of unease through me. I took a deep breath and crept towards Mum's door.

"Are you okay, Mum?" I whispered.

I tried to open her door but there was something blocking it.

"Go back to bed, Quinn. I'm okay. Just a nightmare."

She was lying again.

"Mum, are you okay?" Doubts swirled in my mind.

I heard movement. Mum shifted whatever was behind the door and opened the door slightly. Her fearful eyes peered through the crack.

"I'm okay, Quinn. Just bad dreams. Please go back to bed."

"Hey, you!" Mr Warhurst roared behind me. I turned. He stood there, his rifle pointing right at me. "I told you to stay in your room." Slurring his words, he staggered towards me, his hands shaking as he held the rifle.

"Run, Quinn!" Mum yelled through the crack in the door.

I bolted down the passageway and out into the backyard. Sunrise and birdsong greeted me, but my heavy panting drowned them out—the crazy man was charging after me.

I sprinted towards the cover of the trees, but a loud grunt followed by a thud made me glance back. The crazy man had fallen. Mum, still in her nightgown and wrapped in a blanket, hurried to his side and knelt beside him.

I tried hard to control my breathing. My stomach knotted and my heart pounded. Would the old man have fired the rifle?

Mum stood and walked towards me. "He's okay. Just drunk and passed out. He probably won't remember what's happened. Go back to your room. I'll put a blanket over him." She turned to look at the man crumpled on the ground. "He'll wake up soon. The cold ground will wake him."

I walked up to the man, battling the desire to kick him.

"Go, Quinn. Go back to your room. Please."

I paused.

Mum sent me a stern look. "Please."

I stormed towards the back door, bare feet squishing in the damp grass, my hands balled up tight. Would he have shot me? My mouth tasted gross, like licking a penny. I stopped and turned to look back. Mum was crouching beside the drunken man, fixing the blanket over him. She stood, saw me, and waved me to go into the house.

I pulled open the back door and headed to my room, pausing at the doorway as my feet suddenly felt heavy. The urge to kick the door was strong. I heard Mum's soft footsteps as she entered the house, came up behind me, and stood next to me, resting a hand on my shoulder. I tried to calm my breathing.

"Mr Warhurst's mind was probably in the jungles of Papua New Guinea when he saw you. He could've mistaken you for the enemy and taken a shot at you." A shiver ran over Mum's body.

She continued, her voice quiet. "He served with the Australian Army in the jungles. When he drinks, he sometimes leaves reality behind and thinks he's in the jungle, fighting. Again, Quinn, it's the drink."

"Is this what Dad was like?" How long was it? Four or five years. I can't tell if I really remember him or if it's just from what people have told me or pictures I've seen.

Mum didn't answer.

"Why was he in your room?"

Mum drew in a deep breath and paused for a moment. "He was lost."

"Lost in his own home?"

"No. Lost in his mind."

I didn't understand. Daylight was pouring into the house. I needed to get ready for school. I couldn't leave Mum alone, but I also wanted to escape the madness.

She seemed to read my thoughts. "You best get ready for school. I'm going to be fine."

A shadow flooded the passageway. Mr Warhurst stood in the doorway. He headed towards us, brushed me aside, and rushed to the bathroom hand raised to his mouth. The sound of his puking followed.

"Go to school, Quinn. You'll be safer there."

"What about you?" My mind was a twisted mess.

"I'll stay in my room until he sobers up and I'll barricade the door." She touched my shoulder. "Don't worry, Quinn. Once he's sober, he'll be full of guilt and gentle as a mouse."

I wasn't sure about the last bit. He didn't strike me as a gentle man.

"You should come to school with me. Stay at the post office and come home later."

"That may not be the best thing to do. He may fire me, and then we'll be in a worse situation. I'll talk to him when he sobers up. Now, you get yourself off to school. Grab your lunch pack from the fridge. Go, I'll be fine."

My mum was tough. She needed to be.

The tears came as I was riding the bike. I had to stop to wipe my eyes. I looked around the bushes and up to the clear blue sky. Nature could feel comforting sometimes. I asked God for help.

***

Bruce's bike was propped against a fence post while he was kneeling to study something on the leaf-littered dirt track. He looked up when he heard me approaching.

He pointed with a stick to an insect. I dismounted, set my bike on the ground, and walked over for a closer look. It was an ant with a long, lean body and huge eyes.

"Wow. That's big." The morning's events slipped from my mind.

"Bull ant." Bruce poked it with the stick. "They bite with one end, sting with the other." The ant stood on its rear legs, ready to attack. Bruce threw the stick away. He walked over to his bike and lifted it off the post.

I picked mine up off the ground and wheeled it over to Bruce.

"It's good to keep your eyes on the ground," Bruce said.

"Because of snakes?"

"Nope, still a bit chilly for the snakes, but you might find a gold nugget."

"Have you found one?"

"Nope. But I'd love to. There's just something about gold."

"It makes you rich."

"Yeah, I've heard of people finding big nuggets," Bruce said. "You never know."

"You ever seen a nugget before?"

"Nah, but I always keep my eyes peeled. I've seen people walking around with gold detectors."

"What's a gold detector?" I asked.

"They look weird. Like a box with a pole sticking out of it and a circle thingy at the end. The box has knobs and switches on it. I saw a man with one once—thought he was an alien." Bruce chuckled. "He moved the circle thing along the ground, like he was polishing the soil."

"Polishing the soil?"

"Yeah, like when someone polishes a hospital floor."

I nodded slowly, picturing Mum with a big machine, moving it back and forth over a shiny hospital floor. I couldn't tell if that was a memory or just something I made up.

"Mr Warhurst has a gold nugget." It would be so cool to steal it. I felt a twinge of guilt. I wouldn't actually do it, but today, revenge felt really tempting.

Bruce's eyes lit up. "Really?"

"Yep. I'll show it to you one day."

"Would you? That'd be so cool." A serious look came over his face. "How are you getting on with the old man?"

"Alright, I suppose." I had never lied so much in my life.

Bruce stared at me. "My dad doesn't like him. Thinks he's a grouch."

"I don't really know him. I've only seen him a few times. Mum mainly deals with him." More half lies. I didn't like the feelings that came with lying.

"Well, you make sure you look after your mum. You have any problems, let me know and I'll tell me dad."

I liked Bruce. He was looking out for me, but I wasn't sure why. Talking about Mum had triggered more guilty feelings and the urge to go back and check on her.

Bruce mounted his bike and looked at me. "Well, you coming?"

I gripped my handlebars tightly. "I'm not sure if I should go to school today. Talking about Mum has made me think I should go back and check on her. She wasn't well this morning."

"Okay, you get home to her. I'll tell the teacher. We need to look after our mums. Now go." He pointed towards the farm. "Go," he repeated.

I went. As I entered the track, I stopped and turned to watch Bruce riding along the road. He was pedalling like mad. I would've slowed him down. I turned back towards the farm and started pedalling, feeling guilty that I'd left Mum alone with that man.

June 1964
Edithburra

My dearest Martha,

My heart reaches out to you. I miss you and home so much.

I sit writing to you under a huge deciduous tree, its leaves forming a carpet beneath my feet. I feel now that a large shadow has come over my life. Writing helps me make sense of the mess I've found myself in. You see, we had to move so I could find a job, and it hasn't worked out well.

What have I done? I've put our lives in danger. I've taken on a job as a housekeeper to look after a man and a household while his family travels overseas. Why was I so stupid not to see the dangers it presented?

The man's another version of Harold, and just as violent. I feel trapped. I've no transport and the house, a farm, is many miles away from the main town. I sit and stare at the phone on the wall many times a day, but who can I call? I do not want to alarm my children.

I can still picture the look on their faces when I told them where I was going. They questioned if I was doing the right thing. I just wanted to escape; my grieving blinded me to the foolishness of my actions.

A neighbour appears to be my only hope.

Forgive me for writing to you with such negative things. I know there's nothing you can do, but it helps to share this with you.

I'll pause for now and write some more later.

20 A Trip to School

Off the track and on the dirt driveway, I heard a screech and saw flashes of white in the pine trees. Cockatoos, searching for food.

The house came into view. The screeching ceased, and a hush came over the homestead. I rested my bike against the front of the house. The front door creaked as I opened it. My feet deathly quiet, I stepped inside.

"Mum?" I said in a soft voice, my heart pounding in my chest.

Silence, except for the steady hum of the refrigerator. I scanned the living area. The morning sun filtered into the room, some rays of light shining on the rock collection. I was sure a glitter came from the gold nugget.

A funny sound came from the direction of the old man's room, and it startled me. Snorts mixed with a whistle. The door was ajar. Nervously, I peeked in. The old man lay motionless on his back, like a corpse. His chest rose, and a snort came out.

I stepped back quietly, away from the door, not wanting to wake him. Suddenly, a deep snore burst from his room, echoing through the house. My heart constricted. I turned and peeked back in, expecting to see him awake. He lay there, still dead to the world. I retreated.

Where was Mum? I checked her room. Nothing. I walked down the passageway, birdsong filtering through the back screen door. Stepping outside, everything felt different, like I'd entered another world. The gentle breeze and soft morning light were so peaceful, it made the scary stuff from before feel like a dream, like maybe I had imagined it all.

A wooden picnic table stood under a large tree, most of its leaves gone. Two large black birds perched high in the branches. Tom had told me those birds were ravens, but for some reason they gave off a bad vibe. Maybe it was their blackness.

Mum sat at the table, her back to me. It looked like she was writing a letter.

Kraah, kraah.

"Mum." I kept my voice soft, not wanting to wake the snoring old man. The noisy ravens would probably wake him soon enough.

Mum turned with a surprised look on her face.

"Quinn! What are you doing here?" She stood. "You should be at school."

"Yes, you should be," came the croaky voice behind me.

Kraah, kraah. The ravens flew off.

The old man stood there, resembling a scarecrow: his clothes hung loosely from him, his hair a mess with bits of dead grass tangled in it from the morning, and his face was pale. He walked up to the table and rested his hands on the surface to steady himself.

"Err…sorry about last night. I'm very embarrassed. I shouldn't drink. I'm really sorry. It won't happen again." He rubbed his head.

Mum moved closer to me and looked at the old man. "Is there anything I can get for you?"

"No, you stay there." The old man swallowed. "Let me get Quinn to school. I need to pick up something at the post office."

Mum looked at me. "Maybe it's alright for Quinn to miss a day."

"That's up to you." He coughed. "But he's just started at a new school, so skipping won't leave a good impression on the teacher." His voice was still croaky.

I wanted to jump on my bike and escape. Strange feelings stirred in my gut.

Mum appeared deep in thought. "Maybe you should get to school then, Quinn. Is that okay?"

I was starting to think that Mum's world didn't have room for me. In some ways, I understood as she had a lot on her mind and needed to work hard to keep this job.

"You come for the drive too, Mum. I can show you the bike track I use." I tried to push the things that had happened to the back of my mind.

The old man looked at me. "Yes, and about that bike…"

I sensed I was about to be in trouble. I was sure Mum had asked him about using the bike.

The old man rubbed his eyes. "It doesn't matter."

"Oh yes, that's my fault, Lance. I forgot to ask if it was okay for Quinn to use a bike."

Mum had forgotten to ask. I could've been in even more trouble.

"No, that's okay." He turned and started heading back to the house. "Meet you both at the car. Go and get your stuff."

He still had a slight stagger. Would he be okay to drive?

Dr Jekyll had returned. I wondered for how long.

Mum put her hand on my shoulder. "We'll be okay, Quinn. I'll talk to him."

Mum knew how to handle these things.

The car trip was a quiet one. Both Mum and Mr Warhurst were totally focused on the road ahead. I wondered how drinking affected driving.

I didn't like the quiet. I wanted to say something to break the uncomfortable silence. My mind wandered to unpleasant things.

"Just up ahead is where the shortcut comes out."

They both turned and looked as we passed the track.

More silence.

"It's really thick bush in there. Like the jungle." *Maybe I shouldn't have mentioned jungle.*

Mr Warhurst's chest rose. He let out a deep breath. Mum's eyes were closed. She opened them and spoke.

"Quinn likes to talk. In the past, I've offered him bribes to keep quiet. You know, like don't say a word for five minutes and I'll give you a thruppence."

"Five minutes is an eternity for a young one," Mr Warhurst said with a thin smile.

The old man was right. I'd never made any money being quiet.

We turned onto the school road. Bruce had just pulled up and stood with the boys outside the post office. Rosemary and Jill came out of the building. They all looked in the direction of the car. Bruce wore a surprised look as we pulled up. They started heading up to the school.

"I'll get out here," I said.

The old man nodded.

"Why don't you go in and check out the store, Mum? Lots of goodies."

"He means lollies. Another potential blackmail strategy for you, Elizabeth," Mr Warhurst said.

Mum gave a soft laugh. Her mood seemed to be lifting, and I felt better.

Now, new feelings attacked me. I didn't want my school class to see Mum. All I wanted was to leap out of the car and sprint to the school. I loved Mum at home, just the two of us—but here, in front of my new friends, they might think she was uncool. Maybe even a bit old.

"See ya later, then." I stepped out, shut the door, and headed towards my friends.

Mum was getting out of the car. I shot her a quick smile as I hurried past. When I briefly looked back, she was shrugging at Mr Warhurst.

Bruce walked over to me. "Things okay?"

"Yep."

***

Jill singing from the radio room could be heard in the main classroom. It was soft and had a sweetness to it. Rosemary leaned over. "Jill loves music and singing. There's a radio show on in the morning with music and singing. Mr Hecat lets her listen to it."

When Jill was finished with her radio show, it was my turn in the radio room, as Mr Hecat wanted me to catch up on some math classes.

The radio show was now talking about the government considering a new form of money and briefly spoke about old and new types of money.

"So, how many cents in a threepence?" Mr Hecat asked.

I tried really hard to hear what was being said on the radio. My stomach was full of knots. And then the blow came, more violent this time. He threw me off the chair and kicked me in the ribs. I covered my head.

He forcefully picked me up and dumped me back onto the chair. "You deaf or something?"

Pain shot up my left side. "Maybe...maybe I am," I stammered.

The look on Mr Hecat's face changed, like he had committed some crime.

I rubbed my aching ribs.

"You're going to tell the class that you fell off the chair again."

I felt strange and jumpy, like I was in some crazy movie. *The old man attacked me, but I survived that and I'll make it through this also.* Thoughts bounced around in my head. I thought of paperboy Jimmy. He'd help me. That made me feel a bit better.

Mr Hecat was staring at me. "Well?"

"I fell off the chair," I said softly. Even speaking hurt my ribs. Mr Hecat was disciplining me because I wasn't hearing the radio. I wasn't concentrating. I'd do better next time.

"Yes, I fell off the chair," I repeated, louder this time. Like Jimmy, I'd be tough and strong.

"It's best the class believe that. We can keep your stupidity a secret between you and me. We'll work it out."

"We will work it out," I agreed, but I wasn't stupid. I wasn't. He was, but what could I do? He was my teacher.

"You're lucky I'm here. I'm overqualified to be working here. They don't pay me much. But I'm here because I want to keep my wife happy, and I can help you. Yes, you're very lucky."

He mumbled on. The radio was still broadcasting words like *dollars* and *cents.* I didn't know whether to listen to him or the radio. The words mixed with each other and just sounded like noise. In my mind, I went into the bush, looking for birds.

"Mr Hecat, are you okay?"

Bruce's voice brought me back to the real world. He stood in the doorway.

"We heard a noise and thought it best to check if everything was okay."

"Thank you, Bruce. That was very thoughtful of you. Quinn fell from the chair again. I think the radio broadcast put him to sleep."

"You okay, Quinn?"

"Yes, he's fine, Bruce. Now go back to the classroom; I'll be there in a sec."

Bruce gave a reluctant nod and left.

"You stay here, Quinn. Just listen to the radio." Mr Hecat looked at the machine. "Listen to get some practice. I'll come back and get you in ten minutes.

"Make sure you don't fall off the chair." He grinned. "Again." He added.

He left the room. I stared at the radio, then moved closer and placed my ear against the speaker. The soft cloth covering the speaker offered comfort. It was someone talking about God.

I looked up at the ceiling. "Please help me, God. Please help me," I whispered.

21 There Are Secrets

When school ended, I walked to the post office with Rosemary and Bruce. We passed an empty can on the road and Bruce kicked it along the road a few times, then picked it up and dropped it in a bin outside the store.

"Most probably belonged to a city person. They don't appreciate nature," Bruce said.

I couldn't stop thinking about Mr Hecat kicking me. Why would a grown-up do that to a kid? What kind of monster kicked a child? We found a bench under the big window with posters of all kinds of chocolate bars sticktaped on the inside of the glass. The posters helped take my mind off things.

"You didn't fall off the chair, did you, Quinn?" Rosemary asked.

"I did, I think I fell asleep. It's all blurry." For some reason, Mr Hecat doesn't like me, and I have to deal with it.

I didn't like lying, so I sent a quick sorry to God.

Rosemary nodded slowly, looking like she wanted to say something else.

"How you getting home?" Bruce asked.

Just then, Mr Hecat pulled up. He leaned over and wound down the passenger window. "You want a lift home, Quinn? I noticed that you didn't have your bike."

"Nah, going to hang around with these two."

"Okay, just remember you had a fall. So, take it easy. You sure you don't want a lift?"

"I'm good."

We watched him drive off.

"How are you getting home, Quinn?" Rosemary asked.

"Haven't really thought about it. I guess I'll have to walk." The last thing I wanted to do was get in a car with that monster.

"I can dink you some of the way," Bruce said.

"That sounds dangerous," Rosemary said. "Would he sit on the handlebar or the crossbar?"

"Crossbar. But he'll have to walk on the hilly parts."

"I really don't have a problem walking all the way." Although the pain in my side told me something different. I touched the tender area.

Rosemary saw me and got up and went inside.

"Hopefully she's grabbing us a lolly," Bruce said.

"Hope so. Those black-and-white lollies are nice."

A few moments later, Rosemary appeared with her mum at her side.

"Hello, Mr Quinn. I met your mum earlier. She's a lovely lady. Now, I hear you had an accident at school today."

"Not really, I just fell off a chair."

"You sore anywhere?"

"Not really."

"He's not telling the truth, Mum."

Rosemary's mum tilted her head. "I don't guess you to be

a liar, Quinn. Maybe you have a bruise but don't know about it." She pointed to my side. "Could I have a look?"

I hesitated, but before I knew it, Bruce had lifted my shirt. The one time I hadn't tucked my shirt in.

Rosemary's mum bent and looked closer. "You're going to have a nasty bruise by the look of the redness there. What did you fall on?"

"I don't know. It all happened too quickly."

Rosemary's mum nodded. "Tell you what, Quinn, we'll get Rosemary's brother to look after the shop and we'll drive you home."

"You don't have to do that." I stood. Pain shot up my left side and I grimaced.

Rosemary looked at me, her eyes wide. "Not sore. Sure."

I sat down. "It'll be okay. Just like a bump in footy. Nothing a hot bath won't fix." Though I didn't remember seeing a bath at the Warhurst place. The pain increased.

"I think they're right, Quinn. You need to take it easy." Bruce stood in front of me, blocking out the afternoon sun. "We have Show and Tell tomorrow and you don't want to miss that. I reckon you should bring that gold nugget in for us to see."

"Gold nugget?" Rosemary sounded excited. "I'd love to see that."

The pain moved to my head. How could I get that nugget? I didn't want to disappoint my new friends, and it would feel good to do something the old man wouldn't like.

The car trip home with Rosemary and her mum wasn't a quiet trip. I thought of offering Rosemary a thruppence to be quiet so I could get a word in. That silly thought eased the pain a little.

When we arrived, Mum came out of the house. We all climbed out of the car. Rosemary's mum explained the situation to my mum. I tried to convince them both that I was okay and they eventually stopped fussing over me.

Mr Warhurst had wandered over. He invited Rosemary's mum and my mum to look at the goats. While our mums yakked like we were invisible, I took Rosemary into the house to show her the nugget.

We stood at the rock cabinet. "Wow, that's so cool," Rosemary said. "Can you open it so I can touch it?"

I shrugged. I hadn't figured out how to open the cabinet.

Rosemary ran her hand down the side of the cabinet, as if looking for a latch. Her hand caught on something. She tilted her head. "It's a lock. Do you know where the key is?"

I shook my head. I wasn't sure we should try to open it. My conscience was finally winning over my urge for revenge.

She looked under the cabinet and then at the back, then shrugged. "Oh, well. I look forward to when you bring it to school."

I nodded.

"Do you think he'll let you bring it to school?"

"I'll get Mum to ask him." He might be okay about it after his recent behaviour, but I doubted that.

We strolled out to the backyard and sat down at the picnic table.

"I came here once," Rosemary said. "Katrina invited a few of us to her birthday party last year. We didn't go inside the house, though. It looks a nice house."

"I'm still getting used to it."

"How has Mr Warhurst been?"

"He's okay. Mostly, I don't see much of him." And when I do, it's not exactly pleasant.

Rosemary's fingertips traced idle patterns across the table's surface and then she looked at me seriously. "I like you, Quinn, so I'm going to tell you a secret."

"There you two are!" Rosemary's mum yelled. "We've got to go, love. I'm not sure how your brother will be doing handling the shop."

"Brother?" That's right, they mentioned him before. Don't think my brain was working well then.

"Yeah, Gavin, he's a good mate of Jamie's—Katrina's brother."

The yowie. "I met him when I first visited."

"Well, there ya go." Rosemary looked slightly surprised. "He goes to a private school. He missed the bus this morning. Mum wasn't impressed. Anyway, I'll reintroduce you to him next time he's around."

I walked with Rosemary to the car, where our mums and Mr Warhurst were waiting. She and her mum climbed into the vehicle.

"I like your rock collection, Mr Warhurst," Rosemary said.

I wished Rosemary hadn't told him that.

"You saw it, then?" he asked.

She nodded. They drove off. Rosemary's secret went with them.

Mr Warhurst rushed inside. I could see through the window that he was checking his rock collection. With an angry expression, he came back outside.

"I don't like strangers going into my house, boy. So don't let that happen again."

He was slipping into Mr Hyde once more. "Sorry. I thought you knew the family." Any thoughts of borrowing the nugget vanished.

"The parents, yes; the children, no. You've been warned."

He stormed off towards the shed.

Mum came up beside me. "Sorry, Quinn. We just need to stay out of his way as much as we can. He's probably missing his family."

A writing pad was tucked into Mum's apron.

"You've been writing?"

Mum nodded.

"Who to?"

"My sister in Scotland."

I didn't know Mum had a sister in Scotland. Maybe it was a make-believe sister, like a Santa type person. I'd written letters to the Phantom before, asking him to help me with problems. Was Mum doing that?

"You going to write a letter to my big brother to check on the dog?" I asked.

"I'll do that soon. I can always give them a ring if you are worried about Doggie."

"Nah, it's okay. He wouldn't be able to talk on the phone, anyway."

Mum laughed.

We stood there looking at the shed. A motor started up and a grinding sound filled the air.

"Polishing stones, I'd say," said Mum. "He's got a fridge in there." She paused and bit her lip as she looked towards the shed. "But he has a trip to town tomorrow—for business and to catch up with some friends. He has an early start, so I think he'll go easy on the grog tonight, and he said he may not be home tomorrow night."

Joy filled my heart. I trembled with excitement. "Do you know where the key to the rock cabinet is?"

"No, why?"

"I was going to take the gold nugget in for Show and Tell."

Mum's lips tightened. "I'm not sure if that's a good idea."

"Why not? He's going to be away all day. He wouldn't even know."

"It's too valuable. Take a gemstone instead. Besides, like I said, I don't have a key."

"I really want to impress the teacher and my class."

"Well, do that some other way. Build friendships with them. Rosemary seems like a nice girl, and from what you say about Bruce, he also sounds nice."

More noise came from the shed. The shed door creaked open and Mr Warhurst walked towards us, his boots crunching on the gravel path. As he got closer, he called out, "What's for dinner tonight?"

Mum hesitated and gave me a quick glance. "Mrs Toohey from the post office gave me some lovely fresh rabbit," she said slowly, "and a recipe for a rabbit stew."

He nodded and walked past us.

The more I saw of this man, the more I disliked him. I wanted to go home. But where was home? The People's Palace?

Getcha 'erald!

22 In Possession of Gold

During the night, I climbed out of bed to go to the toilet and tiptoed down the passageway. On the way back to my bedroom, I heard a noise, some mumbling. I peeked into the living room and saw Mr Warhurst standing next to his beloved cabinet, fumbling with a key on a chain. He hadn't gone easy on the grog after all.

"I know you're there, boy."

How had he known?

"Come here."

I hesitated and then entered the living room.

He waved me closer with his hand, his gaze on the cabinet. "I was a real hero when I found this. Everybody wanted to talk to me, but not anymore. They came and they went. Prospectors."

His speech wasn't too bad. Maybe he wasn't drunk. Lonely?

"But that nugget. So special."

I didn't know what to say.

"So rare." He steadied the key, bent over, and unlocked the cabinet. He picked up the gold nugget and placed it in my hand. "Close your fist. Feel the energy."

Its heaviness surprised me. Even in the dim light, it had a golden glow, but it mostly looked like a yellowy, chewed-up piece of gum.

Was there a mystery connected with this nugget? Was that the secret Rosemary was going to tell me about?

"Now off to bed you go." He turned towards me. His face was sad, his eyes teary. He put his hand out for the nugget.

I placed the nugget in his palm and said, "Goodnight."

The old man nodded as he put the nugget back in its resting place.

***

In the morning, after saying bye to Mum, I walked over to the rock cabinet. Mr Warhurst was such a sad man. I was about to head out to the bike when I noticed the key chain dangling from the lock.

A battle commenced in my head. I walked over to the window and looked out. His car was gone.

I returned to the cabinet and felt a strong pull towards the nugget. Bruce and Rosemary wanted so much to see it. Mr Warhurst would be gone all day. Maybe not back till tomorrow. He wouldn't know.

The phone rang as I rode off with the nugget safely tucked away in my backpack.

I met up with Bruce and we pedalled along the bush track and roads to school.

"You seem full of energy this morning, mate."

I did feel good. "It's the country air." Being sneaky about the nugget also had something to do with the good feeling but that didn't seem right.

"Knew you'd work it all out. The air out here makes you come good."

On the school road, Rosemary and Jill were walking to the school building. We parked our bikes under the tree and ran up to them. Charlie and his twin brothers were already on the balcony and they yelled out a greeting to us all.

Mr Hecat's car was parked, so he was already here.

We all wandered into the classroom and said good morning to Mr Hecat. He stood near a table.

After singing "God save the Queen", Mr Hecat pointed to the table. "Okay, place your Show and Tell items here."

We all mingled around the table. Charlie placed a small skull on the table. His brothers set down some big mushrooms and twigs with orange things growing on them that looked like my piece of gold. Rosemary had contributed a bluish envelope with a plane on it and Jill had placed some stamps. Bruce put a jar on the table holding the largest black beetle I had ever seen. I placed the gold nugget next to the jar, hoping the massive bug wouldn't smash through the jar and take off with the nugget.

Rosemary edged closer. "Wow."

"Is that what I think it is?" Bruce asked.

"It is." A warm energy flowed through my body. I felt invincible, like I could wrestle a yowie. I thought of Katrina. I felt a good foot taller.

The old man's nugget was in my possession. Yep, it all felt good.

***

I picked up whiffs of eucalyptus in the wind as I pedalled down the bush track, the backpack bouncing against my back as exposed tree roots sent shudders through the bike frame.

As I neared home, I could see Mum standing at the front door with her hands resting on her hips. She didn't look happy. I got off and parked the bike and headed towards her. My excitement level had dropped a little.

"You shouldn't have done it, Quinn."

"What, Mum?" I knew what she was talking about. My superpowers were draining away.

"The nugget."

I started to feel bad. Real bad. Almost sick. My eyes watered. "I'm sorry, Mum. I just wanted to show the class. Just wanted them to like me."

"But I'm sure they do, Quinn." She looked down the driveway. "Now, quickly return the nugget before he gets home."

My heart pumped faster. "I thought he wasn't coming home till tomorrow."

"That's right, but he phoned this morning and asked if I had seen his keys. I saw them in the cabinet and told him. He was relieved and said he may be home this evening now." She gave me a hard look. "And that's when I noticed something missing."

I picked up my backpack and moved my hand to where I thought I had placed the nugget. No nugget. I pulled out the empty lunch bag and my jumper. I shook them: no nugget. With the backpack empty, I looked inside and saw a ray of light at the bottom of the bag. I pressed my finger against it. A hole. I gulped and turned the bag upside down and shook it.

"Oh no. Please don't say it's not there." Mum placed her hand on her head. "When did you last see it?"

"At school. After Show and Tell, I put it in the backpack." Panic was building inside me.

Mum sat down on a timber bench near the front door. "Oh dear, Quinn. This is not good."

I thought about my backpack and the bumpy bike ride.

A distant hum broke the silence, growing louder, until it became the unmistakable sound of a car engine.

"Quick, Quinn. Go hide somewhere."

I sprinted around to the back of the house, my mind filling with dread. What had I done? Surely, he'd kill us both now. Yet, I couldn't abandon Mum; she needed my help. Scanning for a weapon, my eyes settled on a large stick. Moving to the side of the house, I cautiously peeked around the corner.

It was my teacher.

***

Mr Warhurst didn't come home that night. After dinner, Mum and I sat on the couch in the living room, staring at the cabinet and the nugget.

"Learn from this, Quinn. Temptation will come in many forms. The things we do can affect others. Try and listen to that inner voice when it tells you something isn't right."

I nodded to show I understood. A wave of sickness had washed over me when I lifted the nugget out of the cabinet. Deep down, I'd known I was doing something wrong.

"I'm sorry, Mum."

"I know you are, but we need to make sure Mr Warhurst doesn't find out you borrowed his nugget."

"It was weird that he left the key there just on the day when I wanted it."

"It is, but temptation comes when we're vulnerable. At a weak point."

I thought of the nugget and hoped we had placed it in the same way it had been. "Do you think he'll notice that we moved it?"

"I'll tell him that as I was able to get into the cabinet, I decided to clean the rocks."

"Rocks and minerals. That's what they are. Rocks are made up of minerals." The words tumbled out like I was giving my Show and Tell speech again.

She gave me a funny look. "You sound like you know what you're talking about."

I shrugged, feeling foolish now. I'd dug into those books on rocks and minerals, practicing over and over in my head. But none of that mattered anymore.

"So, Mr Hecat found the nugget on the floor?" I asked.

"He said he thought a piece of fungi had fallen off a twig from Show and Tell. But when he looked closer, he realised what it was." She gave me a slight nod. "Kids throw things around and don't pay much attention to other things on the floor. We adults pick up after you."

"It did look like fungi. Same sort of colour."

"Okay, we're lucky, very lucky, that your teacher found it. But now we need to make sure Mr Warhurst doesn't find out that his nugget left the house."

"I'll tell the class tomorrow."

"You might have to swear them to secrecy."

I thought of the Phantom and his secrets. Charlie's skull and the big, black bug crawling out of an eye socket. I shook my head. Crazy thoughts.

"Your teacher seems nice. He asked if you were healing okay after your fall. How did you fall?"

He pushed me, shoved me. He's not a nice man. I couldn't tell Mum those things. She liked the teacher. But he had saved us. Mr Warhurst would have gone crazy if the nugget was missing.

One thought lingered. Mr Warhurst would find out one day that his beloved nugget had wandered out of the house, and I didn't want to be around when that happened.

23 Secrets Revealed

A few weeks had passed. The old man kept busy with farm things—fixing fences and things like that—as if he had switched off from the world. Even his beloved cabinet got little attention, just the occasional glance. He seemed to do nothing but work, eat, and sleep.

He ignored me too, which allowed me to settle into the groove of living in Edithburra—peacefully, at least for a short time anyway—also helped by the school radio breaking down.

School holidays came. Springtime. The boys kept me busy. We'd go ferreting for rabbits, hunting them and foxes with slingshots. We'd march through the thick bush and build bridges with fern trunks over creeks, pulling leeches off our bodies in the process.

I hardly saw Rosemary until one day when she popped out of the bushes with Jill. They each had a small bucket. Rosemary tapped hers. "Treasures of the forest." She gave me a crushed leaf. I sniffed it. Whoa! It smelled sharp and fresh, like cough drops. It reminded me of the stuff Mum would rub on my chest or put in boiling, steamy water for me to sniff when I had a cold.

I peeked in the bucket. It was a mixture of berries, flowers, and leaves.

"Some of these are secret ingredients to our lollies," Jill said.

I got a bit worried hearing that, but then I remembered I'd eaten their lollies before and was still alive. My skin hadn't turned green, and no horns were growing out of my head, so these forest things must be okay to eat, right?

We decided to all walk together out of the bush and to the store. I walked behind with Rosemary, carrying her and Jill's buckets for them and grabbing and smelling the crushed leaf every now and then.

"Stop smelling. You could get high like a koala," she warned me with a smile.

I looked towards the school as we neared the store. "Back to school soon."

"You looking forward to it?" she asked.

"Sort of, but I hope the radio hasn't been fixed."

"Me too." Rosemary placed her arm in front of me, stopping me walking while she waited for the others to go ahead. "I want to ask you something and I want you to be truthful."

A lump lodged in my throat. "Go ahead."

"You didn't fall off that chair. He pushed you, didn't he?"

"No, I fell."

"Stop it, Quinn. I know you're lying. He does the same to me."

"What? He has pushed you around?"

"More than that. He hits me and tries other things."

"Other things?"

She nodded. “He’s not a nice man.” Her eyes watered. “So, he does the same to you?”

“Yes, he hits me and shoves me around. I don’t understand what you mean by the other things, though.”

“Some men like young children.” Her voice was soft and full of hurt.

Oh dear. I thought of Jimmy and the creeps he had protected me from on the streets of Melbourne.

“That’s not good.” I looked at Rosemary. She was small and fragile. “What can we do? How can we stop it?”

“I don’t know. I noticed Mum looked at me when she saw your bruise. It was like a big question had popped into her head.”

“You’ve had bruises, then?”

She nodded. “Mr Hecat warned me that no one would believe me, and they’d blame me for it.”

“Our parents think he’s great and totally trust him.” I felt my stomach get all knotty. “Maybe if we said something, they wouldn’t believe us, thinking we were just trying to get out of school or something.”

“He said he’d set fire to the store if I told anyone,” Rosemary said.

“What? But you’re telling me.” My chest felt tight. As if now, I’d become a target like Rosemary. But I already was.

“Yes. Because it’s going to be our secret.”

“Is that the secret you were going to tell me about?”

“No, there’s another one.”

I wasn’t sure if I wanted to hear it. “Jill also?”

“No, he doesn’t go near Jill. I think it’s because she reminds him so much of his own daughter who is home schooled. He keeps telling her that and sometimes calls Jill by his daughter's name."

"He's one spooky man." I wondered who else in school could be suffering.

She paused and swallowed. "It's about Katrina. The other secret."

The lump in my throat increased in size.

"She won't be coming back. They're running away. Their dad scares them real bad and hits them. I've seen her bruises, and I know she's telling the truth. Its happened a lot, and her mom gets hit too."

Anger rose. I needed to protect my mum and Rosemary.

"Hey, come on you two," Bruce yelled. "Charlie's buying us an ice cream."

Charlie thumped Bruce on the arm. "No. I'm not."

Rosemary smiled at the boys mucking around. "They help me feel better." She touched my arm. "Don't tell anyone what we've spoken about."

Her touch brought a warm and comfortable feeling. "I won't. But I'm going to work out what we can do."

She gave me a hopeful smile.

The world was a confusing and sometimes frightening place.

***

I stood at my window, gazing up at the dark sky adorned with countless twinkling stars. Among them, one star stood out, so I directed my words to it. "Hello, Dad. Are you good? Because I'm not. How could you have left Mum down here? She needs to be protected. I haven't seen too many kind souls around who could do that. What's happening? Could you ask God to help me?"

I walked over to my bed and sat down. A noise came from the living room. A low, scraping sound. I needed to watch over my mum, so I quietly went out of my room, tiptoed down the passageway, and peeked into the living room.

It was the old man, sitting on a timber chair—he must have dragged it across the floor—admiring his rock collection. His hand rested on the cabinet glass, almost like he was patting the rocks behind it. I quickly retreated into my bedroom before he noticed me.

He hadn't done that for a while. A heaviness settled over me.

That night, I dreamed of Doggie and Jimmy and being on a train. The train part wasn't good—a yowie was chasing me down the aisle.

A soft knock on the door pulled me from my dream world. Mum stuck her head in. "Come get some breakfast, sleepy-head."

I crawled out of bed and made my way to the kitchen.

Mr Warhurst walked past as we sat at the table. He was dressed all in white.

"Warmer weather brings out the tennis players." He swung his racket in the air. "I'll be back in a few hours. Thanks for making the sandwiches." He grabbed a brown paper bag from the kitchen counter and headed for the door. Tennis must get him in a good mood.

He paused. "Did you open the cabinet, Elizabeth?"

Mum shifted in her seat, clearing her throat. "I did—just to get the dust off a couple of rocks. But that was a while ago."

"You touched the nugget, didn't you?" His tone was tense. Good mood didn't last long.

"I did. It's such a beautiful thing."

The comment softened his face. "It is, but I'd prefer if you left the rocks alone."

"Okay. Sorry, I won't touch them again."

He nodded. I could see he was struggling with himself. Maybe he was trying to be nicer.

Mum's eyes fixed on him as he departed the house. She let out a sigh. "Well, I best tidy up and get some letter writing done." She looked at me. "Have you written to your friend in Melbourne yet?"

I shook my head.

"Well, maybe now is a good time."

Maybe. "I might just explore outside for a little while."

"I've got a spare writing pad. I'll drop it on your bed."

"Okay, thanks."

I wondered who he'd play tennis with. I pictured a tennis racket. Where had I seen one before?

I walked around the yard, thinking about going back to school tomorrow. Pressure built in my chest. I wanted to protect Rosemary and my mum from these evil men. Weak men, they were. Jimmy seemed to know how to deal with them. He'd told me he was streetwise. I wasn't sure what that meant. But maybe it was a good idea to write to him. Maybe he could tell me what to do about the teacher.

There was a small table in my room under the windowsill. I sat down, opened the writing pad, and stared out into the backyard, waiting for words to form in my head. I could see some rabbits hopping around in the distance. A pigeon landed on a fence post. It was the type of pigeon that Mr Hecat had shot. I thought about the rifle in the back seat of his car and the mess and *the tennis racket.*

That last thought got my heart racing. I felt sick. Mr Hecat played tennis.

I panicked and ran through the house, looking for Mum. "Mum, where are you?"

I felt like tipping over the rock cabinet as I passed it, and then I saw it. The key chain dangling from the lock.

Mum had wandered into the living room. "What is it, love?"

I was frozen stiff, staring at the key chain.

Mum followed my gaze. "He's done it again, Quinn."

"Is he testing us or something?"

Mum wiped her hands on the tea towel draped over her shoulder. "No, no, he's just being forgetful again. We best just leave it as it is."

My hands were sweaty. Too hot. Too nervous.

"Hey, Quinn? You home?" Bruce's voice boomed through the house.

"Sounds like your friend's here. Go off and play for a while."

My feet felt so heavy. Mum gave me a gentle shove. "Off you go."

"Yeah, I'm here. Give me a sec," I yelled back to Bruce.

I looked at the key chain. It seemed to have a power of its own, pulling me towards it. I felt the urge to grab it. How could a mere key have such a strong effect on me? Was I losing my mind?

Mum seemed to sense my confusion. "Evil has a power of its own, Quinn. Be on guard."

"What sort of power?"

"It's called temptation. It's like there's a force out there, always tempting you to do bad things."

"How do we stop it? Sounds scary."

"Everyone experiences it. It's normal. Like wanting to grab a handful of lollies when no one's watching or taking a toy that's not yours."

"Yeah, I know what you mean." The walls were closing in, so much that I wanted to be outside the house. "I'm going out. I'll see ya later."

"Okay. Just remember that when that little voice in your head tempts you, it's up to you whether you listen to it or not. You're in charge. Think of the Phantom or Superman. They were in charge of their lives."

"Yeah, I might become a superhero. See ya later."

But I was far from being a hero.

24 Fiddling with a Radio

Bruce rested against the crossbar of his bike. "What took ya so long?"

"Talking to Mum." I felt flat. "Do you know where the tennis courts are?"

"Sure, they're not far from school. Up behind the town hall. Hidden behind some big pine trees." He gave me a curious look. "Why?"

"The old man plays tennis on Sundays. Just wondering who he plays with."

"There's a few of them. Dad sometimes goes along on Sundays. It's a bit of a comp. Dad says it's more like a war at times. A few fiery characters."

"Who would they be?" I thought I could guess.

"Dad had a tennis racket thrown at him once. Didn't go for a few weeks after that. Wouldn't tell me who it was, but I found out."

"Who was it, Mr Hecat?"

Bruce laughed. "How did you know?"

"I think he's the fiery type."

"Yeah, and his doubles partner is your mate, the old man."

This was getting worse by the minute. I think Mr Hecat knew Mr Warhurst a bit more than he let on.

"Apparently, they even fight amongst themselves."

My head felt like a battlefield. What would the old man do when he found out that his nugget had made an appearance at school?

"You want to come to my place? And then we can go check out the tennis courts if you want."

I agreed. I needed a change of scenery.

We pedalled towards Bruce's house. When we arrived, a car pulled up at the front of the house and a lady in a tartan-coloured skirt and thick jumper stepped out.

"That's me mum, she's been to church. I go with her sometimes. It's a bit boring, although they tell some interesting stories."

The lady waved and waited for us to come closer.

Church? The only time I'd been to church was for a wedding, but I must have been at one for my dad's funeral. I was sure that was in a church.

"Hello, my boy."

"Hi, Mum." He pointed to me. "This is Quinn."

"Well, hello, Quinn, nice to meet you." Her greeting was warm. "Bruce tells me he's been helping you settle in."

I nodded. "He has."

"I must get over and meet your mum sometime. Is she settling in okay?"

"I think so. Everything's a bit different to the city."

"I imagine it is. We're neighbours and we live nearly a mile apart." She smiled. "I'll have you over for a Sunday roast sometime.'

"That sounds nice." It did.

She looked at Bruce. "You want to come in for something to eat?"

"Nah, just going to show Quinn the shed, then we might ride into the village. I want to show him the tennis courts."

"Sounds like fun." She raised her eyebrows. I think she was joking about the fun bit. "Your dad's there playing. Mr Hecat picked him up." She thought for a moment. "From what your dad tells me, Mr Hecat needs to be dragged to church so the Lord can curb his temper."

She knew about his temper. How would the Lord curb his temper?

She laughed. "I'm sure you don't see his temper displayed in school." She paused. I hated the silence and was about to speak when she continued, "I hope not. If ever his temper appears, you let me know, boys. Now off you go."

Bruce paused beside a hose near a tap. He pointed to the hose. "Like a snake soaking up the sun." He turned the tap on, grabbed the hose, and let the water pouring out of the hose run through his fingers. "Bit hot, the water's been sitting in the hose. The sun is getting warmer." He waited a few seconds and then put it near his mouth, gulping at the water as it gushed out. He lifted his head, water dripping from his lips. "Now the cool water comes."

He handed the hose to me with water spurting out onto the grass. I hesitated.

He smiled. "Come on, city boy, it won't kill you."

It didn't kill me and it was refreshing, although it had an odd taste. Rubbery-like, but I might have imagined that.

He pointed up at a large, corrugated tank. "That's our water supply. We used to jump in the tank and go swimming when we were young. Mum didn't like that, so she made up a story of a big snake that used to crawl into the tank on hot summer days to cool off. Sort of put us off swimming."

The tap water had now taken on a different taste. I wanted to spit it out of my mouth. I coughed instead.

"Us?" I wondered who the other swimmers were.

"Got a few older brothers, but they're away with friends camping somewhere. Near the ocean, I think."

I followed Bruce into his shed. A large bench was covered in wires and odds and ends. "My dad's an electrician."

I must have given him my best dumb look because he continued, "Electricity is getting connected everywhere now. There are some big power stations not far from here. Dad does some work there at times."

Glancing at my hand, I glimpsed the scar from when I was electrocuted at around five years old. I held it up to show Bruce.

He leaned in to have a look.

"I got electrocuted once," I said, rubbing the scar. "My hand was on some bare wires sticking out of an old radio cord when my friend turned it on. I got this huge zap, and my hand locked onto the cord like it was glued there. No matter how hard I tried, I couldn't let go, and I was screaming my head off. My whole body was jerking around like a puppet. One of my brothers ran in and yanked the cord right out of the wall. Saved my life."

"Well, you're lucky you survived. Dad has lost some mates to electrocution."

Had that electric shock messed up my brain or something? Was that why I couldn't handle the school radio? Does static electricity mess with my head now? Nah, it was probably just me being me.

"Dad's taught me a lot about electricity, so I like tinkering around in here." He walked over to a large radio, similar to the one at school. "Familiar?"

"It is." My chest tightened.

"I want to tell you something, Quinn, just between you and me."

Another secret. I nodded.

"I did something to the radio at school. I know what Mr Hecat is doing to Rosemary and to you. So, I'm trying to stop him from going into that room."

My heart moved into my throat. 'You did that for me, for us?"

"Yep." He pointed to some old cameras on the desk. "And I'm trying to work out a way to catch him in the act."

"Take photos, you mean?"

"Not sure yet. Maybe photos."

"Will he call your dad to come fix the radio?"

"Maybe, but I think the school will contact someone in the city and they'll get it organised. Hopefully, it won't be fixed yet."

"Thanks, Bruce, for what you've done."

"That's okay. I like Rosemary and don't like what's going on. She won't tell anyone, not even her mum. Too scared."

"I'd say Mr Hecat threatened her with something."

"Ya reckon?"

I nodded.

"Has he done that to you?"

I shrugged.

Bruce's eyebrows lifted, as if he was waiting for me to say more, but I couldn't. Too many thoughts bounced around in my head.

"Okay, let's go to the tennis courts. We can grab some of Dad's rifles and hide in the shrubbery and shoot Mr Hecat."

I wasn't sure how to respond to that.

Bruce laughed. "We won't do that, Quinn, but we need to work out something. In the meantime, I can do things to the radio to stop it working again once it gets fixed, although he might bring in a radio from home."

I agreed. And at least now I knew I had a good friend in Bruce.

25 Tennis

The tennis courts were hidden behind a bunch of big pine trees. No wonder I hadn't seen them before. They looked kind of cool, like something from an old movie. Tall, scratched-up wooden posts marked where the tennis park started and ended. Some had plants growing up them like green, twisty snakes.

There was chicken wire all around the courts, but it was sagging at the top, like it was tired of standing up straight. The courts and nets looked pretty beat up too. I guess the sun, rain, and wind had been playing their own games here for a long time.

We sat on a timber park bench in a sloping grassy area just behind the court watching a game in play. Silence surrounded the court, as if nature itself was a spectator. Grunts and thwacks seemed to echo louder because of the quietness surrounding us.

Words drifted from the court. "40-Love."

"Friendly game, hey? They call each other 'love'." Bruce laughed.

"Why 'love'?" I'd heard the tennis term before but didn't understand it.

"Dad tried to explain it to me once. Love is naught. He reckons it's something to do with a French word meaning egg. An egg looks like a naught, a zero. Makes sense, hey?"

"Sort of."

"And my dad, being the man that he is, believes there's a lot of truth in that because a naught can also mean a goose egg."

"I'll think of tennis now every time I see an egg."

"But Dad believes it's really just used because people love playing tennis."

"I'll stick with me footy. Goals and points for me."

"That's my dad, serving to Mr Hecat."

Bruce's dad had his back to us. He looked like a fireman with his super wide shoulders and big muscles. CRACK! The sound of the ball being hit echoed loudly across the empty court. Old Man Warhurst was at the net, facing the server. He was crouched over with a serious look on his face, watching every move Bruce's dad made. Mr Hecat was at the back of the court, ready to receive.

The ball whizzed past the head of the server's partner standing near the net. "That's Charlie and the twins' dad," said Bruce. "He's a good bloke but not around much."

It must have been a super important point. Mr Hecat messed up the return, and his racket went flying through the air. SMASH! It slammed into the chicken wire and then it bounced back onto the court.

Mr Hecat's team must have lost.

"You want to have a hit?" Bruce asked.

Before I could respond, he was moving towards the court. We stood on the edge of the playing surface.

Bruce's dad and his partner wandered up to the net to shake hands. Mr Hecat met them and was joined by Mr Warhurst.

As they shook hands, Mr Warhurst spoke, his voice carrying clearly. "Sorry about that display by my partner." He patted Mr Hecat on the back. "He's a work in progress."

I imagined steam coming out of Mr Hecat's ears.

"Yep, I do apologise," Mr Hecat's grumpy voice replied. He didn't look like someone who was truly sorry.

"Only a game," Bruce's dad said.

They all nodded and walked off. As they headed towards bags sitting on a timber log near the exit, two ladies in white skirts jogged onto the court.

"Mixed doubles?" One yelled out.

Towelling off and cooling themselves with beers from a foam cooler, Mr Hecat and Mr Warhurst glanced at the ladies but remained silent. Meanwhile, Bruce's dad and his tennis partner had just grabbed their towels and were wiping sweat from their faces.

With a final swipe at his brow, Bruce's dad tossed his towel back onto his bag. "Okay, just the one set, though. Will you join me, Richard?" Bruce's dad asked his playing partner.

"Why not? But I'd better partner with my wife as I know her game plan," Richard replied in a playful tone.

"No problem, you go with Julie, I'm happy to go with Gail. I could score some treats from the store."

"Only if we win," Gail said. Her tone also sounded playful.

"It's good to see Charlie and the twins' dad home," Bruce said to me. "He's been away for a while. Up in Northern Australia, working on a humongous cattle farm."

I must have worn another one of my dumb looks. Bruce explained, "Humongous, meaning massive, larger than large."

"I know that," I lied.

Mr Hecat and Mr Warhurst were hanging out in the shade of a tree, on their second cans of beer, watching the next game get started. They guzzled down those cans like there was no tomorrow. Like they were in a race. I guess they must be really thirsty and hot after all that tennis.

The mixed doubles game had a different tone. More fun, more laughs.

After confirming Bruce's dad would be alright to get a lift home, Mr Hecat and Mr Warhurst gave a few low-key goodbyes and walked to the teacher's car. I wondered how clean the car was inside. Mr Warhurst opened the passenger door and climbed in. Mr Hecat lingered at the driver's door, his gaze flicking back to where we stood. A slow, unsettling smile spread across his face before he raised a hand in a deliberate wave.

I sensed he was sending me a message. Like, "Look who I know." I'm sure his head had tilted towards Mr Warhurst.

The urge to rush home to Mum overtook me, so I sprinted to my bike and jumped on and started back.

"What's the hurry?" Bruce yelled, pedalling behind me.

"Just want to get home to Mum. I don't like it when the old man drinks."

Bruce nodded. "Okay, we've got a head start. It looks like they've stopped at the store. Let's go."

The track ran alongside the road in parts but there had been no sign of the car as we pedalled along. Approaching the farm, I could hear a car engine. Halting, we peered through the bushes only to find it wasn't Mr Hecat's car. Suddenly, another noise penetrated the air: a gunshot.

"Someone shooting rabbits, I'd say," Bruce said.

"Or pigeons."

"Yeah, could be that, too."

We came out of the bushes close to the Warhurst house and saw a man walking from the front door. He turned at our approach. It was our neighbour, Mr Molloy.

We rode up to him.

"Howdy, Mr Molloy," Bruce said.

I nodded as I didn't know the man as well as it seemed Bruce did.

"G'day, Bruce. You behaving?"

"Always."

Mr Molloy laughed. "I believe you, but a thousand others wouldn't."

"Sure they would."

Mr Molloy ruffled Bruce's hair. "Maybe they would. And how are you settling in, Quinn?"

"Good, thanks."

He smiled.

I could hear the sound of a car.

"Well, you found a good buddy in Bruce. Anyway, I must be off."

Mr Molloy seemed to be in a hurry.

"Hey, Mr Molloy, you still got any of that copper wire?"

"Yeah, sure, Bruce. You want some?" As Mr Molloy spoke, his eyes kept darting above Bruce's head, looking down the driveway.

"Yep, could I? I just want to try to fix something."

"Well, come over and grab some when it suits you."

A car turned into the driveway. Mr Molloy's shoulders sank. "See ya, boys." He started walking towards a gate along the fence. His leaving seemed strange to me. Didn't he want to say hello to his neighbour? The reason why soon became clear.

A door opened and slammed. Mr Warhurst stood towering over the roof of Mr Hecat's car. Mr Hecat stood at the driver's door and seemed alarmed.

"Hey, you!" the old man yelled in the direction of Mr Molloy.

Mr Molloy turned slowly.

"Yeah, you. I thought I told you to stay off my property. Or have you come sniffing around like you used to with my wife when I wasn't here?"

Mr Molloy, now fully turned, took a deep breath and stared hard at the old man. "Steady on, Lance. You don't go making those accusations in public."

"I can do what I want. Now get off my property."

"Oh, I will, and for your information, I was just checking on Mrs Davies to see how she's settling in."

"And it was very kind of him to do so." Mum had appeared out of nowhere, like the Phantom.

Mr Warhurst looked at my mum. "Who asked you to speak?"

I didn't like the man's tone. I thought he got on okay with his neighbour. Either a very sore loser, the grog is talking, or their friendship was always fake. I remembered that time Mr Warhurst didn't wave to him when we drove past once.

"Okay, okay, let's steady on." Mr Hecat had slipped into teacher mode, trying to calm things down. "Tennis didn't go our way today and we're not good losers. But still, we shouldn't be talking to friends like this."

Mr Warhurst rubbed his face. His chest rising, he took several deep breaths. He closed his eyes and then opened them again. Was that some kind of switch?

He looked at Mr Hecat. "He's right. I shouldn't be speaking to you all like that. I just need to go inside and rest for a minute."

He ruffled his hair and looked towards the house. He gave Mr Molloy a quick glance but said nothing as he turned to Mr Hecat.

"Thanks for picking me up, Trevor. Looking forward to our next game."

Mr Hecat nodded and climbed back into the car. His window was down. "See ya tomorrow, boys." He reversed out of the driveway and was gone.

Mr Warhurst made his way into the house, looking like a wounded soldier.

A heavy sigh came from Mr Molloy. "Okay, I'm off. You take care, Lizzie, and anything you need, let me know."

"Thank you for dropping in, Tom. And sorry about that." She pointed to the wounded soldier who had now walked far enough that he couldn't hear.

He used his head to gesture to the old man. "That's okay. I understand your circumstances. Please reach out if you need to."

Mum looked at Bruce and me. "I best go check on Mr Warhurst. You come in soon, Quinn. Thanks for hanging around with my boy, Bruce."

She turned and headed back into the house, the house that was rapidly losing any appeal. It was becoming a prison for my mum, and maybe that's what it was for Mr Warhurst's family.

They had escaped. Should I tell Mum that the old man's family had run away? And that they weren't coming back?

A glumness came over me. I wouldn't see Katrina again.

26 Not a Dream

The old man sat slouched on the couch, his head buried in his hands, his elbows digging into his knees. He looked like a deflated balloon. My chest filled with sadness.

"Lance, are you okay?" Mum asked.

Mr Warhurst slowly raised his head. His eyes were watery and red.

"You shouldn't let that man near you. I didn't trust him around my wife."

"I'm sorry. I didn't know that was how you felt about him."

He looked at Mum. "And you're a pretty thing, so you need to be careful around men like him."

Mum blushed. "Could I get you something?"

"No, I might go lie down. Tennis has zapped me of energy." He stood up and placed a hand on his hip. "I must be getting old." He raised his eyebrows and tried to smile.

We watched him slowly make his way to his room. He walked past the rock cabinet without even pausing to look at his rocks. He must be in a bad way. The key chain remained where it was.

"He's missing his family, Quinn."

"Are they coming back?" My question didn't come out the way I'd intended.

Mum wore a puzzled expression. "What do you mean?"

I shook my head. "I meant, when are they coming back?"

"In about six weeks."

I felt drained. If Rosemary's big secret was true, and the old man's family didn't return, what did that mean for Mum and me?

***

The room was cloaked in a dreamy greyness. Mr Warhurst, Mr Hecat, and Bruce were all standing around the rock cabinet. They turned as I entered the room. Mr Hecat was holding his pigeon-shooting rifle.

In a deep, rough voice, Mr Warhurst said, "He took it!"

I looked in the rock cabinet. The gold nugget was gone.

Mr Hecat raised his rifle and pointed it at me. "Give it back!" he yelled.

"Yeah, shoot him," Bruce said.

A piece of copper wire encircled Bruce's neck. I leaned in closer. The gold nugget hung freely on the wire.

I pointed at it.

They all laughed.

A loud *thump* woke me.

Early morning sunlight flooded the room, but Mum's sudden screams darkened the mood. Loud voices spoke.

"Get off me, you thug."

"Okay for my neighbour but not for me?"

I heard a slap.

I ran to the cupboard and found the cricket bat, then sprinted to Mum's room. The stench of alcohol was strong.

On top of Mum, Mr Warhurst turned to look at me. It was a face that I didn't want to see again. His eyes were like black marbles. Distorted. Beast-like. A real Mr Hyde thing.

"Mr Warhurst, please get away from my mum," I stammered, not sure what to do.

He gave a raspy laugh. "Yeah, what you going to do about it, little boy?"

He grabbed Mum by the throat and tried to kiss her.

I raised the bat and moved towards him. Mum's eyes were wide. She shook her head and mouthed the word *no*.

She gave one powerful heave, and Mr Warhurst tumbled from the bed. His head hit the sharp edge of the bedside table, and he fell to the floor. A thin trickle of blood spread slowly across the wood. Mum jumped out of bed and looked down at the wounded man.

"Quinn, quickly go and get Mr Molloy."

I threw the cricket bat to the floor and burst out of the house, sprinting through the dew-covered grass to Mr Molloy's house. He was in the garden and saw me coming. He threw down his gardening tools and ran towards me.

"What is it, Quinn? Is it your mum?"

"No, it's the old man. He's hurt his head."

We rushed back to the house and entered Mum's room together. Mr Warhurst was sitting up, his back resting against the bed as he held a rag to his head. He gave Mr Molloy a deadly look.

"I told you to stay away from here." His words were jittery.

Mum standing at the end of the bed, shook her head.

"They were concerned for your health, Lance," said Mr Molloy. "Give us a go. We only want to help."

"The boy attacked me with the cricket bat."

Mr Warhurst's head was listing to the side like it was too heavy for his shoulders to support. He could barely focus on any one of us, but I wasn't going to let him blame me for something I didn't do.

"What! I did not."

The old man moved the rag from his head and eyed it. "You did, boy, and you're in big trouble now."

"No, he's not," said Mum. "You were so drunk, you were trying to force yourself on me. The boy was scared. *You* scared him. I pushed you off the bed. You're the one that's in trouble."

"That's a lie; the boy attacked me." He held up the rag. "Look, what's this red stuff?"

"You hit the bedside table as you fell. It's only a graze. The cricket bat would have fractured your skull, and more than likely killed you." Mum's hands gripped the rail at the end of the bed.

"She's right, Lance, and I think you should get up and get out of this room." Mr Molloy moved towards him.

The old man swung an arm in the air, in an aggressive, sweeping motion. "Get out of my house!" He swung his arm again.

Mum looked at Mr Molloy. She shook her head. "It's okay, Tom. He's drunk. Been drinking most of the night, I'd say."

"It's not okay. You and Quinn come with me. You can't stay here." Mr Molloy gestured with his hand for us to come.

"Yeah, all of ya get out of here," said Mr Warhurst.

We did.

27 Rescued

We sat on timber chairs on the front porch of Mr Molloy's house. Mum rubbed her head.

"You okay, Lizzie?" Tom asked.

"Sadly, Tom, I've encountered this behaviour too frequently. I think it toughens you up. Almost like it's part of the marriage arrangement."

"But you aren't married to him, Mum," I said, confused by this adult talk.

Mum looked at me. "No, I'm not, Quinn, thankfully, but I meant living under the same roof with a man." She gave me a tender smile and turned to Tom.

"His siblings have moved on—some married, two joined the navy, another became a police officer. He's younger, a lot younger. A change of life baby some called it. I've tried hard to give our family stability. It's just harder now without a husband. Harder to put up with the darkness that surrounds us." She pointed to the old man's house. "The drunkenness of strangers is starting to alarm me."

Mum normally didn't talk about this stuff when I was around. She must be really tired. My mind started to wander. I looked over at some kangaroos eating the wet grass. They looked so happy and calm. I wished I could be a kangaroo.

Mum and Tom kept talking their grown-up talk. Their voices got quieter. I kept going back and forth between listening and my make-believe world.

"I gave up the grog," Tom said, "It kept bringing up nasty stuff from the war. But a lot of the other fellas, they're hitting the bottle hard to forget things. It's getting real bad, you know. Kids see all this and think it's normal, but it messes with their heads." He let out a heavy sigh. "Old Warhurst, he's still stuck in the trap." Mr Molloy stood.

"When they're not drunk, they're like different people," Mum said. "I think that's what gets me. I know they're trapped and I want to help, you know? Make them better."

"Yeah, it's like two different people," Tom agreed "And some of 'em, well, it's real tough to get them to change their ways."

The morning was crisp, so Mr Molloy suggested we go inside. Mum shivered in agreement.

Mr Molloy's house was different to the old man's house. More homely feeling. I wondered if the large wooden beams holding up the roof came from the giant trees. The timber floor creaked as we walked on it. I looked down at my feet.

"You get used to the creaking," Mr Molloy said. "It's an old house that likes to creak and groan. Bit like me."

"It's lovely," Mum said.

The exposed brick walls made me think of a castle. I wanted to stay here.

Mum stood looking at a large painting on the wall. Mountains and blue sky. A green valley.

"My Emily painted that."

"Emily?" Mum looked closer at the painting.

"My wife. She passed away some years ago. A battle with cancer. Her painting helped her through the latter stages." Tom swallowed.

"I'm sorry to hear that, Tom. She obviously had talent."

He moved to other pictures hanging on the wall. "Our daughter, Susan, picked up her talent. She's an artist and is based in Melbourne." He pointed to a photograph.

"She has your eyes."

Tom smiled. "She seems to be doing okay—has had a few exhibitions, made some money."

"That's good." Mum rubbed her face and bowed her head a little.

"You must be weary, Lizzie." He pointed to a big couch near an open fireplace. "Go sit down. I'll make you a cuppa." He looked at the fireplace. "I can get a fire going if you would like.

She smiled and nodded slowly, then strolled over to the large couch. "The bricks seem to be throwing out some warmth."

Tom nodded. "Yeah, they do that. They carry warmth even after the fire dies down."

"That's nice. I can feel it." She sat down and waved me over, patting the seat next to her.

I sat beside her. The cushions were so soft, I sank right in. I had to sit up, so I didn't vanish. I looked at Mum. Her eyes looked sad, like when she watches those old love stories on TV.

"You okay?" she asked.

My head felt all mixed up. "Are we going back there?"

"I don't know." She took a deep breath and looked out the window. Trees swayed with the breeze. We just sat there, not saying anything.

Some moments later, Tom stood before us with a tray. "I'd offer to accommodate you, but I've only the one room with a bed. You sleep here tonight, and we'll work out something." He pointed to the couch. "I'll sleep on the couch."

"Oh no, we can't let you do that."

"It's okay, done it before many times. I often fall asleep reading. Sometimes I prefer this couch to my bed."

"Let's just see how the day unfolds," Mum said.

Tom nodded. "Okay."

Tom seemed like a nice man.

I could see Mum wasn't herself. Tom suggested she was in a state of shock. I thought I understood what he meant.

Mr Molloy gave her a weird tea with herbs in it. He said it would help her feel better. After a few sips, she seemed calmer and not so jittery. She rose and walked towards the sunny room at the back of the house. I followed her. Sunshine always made things feel better. It helped melt away the bad and confusing things that had been happening.

While Mum dozed and Mr Molloy was busy elsewhere doing chores, I found an old book called *The Silver Brumby*. I'd heard of it but never read it. I flipped through the pages.

The book talked about these horses—brumbies—finding shelter under a big granite rock from the driving rain. That made me think of the big rock nearby that I had once explored with Katrina and her brothers. I read on but couldn't remove the big granite rock from my head. So, I placed the book down and strolled outside.

I found Mr Molloy raking the garden and asked, "Is it okay to go for a walk up to the big rock?"

He stopped raking and held the rake next to him. For a moment, he looked like a Roman soldier guarding the temple gates in one of those old Bible movies. "Is your Mum okay?" he asked.

"Yeah, she's snoozing."

"Okay, off you go, but don't be gone too long."

I set out. The big rock protruded from the landscape sooner than I'd expected. I stood in awe for a moment, staring at the massive grey boulder that looked like it had been dropped from the sky. I climbed the bumpy surface and sat on top, looking out over the valley. It reminded me of the painting in the house. Maybe it was the same valley. I pictured Mr Molloy's wife sitting here, painting. I laid back on the rock and put my hands under my head as a pillow. The warmth in the rock felt comforting, like nature was giving me a hug.

A tree shaded me from the sun. I watched the leaves swirling down and making soft whispering sounds. My eyelids felt heavy. I must have drifted off because the laughter of kookaburras jolted me from my sleep. When I remembered where I was, I smiled and tried to locate the birds. No such luck.

I stood and stretched, then climbed down and wandered back after having a quick wee behind a tree—a country habit I'd picked up.

As I hiked along the leaf-littered track, I thought of Katrina and wondered where she would live if she wasn't coming back. Maybe Melbourne. Maybe my mate Jimmy could help me find her.

My tummy rumbled. It must be getting close to lunchtime, maybe well past lunchtime. I had no idea what the time was. It seemed like hours since the events of early this morning. As I squeezed through the wired fence to enter Mr Molloy's property, I spotted an apple tree. The apples looked inviting, so I grabbed one.

Mr Molloy and Mum looked comfortable sitting in the sunroom. They gave me a wave through the window. I wasn't ready to go inside yet, so I walked over to the boundary fence with the apple in hand. I took a bite. A burst of sweetness flooded my mouth. *Mmm! Nice.*

I looked towards the old man's house. I felt the house was watching me.

28 Remorse

I stood at the boundary fence with my gaze fixed on the old man's house. Many thoughts bounced around in my head while a knot of confusion tightened in my stomach. The sky was blue, and there were no stars, so I couldn't ask Dad for advice.

A door opened and Mr Warhurst stepped out. He scratched his head and moved it from side to side. Shaking off cobwebs?

He saw me. "Hey Quinn, where's your mum?" His voice was loud and croaky. He started walking towards me. My heart started pounding and my stomach churned. I turned and started to head back to Mr Molloy's house.

"Quinn, wait."

I kept walking, taking deep breaths.

"Please, Quinn." He coughed. "Hold on. Let me say something."

I slowed, confused. I turned and looked at the old man, who walked slowly and carefully towards the fence. He looked older. My fear intensified.

He reached the fence line.

"You hurt my Mum," I said, the words heavy with anger.

"It wasn't me."

"It was, I saw you." I clenched my fists.

"No, I mean it's the drink. I have blackouts. I don't remember what I do." His words were slow, pulled from his foggy mind. "The last thing I want to do is hurt your mum."

"Well, it doesn't look that way to me."

"Where is she? Is she okay?"

The scene played out in my mind. What had he been trying to do with Mum? He had said that she was pretty. Maybe he was just trying to kiss her. It was all too confusing.

This Dr Jekyll and Mr Hyde thing was real.

"She's a bit shook up." My voice had softened.

Mr Warhurst let out a sigh. "Could you tell her I'm sorry? I mean, really sorry. I'll get rid of all the alcohol in the house. It won't happen again."

I nodded. "Okay, I'll tell her, but I'm not sure what she's going to do." Traces of dried blood matted his hair on one side. His face was pale, with puffy, hollow eyes surrounded by dark circles. I felt sorry for him.

"I understand." He paused and his eyebrows rose. "And Quinn, what was Jamie's cricket bat doing in your mum's room?"

He really didn't remember?

Leaving Mr Warhurst, I entered Mr Molloy's house through the front door. Out the back, Mum and Mr Molloy were still chatting. I stopped and looked at the painting. I pictured myself walking in the valley, Katrina running towards me.

Tom was speaking. "Did you want me to come with you?"

"No, it's best if I talk to him alone. I'd say he likely has no memory of what took place." She paused. "Besides, we can't just pack up and leave—we have nowhere to go. I'd need to plan an escape, and it'll be hard for Quinn; he's only been at the school a short time." Mum's voice was hoarse.

"But you're putting yourself in danger."

"It's the drink, Tom. It does different things to different men. Changes them. If he stays away from the drink, it could work."

"That's a big ask. His wife used to talk to my wife. He wasn't nice to her and the kids. I wouldn't be surprised if they didn't come back from their trip."

My brain lit up. Did Mr Molloy know?

"Tom, the drink killed my husband. It'll kill Mr Warhurst too. I want to help him."

What did Mum mean, the drink killed Dad? I had no memories of Dad. Did everybody drink?

"Elizabeth, I understand what you're saying. I admire your faith and hope. But can a man truly change?"

"Sounds like you did, Tom."

I thought it best to pass on the old man's message so I walked into the sunroom.

"Yeah, but—"

Their conversation stopped.

"Nice apples, hey?" Mr Molloy was looking at the apple in my hand.

I glanced at the half-eaten apple. "Yes, very nice."

"Maybe you can help me pick them off the tree today."

I nodded, but the words felt heavy in my chest, like they needed to come out. "Mr Warhurst saw me outside. He talked to me."

"Well, he's had a few hours to sober up." Tom looked at his watch. "Wow, two o'clock already. He could well be sober by now. I hope he was nice to you."

"How is he?" Mum asked.

"He said he has blackouts, doesn't remember things. He said the last thing he would want to do is hurt you."

Mum took a deep breath.

"He didn't know how the cricket bat got into your room."

"He wouldn't remember much." Mum's lips tightened.

"He also told me to tell you he's sorry, really sorry. He's going to remove all the alcohol from the house. He promised it won't happen again."

Mum ran her hand over her forehead and looked at Tom.

"Let's go see how he is," Tom said. "Are you up to that, Elizabeth? I'll walk you to the door and stay in the background."

"I prefer it when you call me Lizzie. Less formal. Suits me better."

Tom smiled. "Okay, Lizzie. You sure you're okay to have a chat with him?"

"First time I heard you call Mum that," I said, "I thought you called her a lizard." Why was I telling him that? I must be nervous.

Mum let out a soft laugh. "Sometimes I think Quinn has hearing problems." She gave me a nervous hug and nodded to Tom.

"Nah, Lizzie can sound like Lizard." Mr Molloy winked at me.

He was a nice man.

We walked through the gate, along the driveway, and towards the front door. It reminded me of a scene from a cowboy movie, waiting for the gunslinger to come barging out, pistols aimed at us.

The door opened and Mr Warhurst stepped out. No pistols.

He coughed and looked at Mum, his eyes clouded with confusion. "Umm…look, I'm not entirely sure what happened but I'm terribly sorry as I'm sure I've done something wrong. It's all a bit of a blur." His voice was shaky, and he was fidgeting with his belt. This was neither Dr Jekyll nor Mr Hyde, but a completely different man. He looked sort of…broken.

I watched the old man's Adam's apple bobbing up and down as he spoke, like a marble rolling up and down in his throat. He looked like he'd just escaped from a prisoner of war camp. I supposed I should be happy that he'd escaped, but I felt sorry for him.

And so did Mum. She gave him another chance.

29 Not Coming Back

Mr Warhurst was true to his word. I'd seen no alcohol in the house and it had been a week so far. The other good news was that the school radio was still broken.

Things weren't perfect, though. At times, I knew to stay out of the old man's way. He'd become a Mr Between Man—a bit of good, a bit of bad, but mostly treating Mum nicely. That was the important thing.

One afternoon when I got home from school, I noticed the old man walking to the letterbox. Mum said he did it every day. He must miss his family.

"Has he heard from them?" I asked Mum that evening.

"I think he gets the occasional postcard. He doesn't say much. They're probably just letting him know where they are. I tell him to be patient because it can take weeks for mail to arrive from overseas."

Maybe he should check the stamps on the mail. Someone might have posted them from Melbourne and not overseas. I'd gotten that idea from a movie I'd seen once. I continued to feel bad for the old man. What would he do without his family? Then another thought dropped into my head. What were we going to do?

All these thoughts jumped around in my head the next morning as my bike cruised down the slope towards school. Mr Hecat had been in fine form that week. He had slapped his large wooden ruler against Charlie's desk a few times with the entire class—all seven of us—jumping out of our seats. He'd had Rosemary and Jill in the radio room on separate occasions. I thought the radio was broken? This added to the tension in the classroom.

Whenever Rosemary returned from that room, her eyes looked sad, her shoulders slumped like she was carrying a big, heavy weight. Usually, her eyes would sparkle. I hated seeing her so gloomy and wanted to wave a magic wand and make all her troubles and worries disappear right then and there. I resolved to try and chat with her more and see if I could make her laugh.

My sessions in the radio room resumed. Mr Hecat had brought a small transistor radio as a replacement, which produced a weak and crackly sound. I could barely hear the voices, let alone work out what was being said. Mr Hecat seemed to understand this, and I only got clipped across the ears a few times. Maybe the bigger the radio, the bigger the hits.

I enjoyed the school lunchtimes. We'd all muck around with a plastic footy and Rosemary and her sister would jump in and play too, laughing and running every which way. But one day, Rosemary sat at the lunch table under the tree, not interested in the fun and games. I left our footy match and walked over to her.

"What ya doing?"

She looked up, her eyes watery. "Writing a letter to Katrina." She smiled. "Telling her how you are madly in love with me and not her."

My face heated. I looked over at the footy game and battled the urge to charge back there to rid myself of the uncomfortable feelings attacking my body.

"Just joking, Quinn. Sorry, didn't mean to embarrass you."

My face got hotter.

"I miss her. I miss talking to her."

"Do you think she'll come back here? I mean, somewhere close by?"

Rosemary looked around and raised a finger to her lips. "No, she won't be coming back, and that's sad. Her dad is not a very nice person."

I was about to agree with her, but bit my tongue, as if my words would find their way to the old man's ears. "Well, that puts us in a pickle."

She laughed. "That's a funny saying."

My mood turned serious. "It's not meant to be funny." I missed my dad for the first time. "I don't know what Mum and me are going to do. Where we're going to live. He'll probably kick us out at some point."

"I'm sorry, Quinn. I didn't think about that. Maybe you and I can run away." Her eyes were eager.

I liked that thought, but an image of my mum jumped into my head. "Nah, I couldn't leave my mum with that man."

"Yeah, you're right. I couldn't leave my family. Maybe I just need to leave this school."

"That's a better idea. Is there another school close by?"

She laughed. "Not for miles and miles. And I think that if we left here, they would shut it down. Not enough students."

"Maybe we need to get rid of the teacher."

"Now that's an even better idea."

She looked down at the words on the paper. "I've asked Katrina where they're going to live when they return. I'll let you know if she tells me. Remember, it's our secret. I'm not sure how her dad will react when he finds out they're not coming back."

And Mum and I had best not be there when that happens.

***

After school, as Bruce and I walked down to our bikes, I saw Rosemary rushing to the lunch table under the tree. She looked underneath and around the table and then rushed back up to the school.

"Wonder what she's lost?" Bruce said. "Maybe a hair clip or something." He shrugged.

We mounted our bikes.

"Quinn!" Rosemary's panicky voice came from behind me.

I placed one foot on the ground and turned. She ran up to me, puffing.

Bruce looked at me. "I'll leave you with your girlfriend." He winked. "Meet you at the store."

The heat returned to my face.

Bruce laughed. "You're blushing. Sorry." He rode off, chuckling.

Rosemary waited for Bruce to be out of hearing distance. "I lost the letter."

I wasn't sure what to say. "It must be in the school somewhere."

"It's not, I've looked."

"I'm sure it'll turn up."

"That's not the point." Annoyance crept into her voice. "If anyone finds it and reads it, our secret will be exposed." She kicked a twig lying on the ground.

"No one's going to read a letter they find. It's a private thing. I know I wouldn't."

She gave me a strange look. "They will, because people are nosey."

"Hey, Rosemary." Mr Hecat's voice sounded behind us. He strolled towards us, waving an envelope in the air. "Is this yours? It's addressed to Katrina—your best friend, I believe. So, I'm guessing it's yours."

She tensed and moved towards him, her hand outstretched. "Oh, thank you, Mr Hecat. It is. I was starting to panic."

"Why? Are there secrets in here?" He held the envelope back.

I sensed Rosemary's uneasiness. "I'm sure it's just girlie things."

"Thanks for that insight, Quinn."

"Nah, no secrets," said Rosemary. "I just wanted to tell her I'm missing her."

"Nice. I'm sure her dad is, too," Mr Hecat said.

A hidden message lurked in those words.

He turned to me. "What do you reckon, Quinn? Is Mr Warhurst missing his family? I can't wait for them to come home. There'll be a big party when they return."

His eyes gave me the creeps. It was like he could see right through me. A shiver ran up my spine.

He returned his gaze to Rosemary. "When are they coming back?"

"Oh, I don't know."

There was an element of truth in her answer.

He handed her the envelope. "Your secrets remain hidden."

I sensed they did not.

30 Out From the Shed

It was Saturday morning, and I was munching on a bowl of Coco Pops. Mum stood at the sink, her hand in the basin, staring out the window. Something wasn't right; even my slurping wasn't bothering her.

"You okay, Mum?"

She nodded and continued to stare.

"I'll be back mid-morning," Mr Warhurst said on his way to the front door.

Mum said nothing. After the door closed, she turned to me. Her eyes were watery. "He's drinking again."

I felt sick in the stomach. Life had settled down. My school friends had become my best friends. I didn't want to leave, but Mum needed to be protected. Family comes first, even if it's hard.

"Not getting drunk, though." I hoped that was true.

"That comes, Quinn."

"Maybe not."

She forced a smile and looked towards the living room. "He's left the key chain in the cabinet again. We best leave it as it is."

That worried me. He left the key there when he got drunk.

Mum was sad, and I wanted to comfort her, but I didn't know how.

"I'm sure it's okay, Mum. He knows what happened last time."

She raised her eyebrows and shrugged. "Hopefully you're right. Maybe it's just a one-off."

It wasn't.

Close to midday, we heard a car turn into the driveway.

"I'm off—home for lunch." Bruce said. "Maybe see you tomorrow."

Since it was the weekend, he'd been around for a few hours. We'd been tinkering with an old go-cart in the shed. Bruce joked about the gold nugget, suggesting we could use it as an emblem on the go-cart. He'd probably end up a gold prospector when he was older—he really liked gold.

As Bruce pedalled away, Mr Hecat's car pulled up. Mr Warhurst sat in the passenger seat. I swallowed a hard lump in my throat. They stepped out of the car. Mr Warhurst watched Bruce disappear down a track.

"What was he doing here?" His voice was angry. "Did he steal anything?"

Mum had come out and stood near the front door, wiping her hands on a tea towel. I walked up and stood beside her. I wanted to protect Mum, though I had no idea what was coming. I felt her tension.

"Bruce is not a thief, Lance. He's one of my best students. An honest, reliable lad." Mr Hecat's words seemed to ease Mum's tension.

"Car broke down." A grumpy Mr Warhurst pointed to Mr Hecat. "Thankfully, he came along and pulled over. Not that he's a motor mechanic or anything."

"Thanks for the compliment, Lance." Mr Hecat smiled. "But I'm a good tennis player."

The old man chuckled. "I don't think so."

"Well, I'll be off, then," Mr Hecat said, climbing back into his car. "You right with your car?"

"Yep, just need to make a call. Get it towed back here." Mr Warhurst looked at his rescuer. "'Look, Trev, why don't you stay and have a drink?"

"Ah, not sure. Need to get home." His brows lifted. "On second thought, what's the hurry? It's the weekend."

Mum's tension had returned.

"And don't you worry, Elizabeth, there'll be no drinking in the house as promised." The old man gestured to the shed.

He'd promised he wouldn't drink at all.

The locked fridge in the shed came to mind. Bruce had fiddled with the lock with a thin piece of wire, giving up when he couldn't unlock it. Still, he was streetwise—like my friend Jimmy.

The men headed towards the shed.

***

The clock kept ticking and ticking. Each tick seemed super loud in the quiet room. It felt like forever. Mum told me to pack my suitcase, so I did. My tummy was all tied up in knots, just like Mom's face.

She kept muttering about 'making a run for it' and kept peeking out the window at Mr Molloy's place. But there wasn't any car there. Finally, she said in a tight voice, "We'll need to bunker in."

I thought 'bunker in' was one of those war words, like soldiers having to hide from the bad guys shooting at them. What did she mean? What was coming? She stood frozen, like a statue, her eyes now locked on the shed. I tried not to feel scared, but it was getting harder and harder.

"Okay, looks like the drinking session is over." Her voice was stern.

I moved closer to Mum, pretending to be a soldier. I was going to be tough and protect her. The two men staggered towards the house.

Mum barked out orders like a commander. We barricaded ourselves in her room. I had the cricket bat again, but Mum had a rifle.

She saw me staring at it. "It's okay, Quinn, I'm just keeping it away from him."

"What? Would he shoot us?" I trembled.

Mum shook her head. "Don't think so. But he could turn it on himself. He's a sick man. The grog has hold of him. It's evil."

I'm never going to drink.

Mum locked her door and left the big brass key in the lock. We dragged a cabinet up against the door and moved the bed up against the cabinet. I'd never realised how strong Mum was.

The men's footsteps echoed through the house. We sat on the bed, listening. It sounded like they had settled in the living room. Mr Hecat's loud, slurred voice asked the old man where we were. Only a grunt came from the old man. Their words got louder as they argued about something. There was a crash, and foul language. A door slammed, and then there was silence.

We sat on the bed looking at each other.

"That crash sounded like glass. Could only be his rock collection," Mum whispered.

Mum must be right.

The silence was frightening. "Should I go see if he's alright?"

Mum shook her head with a frown.

The silence remained. With our barricade, I felt safe and my heart no longer pounded in my chest. Mum started to relax in the quietness.

I lay on Mum's bed, staring up at the ceiling. The room was semi-dark, soft moonlight filtering through the partially opened curtains. Mum was asleep. How could she sleep? My mind was racing, and dark shadows danced in the corners of the ceiling.

I slipped off the bed and sat on a chair near the locked window. It was a large, wooden framed window. Our suitcases were packed, parked under the windowsill, ready to fit through if it came to that. Mum had told me to pack only things that I really needed, saying we may not come back.

To let a little breeze in, I lifted the bottom part of the window slightly. I parted the curtains and looked up at the stars. A tight knot of anger twisted in my chest—I was angry with Dad.

Night sounds entered the room. Crickets chirped and frogs croaked from the nearby creek. The calls of nighttime creatures and their rustling filled the air. An eerie shriek broke through the night. A fox, maybe a wild dog, maybe a yowie. I laughed to myself and then I heard movement inside the house. I turned and noticed Mum had shifted. The last shriek had disturbed her briefly, but then she fell asleep again.

Again movement, footsteps coming our way. Mr Warhurst thumped on the bedroom door and hollered, "Get out here and make me dinner, woman!"

Mum sprang from the bed and leaned against the iron bedhead. She gestured for me to do the same. I thought about grabbing the rifle.

"I'm not well, Lance. I need to sleep it off." Her voice was strained and raw. She looked at me and whispered, "He's lost track of time."

"You weak or something? Get out here," he demanded, thumping the door again.

"I'm sick, please leave me alone," Mum pleaded.

Footsteps retreated. The minutes ticked by. Silence filled the house.

Mum stretched out on the bed. "Rest, Quinn. I'd say he has collapsed somewhere, hopefully not on the hard floor."

My mum had a big heart.

I returned to the window. My mind was on the dark sky above when the door handle shook. There was a *thud*. The key had come out of the door and now lay on the timber floor.

Mum jerked upright.

"I have a key, you know." A snicker followed the comment.

He must have pushed the other key out. I could hear him fiddling with the lock, trying to put the spare key in. He got it in, then turned the handle. He grunted.

"What's stopping the door?" He groaned.

"Please go away, or I'll scream."

He laughed. "Who's going to hear you?"

"Your neighbour, Tom."

"He's nearly as deaf as your son."

"My son's not deaf."

"That's not what his teacher told me."

Well, I could certainly hear his shouting.

"He told me the other thing, too." He laughed evilly. "He told me my family ain't coming back. I hit him for that."

The cabinet screeched along the floor. I had heard grog could give you super strength.

"And he told me that your boy took my nugget to school for Show and Tell. You wait till I get my hands on him, the little brat."

Mum pointed to the window. "Go."

"No, you go first."

She looked at me, her eyes wide. The cabinet screeched again. She nodded and rushed to the window. She lifted it up with a grunt and shoved the suitcases out, one after the other they fell onto the grass outside.

Once we were both out the window, we ran with our suitcases. I thought I saw the shadow of a man standing near a tree. Who could that have been? I didn't have time to consider if it was the yowie.

31 The Escape

Tom was on his way to the Warhurst house, a rifle in hand. Mum turned him back to his house. "Please, Tom, no trouble." She did well to turn him because he was like a raging bull.

"That's it." Tom looked at the old man's house. "I'm getting you out of here. I'm sorry, but it's just not safe for you or Quinn. You have to go. That man does not deserve any more chances."

We passed Hecat's car. He stood near some bushes relieving himself, covering his eyes from the headlight glare as we dove past. Tom shook his head. "I hope he sobers up a bit more before he continues his trip home."

We spent a night in a hotel in Willward. Tom knew the owner and they kindly put us up. We were safe there, since nobody knew where we were. Though the noise from the bar below took some getting used to.

Tom had promised to deal with Mr Warhurst. It had dawned on me that the old man had 'war' in his surname. I didn't know if that meant anything, but he was fighting a few battles and we had just escaped from one of them.

In the morning, we wandered around the town. It was super quiet, hardly anyone on the streets. I figured we were going back to Melbourne. Back to the People's Palace, until we worked out what to do next. We were nomads.

We ended up at the train platform where it had all begun. This was where Mr Molloy picked us up and drove us to Edithburra. And then he'd helped us escape Edithburra.

The sound of the train approaching excited me. Train trips always meant adventure. But I just had a funny feeling that this part of the story wasn't over yet. We boarded and found our seats. Mum let out a big sigh. "Did you know, Quinn, that they weren't coming back?"

"Sort of." Rosemary would probably be happy with that answer. I thought of her and my school friends, wishing I could be with them instead of here. The way everything was ending just made me feel so sad.

"Sort of?" Mum queried.

"Didn't know for sure. There was talk of it at school."

She leaned back in the leather seat, her voice soft. "I'm sorry, Quinn. I'm just shunting you around." She shook her head, looking out the window. "What a sad adventure that was."

"It was." But a bit of fear lingered, like the battle wasn't over yet. Would Mr Warhurst come after us?

I dozed off and an image of the rock cabinet came into my mind. Rocks and glass were scattered over the floor. The old man was kneeling, scrambling around, searching. Blood came from a cut on his arm.

The gold nugget. It was missing. He turned to me, as if the dream was real.

Where is it?

I froze. I didn't know. But this was just a dream, right? At least, I really, really hoped it was.

Was the nugget hidden under something in the living room? Or did Mr Hecat take it? Maybe Bruce grabbed it as an emblem for his go-cart—I laughed at that. Nah, it had to be Mr Hecat. He wasn't nice at all.

Where is it?

Warhurst's face was so close I was looking up his nose. He screamed. *Where is it?*

That jolted me awake.

I looked at Mum. She was clutching her handbag tightly. How long before she could relax and not be scared?

I turned to look out the window. There were lots of green fields, all different shades. Maybe one of those was a cabbage patch. Workers with big floppy hats moved between the rows. One of them stopped and bent down to pick up something.

A baby? A baby boy?

Spring 1964
Melbourne

My dearest Martha,

I cannot help but start this letter with a heavy heart, for our lives, Quinn's and mine, hung by a thread. We had to escape the clutches of a dreadful man, a wretched soul he was. I knew it was coming, so I scoured the classifieds and secured a position in a far bigger town. Over 10,000 souls, a far cry from wee Edithburra.

And thankfully, a kind neighbour helped us slip away unseen. We were so blessed by his actions. Though I'm a wee nervous. Will that evil man come after us? I have told no one of our destination, so hopefully we will be safe.

As I write this, I'm at Flinders Street Station, waiting for our train to take us to our secret destination. An hour yet, a chance to catch my breath. Quinn has wandered off, likely found his newspaper friends. I can hear their calls echoing through the grand halls.

I have secured a job as a kitchen hand at a family-run guest house. They seem like kind folk on the phone. I look forward to the fresh start. Just now, I saw Quinn walking towards me. There's a hurt in his eyes, many hurts—secrets he carries from our troubles. He's young, though, and hopefully these scars will fade with time.

He has just asked me for something—he's always hungry—so I'll finish now. I'll write soon to tell you about our new life.

All my love,
Elizabeth

Part 2 – The Wounded Man

Suburbia Melbourne, Australia
1981

32 Rock Bottom

The image was blurry.

The cold of the curb seeped through my jeans, making my backside numb. The scene before me was one of chaos, flashing lights—red, blue, yellow. Ambulance, a police vehicle, tow-trucks. How had they gotten here so fast? All brought about by me and a split-second decision to try and end my life.

My gaze rested on the lady across the road. Early-twenties I'd say. Police surrounded her, their voices soft, trying to calm her down. I knew they were talking about me. She had pointed at me a number of times. I had the urge to wave, a ridiculous plea for normalcy to return. I wanted to tell her I was sorry.

Steam rose from under the crumpled bonnet of my car. The left side revealed dented metal and shattered lights. The lady's car had ended up off the road and now rested on parkland. Her car was badly damaged on one side: lights smashed, fender and bumper buckled.

An officer, his face showing little emotion, approached me. "You okay, mate?"

"I-I'm sort of fine, Officer. Is sh-she okay?" I was trying hard to get my words out straight.

He turned and looked back at the woman. "She's in a mild state of shock." He returned his assessing police gaze to me. "Did you run a red light?"

Reality kicked in. I started shivering. "I th-think I did…I d-decided I'd had enough of life." My actions leading to the accident a clear snapshot stamped in my foggy head.

"It's sad that you had to bring others into your misery."

I nodded and my stomach twisted. "I agree."

"You'll have to come back to the station with us."

I took a deep breath and tasted mint. I had gulped down Tic Tacs to try and conceal the smell of alcohol, a pathetic attempt to mask the stench that clung to me. Who was I kidding?

At the station, they took my blood alcohol reading. Four times over the limit. I was drunk, very drunk and very dangerous, a missile on four wheels. I suggested to them that maybe the mints had affected the reading. The police officer's steely gaze told me he didn't agree. Fingerprints, a mugshot—the process felt surreal. I stood there, my foggy mind seeking clarification.

That was when it hit home. I had nearly killed someone. Standing in the police station, overwhelmed and burdened by what I had brought on myself. I had hit rock bottom.

I stood in the booking area of the police station, trembling and crying.

They'd seen it all before, these officers—the fear, the lostness. One offered to drive me home, his voice kind and sympathetic, but I declined. Paperwork was placed in my palm, a cold reminder of what I'd done and what was to follow.

"Further details of the court hearing will come in the mail," they said.

On that slow walk home, with the streets deserted and a mist settling in, I passed a church building. A white cross on its roof stark against the gloomy night. The branches of a tree in the front yard creaked. I paused and looked at the front door of the church. What lay behind that door? What secrets? With a heavy sigh, I shrugged and continued my walk home, burdened by what I'd done.

A faint sound came from behind me, and I turned, on edge, to look back towards the church. Just the wind. My thoughts went back to the accident. It had felt like something unseen had entered the car, like the wind, and took control. Good or evil, I didn't know, but I'd sensed something.

I shook my head. Was this still the alcohol talking? Maybe not. Maybe there truly was something out there, something unseen.

I walked into my unit. Silence. Just me. Over the years, doors had been shut to others, leading to this isolated existence. I headed to the fridge, opened the door, and grabbed a can of beer, then flipped the tab. Beer bubbled and frothed on the top of the can. I stared at it. Years of hurt and confusion passed before my eyes.

Yes, rock bottom had arrived. I poured the beer down the drain.

***

A noise jolted me from my sleep. Disoriented, I blinked, trying to focus on my surroundings. I placed my hand on the worn couch and pushed myself up. My head felt like a concrete block, my body wanting to fall back on the couch. Then it came again—a soft rapping at the front fly-screen door.

Panic jolted me upright. The door. I'd left it open and only the fly-screen had kept the creatures of the night at bay. A shadow loomed beyond.

"Hello, anybody home?" a man called.

I struggled to my feet. Last night's events—a blur of shame and confusion—washed over me. I collapsed back on the couch and raised my hands to my head. Bile filled my mouth. A dry heave escaped my throat.

More soft rapping. "Hello, anyone there?"

I cleared my throat. "Be with you in a sec." My voice was raspy.

I knew the visit had to do with last night. Taking a deep breath, I pushed myself upright with a groan and steadied myself. Consequences. My actions had consequences and now was the time to face the music. I tried to rub the crinkles out of last night's clothes and gingerly moved towards the door.

In my confusion, I unlatched the door and looked through the fly-screen at the visitor.

The man was tall, around my height, with curly brown hair and deep, peaceful blue eyes. "I'm the father of the victim of the accident last night. Your address was provided for insurance purposes."

My heart pounded in my chest. I tried to speak, but the words caught in my throat, leaving me gasping for breath.

The room swirled as the man's distorted figure opened the door and stepped towards me. I stumbled back, bracing for the blows I expected to follow. But they didn't come. Instead, he reached for me.

"Steady, take it easy. Let's get you to a seat." His voice was calming.

"Look, I'm awfully sorry about what happened…I've been under some stress…a bit lost…grog got a hold of me…" The words spluttered out. My eyes watered.

"I understand. Take some deep breaths. Look, my daughter is fine, a bit shaken, more concerned about her car—"

"Send me the bill, or I can give you money now if you want."

He raised a palm. "Look, my daughter's quite resilient. She'll be fine. She's just returned from overseas and is living with us at the moment. So, try to relax a little." His eyes met mine, gentle.

He wanted me to understand that his daughter was strong. But I had nearly killed her. What sort of man was I dealing with here?

"We'll get quotes and let you know. The car is still drivable. Here's my contact details." He held out a piece of paper.

I reached out, my hand trembling slightly, and took the paper from him. The crisp edge of the sheet felt oddly sharp against my fingertips, grounding me in the moment. I glanced down at the neat handwriting, the numbers and letters blurring slightly before coming into focus.

He continued to look at me, his brow furrowed with concern. "Are you okay?"

As I clutched the paper, a strange shift occurred within me. The sense of impending doom that had been suffocating me—the feeling that I was about to die—began to fade away. My breathing, which had been rapid and shallow, gradually slowed. The pounding of my heart, so loud I thought it might burst from my chest, began to ease.

I looked back up at him and managed a small nod.

"Mate," said the man. "I've been where you're at. Although I'm not happy with the harm you could've brought upon my daughter and our family, I'd feel much better knowing you're going to right your ways and not bring misery to anyone else."

Was this man real? Was I dreaming?

We had found our way to the dining room and sat on chairs across from each other. He held my gaze, his eyes throwing out a challenge. I looked over towards the kitchen sink. An empty beer can lay overturned. I remembered I had poured it down the sink.

He followed my eyes to the can and then looked at me, the challenge still in his eyes.

I knew then that my drinking days had come to an end.

33 Bruno's Burgers

That week turned out to be the worst and best of my life.

The accident had occurred on Friday evening. Sunday came, and I was still jittery. No one needed to know about the accident. The challenge would come when I lost my licence, but I'd face that hurdle when it arose. There was always the option of public transport, so my secret might remain hidden.

Deciding a greasy hamburger and Coke would make me feel better, I grabbed my keys and wallet and headed out of my unit. The carport was eerily empty, since my car had been towed to the panel beaters. Thinking about that made me feel nauseous.

The takeaway shop was only five minutes away and, thankfully, located in the opposite direction of where I'd had the accident. The shop made the best hamburger with the lot, and the thought of squishy egg and juicy meat cheered me up a little. I was there in no time and placed my order. My hands shook as I handed over the money. The cashier seemed to notice, though I was sure I detected understanding in his eyes.

I stood back to wait for my order, letting my eyes wander to a poster of Australian fish species. Over the years, I'd caught a few of them—usually with a beer in hand. The memories churned up a bit of unease, so I headed outside and stopped near a notice board. At a nearby table, a couple were munching on chips, the salty aroma drifted over. I took a sip of my Coke, hoping to shake off the uneasy feeling.

The accident replayed in my mind, the accuracy of my memories uncertain, but the impact undeniable. Tears welled up, blurring my vision. A sudden scrape of a chair behind me made me flinch. I felt like a fragile shell, ready to shatter at the slightest touch. Guilt and shame weighed heavily on me, leaving me feeling lost. The thought of facing court and losing my license filled me with anxiety.

I was a complete mess. I held my hand out in front of me; the shaking had stopped. Was this some kind of withdrawal symptom?

I stared aimlessly at the notice board, my sight gradually clearing. A squash team was starting up and looking for players. That set off a small spark. I could do that. Then the words on a larger notice caught my attention. **Is Alcohol a Problem?** It was a flyer for AA and listed a phone number.

I sensed someone behind me. "Here's your burger, mate."

I turned. The takeaway shop man, wrapped in his stained white apron, stood there with my burger tucked away in a bag. He smelt of grease and salt, and a pen stuck out of his apron pocket.

"Could I borrow your pen?" I asked.

"Sure." He handed it to me. "You want something to scribble on?" Before I could respond, he handed me a piece of paper. He watched me write down the number and then I returned his pen and took my burger. He nodded and went back inside. I put the piece of paper in my pocket.

The chip-eating couple had left, so I went and sat at their table. I unwrapped the burger and started eating. The warm, greasy food helped, gave my body what it needed. The shop was quiet, and I could hear the owners chatting inside and noticed an occasional glance in my direction. I devoured the hamburger like I hadn't eaten in years, and my stomach responded with a loud burp.

Soon, the burger man reappeared outside and walked over to me. He put out his hand for the wrappings.

"Are you okay, mate?"

I stared at him.

"I mean, I noticed you wrote down the AA number. The reason I put the flyer up there was to help people. So, is there anything I can help you with?" He handed me a pamphlet. "My name is Bruno."

***

I unlocked the door and entered my unit. The silence was deafening. The boredom grated on me. A few of my mates would be down at the pub playing pool, and I felt tempted to join them. Although I had doubts about my ability to hold a cue stick steady. I hadn't had the shakes like this before. Hopefully, they'd clear up in a day or so. If not, I best go see someone.

I placed the flyer on the table and went to the bathroom. The four light bulbs above the mirror assaulted my tired eyes. Catching a glimpse of myself, I stopped cold. A stranger stared back at me: hair a tangled mess, beard overgrown, eyes sunken and lifeless. My hand drifted up to touch a network of angry red lines pulsing beneath the surface of my skin, something I'd ignored for far too long. Yesterday, a beer would wash away such concerns, numbing any anxieties.

But the truth was clear now, etched in the lines around my mouth and the tell-tale map on my face. This was the cost of my drinking, and resolve hardened within me. "The tide has now turned," I whispered, the words both a promise and a challenge.

Stepping out of the bathroom, I lit a smoke. It rocked in my hand from a tremor I couldn't quite steady. Observing the smoke curl upwards, I mused about how manly smoking was supposed to be. A humourless chuckle escaped my lips. I'd once thought the same about the drink, but that thought was wavering, and in a big way.

I went and sat on the couch, my gaze drifting towards the stereo. A cassette tape, a compilation of Beatles tracks I had made myself, lay near the cassette deck. With a sigh, I rose and shuffled over to it. Slipping the tape into the deck, I pressed play. As I slumped back onto the couch, McCartney's voice filled the room, reminding me that even when the night is cloudy, there's still a light shining on me.

At the takeaway shop, Bruno had sat down and chatted with me, explaining the pamphlet he had handed me about quitting alcohol. He told me there were some tips there that could help and to ring him anytime if I had any questions. The pamphlet sat on the coffee table near the ashtray and I stared at it. What tips could possibly help me? Bruno's face appeared in my mind, his eyes offering hope. I stubbed out the cigarette and reached for the pamphlet. Skimming the first page, my eyes glazed over. Words swam before me; twelve steps were listed. Tears started flowing at the first step, realising that my life had become unmanageable. I closed my eyes and spoke to God for the first time in many years.

34 Hello, My Name is Quinn

Monday morning. I woke full of remorse. I could not face the world so I phoned in sick to work.

I had tossed and turned all night, figments of the past flooding my mind. So many people to make amends to. I wanted so much to escape from the heavy burden I now felt. The urge to drink strong.

The piece of paper with the victim's father's details caught my attention as it lay on the dining table. It brought sharply into focus the remnants of the accident. I rushed to the toilet and started dry retching.

Head heavy, I returned and sat at the dining table. I took a deep breath and finally confronted the information on the paper. His name was Frank Burgess, and he noted he was the father of Pamela Burgess. He provided a phone number. It was a local number and he did mention that his daughter was living with them at the moment.

I'm sorry, Pamela, for the pain I brought into your life. That last thought stirred a desire in my heart to speak to her, to make amends. Would she be at home, maybe at work? Then I felt bad, thinking that she may still be in shock recovering from the accident. I tried to push the urge to talk to her away, but it remained.

I needed to do it. I walked over to the phone, paper in hand, and lifted it off its cradle, but then quickly placed it back and stared at it. What a battle. A voice was telling me to be strong. I picked up the phone again and fought the urge to put it down again, instead focusing on the piece of paper. My hand trembled as I dialled the number with mum's voice from the past offering words of wisdom. Remember Quinn, it's Mr or Mrs.

A man's voice answered. "Hello."

I was hesitant. "Mr Burgess?"

"Yes, how can I help you?"

"I met you the other day," I said, my stomach knotting. "Regarding the accident."

"Yes, Quinn, wasn't it?"

"Yes, that's right." I took a deep breath. "I was wondering if it would be possible to talk to your daughter because I'm really sorry about the accident and wanted to apologise to her."

Silence, except for the sound of my heartbeat. "She seems in better spirits today. Has a rostered day off work. Just hold on for a second."

The second seemed like hours.

"Hello, this is Pamela," a soft, guarded voice came on the phone.

I cleared my throat. "Hi, this is Quinn from the other night. I…I just wanted to tell you how sorry I am about the accident. I know I can't undo what happened, but I'm willing to do whatever I can to make amends."

"Thank you," she said. "My dad has spoken to me about his visit with you. I'm also sorry that your life has gotten you into this mess. I understand how important it is to forgive." She paused. I thought I heard a sniffle. "So, I do accept your apology. Although your actions have inconvenienced me a bit, I'll be okay." She sounded strong.

"Thank you, so much."

"I just hope you continue to take action to sort your life out."

"I have made contact with AA and realise now my life was getting out of hand." Those words stumbled out. "Again, I'm so sorry."

"It's okay, I know it's hard for us both, but time will help. Thank you for calling."

I heard some shuffling sounds and Mr Burgess came back on. "Thanks for doing that. Good luck with your future. I think what you've done here shows you're on the right track."

"Thanks for your help and understanding." The call ended.

After hanging up, I went and sat on the couch, enveloped in silence for a long while, feeling a mix of exhaustion and relief. It was a start—a critical step towards healing and recovery.

***

I attended my first AA meeting that Wednesday night at an old Baptist Church in Hawthorn, with Bruno by my side for moral support. The group, made up of around seven or eight men from various occupations, welcomed me with friendly faces etched with stories.

There was no pressure to contribute to the meetings.

As mentions of a higher power drifted in and out of the conversations, my mind wandered. During the accident, time had seemed to stand still, and I felt like a distant observer of what was happening. Later, I wondered if this had been some kind of spiritual intervention—not to excuse what I'd done, but to redirect the destructive path I was on. One thing was clear: some force was now directing my life.

Bruno said that I had been blessed with what AA called the gift of desperation. He explained it as the rock bottom experience that removes the desire to drink ever again. Sometimes it would be forced upon a person by a higher power in the form of a drastic event. Bruno said that was my encounter, a turning point that had forced me to confront my demons head-on and that I now clung to.

After the first meeting, I stayed and had a cuppa with some members of the group. The scent of alcohol was detectable on one man. I realised then that we were all at different stages but fighting the same battle.

I started attending church with Bruno and working through the twelve steps. Bruno shared his story with me and understood my pain, as he had walked the same path. He filled me with hope. He explained that the twelfth step was about giving back and helping others on their journey. Bruno became what they call in AA, my sponsor.

At the third meeting, when there was space for introductions, I finally took a deep breath and introduced myself. "My name is Quinn," I said, my voice surprisingly steady, "and I'm an alcoholic." The words hung in the air for a moment, then relief surged through me, as if I had finally released a pressure valve. The hisses of worry and shame quieted.

Group members responded with "Hi, Quinn."

I coughed to clear my throat. "Hi to you all…I might start by saying that looking back, I realise my understanding of alcoholism was wildly inaccurate. I'd picture a man in dirty clothing lying in a gutter." I paused, took a breath, and looked around the room. No one here fit that stereotype. Instead, I saw faces marked by experience. Some were lined with worry, others hardened by life.

"I started drinking when I was young. I was in the 'cool group' at school. Whatever that really meant—maybe the group that didn't want to be at school." A few people chuckled. "And every weekend, we'd drink. Alcohol soon had control of my life, and I could do very little without drinking. Eventually, I was expelled from school, but that had more to do with smoking." There were some laughs. "Still, my life was getting out of control. And it stayed that way for twelve years—" I welled up, but words still wanted to flow.

"I couldn't see the problem. Everybody else had an issue, not me. A few long-term and short-term broken relationships later, I realised I had totally lost my way. Remorse—an emotional heaviness—controlled my life, and I wanted to end things, to be free of it. I tried. Ran a red light. But wasn't successful and nearly destroyed the life of another person." I took a long breath. "And here I am."

Soft applause greeted my declaration.

"Thank you, Quinn," Gary, the group leader, said. He was a middle-aged man with kind eyes and a calm demeanour. "We're glad you found us."

"Could I just say one more thing?" My candour surprised me. "I'm working through the AA steps at the moment, and the step about making amends with the people I've hurt—

and there's a few of them—deeply connected with me. I felt terrible for the lady that I involved in my misery through the car accident. I contacted her recently and, although she was hesitant at first, she warmed to my apology. Her dad helped bring that together, and it was a healing time for us both. I felt a sense of closure from the accident."

"Thank you, Quinn. They are great words of encouragement," the leader said.

I looked at Bruno and nodded. I was thankful.

From that point on, I resolved to rebuild my life. The words 'one day at a time' found in the AA readings became my mantra, whispered regularly as I climbed my way back towards a normal life. When anxieties about the future threatened to overwhelm me, I'd focus on just getting through today. It was the most valuable advice I'd ever received, helping me stay sober and grounded in the present rather than drowning in worries about tomorrow.

Smoking went out the window too. There seemed to be a connection with drinking, some kind of interplay between the two habits. I still had the odd cigarette, but the desire soon faded. Gambling even invited itself into this interplay—and it, too, eventually departed.

I knew times of deep reflection were coming. And hopefully, times of healing, too.

35 The Course

I leaned towards the mirror and ran a hand through my thinning hair. It was receding a bit at the front, with more scalp showing at the rear, as was pointed out—in a nice way—by observant family and friends. I wasn't sure if the thickening shampoo was working, but I wasn't overly concerned. *It is what it is.* At least it looked healthy.

Leaning in closer, I smiled. The spider veins were hardly noticeable. I remembered them as a warning sign connected to the drinking. My eyes were clear. Were they grey or blue today? I scratched my chin. The beard was trimmed well and close to the face. I'd come a long way in a few months.

As I stepped back from the mirror, my self-appreciation exercise continued, and I realised it wasn't just my appearance that had improved. With the brain fog lifted, my thinking was sharper. I no longer relied on alcohol as a coping mechanism. Now, I could think clearly, which had led to considering a job change. Something to be pondered.

Hitting the stores had become my new pastime, along with getting fit—both a whole lot better than drowning my sorrows. I took one last look in the mirror. The new dark blue shirt complimented my black jeans. No need for a jacket, since the nights were still warm. A knot of nerves twisted in my gut, but I was ready for the course. I tapped my back pocket to make sure I had my notebook. My thoughts went back to my court appearance.

The judge had given me a frosty glare over his glasses and told me in strong words that I needed to attend a mandatory drink-driving course as part of my conviction. A scoff had escaped his lips when I'd declared my intention to quit—he'd probably heard it all before. He added that this course was going to help me achieve my goal. He did offer some words of encouragement, something like "Good luck".

By attending and completing the course, I'd have my disqualification period reduced. A question nagged at me: was that truly the goal for some people—to shorten their sentence rather than conquer their addiction? Maybe this course could be another nudge to further right the ship. Well, I was on my way.

En route to the course, I passed the Grand Hotel, a lapse in judgement. I glimpsed Prouty at the bar. Our eyes met, and he gestured for me to join him. The pull was strong. The problem was I had time, as I always had a leaning towards being early for appointments. I'd avoided situations like this before, but now I was caught out.

I entered the bar. My senses were attacked by lingering smoke and the smell from cigarette butts and stale beer mixed together in the steel trough that ran the length of the bar. The sight triggered nausea. Alcohol had dulled the senses of the drinkers. I wanted to retreat back to the street, but I'd already committed to being here.

Prouty jumped up to greet me. "Where ya been, mate? Your drinking buddies have been asking about you. Rumour has it that you're on the wagon." He took a sip from his glass. "Is that true?"

"It is." The smell from his glass stirred up repressed feelings. "Got into some trouble, lost my license. So I need to stay off the stuff."

Toby, eyes glued to the racing form guide, let out a gruff sound. "Sure, Quinn. Pull the other leg, it plays 'Jingle Bells'." He didn't even look up.

A few laughs echoed nearby, including from Lucy the barmaid. "Want a pot, Quinn?" she asked.

"Nope." I needed to get out of there.

"What about a 7-ounce?"

Before I could react, a frothing glass of chilled beer appeared before me. Its familiar scent teased my senses, awakening dormant urges. I needed fresh air.

"Bet that won't even touch the side of your mouth. Be gone in one gulp." Prouty smirked.

A mild panic bubbled up. Scanning the room, my eyes locked with those of a girl seated near the pool table—the girl from the accident. Her eyes widened in shock, then filled with a deep, wounded look. Without a word, I turned and fled.

Outside, I gulped down the cool night air, hoping it would steady my nerves. Lesson learned. I wanted to race back in and tell the girl that wasn't me anymore. But I didn't want to go back in there. Maybe an encounter with her at another time would fix things up. I let out a heavy sigh and trudged on. As I made my way to the community centre, I realised that the constant pressure from others to drink would continue to be a challenge.

Approaching the community centre, I observed others filing in. Gripping my notebook and pen, I clicked the pen top repeatedly, mustering the courage to enter. My ordeal at the Grand Hotel stirred up haunting memories of how I used to rely on the grog in moments like these.

I moved towards the entrance. Sheets of paper, taped to the walls, served as makeshift signs guiding attendees to the training room. I found the room, which was narrow with a long table. Some attendees had already taken their seats, and the soft hum of conversation filled the air.

A tall young woman I assumed was the instructor stood at the front of the room, her posture confident but approachable. She appeared to be in her mid-twenties, with shoulder-length, neatly styled brown hair. Her attire was professional yet comfortable—medium wash jeans, a loose-fitting cotton-blend floral print blouse, and an unbuttoned cardigan sweater. She wore oversized glasses with black frames.

As I entered the room, she gave me a warm smile and asked my name. With a nod, she checked my name off a roster. She then gestured towards the long table, still smiling. "Your name is on a place card on the table. You're seated on the right side. You'll also find a name tag there to put on."

I smiled and went scanning for the card. I found my name, clipped the tag on, and sat down at the long table. Another man had entered behind me, looking like he'd just come from a construction site. Sweat and dust clung to him. He sat on the opposite side of the table. I got a brief look at him. He had an angry, weathered face with a scar under his right eye.

Before I looked away, he pointed to the scar and said, "Shrapnel."

Suddenly, the seriousness of the situation dawned on me. What was I doing here, with all these strangers? Gloom settled on me. Glancing around the table, I saw only grim faces. No one was happy to be here.

My emotions and thoughts were a tangled mess—a familiar feeling these days, ever since I'd quit the grog. A wave of euphoria had washed over me initially, like a heavy weight being lifted. I felt lighter, but beneath it, emotions brewed raw and unfiltered, emotions that were previously covered by the thick fog of alcohol. Maybe this course would help. I just didn't know how.

Six others sat at the table besides me. The class at Edithburra had been the same size, with the same gender break-up: five men and two women. I frowned wondering why I was making this comparison with Edithburra?

The instructor stood at the head of the table, next to the overhead projector, and flicked it on. Her name was projected onto the screen.

"Greetings to you all," she said. "My name is Lee Trewin." She pointed to the screen. "I'd like to welcome you to this course. It's a community-based program to help reduce your likelihood of reoffending and also to explore the hazards of drinking and strategies to avoid drinking while driving."

"And to reduce our sentence," the construction worker added. His name was Vince. He seemed to find his comment amusing. A few others did, too.

"Yes, that's right." The instructor smiled. "Helps with that as well. Let's continue." She changed the slide. "Here are some rules."

They were simple rules. We were to attend all sessions and be in a sober condition with no alcohol before or during the course. The class chuckled at that one. We had a lot of learning ahead of us.

I forced myself to attend all sessions. Most of us did. The course was confronting. I was lucky not to be in prison. I could see now how drinking had taken hold of me, letting some other entity seize control of my thoughts and actions. Whatever it was, it had been bent on destroying my life. "Under the influence" was an apt description of being drunk. But now, I dared to hope that I'd been set free, that the dark entity had been banished. The demon drink gone.

Welcoming the sessions, I soaked them in like a sponge. A hunger for understanding grew within me, driving a desire to gain insight into the reasons behind my drinking and the essence of who I was.

36 The Final Session

At the final session, emotions ran high. Shame and anger flared; old wounds reopened. The lack of respect—eyes rolling from some of the young—towards Vince disturbed me. I sensed an eruption pending, and it came.

Vince shot to his feet, slamming his fist on the table. "You people have no idea what a stupid war does to someone. It rips you away from reality. You don't know how hard it's been for me to sit here, listening to your petty stories. You all need to go fight in a war."

He paused, his breath shaky, his eyes scanning each of us. His anger softened, giving way to tears. "But Lee is right," he added, his voice quieter now, more controlled. "That grog is stunting our growth, getting us into trouble." He turned to Lee. "I'm sorry for my outburst, but geez it's hard not to drink."

"It is hard, Vince," Lee agreed, seeming unphased by Vince's display of anger. "War is a terrible thing, and its impact on the mind is profound. Researchers are now delving deeper into trauma, recognising how it shapes us." She paused, glancing at her notes. "Alcohol often becomes a coping mechanism, eventually turning into a full-blown addiction. But addictions can be broken." Her gaze shifted around the group. "I want each of you to reflect on your relationship with alcohol. There's often a deeper issue driving the need to drink. Understanding what that is can be the first step towards healing."

"Yeah, Lee is right." The urge to speak was overwhelming, thoughts and feelings having been bottled up for too long. "These sessions have made a few things clear to me. Somewhere along the way, I lost my direction in life." Glancing at Vince and seeing the pain in his expression, it felt important to add. "Without taking away from Vince's experience, but I felt disconnected, too. I fell into the drinking culture, thinking it was just what you did. My siblings showed me the way, and peer pressure did the rest. People laughed, sometimes with me, sometimes at me."

I noticed others nodding in agreement. "Alcohol became my crutch for every little problem. My personal growth was stunted, and the years took their toll. Relationships broke down. I threw caution to the wind but regret always followed. Eventually, I was drinking to escape from the things that drinking had caused."

"Hear, hear!" said Graeme, the youngest member of the class, offering his encouragement.

I continued, "The remorse for my actions led to guilt, shame, self-loathing. I'd drink to escape those feelings, but they were always waiting for me the next day, like a smiling, welcoming face. The remorse was heavy on my chest, and I'd replay my regretted actions over and over in my head. I'd created a painful loop, numbing my remorse with alcohol.

The car accident, where I ran a red light, was an attempt to escape from the cycle I'd trapped myself in. How selfish and self-centred that was."

A soft round of applause came from the class. I wasn't sure where all these words had come from, but I needed to get them out, to share them.

"Well said, Quinn. Thanks for sharing," Lee said, her voice encouraging.

I noticed my hands were shaking. The speech had taken something out of me. But then, one by one, others began to speak up, too. My words had given them the courage to share. Difficult pasts seemed to weave a common thread through all our stories.

"As we've discussed," Lee finally said, "confronting the past isn't easy. Many people are unwilling to face it, and I'm not saying everyone has to, but for some, it helps. Some don't want to see, some don't want to hear. The drinking culture is strong here in Australia."

Lee handled our different personalities well. Despite the charged atmosphere, she offered space and a compassionate ear, never pressuring anyone to share more than they were comfortable with. My heart went out to Vince. He had fought in Vietnam. I could see a simmering anger behind those war-torn eyes. He reminded me of an old man in Edithburra.

I sensed a collective sigh as the final session came to an end.

***

As the course concluded and Lee offered final words of encouragement, participants filed out with mixed expressions. Some exchanged contact information, discussing the support groups they planned to attend. Others looked uncertain, perhaps grappling with the changes ahead.

After saying my goodbyes to the other attendees, I decided to use the restroom before my walk home. Exiting the restroom, I found the place deserted, except for Lee walking ahead, carrying a box of her training material. I caught up with her.

"Do you have far to go with that box?" I asked.

Lee turned and smiled. "Nope, just out to the car park at the back of the centre."

"Well, let me carry it for you and walk you to your car. You never know what may be prowling out there."

"Cats," she said with a wink, lifting the box towards me. "Thanks. I'll take you up on that offer."

"You enjoy doing the classes?" I asked as we walked to her car.

"Some classes are better than others," Lee said. "Some just don't get it. It's a massive culture problem. But others will eventually stare at their glass of liquor and start pondering the things we've covered. In time, the light bulb will go on." She turned to me and smiled. "Stay with it, Quinn. It's a journey—a hard one, but a rewarding one."

We reached her car, and she opened the hatch, gesturing for me to place the box inside.

"Thank you, Quinn." She gave me a hug.

My body tensed—a conditioned reflex to keep others out of my personal space—but I soon relaxed as I sensed the warmth behind her embrace. The course had helped bring down some of the walls around me, and I realised with a jolt, that there had been very few genuine hugs in my life. A sadness touched my heart.

Lee handed me a business card. "I'm a social worker and counsellor. If you ever want to talk about things, give me a call." Her eyes were filled with genuine concern and kindness. "Not too many people beat the bottle. The gate is narrow, and not many find it."

I looked at the card, thinking it might be a ticket to help me navigate the maze I'd found myself in. When I lifted my eyes to Lee, the tenderness in her expression made me feel understood and comforted, as if she truly cared about my well-being.

"Give me a call. I'd love to know how you're progressing."

"I may take you up on that."

She smiled and climbed into her car.

Walking home, the cool evening air nipped at my face, refreshing and invigorating. As I reached the main street, I crossed to the other side of the road to avoid passing in front of the Grand Hotel. I noticed Vince standing at the entrance to the hotel, caught in a silent battle, pulled in two directions. Thankfully, he turned and walked away.

I continued my walk home, reflecting on the past five sessions. The road ahead wouldn't be easy, but I felt a newfound determination. This course hadn't been just about reducing my sentence; it was about changing my life.

***

Two months after the course, Lee's words still echoed in my mind: *It's a journey—a hard one, but a rewarding one.*

She was right. There were days when the weight of social expectations threatened to pull me under. The relentless pressure to conform felt like a churning current, dragging me in the opposite direction of where I wanted to go.

Loneliness crept in as I realised how central alcohol was to social life. From catching up with friends to unwinding after work, even celebrating—raising glasses and cans to the sky in some bonding ritual—drinks were a constant.

In an effort to break free, I sought solace in the Dandenong Ranges, running and hiking on the outskirts of Melbourne, where we had made our home after Edithburra. I was drawn to hilltops, where I could gaze down at the patchwork of rooftops during moments of introspection. Among those rooftops was the retirement village where we had settled Mum after I was removed from the schooling system and entered the fray of the world.

Thoughts of Edithburra often intruded on these moments of reflection. Why did these memories resurface so persistently? Was it a yearning for the simplicity of that time? The towering trees, the winding bush tracks, the friendships, the rocks, and that gold nugget. Yet, beneath this idyllic veneer, shadows of darker memories lingered.

It was during one of these hilltop reflections that I decided to reach out to Lee. I needed to speak with someone who understood such matters. I craved a listening ear, not a clinical diagnosis. Lee, with her genuine empathy, felt like a better fit than a doctor's sterile office. So, I made an appointment.

37 Chat One

I took a week off from work to recalibrate. Adjusting to a life without drinking has been a challenge. Most of my colleagues are puzzled by the new me, and only a few know about my driving offence. I might have to bring it up during my next security clearance briefing—though I might be gone by then.

I'd been working for a defence-related organisation based in Melbourne's Victoria Barracks for many years, but I could feel the undercurrent pushing me towards a job change. The organisation was relocating interstate, offering redundancies. I had submitted my paperwork, aware that I could still change my mind.

Well-meaning advice from a family member had initially led me towards a government career, emphasising the security aspect—I'd always have a job, on my terms at least. They were right; I'd ended up in a management role where it seemed nearly impossible to sack anyone. The best solution often seemed to be moving the problem elsewhere: special projects or another organisation.

Edithburra jumped into my head. And Mr Hecat. Was he an example of moving a problem on? Sweeping it under the rug? That thought disturbed me. Memories of his treatment, long buried, surged to the surface. Had alcohol numbed not just the pain, but also the truth of his actions? What I'd once dismissed as mere discipline revealed itself as clear-cut physical abuse. The realisation hit me like a sudden wave, stirring anger and confusion within. It was definitely something I needed to deal with.

With my mind free of alcohol's fog, several issues were starting to crop up. The idea of changing jobs was a recurring one, but I had no idea what I wanted to do. This seemed a common problem amongst my friends and colleagues—most just put up with jobs they disliked. My thoughts went in circles.

Part of my week-off strategy included a visit to see Lee, my course instructor and now counsellor. It was Monday morning, and I sat in the small reception area, flipping through the pages of a magazine while waiting to be called. I hoped this visit would help untangle the jumbled mess in my head.

"Quinn."

I quickly closed the magazine and placed it back on the table, then looked up.

Lee greeted me with a warm smile, gesturing for me to follow. Her casual dress and bold yellow jewellery caught my eye. We entered her cozy office, a striking contrast to the cold environment of the drink-driving course.

She gestured towards a chair, and I took a seat. "So good to see you again," Lee said, settling beside me. "Sometimes a desk can serve as a barrier." She smiled. The scent of lavender and the gentle hum of the air conditioner created a soothing atmosphere. Framed sporting photos directed our initial conversation. I relaxed, grateful for the easy conversation.

Lee then switched to counsellor mode. "How have you been?"

I paused to assess my thoughts.

Lee grabbed her notepad, eyes locked on me. My throat constricted, thoughts whirling.

"I like to doodle," she murmured, sketching a bird.

I forced a chuckle. "I'm okay. Still sober."

"That's great," she said, warmth in her eyes. "Are things surfacing now, without the alcohol?"

"Mind's racing. Like a dam about to burst."

"Good you've come," she said, softly. "Had counselling before?"

My stomach knotted. "Yeah, once. During the dark days. Depression, drinking...a mess. Doc prescribed pills and warned against mixing with booze. Bad combo. Dredged up ugly memories."

"The doctor missed the alcohol problem?"

"Guess so. Unless the meds were a hint."

"Didn't work, I take it." Her smile was wry.

"Nope. Kept drinking. Life kept spiralling, each turn steeper."

She nodded, her expression thoughtful. "What brings you here today?"

"Need to sort out the mess in my head," I admitted. "Feel like my life has stalled.'

"You've already taken a big step by quitting drinking," she replied, her voice reassuring.

I relaxed slightly. "Took a while to realise I had a problem. Just felt...off track."

"Until the accident," she prompted.

"Yeah."

"You once said you wanted to die. Still feel that way?"

"No," I said, surprised by my own certainty. "Now it's more...searching for meaning."

"A worthy goal," she smiled.

I hesitated. "Maybe. But it's damn hard work."

"Like digging for gold," Lee suggested. "Rewarding, but messy."

Edithburra flashed in my mind. "I've got a gold story…but that's for another time."

"Looking forward to it," she said, and I believed her. "Do you read?"

"I've been looking for resources."

She plucked a book from her shelf. "*Man's Search for Meaning*. Borrow it if you'd like."

Her offer surprised me. I wasn't used to such kindness. "You sure?"

"Absolutely," she nodded, handing it over. "Now, tell me about your background."

Okay, here we go. "Mum said I was found in a cabbage patch," I said with a half-smile.

"Playful," Lee observed.

"More like passive. Avoiding conflict, bottling things up."

Lee nodded. "That cabbage story could well be a form of evasion. Some parents struggle with tough talks."

I swallowed hard. "Makes sense."

"Lost my dad young," I continued, stomach knotting. "We moved around a lot after."

"I see," Lee said softly. "Would you feel comfortable telling me more about your dad?"

I sighed. "Not much to say. He died when I was around four."

"How?" Lee asked gently.

My eyes darted to the window. "I'm not sure." The words felt leaden. Truth and lies tangled in my mind, a story I wasn't ready to share. My hands fidgeted with the borrowed book.

Lee doodled a star. It sparked a memory.

"Mum said Dad became a star in the night sky," I found myself saying. "It was how I sensed him and reacted to his presence after he was gone."

Silence stretched between us, broken only by the clock's ticking. I shifted uneasily.

"There's more about Dad," I blurted. "Let's just say...his death wasn't what I'd been told."

Lee nodded. "Did you want to explore that?"

"Um…yes…maybe not right now though."

"That's fine, but I feel it could be something we need to explore."

Lee was right. There was some tangled mess about dad in my head.

"Tell me about your family." Lee said.

"Mum called me an afterthought. Bordering on a mistake. Behind that, I gather I derailed her plans."

"Siblings?"

"Three brothers, one sister. All much older." I sighed. "Teenagers when I was born. We never connected much."

Lee sketched stick figures. "No bond at all?"

I laughed dryly. "At gatherings, sure. Until the booze kicked in."

"Then what?"

I hesitated. "Old wounds surfaced. Anger. Accusations. Things I didn't understand as a kid."

"All siblings drinkers?" Lee asked.

"The men, yeah. Always have been."

"Still?"

I nodded. "I'm the odd one out, climbing out of that trench." I sighed. "Watching others get drunk while sober is...enlightening. Funny, but sad."

Lee agreed. "Past relationships?"

"A few. Drink killed most. One sober relationship ended badly. Rejection hit hard."

"Particularly sensitive to rejection?"

"Isn't everyone?"

"Some handle it better," Lee hinted.

I paused. "Oddly, I often think of two girls from Edithburra. Katrina and Rosemary. From when I was ten."

"Emotional impact, perhaps," Lee said. "Memory is complex."

I pondered that. She was probably right.

We shifted to lighter topics—sports, friends. A welcome respite.

"I think that's enough for today, Quinn," Lee said, softly. "We've opened some old wounds, but it's part of healing."

Exhaustion hit me. "Talking helps. Brings the hurt up."

"Exactly," she nodded. "Recognising the influence of your past is the first step. We'll develop strategies in future sessions."

Lee squeezed me in for Friday. "Don't forget your homework," she smiled, tapping the book.

Leaving the community centre, I felt lighter. Talking had lifted a weight. For the first time in a while, I felt hope.

38 Chat Two

Lee sat beside me again, ensuring the desk didn't come between us. A fountain trickled nearby, adding calm. I hadn't noticed that on the last visit.

"What did you get from the book?" Lee asked after greetings.

"It changed my view on hardships," I began eagerly. "They're inevitable but offer growth. I can't control the past, but I can control my attitude. Helping others gives meaning. And hope...hope's crucial."

"Impressive," Lee smiled.

"I've been reading Proverbs too," I added, surprising myself.

"'The fear of God is the beginning of wisdom'?" Lee quoted.

I nodded. "Religion is tricky. Everyone tiptoes around it. That fear of God...it's in me. Maybe from Mum."

"Children often adopt parents' beliefs," Lee explained. "Often superficially."

"I think old Bible movies shaped my religious views more than the actual stories in the Bible," I admitted.

Lee chuckled. "TV often does that."

Her openness encouraged me. "Lee, I'd decided to quit drinking before the course."

"I sensed that," she nodded.

"The course confirmed it. But AA meetings after my accident...they really hit home." I paused. "I realised alcohol had me chained. I needed something greater than myself in order to break free."

"You're doing well, Quinn," Lee said warmly. "Sounds like the twelve steps resonated with you."

"The 'higher power' concept really clicked for me," I said. "Gave me purpose. Ties in with your book too." I hesitated. "Feels odd talking about religion. But God...he filled this hole in me. Like he was waiting. I've handed him the wheel."

Lee smiled warmly. "Having a superpower directing you can't hurt."

I chuckled, feeling lighter.

"How did you feel about the cabbage patch story? Or about being called an afterthought?" Lee asked.

"It's been on my mind lately. This feeling I wasn't wanted, just an accident." A heavy ache settled in my chest.

"I'm sure that wasn't the intention, but those comments can form a pattern. Losing your dad probably complicated things."

My chest tightened. "I want to share the truth about my dad."

Lee leaned forward. "Go ahead, I'm listening."

"Dad served in World War Two. Mum said it changed him." I paused. "I used to believe he was a star in the night sky, that he died of a heart attack." I took a deep breath. "But when I was around fifteen, I found out through a mate that my dad took his own life. At first, I thought it was just some cruel joke. Mates could be mean. But Mum confirmed it."

Lee's eyes dipped.

I closed my eyes, reliving the moment. "His mum had told him. I didn't even know she knew my mum." I shook my head. "It felt like everyone knew but me. What kind of secret is that?"

"Must have been quite a shock," Lee said softly. "Another layer added to the pattern."

"Yes, I've started to see that." My throat tightened. "Hearing from a third party hurt me but the sad thing is...I made it all about me, not how it impacted Mum."

"That shows progress for you to see that."

Tears welled up. Lee offered water and tissues.

"Sorry," I mumbled, embarrassed. "It's the first time I've brought this up with a stranger. Such strong emotions attached to…I'm not even sure why."

"Don't be sorry," Lee said. "Suicide was taboo in those days and still is for some families. Your family likely tried to protect you. Probably embarrassed by what happened."

Anger flared. "How did my friend even know and me not know?"

"It doesn't matter now. Remember, it's attitude, not hardship, that counts."

I exhaled slowly. "You're right."

"Thank you for sharing, Quinn," Lee said. "Understanding these things will bring peace."

Edithburra floated into my mind. "I've met other men affected by war. And the private wars they wage with themselves after."

"Trauma is widespread," Lee said. "War, accidents, assault, abuse. Many turn to substances to escape."

"Not a nice world," I sighed, feeling weary. "Even on the course. What was his name? Vince? He was war-torn."

"Yes, it was Vince. I've heard he's doing well."

We shifted to lighter topics before scheduling next week's session.

Leaving, I felt that familiar lightness, but unease lurked beneath. Patterns from my past were emerging. The root of my struggles? Or chances to heal?

The answer eluded me, but I knew I had to keep going. No turning back now.

39 A Searching Chat

Things happened quickly with the relocation of the organisation. I confirmed that I was happy to accept a redundancy, which amounted up to quite a few weeks' pay—plenty of time to find another job or take an extended holiday. My work had involved computers, and I sensed that this background would offer opportunities elsewhere as more and more companies were starting to invest in technology. I was eager to move on and the process unfolded rapidly.

Murmurs of resignations and uneasy glances swept the workplace as we took turns entering the manager's office. The expressions of those exiting were mixed: Heather, one of our team, but a temporary officer, was particularly distraught, while other team members consoled her.

Despite the situation, a sense of calm settled over me. Change often brings personal growth, or so I've come to learn. It was lunchtime, and we gathered outside in the autumn sun, our conversations subdued and quiet. I noticed Heather sitting in a patch of sunlight, surrounded by fallen gold and red leaves, so I walked over to her. She seemed calmer. "Hi, Heather, you okay?"

Heather looked up at me. "A bit better, thank you, Quinn. It's all a bit of a shock but in some ways I'm glad it's happened. Although I've only been here a short time, I've been getting far too stressed with the work, and the family will see this as good news."

I nodded. "Yes, things have moved quickly. In some ways it's good to get it over and done with, less stress."

She gave me a smile. "Might even take the kids for a drive up to that place you keep telling us about although your story about the leeches is a bit off-putting."

"Nah, just made it up."

She laughed. "I know you didn't. I've encountered those bloodsuckers before." Her eyebrows lifted. "You got any plans?"

"Now that you mention it, I might make a trip to Edithburra myself. Be nice to have a break. No mad rush for another job at the moment. I only have me to look after."

"Not for long. I'm sure there's a lady waiting for you in the wings."

"You never know."

Heather stood and we hugged. "Take care, Quinn. I've enjoyed working with you."

"You also, Heather." I felt for her; her entitlements wouldn't be so great due to her short time here, but it sounded like it would turn out to be a good thing family wise. It sort of emphasised the importance of finding the right job.

***

I rushed to Lee's office for our last session before her overseas trip. Boxes filled the room—she was relocating to another area when she returned.

"Looks like I'm not the only one packing," I joked.

Lee's face turned serious. "Are you moving?"

"No, accepted a redundancy today."

"How do you feel about that?"

"Strangely at peace." I smiled. "It's pushing me to find what I really want. My search for meaning. I keep thinking about Edithburra, being in nature away from the big smoke."

Lee looked intrigued and gestured toward the seats. "Edithburra? We haven't really discussed that. Is it something you want to talk about?" she asked as she sat down.

I joined her. "Edithburra occupies a large space in my mind, even though I was only there for a few months when I was ten."

Lee nodded. "They say time stretches for young minds."

"Mum says it speeds up as you age."

"Younger brains process more, have more storage," Lee suggested.

I nodded seriously.

She laughed. "Life feels more routine later. Now, tell me about Edithburra."

"Mum worked as a housekeeper there, assisting a man with his household while his family travelled overseas."

"Where is it?"

"A small town in south-eastern Victoria. Fewer than 100 people. I went to school there—just seven of us. It catered for all primary school grades; I think we had from grade three to grade six."

"That's small," Lee remarked.

"The teacher was rough. Slaps, threw me around, kicked me." I paused. "And the girls...I hate to think."

Lee's face darkened. "Many things from 60s schools are coming to light. Do you think you have scars from then?"

"Possibly. Let me tell you more," I said. "The home-owner—I refer to him as the Old Man—was obsessed with a gold nugget. Later, I learned Mum had one too, from Dad's funeral."

"A tangible connection to her husband," Lee suggested. "It's interesting that both had a gold nugget. I'm sure you'll bring it together for me."

"I will. But that's not all." I tensed. "The Old Man hurt Mum."

Lee's eyes widened. "Did you know at the time?"

"I must have, but I buried it. Pretended it was normal."

"That's not uncommon," Lee assured me. "Those memories are likely still there. Returning to process them might help you heal."

"I agree. Now, about the gold. After Edithburra, we moved to a bigger town. One day, I came home from school to find a police car parked outside."

Lee listened intently.

"Inside, Mum was on the couch, distraught. A neighbour was comforting her while the police talked to her."

"That must've been confronting," Lee said.

I gave a brief nod. "Mum was angry. 'He was a pig,' she said. Then, 'We didn't steal anything.'"

Lee focused on my face.

"Mum demanded, 'Has his family come back?' She was ignored. A cop searched her bedroom. He tried to send me out to play, but Mum kept me close."

Lee shook her head.

"The officers told Mum that Mr Warhurst—the Old Man—accused her of stealing a gold nugget from his rock collection. It was of considerable value and sentimental importance."

"She reluctantly handed over her handbag and made a comment that it wasn't the same one. The officer searched and pulled out a gold nugget that was in the shape of a heart. Mum collapsed into the neighbour's arms. They bagged the nugget and left."

"Oh dear," Lee said softly. "Was it your Mum's?"

"Yes. Hers was heart-shaped, the Old Man's like a blob of gum. They took it. The Old Man dropped the charges after that."

"But he kept your mum's nugget?"

"Yes."

"And his?"

"Not sure."

"He must have known it wasn't his."

"You'd think so."

"That must've been shocking for you, and painful for your mum," Lee said.

"Yeah. We left Edithburra like runaways, but they found us." I paused. "Those memories got buried."

"I don't think you just want the bush," Lee suggested. "You're searching for a gold nugget. Healing awaits in Edithburra."

Maybe she was right.

"You could also find those girls you mentioned before," she added.

"Yeah, Katrina and Rosemary." I smiled. "It'd be interesting to see where life took them."

Finishing up, we spoke about holidays and travel. I'd miss Lee during her holiday while I went digging for gold. But perhaps Edithburra held the key to unlocking buried truths and healing old wounds.

Still, thoughts lingered. What else might I unearth in Edithburra?

Winter 1981
Melbourne

My dearest Martha,

It has been some time since I put pen to paper. There's been no shortage of days since I last wrote. But I am a bringer of good news. My family have me settled in a comfortable unit. They call it a retirement village, although I'm not retired and walk down to a local guest house where I help out in the kitchen daily. The kitchen staff are a mad bunch, so I fit in nicely.

And there's more good news, another glimmer of sunshine through the clouds. My youngest, wee Quinn, seems to have found his way. He went off the rails for a good while, the wounds of the past holding him tight. I could only watch with a heavy heart as he struggled.

Maybe I didn't give him the best start to life, and his father's death did not help. And I made it worse by not telling him how his dad died—a secret that weighed heavy on my heart. Him finding out the truth just sent him further off the rails.

But he seems to have finally righted himself. It's almost a miracle, like something out of a storybook. He says there's a higher power looking after him now—something they teach at these AA meetings, I believe. Whatever it is, it seems to be working. He's much warmer towards me now, more concerned about others than himself. A world of difference from the young man he once was. But I understand he needed to sort himself out first. He is driven to find the meaning of it all.

He sees me regularly and gives me updates on his discoveries. I wouldn't be surprised if he ends up in a monastery, although I'd prefer that he find a nice lassie to settle down with.

A lot of the time, what he talks about goes over my head.

My heart does feel heavy. And in some ways, I know that my passing will bring peace. I've carried many burdens through life. I look at Quinn and see that he's unloading his burdens. I wish that I could do that, but I do not know how.

He's told me he is going to go back and visit Edithburra. I felt sick in the stomach at the mention of that place. But it's his way of dealing with his issues. I don't know what he'll find there. It's been many years; it may even be a ghost town now. Maybe he'll encounter those ghosts that remain. I shudder at the thought.

He talks about getting my gold nugget back. It was given to me at Harold's funeral by a caring man. But the nugget was taken from me in unpleasant circumstances. Quinn, my knight in shining armour, might well recover his mother's gold.

I'm being a wee bit silly here.

But I know the old man's gold will never be recovered. It was taken from him and is now hidden from him. I know the pain that would've caused him. I also know who has it.

I miss you terribly, Martha. It would be a comfort to see your face again. Maybe when the Lord shows His face, we can be together again. Until then, take care of yourself, my dear.

All my love,
Elizabeth

Part 3 – The Healed Man

Victoria, Australia
1981
Early Spring

40 The Hitch-hiker

An hour and a half had ticked by since I merged onto the freeway. It felt good to be driving again—to feel the simple freedom of getting in the car and just driving. I'd sold my old Holden, along with the memories it carried, and switched camps, buying a sporty Ford Cortina. It felt like an olive branch to myself—a way to start fresh. Its affordability and practicality suited me, and I hoped it might bring back the simple joy of being behind the wheel. This was its first long trip.

The grey bitumen road stretched out before me, unwinding through a landscape of rolling green hills. Wildflowers dotted the side of the road. The steady hum of passing engines filled the car, punctuated by the occasional rumble of a passing truck.

The initial rush of escaping the city had faded early on, replaced by a dull ache in my chest and a whirlwind of thoughts. Why was I chasing these ghosts of the past, as Mum had so aptly put it? What was I hoping to find at Edithburra? Was it a person, a place, or something more? I knew it was more than the gold nugget.

Up ahead, a person walking on the side of the road paused and turned towards traffic. It was a man around my age with a shock of curly black hair. He thrust out his arm and extended his thumb in a back-and-forth motion. As he looked at my car, a smile crossed his face.

I still had forty or so minutes left before I would turn off the freeway, so some company could be good. I pulled over and leaned across to open the door.

His footsteps crunched against the gravel as he ran to the car. He leaned in, puffing. "Thanks for stopping."

"No problem. Where you heading?"

"As far as you'll take me." He smiled. "The next town will be fine."

I ushered him inside with my hand. "Jump in."

Once he settled in, I checked the traffic flow behind me and merged back on to the freeway.

"Thanks for doing this." He put out his hand. "My name's Rod."

I gave him a quick shake. "My pleasure, Rod. I was getting sick of my own company. I'm Quinn."

He chuckled. "Me too. Not many cars stop these days."

I recalled the seventies. "I think the world's changing. It's not as safe as it used to be. I used to hitch-hike everywhere in my youth."

"Well, you're safe with me," Rod said.

Despite Rod's kind demeanour, unease crept into my thoughts. Plenty of untrustworthy people said, "You can trust me." If someone meant no harm, why would they emphasise their trustworthiness?

Rod continued, "But I think a lot more people have cars nowadays, so hitch-hiking isn't as common."

I was probably overthinking things. My mind was all over the place. I settled into the traffic flow again, telling myself to relax.

"Why hitch-hike?" I asked.

Rod pondered my question. "I suppose the main reason is that I don't own a car, but I also see it as an adventurous form of travel. You just never know who's going to pick you up."

The unease remained.

"Why did you pick me up?" he asked.

"Thought it would help you out a bit," I replied. "Help you with your journey."

"So, you took pity on me." He laughed. It was a genuine laugh, and I relaxed. "Where are you heading?" he asked.

"Edithburra."

"Edithburra…know it well." He coughed. "Nothing there, though. You got relatives there or something?"

"Nah, just taking a trip down memory lane."

Rod turned serious. "I've heard it said that the good old days aren't as good as we remember. I think we relive the positive moments more than the darker ones."

"That's a bit deep."

He laughed. "Sorry. I've been studying psychology and I'm starting to think that may not be a good thing."

I chuckled. "I agree, it can make life more confusing."

"It's simple, though, when you think about it. Recalling positive memories feels good, triggering happy chemicals in the brain. Those darker memories, on the other hand, are a whole different story."

This man goes rather deep. The uneasy feeling returned.

Rod went on, "Something must be drawing you back to the little town. Hopefully, good memories."

It was my turn to get serious. "Someone suggested to me that a trip down memory lane can sometimes help navigate a time of transition, self-exploration."

"That may well be the case."

I tried to alter the course of conversation. "Can I ask where you're heading after I drop you off?"

"I suppose it's a bit opposite to you. To be honest, I think I'm just running away." He turned to look out the window. "My life is a mess. Just got divorced. Nothing to tie me down. Decided to leave Melbourne. I'm just going to wander until I'm sick of wandering." He returned his gaze to the road ahead. "I grew up around this area, so I may spend some time here. I have sufficient funds to keep me going for a while."

"You a drinker?" I asked.

His forehead creased. "Nope. Why do you ask?"

"Just found the drink screwed me up badly."

"It does. Drink is evil."

There was something behind those words, but I didn't pursue it.

"You off the grog, now?" he asked.

"Yep, close to nine months sober."

"Well done. Not an easy thing to do. Cold turkey?"

"Yes, but AA helped."

"It's good that you're open about such things. Normally, people like to keep these things to themselves."

We passed a large billboard advertising a local church. "That helped." I pointed towards the sign.

He followed my finger, then glanced over at me, his brow furrowed in thought. "Church helped you, you say? In what way?"

"Sort of. I found that digging into the spiritual side helped."

"What ya mean by digging?"

I gave him a quick glance and a smile. "Lots of reading—Bible and other self-help type books. Talking to people that had found their way home, as they put it."

"Home?" His eyes fixed on the road. "Interesting way of putting it. Anyway, good on ya. Keep at it."

I sensed that the conversation was drifting away from the topic and detected a hint of guardedness, a slight detachment in his tone. He turned to take in the passing scenery.

Had I said something wrong? We drove on in silence for a while, the low volume of the radio filling the space between us. Eventually, it became too much for me.

"Have I said something to offend you? You seem to have gone quiet."

He turned and gave me a small smile. "Not really. I've just got some dark memories from school that involve religion. I'm just waiting for them to drop out of my head."

I nodded, understanding dawning. "Sorry to hear that." I didn't press; it felt like fragile ground—for him, and for me.

"It's alright," he said, his eyes focused back on the road. "Just one of those things, you know? Ain't like it defines me or nothin, but it's stuck with me over the years. Just a single experience in a messy, complicated life."

I offered a reassuring nod, impressed by his perspective and how he carried it.

The radio played softly, filling the car with a melody I liked. "You okay if I turn that up a bit?" I reached for the volume dial, glancing at Rod.

"Sure," he said with a smile. "I like the Beatles."

I turned the volume up.

The *na-na-na-na-na, na-na-na-na* melody filled the car.

"I suppose 'Hey Jude' is an optimistic song," I said. "You know? Make things better."

"Maybe it is. Goes on a bit though, doesn't it? Repetitive."

"Seven minutes, I think."

Rod nodded.

A comfortable silence settled in as the music played. The long melody seemed to stretch on, mirroring the quiet road ahead. Maybe it was just the music, but I couldn't help but feel a strange sense of connection to the man beside me. We were both on journeys, each with our own burdens, but for a moment, we were sharing the ride.

Up ahead, a police car was parked on the side of the road. Rod suddenly lurched forward in his seat, clutching his stomach. "I'm going to be sick." He took a deep swallow. "Could you pull over?"

As soon as I stopped the vehicle, Rod flung the door open, jumped out, and started puking on the side of the road. I glanced towards the police car, wondering if there was a connection to the sudden bout of sickness.

Rod had knelt on the side of the road and was clutching a clump of damp grass. He wiped his face with it, giving. me an 'oh well' look, before pulling a handkerchief from his pocket for another wipe.

I wasn't sure what to do.

"Ugh, I'm going to stink. You drive on; I'll walk until I find a place to, uh, freshen up." He rubbed his tummy. "Stupid servo hot dog. Knew it tasted a little sus when I first bit into it. Should've stopped eating it then."

I felt queasy myself.

"I'm happy to drive you to the next service station to freshen up." Why had I said service station instead of servo? Country folk liked to shorten their words. I used to too. Maybe I'd turned into a city person, trying too hard to sound proper. I was overthinking again.

He seemed to consider my offer, scanning the road ahead. "I might take you up on that. Not sure how far I'd need to walk, and I doubt I'd be welcomed into another car smelling like this."

A valid point. He climbed back into the car and wound down his window. I did the same. The breeze would have to be our air freshener. I drove on, hoping the air flowing into the car would deal with the pungent odour attacking my nostrils.

"I think the fresh air is helping," Rod said with a pleading look.

As we drove past the police car, Rod looked back. "That was Fitzy."

"You know him?" I asked.

"Yep, old school mate."

"Big school, hey? Bet you it was nothing like the school at Edithburra that I went to."

He laughed. "I know what you're getting at. We had a few students at our school from Edithburra. They used to bus in."

My heart skipped a beat.

We pulled into a servo up ahead so Rod could freshen up. He dashed to a restroom, then emerged and went into the servo. I went in to pay for fuel and saw him hovering by the sweets aisle. He reached out and grabbed a bag of what looked like mints. A good idea.

We strolled out to the car and were soon back on the freeway.

"Did you know many people there?" Rod asked.

"Huh?"

"Edithburra, did you know many there?"

"I was only there a short time." I reflected for a moment. "Funny, when I think about it, I can only remember one family surname. And, of course, the teacher. His name was Mr Hecat."

"Hecat." Rod wore a thoughtful look. "Funny name. Never heard it before."

"It was a weird name," I agreed. "The family name I remember is Warhurst."

"Ah yeah, the Warhursts."

There was something different in his voice.

Rod continued, "I played footy with Jamie Warhurst." A smile flitted across his face. "I had a bit of a crush on his sister, but then, a lot of us footy boys did. We were all young then, under 12s, I think, with hormones just kicking in. She'd come and watch the games, pretty as a picture. But then the whole family just seemed to vanish off the face of the earth. At least, that's what we thought."

"A yowie most probably got them," I blurted out, my thoughts confused.

Rod laughed. "That could be true, but you know there's no such thing as a yowie." He winked. "There were rumours at the time that their old man did away with them." He let out a small chuckle. "He was a creepy guy."

My stomach churned. "Yeah, I know. I lived with him for a while."

I glanced at Rod. His eyes had widened. "What! Really?" He turned to face me; excitement flickered in his gaze. "Did you fall in love with Katrina?"

"I did." Bittersweet memories resurfaced. "But she left on an overseas trip, and I never got to see her again."

Rod's demeanour shifted, a glimmer of empathy shining through. "That's sad." He leaned in as if imparting a secret. "But listen up, I'm a bringer of good news," he confided, his tone hushed. "She's alive and well."

41 Old School Friend

The strong scent of mint had replaced the unpleasant odour from Rod's bout of sickness. Willward soon came into view as the speed limit dropped. We passed the faded 'Welcome to' sign, and houses with lawns replaced the paddocks. I pulled up on the main street and parked the car, the revelation about Katrina still swirling in my head.

I turned off the ignition. "Well, here we are—time for a stretch." We climbed out of the vehicle and stood on the footpath.

Rod put out his hand to shake mine. "Quinn, thanks for the lift." He sighed. "Sorry about getting sick."

I shook his hand. "No problem. Added another dimension to the trip."

Rod chuckled. "It did." He gave me a serious look. "Maybe we were meant to connect."

"Could be. As my mum would say, 'The Lord moves in mysterious ways.'"

"He does." Rod looked around the street. He turned to me, a hopeful glint in his eyes. "Think I might stay put for the time being. Our chat rekindled feelings about this place.

Maybe I'm being called back." We stood there for a moment and then he nodded. "Well, I'll be off now. You take care." A smile passed over his face. "And good luck with Katrina."

He began to walk away, then glanced back. "My full name's Rodney Green. If you ever settle down around here, which I might just do, you'll find me listed in a local phone book at some point." He nodded. "And your full name?"

"Quinn Davies. I'm in the Metro phone book. Not too many 'Q. Davies', I'm sure."

"Well, who knows? We may speak again. I'll see ya later, Quinn Davies."

Off he strolled, disappearing into the heart of Willward, leaving me with a tangled mess of emotions and a head full of questions about Katrina. Rod walked past a hotel which triggered a memory. It was the hotel that Mum and I had stayed at after our escape from Edithburra.

My mind tracked back to that night. What had once seemed like an adventure then, now revealed itself through mature eyes, as a frightening time for my mother.

I snapped back to the present, faced with a dilemma. Rod had mentioned Jamie's recent visit to Melbourne. He'd seen Katrina there, living with some bloke in Hawthorn, not far from me. Finding a Warhurst in the phone book would be easy, assuming the listing was in her name.

I felt the urge to do a U-turn and head back to Melbourne. But was Katrina the reason I was chasing ghosts in Edithburra? No, something else was drawing me.

I ate lunch at the hotel, occupying a table with a view of the staircase leading up to the accommodation. I had once walked those stairs, the memory stirring a pang of nostalgia within me.

A prickling sensation at my nape made me glance around, and my gaze landed on the bar. The barmaid flashed me a smile as she softly sang along to a song on the radio. There was something oddly familiar about her, but I couldn't quite place it. Perhaps when you delved into the realm of ghosts, familiarity became a recurring theme—the past constantly seeping into the present.

I couldn't shake the feeling that the ghosts were playing tricks, sending out familiar faces as decoys to distract and confuse, to disrupt my journey of exploring.

My plate sat empty, a half-full glass of Coke beside it. The barmaid emerged from behind the bar, a cloth in her hand and a radiant smile on her lips.

"Can I grab your plate?" she asked.

"Certainly." I shifted my arms out of her way. "It was a nice meal."

"I'll tell the chef." She smiled as she picked up the plate and glanced into my face. Her gaze lingered for a moment. "Is your name Quinn, by any chance?"

The realisation struck: *The decoy knows me.*

I coughed. "It is." I scrutinised her face, and then it dawned on me. "Jill?" Rosemary's sister?

She smiled. "You remember?"

"I do, but it's been sixteen, seventeen years since I last saw you. I think it's your eyes. You and your sister both had the bluest eyes."

"And it was your eyes also that gave you away." She tapped her chin. "And that cute dimple."

I felt my neck warm.

She glanced around the bar, but nothing seemed to require her immediate attention. "Where did you go?"

"What do you mean?"

"You just vanished. We were all so upset thinking that something had happened to you."

My mind raced. "Mum and I needed to escape."

Jill wore a knowing expression. A second time, she glanced around the bar area and then up at the large clock on the wall. "Are you going to hang around for a little while?"

"I am."

"I'll be finished work in an hour." She looked down at my Coke. "I'm sure you don't want to stay and consume too much of that stuff. Maybe go for a stroll and meet me at the front entrance in about an hour, say two-thirty?"

I stood. She was tiny. "I'd like that. How's Rosemary?"

Her mouth turned down. "Go for a stroll. We can talk about the past when we catch up."

I watched her head back to the bar to serve a customer. Her strides seemed to have lost their earlier vitality.

I paused by a large painting on my way out. Rolling hills, trees, and towering tree-ferns filled the canvas. The painting resonated with me, though I wasn't sure why. In the bottom right-hand corner, I noticed a signature. Leaning in for a closer look, I made out the name: Susan Molloy.

Hey, Rod, I just remembered another surname.

Mr Molloy had helped with our getaway, using his connections at this hotel to provide accommodation for the night. Maybe his connections were how the hotel had acquired this painting.

Footsteps descended the stairs. An older man paused next to me, his gaze also drawn to the painting.

"She's doing well," he remarked.

"Huh?" He'd caught me off guard.

"The artist. Susan Molloy. She's based in London. I think she still uses her maiden name. Got the talent from her mum, who did similar paintings." He turned his attention to me. "You local?"

I shook my head.

"Thought not," he mused, scrutinizing me further. "You look familiar, though." He chuckled and tapped his temple. "I've got so many faces stored up here, everyone starts to look familiar."

He returned his gaze to the canvas. "Do you know the Molloys?" he asked.

"They lived in Edithburra in the sixties, right?" I queried.

"Sure did, and still do. Just Tom, though. He never remarried after losing his wife. Over the years, his daughter has come and stayed when she wants to get away from the rat race."

I remembered Tom. "Does he still live in the same house?"

The man paused. "Yep, still there." He scratched his head. "Although the last time we chatted…he spoke about getting a smaller property. Too much grass to mow." He smiled. "Then again, I don't think he'd ever leave his roses. He's probably bought some sheep to eat up the grass."

An image of Tom pruning a rose bush dropped into my head. "So, you've been there?" I asked.

"Oh, yes. Many times. I'm his brother."

I sensed a faint resemblance. My gaze drifted to the stairs. "I stayed here once. Way back in the sixties."

"So, you're the boy, then?"

"Sorry?"

"I used to be the owner back then. Now I have a permanent room upstairs. Part of the agreement with the new owners."

I was puzzled. "You remember me?"

"The police came looking for you and your mum. I think my brother's neighbour made some accusations, so they paid Tom a visit. He told them you had stayed here the night." His mind seemed to wander. "People were spreading rumours you'd been murdered. But we quickly put that story to bed. Told the coppers you jumped on a train and that was the last we saw of you."

I estimated this man to be in his late sixties. His face was etched with laughter lines that mingled with life's challenges. He had a well-rounded tummy and his cheeks had reddish-blue, purple lines. I suspected a fondness for drink.

He gestured to the bar and asked, "You want to join me for a drink and a chat?"

Uncertain what steps to follow in my journey into the past, I decided to just go with the flow. "Sure, but I'm a teetotaller. Gave up drinking; caused too much trouble."

I detected something akin to respect in his eyes. "Well, you're more of a man than I'll ever be. The drink's got me in a vice-like grip, and trouble sometimes follows." He gave a guilty smirk.

His comment lifted my mood. Praise for not drinking was rare; most people found abstinence strange.

"My dear brother Tom also gave up the bottle. A long time ago. He's also more of a man than I."

Jill smiled as we made our way to the bar. "So, you couldn't escape the clutches of our dear Fred?"

"What? You know the lad?" Fred asked.

"I do. An old school friend." Jill winked at me as she grabbed a glass and started pouring a beer. "You want another Coke, Quinn?"

"Might go for orange juice this time."

My new friend Fred seemed lost in thought. "It must have been at that small rural school, then."

"It was," Jill confirmed as she placed the beer in front of Fred. "It closed the year after you left, Quinn."

"Really? Why, what happened?"

"They couldn't recruit another teacher."

"What happened to Hecat?"

"Car accident." A long sigh escaped Jill. "It's a long story, but in short, the school never recovered after Hecat's accident." Sadness flickered across her face. "Let's save the details for our chat over coffee."

"Good idea," Fred agreed. "Not good to dig up things from the past. Slows you down." He tapped his temple. "Years of wisdom up here tell me that."

He seemed to enjoy tapping his head.

He glanced at the glass of beer in front of him. "Hmm, maybe there are still things for me to learn yet."

I understood reflective Fred. I was curious about the past but had no plans of getting stuck there. That was the plan, anyway. I had no idea what lay before me, but I wasn't afraid to delve deeper.

42 Chasing Ghosts

The café was just a short stroll from the hotel. Jill was still dressed in her casual bar uniform—jeans and a long-sleeved white T-shirt embroidered with the hotel logo. She had a denim jacket draped over her arm. The weather was cooling down, though the sky remained clear and blue. We opted to sit outside and soak up the sunshine.

Jill rolled up her sleeves as she grabbed a menu, motioning for me to do the same. "Best burgers in the world. Pity you've had lunch." She smiled. "Maybe next date."

She was cute, just as I remembered her. I'd once had a crush on her sister. Funny, how age seemed like such a big deal when you were young—two years' difference felt monumental. Now, it was nothing. Then again, Rosemary was older than me. That was a definite no-no back in those days.

"Hi, Jill." A young lady stood next to us, pad in hand, neon bracelets on her wrist. She gave me a cursory glance before returning her attention to Jill. "You want your favourite cake and coffee?"

"Thanks, Donna. That'd be nice." Jill pointed to me. "Maybe we should test the cake out on this stranger, too."

Donna looked at me, raising her eyebrows as if for confirmation.

I nodded. "I think I can trust you two ladies."

Donna chuckled. "He's a brave man, Jill."

"He is."

"Coffee also?" Donna asked. "Jill has cappuccino. That good for you?"

I nodded. The only coffee I usually drank was instant and black, a habit from those dark hangover days to help sober up.

Donna smiled warmly and wandered off to look after the orders.

Jill smiled at me. "You've aged a little."

I rubbed my face. "Nicely, I hope."

She moved her head from side to side, studying me. "Not too bad."

I detected a toughness in her. From working behind a bar? "Well, it's been a long time, maybe seventeen years, I think."

"It has, and I'm wondering what's brought you back."

Some sparrows rummaging under a nearby table caught my attention. "That's a good question." How much should one disclose? The sparrows flew off at the sound of approaching footsteps.

Donna placed the cakes in front of us. "Coffee coming."

When she left, I continued, "My mum says I'm chasing ghosts of the past. She may be right. Edithburra had a big impact on my life and I'm not quite sure why."

"You weren't there for long." Jill picked up a fork and dug into her cake.

"Funny that. Yes, not long at all. But I think I was at an impressionable age."

"So, we left a good impression?" She smiled around her mouthful of cake. "Hmm, nice." She pointed to the plate in front of me. "Have some."

I complied. It was indeed nice. Donna returned with coffees. She placed them in front of us, along with the bill. I gestured to it. "I'll look after that."

"Thanks." Jill smiled. "What ghosts were you hoping to encounter? Edithburra's not quite a ghost town yet."

"You still live there, then?"

"Nope, sharing a house with a friend here in Willward. Mum still runs the store. Bit different now, but still the best lollies in the world. More customers now, mainly tourists. The town is well-known for its beauty."

"Maybe that's what's drawing me back. The simplicity of that time."

"But it was mixed with dark stuff."

I didn't know how to respond to that. She could only be referring to dark times *she* had experienced.

"I picked up a hitch-hiker driving here, and we had a good chat. You may well know him—Rodney Green."

She laughed. "Yep, Rodney. Always the charmer, chased after everything with a skirt. He was a good mate of Katrina's brother Jamie and my brother Gavin. You remember them?"

I nodded, though I had only vague recollections of them both. Gavin more so, as a pretend yowie.

"Apparently, he got married and moved to Melbourne. He's back, then?" Jill asked.

"Said he's divorced now and trying to sort out his life. Thinking about settling back down here."

Jill sighed. "Life," she muttered, "throws so many curveballs."

"American saying, creeping into our culture," I suggested.

"It's the movies," Jill conceded with a smile.

I nodded. "Anyway, Rod was being philosophical about life and suggested that recalling positive memories feels good, triggering happy chemicals in the brain, whereas the darker memories are a whole different story."

"Didn't realise Rod had such wisdom in him," Jill said.

It was time to be honest. "I think I'm here for the darker memories," I said, bracing myself for the heaviness that would inevitably follow the admission.

"I would say you are," Jill replied, her gaze dropping to her hands, "because there were a few of them."

Jill's eyes connected with mine, and I felt a tug of connection.

"About the school?" I asked.

"Some really dark memories there. Did a lot of damage to Rosemary. She's still struggling."

Sadness filled my heart.

"Hecat," Jill continued, "was a monster. He did horrible things to Rosemary." Jill's eyes watered. "And to a lesser extent to me. He would put me in the wardrobe in the radio room as punishment and then he would do things to her. I could only hear…" Jill scrunched her lips together and took a deep breath. "No need to say any more. Too painful. You can work it out."

To alleviate some of Jill's burden, I shared my experience. "He used to throw me around like a rag doll."

"We knew, Quinn. There was nothing any of us could do." A razor-thin smile crossed her face. "But fate catches up to you."

"What do you mean?"

"Oh, of course you wouldn't know. You vanished off the face of the earth."

I detected a hint of resentment.

"The very same night you vanished, Hecat was involved in a car accident."

I wasn't sure how to react to that.

"Is he still alive?"

"Wheelchair-bound. Spent many months in hospital. We had relief teachers who were just as bad as Hecat. It seemed lots of problem teachers in the schooling system were just passed on to other schools. Rural schools were perfect for those sorts of people."

Hecat had affected me but not to the extent of the damage he had inflicted on these girls. He was a monster. A perverted creature.

Regret crept in. The thought of what school would've been like the day after we escaped intrigued me. "I had no chance to say goodbye to any of you." Now I was tearing up. "I treasured the friendships I had developed in that short time."

"Then why did you go?" Jill said, then corrected herself. "Sorry, Quinn, that's not a fair question. At that age, you had no say in such decisions."

"You're right, Jill. It was all just an adventure for a ten-year-old. Mum needed to escape from that man we lived with. He did some nasty things to Mum. His family had deserted him, and when he found that out, it sent him into a fit of rage. We bore the brunt of his anger; we needed to escape."

"You're talking about the Warhursts, aren't you?"

I took a deep breath. "Yes. We ended up in a much larger country town, with hundreds and hundreds of students at school, not like at Edithburra"—I raised my eyebrows—"and

I just went through the process of building my next new life. You see, I'd done that many times before. Even before Edithburra. From memory, I was in grade four at Edithburra, and I had already been to five different schools."

"That would've been hard."

"It was, but I didn't know that at the time. Each new school, I'd go through a process of starting over again. You know, making friends for a short time and then moving on. I got good at it. Never really stayed in contact with any of my school friends. Can't explain why."

Jill hugged her coffee cup, seeming lost in contemplation. "So, there ya go. We've addressed the past. Do you feel any better?"

She could be abrupt at times. A skill set likely honed by bar work.

"I think Edithburra just…I don't know, pulled all my emotional baggage into one place. I lost my dad at an early age. Mum was too tied up in grieving to show much love and affection. Except for ripe raspberry lollies and Phantom comics." I chuckled. "In my teenage years, I fell into the trap of drinking; the past fueling the rage and confusion inside."

I took a deep breath and debated whether or not to say more. "I tried to kill myself not too long ago."

Jill just shrugged.

I was surprised by her response.

She let out a sigh. "I think a few of us have considered that. I saved Rosemary once when she took an overdose. The twins…you remember them? They've also had issues. Their dad was never there for them. They got into alcohol and dope in a big way."

All so sad.

Jill continued, "It wasn't that Edithburra had a dark cloud hovering over it; it was just the way society was. Lost its way, for whatever reason. Not much love anymore; too much focus on self."

She took a sip of her coffee. Her cake was long gone, and she had her eyes on mine. "Better eat up or I'll grab it."

I looked down at the cake. My appetite had vanished. I pushed the plate towards her. "Eat. Your hotel lunch filled me up, and this topic of conversation has taken my appetite away."

"Oh, I'm sorry, didn't mean for that to happen." She gave me a genuine smile. "What are your plans? I might be able to fit in with them depending on my roster. You know, be your Edithburra Ghost Guide."

Maybe I'd let her. Jill had turned out to be an interesting young woman.

"You know, there's two things we haven't covered," I said.

She gave me a puzzled look.

"Yowies and gold."

Her expression didn't change.

I shrugged. "Maybe it's the gold I'm pursuing, because yowies aren't real."

"Aren't they?"

Did she know something that I didn't?

43 The Yowie Question

Jill and I planned to catch up again later. She had been a pleasant surprise. By coincidence, she had a few days off and wanted to experience my journey back to Edithburra. I resolved to go with the flow.

Overcome by nostalgia, I booked a room for a night at the hotel before driving on to Edithburra in the morning. The grand old building, with its peeling paint and aged façade, felt the perfect backdrop for my ghost-themed search for meaning. Haunted stories always seemed to cling to places like this, and this establishment was no exception. A framed news clipping near the stairwell caught my attention, the headline boasting the words "haunted" and "ghost".

I read no further. I didn't want such things cluttering my mind when bedtime came—I valued my sleep.

My hotel room was cozy and, as far as I could tell, ghost-free. I placed my bag on the neatly made bed, grabbed a folded towel and my toiletries bag, and headed off to the shared bathroom for a quick shower. I needed to refresh before catching up with Jill and wash away any lingering reminders of Rod's sick episode in the car.

The country air had a bit of a bite, so I pulled on a worn, navy-blue jumper over my black T-shirt and jeans and headed out to meet Jill. We strolled for a while, grabbed some takeaway—hot chips and dim sims—and settled on a park bench. The night air was crisp, and a stunning sunset painted the sky above the distant hills.

"You know," Jill said, juggling a hot chip in her hand. "I had a crush on you once. But you seemed more interested in Rose and Katrina."

Her forwardness took a bit of getting used to, but it was nice, in a funny sort of way. Now, how did one respond to a statement like that?

"I thought you were pretty." I paused, looking at her as the sunset bathed her face in a warm glow. "Still are." It was a genuine admission, and I felt a stir in my heart.

"Ah, shucks." She laughed, a little embarrassed.

I smiled with her. "I have fond memories of you singing and dancing to the radio at school. So free and relaxed."

"Escapism, I think," she said with a soft chuckle.

"What did you do after the school closed?" I popped a dim sim into my mouth. It was just the right temperature and tasty.

Her eyes were alert and clear. "Mum had been a Christian for some years and really grown in her faith. She chose to homeschool us, hoping to protect us from the growing secularism of the outside world. It felt like society was turning away from faith and the Christian values that had always guided us."

Secularism was a word I was encountering more and more as I delved into religious things. Some saw it as a threat to traditional values and customs. Others were worried about moral decline. "For a while, I couldn't quite figure out the whole Christian bit," I replied. "I mean, we live in a Christian nation—at least that's what I thought—so I assumed we all must be Christians. But that always felt shallow. I wore a crucifix more as an ornament, a token belief in God. Yet, it never sat right. It's funny how religion was rarely discussed back then. Maybe as a nation, we were already drifting away. But, in the end, my belief in a higher power helped me give up the grog."

"That's good, because drink can be evil. I see it at my workplace, and it's sad what it does to people." She shook her head. "Such a culture thing, too."

"Tell me about it. I was completely caught up in it."

She placed her hand on my leg. "You've done a great thing, Quinn."

With all this encouragement, I might have to move here.

Jill turned serious. "I went Mum's way; Rose went the other way. Your old way." She tapped my leg and removed her hand. "Boys would flock after Rose because of her 'out there' attitude. I was a goodie-goodie, so they didn't come after me too much, thankfully."

"And you work in a hotel," I said.

"Funny that. I tell you, if you want to see where society is heading, spend a shift with me."

"I can imagine."

"But there is a funny side to it. I hear stories. There's one you would be interested in."

I leaned forward.

"Some local lads. Some bored, get-up-to-mischief types were at the bar chatting. I was leaning back, cleaning glasses and listening. They spoke about the yowie. I wasn't sure of when their story took place."

I snickered.

Jill smiled. "They went after the mythical beast and found him. He was a rough sleeper, a swaggie, who lived in the bush. He always wore a long, dark coat, and had a long unkempt beard. They netted him, the poor thing, but they let him loose when they realised he was human. They say he still lives there in the bush, but I'm sure he's moved his camp away from where they found him."

"Well, that addresses the yowie question," I said.

"Yes, but he may be connected to the other part."

"Other part?"

"The gold." Jill stretched out her legs and then tucked them back under the seat as a bike rider passed. They smiled at each other.

I wasn't sure where this was heading.

"I'm sure you know Mr Warhurst had quite a rock collection. You may not even be aware that he had valuable rocks hidden in his big shed."

"Nope, I wasn't. I only knew he cleaned rocks in there."

"Well, the story goes that the yowie also had a good rock collection, and it may well have been gathered from Mr Warhurst's shed."

I laughed. "But no gold, I bet."

"Don't know, but there was talk that the yowie had broken into the Warhurst house at some point."

That sent shivers down my spine. "Fascinating." I stood to stretch.

"It is." Jill also stood and studied me. She seemed to sense my unease. "Can you walk me home?"

"Sure, lead the way." I hoped the walk would banish the shivers.

She surprised me by tucking her arm in mine. I was getting used to her forwardness. "You know," she began, "apparently Mr Warhurst lost the plot after you and your mum bolted."

"I can imagine." The image of a desperate and heartbroken Mr Warhurst flashed into my mind.

"Rose explained it to me," Jill continued. "His family deserted him."

"I think 'ran away' is a better way of describing it." My words were sharper than I'd intended.

"Yes, maybe. But he was devastated."

Jill was probably right. It would've been a terrible shock for him, especially with alcohol clouding his judgement. Silence descended upon us as we took in the evening sounds, nature bedding down for the night.

Jill's voice was soft. "Mum found him one day, lying on the side of the road. Rifle beside him. Middle of winter, close to death, mumbling about the yowie having his gold."

A cold dread came over me. "I knew his beloved piece of gold had been stolen. The police found us and searched our belongings. They discovered a nugget of gold that had been given to Mum at my dad's funeral—years before we came to Edithburra. It was a treasure she held dear to her heart. She carried it always. I'm sure the proceeds from selling it would've helped us, but she never parted with it. The police took it." I choked up, the memory still raw in my mind.

Jill stopped walking and turned to face me. "That's so sad," she said softly. "Did Mr Warhurst bring that to the police's attention? That it wasn't his?"

"I don't believe he did," I replied, shaking my head.

She frowned, her eyes growing distant. "It's all connected," she murmured. "Life, Edithburra, the nuggets, your dad's death. Somehow, it's all tied together."

We turned onto a quiet street lined with trees. The houses few and far between, each with a spacious front yard. She pointed to a cute little cottage. "Did you want to come in and have a cuppa?"

My legs went weak. Why did her simple invitation make me nervous? I needed to push myself out of my comfort zone, keep building my social skills, no longer aided with the false confidence of alcohol.

Jill seemed to pick up on my nervousness. "You don't have to."

"No, I'd like to." I forced a smile. "I'd love to have a cuppa with you."

A knowing smile played on her face. "Much more relaxing than getting drunk, right?"

I chuckled. I liked her sense of humour. "Yes, I agree."

We walked up to the entrance. "My flatmate also works at the hotel." Jill unlocked the door. "She's covering the shift after mine, so won't be home until closing time." She shot me a cheeky smile. "I'm not telling you this for any reason other than to cure your shyness."

I shook my head and gave her a genuine smile. "You're funny." And cute. I kept that last part to myself, silently appreciating her thoughtfulness.

After entering a small passageway, she gestured towards a comfy-looking couch, one that you could sink into. "Grab a seat. I'll put the kettle on."

I looked around the room. There wasn't much on the walls, just a few landscape pictures. My mind drifted back to Jill's yowie story. Was that where the gold nugget was? Hidden in some strange bushman's camp?

The kettle hummed as Jill bustled around in the kitchen. Cupboard doors opened and closed, and cups and spoons clattered. I took a deep breath and found myself sinking deeper into the couch, more relaxed than I had felt in a long time. *It's been a long time coming.*

"Here we go," Jill announced, setting a plastic, wood-grain tray on the coffee table, its edges worn and chipped with years of use. The matching teapot and mugs looked like the work of a local pottery class. The silver milk jug and sugar bowl had a British touch.

She disappeared into the kitchen and returned moments later with a serving plate stacked with slices, alongside neatly folded floral paper napkins. "Mum makes the best home-made hedgehog slices."

The mention of the slices stirred a vivid memory of Katrina—her voice, her smile, and the sight of her shaking a brown paper bag. Yummy.

"You okay, Quinn?"

"Huh, sorry." I pointed to the plate. "It's just—this is only the second time I've seen these. Funnily enough, the last time was in Edithburra. Mrs Warhurst made them, and Katrina said the same thing: her mum made the best hedgehog slices. She even had to convince me they weren't animal-based."

Jill laughed. "A hedgehog competition between mums." She sat down and poured tea into the cups. "Help yourself to milk and sugar."

I stuck to black tea.

She picked up a slice, wrapped it in a napkin, and handed it to me. "Bet you were smitten with Katrina then? Most boys seemed to be."

I accepted the slice. "Yeah, I guess I was, but I was only ten." A blush crept up my neck. "But as you said, I liked your sister, too. And there were others over the years." I paused, surprised by my candour. "Why am I telling you all this?"

Jill laughed warmly. "And I just naturally drifted into the background, right?" she teased, a playful glint in her eyes.

The blush resided as I warmed to her humour.

Jill pointed at the hedgehog slice. "Maybe…maybe that's why you've been drawn back here." She punched the air playfully. "Problem solved."

"It would be nice if it were that simple."

Jill's smile softened. "It can be, Quinn. Just keep moving forward. Learn from the past, don't dwell on it. We all have our ups and downs, but the key is to keep moving forward." Her eyes met mine, a hint of empathy in them. "I think you're well on your way. What you're up to now isn't a search for meaning…it's more like a treasure hunt, wouldn't you say?"

I half expected Jill, with her blunt honesty, to blurt out that she was the treasure, but maybe there was some wishful thinking at play there.

I thought of Lee, my counsellor. That could well be Jill's forte also.

We sat in silence for a moment, sipping our tea and munching on the hedgehog slices. Then Jill stood, retrieved a worn-looking photo album, and sat back down. We flipped through the pages, sharing a few laughs. Between sips of tea and too many hedgehog slices, time seemed to slow.

There weren't a lot of photos of those days, but enough to stir something inside me. A heaviness loomed. Jill must have sensed the shift in my mood. She closed the album with a gentle sigh and smiled. "It's been a big day for us both. You were the last person I expected to run into today, and it's been so lovely." She nodded. "I think it's time to send you home to bed, to rest up for the rest of your adventure."

I nodded, standing with my emotions tangled up inside. I smiled. "Thanks for such a lovely time."

She hugged me. "I enjoyed it too, and I look forward to exploring Edithburra with you. Now off you go."

As I walked out into the cool night air, hedgehog memories lingered in my mind, but they soon passed as I looked to the stars in the sky. I hadn't spoken to my dad for a while.

I'm getting there, Dad.

44 Ghosts and Gold

I returned to the hotel and entered through the guest entrance. I caught a whiff of stale beer—a stark contrast to the fresh air I had been enjoying. A peek through the doorway to the bar revealed a boisterous scene.

Fred was perched on a barstool, clearly under the weather, as were his companions. Their laughter boomed through the room. The barman smiled and shook his head while a barmaid wandered the floor, collecting empty glasses. I assumed that was Jill's flatmate. The atmosphere beckoned me to join, but I moved on.

I turned my attention to the stairwell. The warm sunlight that had bathed it earlier in the day had vanished, replaced by dim, flickering light that cast long shadows, enveloping the space in gloom. I passed the ghost story clipping and began to ascend the stairs.

Reaching the stairwell landing, I nearly collided with a man staggering towards the stairs. His clothes were rumpled, his face pale, and his eyes wild. "Woooaaah," he slurred, reaching for the support of the wall. "Thought you were another ghost for a second there!" He laughed and pointed to a room at the end of the passageway, his finger shaking.

Thankfully, the room he gestured towards was not mine. "A ghost?" I asked, my voice wavering as a chill of the unknown crept over me.

"Yeah, right there!" He pointed to the room again. "Walked right through that door…I mean, right through it!"

He retraced his steps and peered back into his room for a moment, then retreated inside. A beat of silence, then his head poked out, eyes darting to either side like a caged animal's. He gave a confused shrug and slammed the door shut; the sound echoed eerily down the empty hallway. It was as if I didn't exist.

Any trace of fear I'd felt had departed at the humorous scene. Smiling to myself, I entered the haven of my room and bolted the door, just in case.

I was soon under the bedcovers, drifting towards sleep, when I heard footsteps echoing off the timber floorboards. They stopped outside my door.

Booo! Booo!

I bolted upright, heart pounding, as a chorus of boos spilled through the thin door, followed by high-pitched giggles, jumbled and clashing together. My lips tightened as I fought off the adrenaline rush. Then a deep, familiar voice boomed, "There you are, hiding from ol' Freddy!"

I stifled a laugh as the footsteps and giggles retreated down the passageway. The resident ghost now exposed—none other than a tipsy ol' Freddy. Sinking back into the pillow, warmth washed over me. This whole experience, from reconnecting with Jill to the 'haunting' felt strangely fated.

I thought of Mum and my chasing past ghosts. This would be a good 'ghost' story to tell her. I hoped to catch up with Fred's brother Tom, so I had a story to tell him as well.

I smiled. What did tomorrow hold? I wasn't sure. But I was grateful for the unseen force guiding my steps, for the unexpected twist of fate that had led me here. I thought of Jill. Sleep came easy that night.

I woke to a soft thud outside my door. Probably, the courtesy newspaper. A smile played on my lips at the memory of the playful 'haunting' from the night before. Sitting up, I blinked and rested my feet on the floor. Opening the curtains flooded the room with sunshine, signalling a beautiful day ahead. Grabbing my toiletries and towel, I went to freshen up. When I opened the door, I spotted the newspaper waiting for me. Tossing it on the bed, I decided to read it later and headed off to have a shower.

I returned to the room and packed my things. I had no idea where I would be staying that night. Surely there would be accommodation in Edithburra, as it was a weekday. Jill, my tour guide, popped into my mind. Where would she stay? Her mother's, of course.

I tucked the newspaper under my arm and went searching for a light breakfast. Passing the entrance to the bar, I noticed a few people sitting at tables, eating. I wandered up to the bar.

"Good morning, sir. After some brekkie?" the barman asked.

I nodded. "Now, that's a good idea."

He gestured to a blackboard positioned behind him. Eggs and more eggs. I opted for some scrambled eggs on toast and a glass of orange juice, paid, and found a vacant table. As I waited for my breakfast, I unfolded the newspaper. The headlines were dominated by news of the Painters and Dockers Union. Another grim report detailed a shooting and murder. It reminded me of my paperboy friends. Had any succumbed to the city's underworld? I often reflected on the toughness ingrained in those boys from an early age, shaped by their experiences growing up in a harsh city environment. The thought of tracking down Jimmy lingered—reconnecting always in the back of my mind.

The scrambled eggs and juice arrived. Just as I was about to take a bite, I glimpsed someone who resembled Jill passing by the entry door. My heart skipped a beat. What was going on here? Was something brewing in my heart? I shook my head, pushing aside thoughts of the Jill look-alike, and took a sip of juice before returning to the meal.

"Sprung." Jill stood beside the table, a mischievous glint in her eyes.

"What are you doing here?" I asked. "Thought you were having a few days off?" A pang of disappointment hit me; I had been looking forward to more time together.

"Just collecting my pay." She gave me a knowing smile. "But even if I was working, I'd find a way to sneak away and spend time with you." She chuckled. "Sorry, maybe it's too early for mushiness."

I chuckled. "You're something else."

"But you like me, don't you?" she teased.

"The only reason I'm still around," I joked back, although I couldn't help but wonder if there was truth in my words.

She nodded, seemingly satisfied with my response, and then moved towards the exit. "Remember to pick me up around nine. I'm looking forward to our adventure."

After finishing my breakfast, I returned to the room for my bag. With some time to spare, I settled onto the bed and resumed reading. My mind, occupied by thoughts of a gold nugget, was naturally drawn to an article detailing someone's discovery of a significant nugget. The article recounted the tale of a man who'd dreamt of finding a massive gold nugget, only for his dream to become reality two weeks later.

The man unearthed the world's largest nugget found with a metal detector, weighing a staggering twenty-seven kilograms—just under a thousand ounces. While bigger nuggets had been discovered in the past, this was the largest find with a metal detector. Its estimated value ranged widely, with some suggesting it could fetch over six hundred thousand dollars, while others speculated it might sell for over a million. In fact, a Las Vegas casino, eyeing the treasure, was reportedly offering more than a million dollars.

The prospector dubbed the nugget 'Hand of Faith', a fitting title given the remarkable journey leading to its discovery and the blessings it promised for him and his family.

The amusing thought of becoming a prospector myself entered my mind. My previous encounters with gold—tiny nuggets no bigger than a large button or resembling a piece of chewed-up gum, both lucky to weigh an ounce—made it seem like a whimsical notion. But then again, an ounce of gold is still worth good money.

I flipped through the rest of the paper and then grabbed my bag and left the room.

When I pulled up a few minutes before nine, Jill was leaning casually on her fence. Maybe, just maybe, I'd already discovered a treasure.

45 Start of the Tour

I pulled over and Jill jumped into the car, bringing with her a surge of infectious energy. "Ready for your adventure, mister?"

"I am." A mixture of excitement and uncertainty brewed in me.

She buckled up, giving directions. "Just follow the road to the end of the street and turn right. We're looking at maybe forty minutes' drive." She rubbed her hands together. "Just in time for cake with Mum. I told her you're coming. She's excited."

Apprehension briefly gripped me. Whether it was the mention of seeing her mum or just the thought of going back to Edithburra, I wasn't sure. I shifted the car into gear and followed her directions, though the apprehensive feeling lingered.

"This may sound silly, but I've forgotten your last name," I said.

"Not silly, been a long time. It's Toohey." Jill gave a reassuring pat to my leg. "I have a confession, Mr Davies. I checked your name in the hotel register." She smiled. "This is going to be good for us both."

I nodded, not really grasping what she was getting out of the adventure. As I turned right, following her directions, she continued, "This is the main road. Basically, we just stay on it." She glanced at the changing scenery. "You have any plans?"

"Cake with your mum, that's about it."

"You want to go visit where you used to live, to the Warhurst house?"

"Not sure."

"Rumour has it, he's a changed man."

"Really?" That intrigued me.

"Yeah, drops into the store every now and then. Likes his lollies now. No grog anymore, I believe. A bit like you."

I nodded, trying to absorb what I was hearing. "I wouldn't mind catching up with Tom."

"Ah yeah, Tom's a good bloke, our friend Fred's brother," Jill said.

"Fred, the ghost." I smiled wryly.

She gave me a puzzled look. "Actually, Tom helped me secure the job at the hotel."

"Yeah, I remember him as a helpful fellow. His brother was a bit under the weather last night and stood at my door with some of his mates, pretending to be ghosts. You know, boos and aaahhs. The giggles gave them away."

She laughed. "Fred has quite the reputation. I'm sure when he eventually moves on to the other side, he'll return to the hotel in true ghost form."

I thought of Fred's earthly brother. "Yeah, I think I'd like to catch up with Tom. He helped us a lot." A sense of gratitude lingered deep within my memories of him

"Well, there ya go, we've got a bit more of a plan." She shifted in the seat. "We staying the night at Edithburra?"

She had a knack of making me blush. And she seemed to sense it.

"I said to Mum that I'll stay over. No room for you, sorry." She sent me a playful smile. "We have visitors."

Anxiety welled up within me at the thought of more people.

"There's a nice, comfy motel," Jill said, straightening. "You might get a discount. It's run by Bruce. You remember Bruce?"

A clear image of a youthful Bruce poking a bull ant with a stick dropped into my head. "I certainly do. Had some great adventures with him." Excitement replaced the anxiety. "That could be a good idea. I look forward to seeing him."

Jill nodded. "You must be impressed with your tour guide?"

"Oh, I am." I chuckled.

We both laughed, camaraderie growing between us. Being at ease with each other helped us settle into our plans.

I thought of the gold article. "I read an interesting story in today's paper about a prospector discovering a huge gold nugget. Apparently, they could end up selling it for over a million to a Vegas casino."

"Wow, now I know the real reason you're back. You're looking for gold." Her playful tone sparked a mix of amusement and unease within me.

"May well be." I nodded. "I'm in search of my mother's gold nugget. The one I believe Mr Warhurst came into possession of many years ago. I'd love to recover it for my mum as it held more than just monetary value for her."

"Maybe he did try to get it back to you." Jill's voice had softened. "But he couldn't locate you."

"I doubt it."

"Maybe not straight away, but perhaps as time wore on, guilt got the best of him, and he went looking."

Part of me wanted to believe Jill's theory. "Well, then, we may have to visit Mr Warhurst and find out."

"Funny…I remember the police coming to our house not long after you ran away," Jill said. "They were interviewing everyone. Talked about Warhurst's rocks being stolen—and his precious gold nugget. I told them it was the yowie, but no one believed me. Except Bruce."

Good old Bruce. Ever the faithful friend.

Silence settled into the car, letting the majesty of the scenery take hold.

"Beautiful," I said, gesturing to the rolling green hills before us. The sight was marred by the occasional roadkill, a grim reminder of my first trip into Edithburra with Tom. I recalled sitting between Tom and Mum in his ute, counting the roadkill we encountered along the way, and wanting so much to sit in the back, in the ute's tray, wind blowing in my face.

"You seem lost in thought," Jill observed.

"Yeah, just reminiscing about my first trip along this road in Tom's ute, and all the roadkill."

"Some things never change. Tom still has the ute, and we still have all the roadkill."

"He must have racked up some kilometres on that ute."

"Sure he has. But he's a handy man. Most probably replaced the engine a few times."

A twinge of inadequacy crept into my mind. These rural folk were handy people.

As the curves in the road multiplied, I leaned forward and focused, noticing the trees getting bigger and the appearance of large tree-ferns. Slowing to navigate a bend, I rolled down the window and drew in a deep breath.

"I bet that triggers some memories," Jill said.

She was right. The scenery was intertwined with my memories, both good and bad. I cherished the freedom of the hill country, despite the mix of emotions it evoked.

"Does it look the same?" Jill asked.

"Funny you should ask that. I was just thinking it seems a bit…different. Less magical, somehow."

"Maybe it's not the place that's changed," Jill said.

I glanced at her. She wore a knowing smile.

Jill continued, "Maybe it's just the way we see it. You saw it through a child's eyes back then, full of wonder. Now nostalgia might be colouring your memories a little."

"But it's still an amazing place—the scenery, the trees." I snuck another look at her. "You ever thought of becoming a counsellor? I think you've got the skill set there. Empathy and understanding."

"Well, thank you, Quinn." She chuckled. "That's a nice thing to say. I may start charging you soon…we need to turn off up ahead."

Memories came rushing back as I caught sight of the store's façade, with two kids sitting on a bench out front, hands deep in brown bags. "Wow, this is like stepping back in time. The store looks exactly how I remember it."

"That's because it hasn't changed much. Mum's holding on to the old charm it's always had." Jill pointed to a driveway tucked next to the store. "We can park there."

I followed her instructions. Stepping out of the car, I turned towards the school. My heart sank a little. It was hard to make out the school building with the trees larger and the shrubbery thicker.

Jill followed my gaze. "Not a school anymore," she said gently. "Someone bought it many years ago and renovated it. It's now a private residence."

A twinge of disappointment stabbed at my chest. I had harboured a secret longing to revisit the school, to maybe somehow walk through the classroom again. To relive those days, to find closure. That dream had just vanished.

Jill must have sensed my dejection, for she tucked her arm in mine. "Come, let's go say hello to Mummy. She's been looking forward to seeing you." She looked at her watch. "9:45. Good timing. I told her we would be here around ten."

A gentle laugh escaped me. She was such a sweet thing. Her kindness helped me deal with the unexpected disappointment.

We stepped into the shop through a creaky door. The same creaky door? A bell jingled. The same bell? It was the same lolly shop, and the familiar sweet smell hit me—surprising me that I could still remember it after so many years. Shelves were lined with jars filled with colourful treats and packets. The retro design on the packets transported me back in time. In a fleeting moment, I saw us school kids, wide-eyed and eager, gazing up at those very shelves.

A young girl with bright eyes and curly brown hair suddenly appeared from behind the counter, squealing,

"Auntie Jills!" She ran around the counter and charged towards Jill, wrapping her small arms around Jill's legs.

Jill grinned at me. "This is Betsy, my favourite niece."

Betsy detached herself from Jill, tilted her head up, and eyed her aunt. "I'm your only niece."

"Still the best," Jill responded playfully.

Betsy giggled. "You're silly, Jills."

"Why don't you grab this man here a lolly?" Jill suggested.

"He your boyfriend?"

Jill's eyes sparkled. "Nah, found him lurking outside. He's in need of a lolly."

Betsy's eyes narrowed. "You're fibbing, Jills. He's your boyfriend!"

"Okay, he's a boy, and he's a friend."

Satisfied with this answer, Betsy ran through a door behind the counter.

"Rose's daughter," Jill explained, her voice heavy.

That sent a jolt through me. How old was the girl?

Jill gave me an understanding look before switching to a more serious tone. "You've returned to a world you left behind a long time ago. Now you're seeing the ripple effects of choices made back then—some good, but mostly bad."

She paused, taking a deep breath. "Life's been a battle ever since…something—whether it was abandonment, betrayal, or mistake—fractured not only our family unit but also others in the local community. It's like a snapshot of life's complexities. I don't think this was our destiny. Somewhere along the way, our ancestors—and society—lost their way, and now we're left to bear the burden of it."

Her touch on my arm brought a surge of unexpected peace through me.

"Why have I returned here?" My thoughts were a tangled mess.

"You've returned for a reason—to relive old memories, to find gold. Let's leave the heavy talk for now. Sorry about that."

I wanted to embrace Jill, to show her how much her words meant, but such displays of affection still felt unnatural to me.

46 Hello, Rose

Betsy's sweet voice preceded her emergence from the doorway behind the counter, accompanied by two ladies. Jill's mum hadn't changed much, with perhaps just a few more lines etched by time. The woman beside her, who I assumed to be Rose, had changed dramatically. She seemed fidgety, her face gaunt, shadows lingering under her eyes. Yet there was a noticeable alertness in her eyes and a sense of moving away from past struggles.

"Well, hello, stranger," Jill's mum greeted me, approaching with a grin. She reached out and gave me a thorough once-over. "My, my, you've turned into quite the handsome man." This family had a knack for making me blush. "How long has it been?"

I cleared my throat softly. "About seventeen years."

"First time back?"

I nodded.

Mrs Toohey turned to the side, motioning for Rose to step forward.

She appeared nervous. "Hello, Quinn," Rose greeted me softly, extending her hand.

I shook it gently. "Hello, Rosemary." My heart ached and tears welled up in my eyes. It was as if years of pain surged through her arm and into mine.

The urge to embrace her was strong, and I followed through. It started as a tentative hug, but a wall seemed to crumble as our shared pain radiated between us and the hug deepened. When we pulled away, I sensed a healing had occurred, for both of us.

Rose's eyes were watery. "I needed that." She took a deep breath.

"You both did," Jill interjected. "I sensed…"

"Healing," Rose added, nodding softly. "So good to see you again, Quinn." She smiled. "It took me a long time to forgive you for leaving."

A twinge tightened in my chest. "I'm beginning to see now how much I underestimated the impact of Mum and me leaving the way we did. Back then, it seemed so routine—just another stop in the nomadic life we were thrust into."

"We didn't get it back then, Quinn," Jill said. "But when we found out Katrina and her family weren't coming back, we started to think maybe the same thing was happening with your mum—that things were so bad, she had no choice but to escape.

"Didn't we all?" Rose said with a wistful sigh.

"Children, this is a happy place. Let's keep the atmosphere positive." Mrs Toohey gestured towards a nearby table and chairs. "Go sit and I'll fetch some treats."

We wandered over to the chairs. Betsy followed her grandmother back through the door.

"Mum always wants to dwell on the positive," Rose said.

"Not a bad thing to do," Jill chimed in.

Rose ignored her sister's comment. "So, Mr Warhurst was also a nasty piece of work, a bit like our dear Mr Hecat." She took a deep breath, attempting a smile. "But that's all behind us now. There are scars, but they're healing."

Uncomfortable sensations churned in my stomach, and a lump formed in my throat.

As if sensing the tension, Jill suggested, "Let's go sit outside. Some fresh air would do us good. We don't want to stain the shop with bad vibes."

We followed her lead.

Mrs Toohey found us outside, where our conversation had taken on a gentler tone. A group of cockatoos clustered next to a nearby pine tree, and the sight of them rummaging around the grass for seeds added to the tranquillity.

"We're tea drinkers, Quinn," Mrs Toohey said as she placed a tray on the table. "Hope that's okay. Although we can get you a soft drink if you wish."

"No, tea's fine." The air was cool. A hot drink would be nice.

Jill arranged the teacups and saucers on the tray. A small pitcher of milk, a sugar bowl, and a generously sized teapot accompanied the cups and saucers.

Betsy's excited voice filled the air as she brought out a small bowl of lollies, while her grandmother followed with another tray bearing cake.

As we engaged in light chatter, enjoying our tea and cake, my gaze lingered on the bowl of lollies. Betsy noticed and playfully pretended to drag the bowl away, flashing me a mischievous smile only a child could muster.

The fresh air seemed to enhance the flavour of the cake, making it even more delightful.

"You know, Quinn, I think Betsy's getting close to the age we were when you came to our school," Rose said.

I glanced at Betsy, struck by the innocence she radiated. "Now that's hard to get my head around."

"Why?" Rose asked.

"For some reason, my memories of those days seem more adult-like."

"Perhaps that's what happens when innocence is taken away," Jill suggested.

Their mum nodded in agreement. "My Jill has always been a deep thinker. I'm not sure where she gets it from, but I'm proud of her."

"You're right, Quinn," Rose agreed. "It's challenging to look back at those times through the eyes of a child."

"But you were children," Mrs Toohey said, her voice catching. She reached out to Rose, placing a comforting hand on hers. "I'm so sorry, my love, for what you went through."

I tensed anticipating Mrs Toohey's next question.

"Why didn't you say something, Quinn?" Mrs Toohey asked gently. "I'm not challenging you, just curious. As I was with my own girls."

I let my mind wander back to those difficult days. "That's a good question," I mused. "Funny enough, I've always brushed it off. Mr Hecat seemed to balance his bad with his good—a Dr Jekyll and Mr Hyde type of person. I think my life up until that point was one of 'Well, that's the way the world is'. I probably already had some walls up and really didn't know how to process what was happening."

"Yes, nothing to compare it to. No instruction book, I suppose," Jill said. "We were exposed to the ugly reality of the world before we knew how to deal with it or process it. We had to mature quickly."

"It was only later, after Hecat was involved in that car accident and became immobilised, that the truth came out," Mrs Toohey said. "Did you know about his accident?"

"I wasn't aware until Jill recently told me."

"Well, my dear Rose had the courage to speak up. He had threatened to burn the shop down if she told anyone what he was doing to her. And sadly, I never dwelt on those times when I sensed something was amiss. You know, we parents trust teachers and the like. Trust was a big thing in those days, but that's long gone."

A heavy sigh escaped Rose's lips.

Mrs Toohey looked at her daughter, concern evident in her eyes.

"It's okay, Mum. The scars are still healing, but I want Quinn to hear these things."

I felt as though I'd been hit by a sledgehammer. My trip back here was indeed uncovering some ghosts from the past, and not at a gentle pace.

"We reported him to the authorities, and sadly, it appears there are a number of teachers like him in the system. The education department just doesn't seem to have the structures in place to address these issues. They're still trying to work out processes."

Frustration edged Mrs Toohey's voice. "And we know it's not just teachers behaving this way. So many men out there, still wrestling with grim wartime memories—escaping them through alcohol and violence."

For a moment, silence settled over us. The sounds of nature filled the pause—the rustling of leaves, a bird calling from the trees, the faint hum of insects. We sipped our teas and nibbled on pieces of the tasty cake.

Betsy pushed the lolly bowl towards me. "Here, try this." She gestured for me to open my hand and when I did so, she dropped a black-and-white lolly into my palm. Pointing to her mouth, she grinned, "Suck."

I did as I was told and soon a liquorice taste flooded my mouth. Déjà vu struck. Her eyes were wide, clearly expecting a reaction.

I grinned. "Yummy."

Betsy giggled.

"Hey, Quinn," Rose said. "Want to go for a walk? A nostalgia type of walk?"

I nodded. "Yeah, I think I'd like that."

"Take him down the track," Jill said. "Bruce and Quinn used to ride home along that track."

"Good idea. You want to come?" Rose asked.

"Nah, I'll keep Betsy occupied and spend some time with Mum." A sly smile crossed Jill's face. "I trust you won't run off with the man."

47 Walking and Talking

We passed the tennis courts. I couldn't help but note their enduring charm. The chicken wire surrounding the courts looked new, devoid of the vines I remembered snaking in and out of the mesh. A sizeable brick wall stood adjacent to the courts, likely a practice wall.

Walking with Rose felt surreal, especially since we hadn't seen each other for over seventeen years. We'd shared a bond during our school days, a closeness that I now realised stemmed from the challenges we'd faced together.

"Bet you're finding Jill lovely and knowledgeable," Rose said. "I say that not out of jealousy, but out of respect. She's been my partner in healing, attending most counselling sessions with me."

"She does seem wise, and she is lovely. I always remembered her being cute and bubbly."

"Bit different from you and me."

"Yeah. My mind has been uncluttering since embarking on this trip. I think we did okay back then, considering what we were going through. It's like we discussed earlier—the loss of innocence, when we start to see things through adult eyes. I think that's when the problems arise."

Rose seemed to ponder my statement. "I think it has something to do with the development of the brain. We were at such a vulnerable age—right when we were starting to form our own beliefs and sense of self. Being in the early stages of puberty, everything felt more intense, more personal. That's probably why it affected us so deeply."

"You're sounding like Jill." I smiled.

"Mum got us into some Christian counselling services, so you might detect that influence in Jill's words of wisdom. Our faith has been a saving grace for our family."

She brushed her hand against some leaves, then continued, "It is nice to see you again. I thought of you a lot over the years, wondering what happened to you. Thankfully, Mum found out through Mr Molloy where you vanished to, so that brought some relief."

In the background, I heard Betsy's voice. We turned to see Jill and Betsy, tennis rackets in hand, heading towards the courts.

"They'll be hitting some balls on the rebound wall. Betsy is good at sports." Rose smiled. "Isn't she lovely? Her dad will be home from work later in the day. He's a builder. Lots of people escaping city life now, so renovations are keeping him busy. I suppose you noticed that with the old school."

I nodded.

"That's how we met. His name's David, but we call him Davey. He was doing some renovations at the school. I jokingly asked him to burn the place down." She chuckled. "To be honest, I think he would've burnt the school down if he believed I was serious," Rose added with another laugh. "He just didn't realise I was serious.

Rose reflected for a moment. "We were both lost at the time, tangled up in drugs and alcohol." She gestured towards Betsy. "She kept us together. We've stuck it out through thick and thin. Been together ten years."

"That's nice. I've been a bit slower in getting my life together. I've had to battle my way through alcohol. It nearly ruined my life. Correction: it did."

Rose gave a knowing nod.

I continued, "Been getting counselling and found help through AA. And connecting to a higher power has really brought some healing."

"Faith. Yes, it does that," she mused, pausing beside a flowering bush. "Betsy's so full of life. She sees the world with child-like wonder." Rose gently touched a flower. "We all start off like that, but then life throws challenges at you that squash those feelings. We ignore the effects of those challenges and bury our emotions so we can stay child-like."

She was as wise as Jill.

Rose continued, "But these things eventually bubble up to the surface, and we don't know how to deal with them, so we push them down again, even while knowing they'll return. Or we seek help from the wrong things."

"Drugs and alcohol," I said.

"And whatever else that will keep us from the truth."

A parrot landed on the bush and started feeding on a flower.

"Lovely, hey?" Rose gestured towards the bird.

"It is."

Out of the blue, she said, "I think you need to go see Mr Warhurst."

Her comment caught me off guard. "I think I'm building towards that."

"You know, I've kept in touch with Katrina. She has no forgiveness in her heart. She hates her father." Rose's eyes held a flicker of resilience, a silent understanding of Katrina's pain.

"That's sad." I pondered my own journey with forgiveness. Had I forgiven Mr Hecat? Had I forgiven my dad for abandoning me?

"I visited her not too long ago. She lives in Melbourne."

"So I hear."

She gave a knowing nod. "I think we can help her. You and me."

"How?"

"Go visit her dad and we can work it out from there."

Our conversation was interrupted by voices behind us. Jill and Betsy appeared.

"Bet you thought we were a yowie," Jill said.

Betsy growled and raised her hands like claws.

"My, what have you two been smelling?" Rose laughed. "I've heard some plants around here can cause hallucinations.

We all joined in the laughter.

"Best we head back. Lots to do and see. Maybe we can go on a long hike tomorrow," Jill suggested.

"That sounds nice," I said with a nod.

"Quinn staying over, then?" Rose asked.

"Yep, need to go book him into the motel."

"Well, Bruce is in for a little surprise," Rose said, looking at me. "Bruce hasn't changed a bit."

I smiled, looking forward to that encounter.

Jill and Betsy turned and ran off in the direction of the store and we trailed behind them.

"You know, Quinn, you and I were vulnerable. No dads to protect us." Her tone was serious. "The Hecats of this world prey on people like that. It's a cycle of harm—fathers, screwed up by their own dads, abuse or abandon their families, and then the vultures move in."

Her words were heavy but rang true.

She continued, "I've broken free from the chains of the past, and forgiveness was the key." She glanced at me. "I'm just rambling on, hoping that some of these words can help you. I can see you've come back here for a reason."

"Thank you, Rose. All food for the mind," I answered genuinely.

She smiled and pointed to the sky. "Look up there."

I followed her gaze, spotting a wedge-tailed eagle gracefully gliding on air currents.

"Magnificent birds, they are," Rose said. "Can I share one of my favourite Bible verses with you?"

"Sure." I was intrigued and still hadn't moved on much from the Book of Proverbs.

"It goes something like this. 'They that wait upon the Lord shall renew their strength; they shall mount up with wings as eagles; they shall run, and not be weary; and they shall walk, and not faint.'"

"Wow, that's in the Bible?"

"Indeed. Encouraging, isn't it?" Rose pointed to the sky. "Coincidence, you reckon?"

I looked up. Lots of coincidences were happening of late. I felt a tug to delve deeper into the Good Book.

As we approached the store, I noticed an old ute parked

out front. A pang of anxiety shot through me. It might be Tom's car—hopefully he hadn't brought his neighbour along. I wasn't prepared for that encounter yet. I hauled in a deep breath. My walk down memory lane was moving at a brisk pace.

Jill stood at the entrance to the store. Her presence gave me encouragement.

"Okay, sis, I'm taking over the caretaking of this lost soul," Jill declared.

Rose shook her head. "Do you find her amusing, Quinn?"

I couldn't help but smile. "Actually, I do."

Rose's eye's widened as she grinned. A blush crept up the back of my neck.

"He doesn't really. I'm just his guide; without me, he'd be lost," Jill teased.

Rose gave me another look, a flicker of amusement in her eyes. "You sure?"

I shook my head slightly; my hands gestured uncertainly. The blush had subsided, but something stirred within me. My heart warmed.

"Tom's out the back fixing up something for Mum," Jill said. "I told him we may drop in and visit him this arvo. Tom said he'd like that; he'd love to see you again. He even said to come for lunch, so we'll drop in around lunch time."

Jill's eyes met mine. I detected a hint of uncharacteristic shyness.

Her voice softened. "Let's go, Mr Quinn. We've got places to be and people to see. We're quite in demand."

48 Complex Creatures

Bruce hadn't changed a bit. He practically jumped over the receptionist desk to give me a hug. "Man, it's so good to see you again. You ain't changed one iota."

There was something about genuine friendships—no matter how much time passes, the connection remains. This was what Bruce and I shared. In the short time I'd lived in Edithburra, we'd formed a bond much like the one I had with Jimmy in Melbourne.

Bruce refused to accept payment for my accommodation so long as I promised to return again soon. He even mentioned having a honeymoon suite, though I wasn't sure where he was going with that. He gave Jill a wink. It was her turn to blush.

As we had to shoot to get to Tom's, we arranged to have dinner later that evening, and Jill was happy to accompany me. My schedule was rapidly filling up—Jill's mum also wanted to spoil me. She settled for lunch the next day instead.

When we left the motel and I climbed back into the car with Jill, I broached the topic that had been swirling in my mind. "Friendship's a curious thing. We seem to connect to some people and not others. I had a special mateship with Bruce, and it's still there after all these years."

"Yeah, I know what you mean," Jill replied. "I think it's sometimes how open a person is. You know, how willing to share or disclose things about themselves."

I thought of Bruce and Jimmy, both of whom were open books.

Jill continued, "A sense of humour is also important for connecting with others. There's nothing worse than when one of your jokes goes over someone's head."

"Well, that depends on the joke," I teased.

"Maybe. But I can sense when someone isn't on my wavelength."

"Yeah, you can still be friends, but there's a lack of depth," I said.

"I think we've connected well, and I detect snippets of humour in you that I'm sure will burst through in time."

She was right. There was a closeness between us, a nice closeness. I searched for an appropriate joke.

"Come on, tell me what ya thinking," Jill challenged.

"I like you. Love your sense of humour. Love your openness. Reckon you're the best tour guide I've ever had."

"Shush, I'm blushing."

We both chuckled.

"Turn left up here," Jill instructed.

Silence entered the car as we navigated the winding road.

"There's a park coming up soon. I just need to use the ladies' room before we get to Tom's. I could wait until then, but the park is special. You can sit somewhere and absorb yourself in nature."

It was a good suggestion. After we stopped, I climbed out of the car and settled onto a log that marked the boundary between the parking area and the park's grassland. Jill wandered off towards the amenities block, tucked away at a distance near the picnic area. The day's chill was lifting as the afternoon sun spread across the park. In shaded spots now touched by sunlight, pockets of mist rose like ghostly veils. That thought made me smile.

In returning to Edithburra, I hadn't anticipated how quickly past connections would come together. I'd made the right decision in returning. My thoughts drifted to Mum and the scars she carried. Unlike me, she didn't appear to chase the ghosts of the past. I wondered how she managed her scars—perhaps by shutting herself off from others, only revealing the flippant side that others could laugh with. But few ever delved deeper with her.

I was beginning to see some of my mum's personality traits in me. Like her, I had a flippant side that I used to gain acceptance from others. I'd once been the life of the party, especially in my drinking days, seemingly without a care in the world. But now I understood how I operated. Mum could never say no; she avoided conflict at all costs—a testament to her scars. Yet, avoidance only created more conflict. She would insist that was the way she was, that people couldn't change. I begged to differ.

Jill returned and settled next to me. "You okay? You seem distant."

"I'm okay, just lost in thought."

"The scenery can have that effect."

"Just thinking of my mum. She must have a lot of scars."

Jill nodded. "I think all parents do. Some just hide it better. Back in the old days, you got on with life."

"Yep, my mum is in a fixed state. She's one of those who believes others can change but believes the opposite for herself. But maybe it's a bit more selective tied in with her own experiences. It's complex."

"Well, you must have spooked her then, with the new you."

I chuckled. "It's funny you say that, because sometimes I get the feeling that she thinks I'm just putting on an act and that the old me will resurface eventually."

"That's weird, but I get it. It sounds like she's afraid of change. The 'old you' would help her avoid facing her own need to change."

I gestured to the car. We climbed back in and I drove off.

"We're complex creatures," I mused. "Maybe there's an element of shame in wanting to change yourself. You know, not liking who you are."

"Yes, it's complex, and we could well be miles off track."

We drove for a while in comfortable silence, my mind grappling with the complexities.

Jill leaned forward. "Just up ahead, Tom's house is on the left, just past the big pines. The Warhurst property is just behind those big trees. We'll pass their driveway soon." Jill pointed to a row of towering, deep green trees, their arrow-shaped foliage thick at the base but narrowing as it reached towards the sky.

"I remember those trees. I thought they looked like rockets, and now they seem to be reaching for the moon."

"I suppose they do look like rockets." Jill chuckled. "I think deep down you're a bit of a romantic."

I wasn't sure what she meant by that comment, but then she explained, "There always seems to be a connection between the moon and romance."

I glanced at her. She was looking ahead, her side profile revealing delicate features and gently curved lips. I found myself enjoying her company more and more.

She intercepted my gaze. "What ya looking at?"

Sprung. I quickly blurted out the first thing that came to mind. "Just noticed you have a big pimple."

She quickly put her hand to her face.

"Just kidding. You have lovely skin."

She shook her head. "Oh, men." She smiled, then added. "Slow down a bit here."

A sense of familiarity settled in as we passed a dirt driveway, marked by a huge sign between two large posts, tilted on one side, perhaps due to a loose bolt. The sign was weathered, the letters barely decipherable, but I recognised what it was meant to spell out: WARHURST FARM. However, some letters had faded more than others, leaving the letters WAR T FA… I paused, realising it revealed the words WART FARM.

"Wart farm," I said, gesturing to the faded sign.

Neither of us laughed. There was something melancholy about the sign as we drove past the driveway.

"That's Tom's house up ahead."

Tom's house came into view. Its whitish façade contrasted with the surrounding greenery, its rustic tin roof giving off a charming feel. I realised my perception had changed since I first saw his house; the spaciousness and emptiness now seemed appealing, almost natural.

I briefly glanced back at the Warhurst property. Overwhelming feelings lingered, a mix of unease and unresolved memories.

Spring 1981
Melbourne

My dearest Martha,

Greetings from the retirement village. I've settled in quite nicely here. It's comfortable; I tend to keep to myself, perhaps a bit too much. I think people have given up on me. When I first arrived, they came knocking on the door regularly. I soon tired of their visits. When the knocks came, I would just sit quietly and not budge. Sometimes, I'd even crawl along the floor to turn the TV off. How silly of me! I've gradually become more of a loner over the years. I don't fully understand why, but I'm sure it's connected with losing my Harold. I also find socialising draining, and I simply don't want any more dramas in my life.

Thank goodness for the television; I find a lot of comfort in TV shows. Some friends in the past suggested I should get into TV.

I've been told many times that I make people laugh and they enjoy having me around. I think people like my lack of seriousness. Though not everyone likes this flippancy. But in some ways, I understand how actors and comedians must feel—it's hard work and draining to entertain others. Yes, I know that's not what life is really about.

Maybe I don't trust people; they can be intrusive and gossipy. But then again, I've come to realise that these are just human traits. Yes, I'll admit to indulging in a bit of gossip, but I only share this with you. I've noticed a certain pleasure in sharing and also receiving gossip. It's not good, I know, but perhaps that's why so many people gossip. We can get addicted to so many bad things.

I believe I mentioned in my last letter that my boy Quinn has gone off chasing ghosts, revisiting a place from the past. I'm puzzled as to why he's doing this, but I understand it's something to do with his healing. He's really immersed in it. Perhaps a bit too much, I think. He talks about retrieving my gold nugget from that cruel man, but I hope he doesn't venture anywhere near that man. The mere thought of the man makes me feel sick.

I had a dream of the place Quinn's visiting. Dreams are peculiar, aren't they? I stood, at least I think it was me, on a porch with Quinn and the man that helped us escape. I reckon we were at his house. We watched from the porch as a man dug a hole. It reminded me of a scene from a graveyard. Even though the man had his back to us, I knew exactly who it was. I found myself hoping that he was digging his own grave.

Oh dear, I don't like having such thoughts. Bad memories cling to me like stains on a white blouse. How can I be released from them?

I'm sorry, dear. My letters to you help me see and try to understand things. I don't mean to burden you with my troubles.

When we meet again and hug, things will be righted.

I'll write again soon.

Love,
Elizabeth

49 Visiting Tom

Tom's ute sat snugly in a carport beside the house. Memories of his home flickered in my mind. They were only fleeting memories, but I did recall him tending to his row of rose-bushes out front. The plants looked well-cared for, healthy and neatly trimmed.

I parked the car in a gravelled area, and as we stepped out, I inhaled deeply. The fresh country air continued to offer a welcome change from the stale, heavy air of the city. My mind began to unwind, thoughts dissipating like morning mist. My gaze wandered over the expansive landscape until it settled on the neighbouring property—and my mood soured. The house looked the same, yet somehow more neglected, and it seemed closer than I remembered. Perhaps my memory had played tricks on me.

"You alright?" Jill's voice broke into my thoughts as her gaze followed mine. Before I could respond, a voice came from behind us.

"Well, hello."

I turned to see Tom approaching. He looked thinner than I remembered, the addition of a grey beard further distorting the image I'd held of him. Still, he looked strong. I reached out to shake his hand, but he pulled me into a warm embrace instead.

"How old are you now?" he asked with a grin.

"Twenty-seven."

"Wow…about seventeen or so years since I last saw you." He turned to Jill. "And how's my lovely Jills?"

"Doing well thanks, Tom. You're looking good."

"It must be the fresh air and my garden," Tom joked, gesturing towards the house. "Come inside. I'm experimenting with baking. You two can be my guinea pigs. Also, I've put some sandwiches together."

As we stepped onto the porch of Mr Molloy's house, I mused on how I sensed a closeness to Tom, and it seemed so natural to refer to him by his first name.

"Thanks for coming to visit," Tom said. "I was so excited when we arranged this visit. I've often wondered how you and your mum have fared over the years. How is she?"

Tom's question caught me off guard. Despite my thoughts of her, she wasn't one to share much about her life, especially with me. I couldn't recall many instances where I'd delved into her personal affairs.

Jill noticed my hesitation and nodded towards Tom, as if urging me to respond.

"It's okay, Jills. He's deep in thought," Tom said.

I cleared my throat. "Yeah, sorry about that. It's not a question I get asked a lot. I was just thinking of how to answer."

"I well understand," Tom replied. "Returning here must be stirring up a whirlwind of emotions."

I nodded. "After we left Edithburra, we eventually settled in another town closer to Melbourne. It was much bigger than Edithburra, with a big school." I chuckled.

"Wouldn't take much to be bigger than our old school," Jill joked.

After a brief bout of laughter, I continued, "After I finished my schooling we settled in suburban Melbourne and in time, Mum moved to a village complex. She has her own unit and seems content. Just does her crocheting and watches TV and keeps to herself. She's a private person. I think she never really recovered from losing my dad."

"And maybe a few other dramas," Tom added.

"Yeah, and that too." I sighed, feeling the weight of unresolved issues. "We never properly thanked you for all the help you gave us. Mum would love to see you again sometime."

"You never know," Tom mused. "That was quite an eventful time." He gestured towards some timber chairs on the porch. "Grab a seat, and I'll get those baked goodies and sandwiches. You want tea or something?"

"Tea would be lovely," Jill responded, "but let me come and lend a hand."

"Always nice to have a woman in the house, especially for tea-making." Tom smiled.

"You want a cuppa, Quinn?" Jill asked.

"Sure, that sounds good."

Jill and Tom headed indoors, leaving me standing alone on the porch. Leaning against the railing, I gazed towards the house—the old man's house.

Memories flooded my mind—Katrina's infectious smile and the warm welcome from her family when we first arrived. Nostalgia enveloped me, transporting me back to those simpler times. Lost in a daydream, I barely noticed Jill and Tom approaching until they were near.

Tom and Jill set the tea and food on the table and then walked over and joined me. It was then that I noticed a figure digging at the rear of the old man's house, his back to us. I knew who it was.

As if sensing our gaze, the old man turned. My heart skipped a beat. He looked towards us and waved before returning to his task.

"He's different now, Quinn. Changed." Tom motioned for us to take a seat. "Come, sit down and enjoy the biscuits and sandwiches."

I tried to steady my breathing.

"Quinn knows how people can change, Tom," Jill said. "He's had to do some hard yakka himself."

Tom searched my face. "Really?"

I breathed deep. "Yeah, I lost my way for a while."

"Well, I can understand that." Tom sympathised. "Life didn't give you a solid platform to work from."

Jill poured the tea, nudging a cup towards me and indicating the milk and food. Tom took a small sip from his cup.

"I think I need to tell you about that night," Tom said. "Particularly what happened after I left you."

"Yes, I'm curious about that." I reached for my cup, sticking with my recent preference for black tea.

"After settling you and your mum in the hotel, I headed back home. Most roadkill happens at night. I had to be cautious driving back from Willward."

"By the way, I've met your brother, Fred," I interjected. "He speaks highly of you."

"That's nice to know. Was he up to his usual mischief?" Tom said with a smile.

"Oh yes, tried to spook me—and maybe other guests—with a ghost routine. Stood outside my door with a few of his drunk mates and gave a chorus of jumbled boos."

"Funny and sad at the same time," Tom remarked, his tone shifting. "On my way home that night, not far from here, I noticed a spotlight beaming into the sky."

A nagging sense of discomfort settled in.

"It could have been mistaken for people spotlighting rabbits, but the light was stationary and shooting skyward," Tom recounted, his voice now serious. "My heart sank as I realised there had been an accident. I pulled over near a large dead roo, likely the cause of it. I grabbed my Dolphin Torch and went to investigate."

Jill and I listened intently, pausing to sip our tea.

"There was a mangled car, which had come to rest on a fallen tree trunk. Its lights were beaming into the sky. It looked like it had rolled several times. I climbed through the buckled fence and headed towards the vehicle. As I got closer, I realised it was the teacher's car."

I nodded, recalling that Jill had touched on this during one of our previous chats.

Tom continued, "Hecat was in a semi-conscious state, in a lot of pain. I did what I could to make him comfortable, then rushed home to call the authorities."

"He ended up a paraplegic, no use of the lower half of his body," Jill added softly. "The next day at school was chaotic. Rumours swirled about the car accident. You weren't at school, and no Mr Hecat. We knew sometimes that he drove you to school. My memories of that day are quite vivid."

"Yes, my memories too. Strong feelings tend to stick with us, don't they?" Tom gestured to his neighbour's house. "Lance took the accident hard; he blamed himself. They had been drinking and arguing, and finding out that his family had deserted him—along with you and your mum disappearing—sent him over the edge."

A shadow of gloom passed over me. "And here I was, starting a new life, unaware of what I had left behind—the engulfing chaos." What had triggered the old man's transformation?

Jill spoke up, her voice gentle. "Mr Warhurst had lost his grip on reality. I think I mentioned to you, Quinn, that Mum found him one day, lying on the side of the road with a rifle beside him, close to death in the middle of winter. He was rambling about the yowie stealing his gold."

"He often went hunting for the yowie-come-bushman," Tom added. "He believed the rumours that the bushman was just a homeless man who visited properties when owners were away or asleep."

Jill shuddered.

"Lance was convinced that the bushman had stolen his cherished nugget—in fact, he blamed everyone. With his family gone, it was the one thing he felt he could recover."

"Quinn, you doing okay with all this?" Jill asked, her eyes showing concern.

I nodded.

"Have a boost. Grab a biscuit; they're lovely." she added, giving Tom a smile.

Tom returned her smile. "Thank you, Jill. Before you leave, I'll give you a plate for your mum."

"She'd love that."

"Speaking of Jill's mum, she played a significant role in Lance's transformation." Tom said.

"She was just practicing what she preaches, Tom, loving her neighbour as you do also," Jill replied.

"I'm grateful for you both sharing these things with me," I said. "They are important to know about."

"They are, and I'm sure Jill will fill in the gaps for you," Tom said. "Now, Jill, I bet you have some entertaining pub stories to share."

Jill laughed. "I do, but most involve your brother."

"Oh dear, let's move on, then." Tom grinned. "Quinn, what do you do for work?"

"I'm currently between jobs. For a while, I worked for the government in the computer side of things. I might go back to it, but for now, I'm taking time to decide my next move."

"Yes, technology, computers and the like are starting to take off. I often wonder where it's going to take us," Tom said.

"He's thinking of becoming a gold prospector," Jill joked, with a mock-serious expression. "Maybe he'll buy a whiz-bang metal detector."

I nodded along with a smile, but my thoughts were elsewhere. A persistent tug at my heart urged me to go and say hello to the old man, to say hello to Lance. Standing, I hesitated before asking, "Would it be okay to go over and say hello to Mr Warhurst?"

Both Jill and Tom nodded, sharing a knowing glance.

"I think he'd like that," Tom said. "It might be best if it's just you that goes over to say hello for now—one-on-one. It could be less overwhelming for him."

I nodded and turned towards the Warhurst house.

50 Visiting the Old Man

The grass felt soft beneath my feet as I walked. A tiny skink darted away, avoiding the steps of the giant moving through its territory. As I drew closer, a knot of apprehension formed in my stomach. The old man rested on his shovel, his gaze fixed on the hills, before he resumed digging.

How old was he? I'd instinctively referred to him as 'the old man' when I first arrived. He must have been in his early forties then. Old, at least through the eyes of a ten-year-old, with his weathered, crinkled appearance. Perhaps now in his late fifties, he was no longer an 'old man' in the eyes of a young adult.

His grunts grew louder as I approached. He paused again and, sensing my presence, turned around, a thin smile cracking the dust on his face.

"You come to help?" He glanced behind me, towards Tom's house. "You the only one with muscles?" He chuckled, shoving the spade in the soil and walking towards me.

He hadn't changed much. If anything, he looked healthier, though still lean.

"Are you a friend of Tom's?"

He suddenly stopped in his tracks, shock registering on his face. His eyes bulged and his jaw dropped open.

"Quinn?" he asked gingerly, gripping a post on the side of the house for support.

Feeling awkward, I hurried towards him.

"No, it's okay. Just got a bit weak in the legs. This is totally unexpected." He looked towards a nearby garden bench. "I need to go sit there. Come with me?"

With his balance regained, he led the way to the bench. My heart swelled with empathy, a feeling I hadn't anticipated. He sat down, tears welling in his eyes. "I'm so sorry."

I sat beside him, offering comfort. "It's okay, I haven't come to dwell on the past. I just wanted to visit." To be honest, I wasn't entirely sure why I was there myself.

He remained silent, his lips trembling as if he struggled to find the right words, his complexion pale. He rubbed his throat and let out a dry cough. "I think," he said, his voice hoarse, "I need a drink of water."

He went to stand, but I gestured for him to stay seated. "Let me go get you some water."

"Must be the digging…." He pointed towards the house. "It ain't changed much."

As I headed inside, he let out a loud sigh. Glancing over towards Jill and Tom, I gave them a thumbs-up.

I only had fleeting memories of the house's layout, but it was fairly straightforward. A short passageway opened up into a large room. I smiled to myself when I saw the potbelly stove.

To the right, against a white wall and near the window, stood the glass cabinet. Katrina's words echoed in my head.

"We collect stones." I was drawn to the cabinet. There was no gold nugget. Through the window, I could see Mr Warhurst getting restless on the bench, so I hurried to the kitchen, found a glass, and filled it with water before returning outside.

Mr Warhurst was sitting upright now, seeming to have regained some strength. I handed him the water and he took a big gulp before turning to me. Nearby, a timber log had been converted to a makeshift seat, so I sat there, deciding not to join him on the bench. Hopefully, face-to-face communication would facilitate a better connection between us.

Taking a deep breath, Mr Warhurst spoke, his voice strained. "Thank you for doing this, for coming to see me. I've carried the weight of regret for many years over the way I mistreated you and your mother."

I sighed inwardly, unsure how to respond, then simply nodded.

"I've been on the wagon for many years now, thanks to Tom." He looked over towards Tom's house. "And Jill's dear mother."

"I'm the same."

"Huh?" Mr Warhurst's expression shifted, showing a mix of surprise and curiosity.

"I mean, I'm on the wagon, too."

I couldn't decipher his expression. "Sadly, I was probably one of the reasons you went off-track."

"Yes, you were one of them," I said honestly. "But strangely, I think it was more the way the schoolteacher treated me. He was a violent and abusive man."

Mr Warhurst lowered his head. "So I heard."

"I remember more that went on at school than what happened here, but I think all the memories tie together somehow. I'm still trying to understand."

Mr Warhurst rubbed his head. "Quinn, I mean this sincerely: I'm so sorry for how I behaved." He took a deep breath. "Is there anything I can do to make amends? For you to forgive me?"

"I hold no grudges," I said, understanding the importance of forgiveness from the AA program. It was a double-edged sword, allowing me to set others free while ensuring I harboured no resentment for how this man had treated me.

"Thank you." His words carried weight—regret and hope. He stood. "Come inside?"

Leading the way, he guided me into the house, heading straight for the cabinet. "It's funny how that gold nugget that once sat there had a hold of me. It became an obsession. I don't fully understand it, but I've been reading a lot of the Good Book and it talks about idols, making metal gods for ourselves—worthless idols that cannot see or hear." He paused and seemed distracted. "Give me a sec."

He walked off to a room, returning with a small box.

"Are you in contact with Katrina? I sensed there was a possible romance brewing when you first met. Parents sense these things." He sent me a warm smile.

"We were pretty young, then," I acknowledged, recalling the connection I'd felt with her even at that tender age.

"Yes, you were both young." Mr Warhurst's gaze drifted, as if he were lost in memories. His eyes watered. "I understand why they did what they did. Katrina was my favourite—though you're not meant to have favourites as a parent." A thin smile appeared on his face.

"I haven't seen her since those days. I know she lives in Melbourne."

"Really?" Mr Warhurst's eyes widened. "I didn't know that."

Had I shared something I shouldn't have?

"I seek forgiveness from them as well, but they refuse to communicate with me."

A sense of brotherly love swept over me. We needed to help each other. He was a changed man—I could see it in his face, in his eyes. There was a peace there now. I held no resentment towards this man. My own journey had given me the strength and understanding to forgive.

"When I get back to Melbourne, I was thinking of catching up with Katrina. Maybe I can have a chat about you with her."

His eyes brightened at my suggestion. "Could you?"

"I could, and it's a start."

He glanced over my shoulder, through the window. "Looks like your friends are coming to visit."

I turned to see Jill and Tom heading towards the house.

"Quinn," Mr Warhurst said, drawing my attention back to him. He handed me the small box, a matchbox. "Open it."

I did as instructed, and peace flooded me.

"Yes, it's your mother's gold nugget. Take it and give it to her and tell her how sorry I am for what I did." He drew in a deep breath. "I did try to track you down, but time seemed to have covered your tracks."

I looked at the nugget and pictured the joy on my mother's face.

"And, Quinn, I've come to understand one thing: faith is more precious than gold."

51 Faith More Precious Than Gold

Lance Warhurst invited his guests into the house.

Jill gave me a questioning glance as she entered the living area. Her caring nature warmed my heart and I responded with a gentle nod and smile.

Lance spoke, his words tinged with nervousness. "I suggested to Quinn that he was the only one with muscles, which is why he wandered over."

Jill chuckled. "I didn't notice him grabbing hold of the shovel."

"Nah, I'd finished. Just working on a new garden bed," Lance explained. "You lot want tea or something?"

"We're good, Lance, I just fed them," Tom advised.

"Has the house changed much since you were last here, Quinn?" Jill asked.

Searching for familiarity since entering the house had yielded only fleeting memories. "Not sure. Wasn't really into furnishing and layout when I was ten." A soft laugh escaped me. "But I do remember the potbelly stove. It was the first time I ever saw one." My gaze drifted to the rock cabinet.

"And the rock display, too. For some reason, I connected with those rocks." I touched the box in my jeans pocket. I considered mentioning it but sensed it might not be the best moment.

"Yes, you did strike me as someone who appreciated nature," Tom said.

There was a slight tension in the air, an awkwardness. Lance seemed unaccustomed to having people in his house. "Would you like to come sit in the lounge room?" he asked.

"It's okay, Lance," Tom said. "I think these two young ones need to be on their way. They're only here for a few days and have a few people to catch up with."

Lance's eyes were on me. "We had a nice chat, me and Quinn," he said. "Seems we both had a battle with the bottle and righted our paths."

"Me also, many moons ago," Tom added.

Jill nodded, her expression warm. "It takes a lot of strength to overcome something like that. I'm really proud of all of you."

Lance didn't press us to stay longer. I understood his reservations.

"Have you heard from Evie or any of the kids?" Tom asked.

Lance shook his head, his expression sombre. "Nope." He glanced at me, seemed to consider saying something, but then changed his mind.

Wanting to offer some encouragement, I spoke up. "I mentioned that I'll put in a good word with Katrina if I catch up with her in Melbourne."

Lance lowered his eyes. "I'm afraid they'll all have a frozen image of me."

"That image will melt in time, I'm sure," I suggested, though the words felt awkward. I knew people could change. We had.

I walked over to Lance and shook his hand. "I'll come see you again sometime." Taking a deep breath, I added, "I understand…and we're good. I hold nothing against you."

His eyes welled up. "Thank you, Quinn, I hope you do visit again. I could teach you about rocks and how beautiful they are. They have an energy all their own."

I could almost feel that energy escaping from the box in my pocket.

***

Once in the car and back on the road, I couldn't shake thoughts of Mum. I knew she loathed Lance. Hopefully, the little box in my pocket would ease the dislike she felt for him. I was coming to understand that an unforgiving heart was a weight on a person—it held them down.

A gentle nudge from Jill brought me back. "You okay?"

It was awkward, but I managed to retrieve the box from my pocket without running off the road. I handed it to Jill. "Take a look inside."

It was a worn matchbox, plain with no markings. Jill pushed one end, glanced at the contents, and then looked up at me. Her eyes widened. "Is this what I think it is?"

"Yep, my mother's gold."

"Wow. He must be a changed man, giving this up."

"He is. And he said something that stuck with me."

Jill tilted her head, waiting.

"He said, 'Faith is more precious than gold.'"

Jill nodded slowly, thoughtfully. "What do you think faith means to him?"

"I've been pondering that. Gold was everything to Mr Warhurst, and it's the most treasured, perhaps the most coveted metal on earth."

"Yeah, it does crazy things to people," Jill said. "Reminds me of the old gold rush stories. The greed, the obsession."

"What do you think about the faith bit?" I asked.

"Trust comes into play somewhere," Jill said, her eyes on the road. "Like how I trust your driving. I have faith in you."

"Maybe it's about believing in something or someone," I added.

Some kangaroos were grazing on the side of the road. I slowed down as we passed them. They raised their heads and gave us a brief, indifferent look. What incredible creatures! I refocused.

"So, I guess trusting gold doesn't get you very far," I said, shaking my head. "I can feel a headache coming on already. Heavy stuff."

"It's not everlasting," Jill suggested.

"What? The headache?" I joked, hoping to lighten the mood.

Jill shot me a stern look. "Mr Warhurst's gold was taken from him and he grieved its loss. But faith—maybe that's something that lasts forever." Jill looked at the contents of the box again. "A complete trust in something or someone," she murmured.

"Just a piece of rock," I said.

"Do you have faith, Quinn?" Jill asked, turning to face me.

"I think I do. What about you?"

"You're not giving away much," Jill observed. "As for me, faith is a cornerstone of my life. I have a deep, personal relationship with God, though I struggle with church and religion from time to time."

"I believed in something but never really pondered it much. Since giving up the drink, I've started reflecting more. Now, I'm at the point where I believe a higher power is guiding me—maybe even helping me. It's like a relationship that's growing."

"That's lovely, Quinn. I have to admit, going to church with Mum is helping me understand more. It feels like we need to be fed—like sheep, I suppose."

"And we need a shepherd to guide us, to take us on that journey. Maybe we're being refined," I said.

"That's a clever thought," Jill said. "Maybe that's the exchange that took place within Mr Warhurst—he swapped gold for faith and is now on a different path."

"I think you're right," I agreed. "Faith is something you can't see, and it's often tied to religion because religious folk believe in the unseen."

"Yet, my mum would say she sees God everywhere. Nature, she would say, surrounds us with God's creations."

I let out a light chuckle and pointed at a faint remnant of a rainbow in the distant hills. "I'm starting to appreciate these little coincidences. It feels like some kind of confirmation."

Jill glanced at the fading rainbow. "It's nice talking to you, Quinn. You're very open."

"Talking things through helps me understand myself better. Not everyone likes to share their thoughts." I gave her a sidelong glance. "But you're a gem," I added with a wink. "Just keeping on topic…you know, gold, rocks."

"Ha, ha, very funny. You need to turn left ahead."

Next up, Bruce. Did he know how much the old man had changed? I had vague memories of dealings between the two. I didn't think the old Mr Warhurst had liked and trusted many people in his previous life. From memory, he'd even accused Bruce of being a thief.

Yes, people could change. If they wanted to. Really wanted to.

52 Edithburra Motel

A large sign jutted out from the roadside, its big, bold lettering announcing vacancies at the Edithburra Motel. Hosts: Bruce & Pamela Weir. Five hundred metres. We'd soon be there, with Bruce expecting our arrival in the early afternoon.

"See that building on the right with the green roof? That's the motel. It just looks different, coming from a different direction.

Jill was right. We had parked out on the road during the previous brief visit. I would've missed it from this angle.

Things were moving at a whirlwind pace. There was so much to absorb, so many things going unnoticed.

"We'll park in the car park this time, just up ahead." Jill said.

I pulled into a spacious gravel car park, its boundaries marked by weathered, treated pine logs. Only one other car was in the lot. A short, gravel path led to a narrow, single-story building with a low-level timber deck, with several doors facing the road. Chairs were positioned near each door.

A bearded man sat on a plastic chair, cradling a steaming mug in one hand and a cigarette in the other. The worn baseball cap perched on his head cast a shadow over his face, obscuring his features. Smoke from his cigarette drifted lazily into the air. He gave us a nod as we stepped onto the deck. A few steps past him, a doorway stood with a sign protruding overhead, clearly marking the office entrance.

The smoker stood as we passed. "Jills?"

Jill seemed to freeze, her eyebrows shooting up. "Jamie?"

The man stepped closer. "Yes, it's me, Jamie. Long time no see."

"The beard caught me out," Jill said, her voice tinged with nervousness. "I thought you'd moved away."

"I did, but I'm back to visit my little brother. He's at the funny farm." Jamie looked at me. "Who's your boyfriend? You checking in for a night of fun?" He winked at me.

Jill coughed. "Nope, just visiting Bruce."

"And"—he gestured towards me, then gave me a harder look—"there's something familiar about you."

She pointed to me. "A face from the past. You remember Quinn?"

I had a feeling that Jill hadn't wanted to introduce me, but circumstances had forced her to. Then it dawned on me—this was Katrina's brother.

He moved closer to me. "Nah, it's not." Another step closer. "You're not *that* Quinn, are you?"

I nodded.

He pushed me and I nearly lost my balance. Jill stepped between us. "What are you doing, Jamie?"

"What do ya mean, what am I doing? Don't you remember, this creep and his mum stole some of our belongings and took off leaving Dad to fend for himself while we were away overseas."

"But you never came back," Jill asserted.

He gave Jill a questioning look. "No, we didn't come back, but I spoke to Dad at some point, and he filled me in on what this jerk did."

I regained my composure and challenged Jamie. "What did we steal?" I asked, trying to steady the adrenaline rush.

Jamie laughed. "You stole my dad's gold. Our gold." His fists curled.

"It was the yowie, Jamie." A voice came from the direction of the office.

Jamie shifted his gaze to behind Quinn, "Oh, g'day, Bruce. I've heard that rumour too." He angrily pointed at me. "But I reckon it was him."

"It wasn't, Jamie," Jill chimed in. "I've heard that some people tracked down the yowie. He was just a homeless man who lived in the bush. They found many stolen items at his camp. The police got involved."

"Really." Jamie didn't seem to believe her. "Bet you there was no gold."

Jill shrugged and shook her head. "I don't know. Besides, Jamie, it was a long time ago. Your dad doesn't seem bothered by it anymore."

"You visited him, then?"

"Yep, me and Quinn."

"Well, that would've gone down well."

"It did," Jill confirmed.

Jamie looked like he didn't want to hear that.

"Hey, Jamie," Bruce jumped in. "When was the last time you saw your dad?"

Jamie pressed his lips together.

"Been years, hasn't it?" Bruce said. "You should go say hello while you're visiting."

"I'll think about it." He gave me a look.

"He's a changed man, Jamie," Jill added.

"Nah, he's a creep, just like your friend."

"Are you going to settle down, Jamie?" Bruce asked. "Or do I need to send you off somewhere else?"

"I'll settle." He gave Jill a look-over and took a deep breath. "Good to see ya, Jills." If that was his attempt to fix things with Jill, he was a long way off. He turned and went into his room, closing the door behind him.

Bruce turned to me and spoke in a hushed tone. "Well, that's quite a grand welcome for you, Quinn." He came forward and gave me a hug, then did the same to Jill.

He gestured for us to enter the office and then through a door that led into a combined kitchen-living area. A lady seated on a couch stood to greet us.

"This is Pam, my wife." Bruce smiled at her warmly as she approached and hugged me. I was getting used to this type of greeting.

"It's always nice to meet another student from the old school," Pam said with a smile. "There weren't too many of you."

"It's all about quality, love, not quantity," Bruce added, returning the smile.

They looked like a pairing made in heaven.

"We've put a roast on for dinner, but it's still a few hours before we eat," Bruce said. "Just thought it would be nice to catch up and reminisce a bit."

"Won't that bore Pam to death?" Jill joked.

"Maybe, but I'll bring her into the conversation. She likes listening to stories and things."

Pam gestured towards a large, comfy-looking couch. "Tea? Coffee?"

"Tea would be nice," Jill replied.

"I'll go the same," I said.

Pam wandered off to prepare the drinks.

"That gold nugget nearly brought an end to this town," Bruce said, shaking his head. "Old Man Warhurst was on the warpath after you took off. Everyone in town was accused of stealing it. But in the end, he believed you and your mum stole it. The dust settled when he came to that conclusion. But I think there were a number of things going on with him, then. Particularly with his family doing what they did."

I thought of the old man. "We just spent time with Mr Warhurst. He's a changed man."

"He is. I believe it's some kind of miracle," Bruce said.

"I've seen Jamie in the Willward Hotel a few times. I think he works at one of the power stations," Jill said. "I didn't think he ever ventured out to Edithburra."

"He drops in every now and then to check on his brother."

"His brother lives here, then?" Jill asked.

"Nope. He has been staying at a centre close by for some therapy."

"That's right, he did mention the funny farm," Jill said.

"Sounds like the Warhurst family is still connected to Edithburra," I suggested.

Bruce nodded. "Except for Katrina. I haven't seen her since they left and you came to the school. The boys stay connected and visit with each other regularly, but they stay away from their dad."

"There must be something about this place," I said, "a drawing power. I definitely felt a pull to return."

"Hmmm, could be," Bruce's eyes narrowed as he continued. "They're off the rails a little. Both violent types. At least the younger one is trying to fix himself."

Pam came over, carrying a tray.

"Just following the patterns of their dad," Pam suggested, setting the tray on a large coffee table. "You might want to keep your eye on Jamie. He loves stirring up trouble and getting into fights."

"We aren't here for long," Jill said. "Quinn's heading back home tomorrow."

I thought of the old man and his family. Jamie's reaction to me had been unsettling. Sometimes people were oblivious to the effect their actions had on others. Friends and family alike.

It was good to visit Lance Warhurst. I sensed an atmosphere of healing. The past was finally dissolving.

53 Coping with Memories

"Did Lance tell you he spent time at rehab?" Bruce asked.

Pam's brow furrowed. "Bruce can be blunt. Do you remember that from the school years, Quinn?" Pam gave Bruce a stern look. "Not everyone feels comfortable sharing everything, especially something so personal."

Bruce shrugged. "Not this mob. We have a shared past."

Pam sighed. "Perhaps, but Mr Warhurst may not want you sharing such things. Rehab is a difficult journey, and some people need privacy to heal."

"It's cool, Pam. Mr Warhurst was quite open about everything," Jill said. "Quinn is on a journey to understand his past. The more things get talked about, the more his memories may clear up." She gave me a hopeful look.

Pam offered a hesitant nod. "Some may be unwanted memories."

"My darling Pam works at the rehab clinic," Bruce advised. "So, she gets a bit protective when rehab topics come up in conversation. Rehab is a hush-hush topic for many. Most people want to keep their time there a secret."

I pondered Pam's comment. "Shouldn't we want unwanted memories to surface, even if they're painful?"

"Memories are complex things," Pam answered. "They can decay over time, and pain may even have disconnected some segments of the memory, so you may be bringing up memories that aren't actually accurate. So, we need to manage the emotional response when they're called up. If there are negative associations, we need healthy coping mechanisms."

"You may be wondering…" Bruce started, a slight grin on his face, "well, my dear Pam is actually studying to be a mental health nurse. Impressive, hey?"

"Very impressive," Jill agreed.

I nodded. "Yes, impressive. What a complex field to study! So, with memory recall, it really boils down to having a coping strategy for the negative memories?"

Pam replied, "Yes, but medicine can also be part of the picture in some cases."

"Like the feel-good pills? Tranquilizers?" Jill chimed in. "Mum and Rose have told me about them."

I wondered what Jill's mum knew about them. It made me curious about the extent of her knowledge and whether it came from personal experience or her dealings with Rose.

Pam smiled. "Medication can be crucial for some people to function normally, but at the rehab centre, we try and help people in non-chemical ways. For example, the steps used in Alcoholics Anonymous can be helpful for other addictions as well."

Rising from her seat, Pam gestured towards the oven. "Just going to check on dinner." As she opened the oven door, a delicious aroma filled the room. Catching our expressions, she glanced over with a pleased look. "Bruce has put together a nice roast. The smell is heavenly, isn't it?"

The food smelled lovely, but my mind remained preoccupied with the weighty topics that had kept me company on this journey. The presence of these thoughts was not unwelcome; instead, these deep conversations were propelling me towards growth and understanding.

Jill smiled at me, perhaps sensing my busy mind. "These chats seem to follow you."

"You read my mind, but it's okay. I feel close to people when we all open up." I returned her smile.

The afternoon was disappearing, and before I knew it, we were seated at the dining table, and the roast was being carved, filling the room with a meaty fragrance complemented by the earthy aroma of herbs.

Bruce had moved to the oven and stood stirring the gravy. "I just love making gravy from the pan drippings. Something about the smell."

Pam placed a tray of roasted veggies on the table. In that moment, I resolved to learn how to cook when I returned home—or at least graduate from the canned and frozen stuff and takeaway.

Bruce moved to the fridge and opened the door. "Did you want a beer, Quinn?"

I sensed Jill's eyes on me. "Not a drinker anymore, Bruce. Had to give it away. It caused too much pain in my life."

"Good on ya, Quinn," Pam said. "Makes you more of a man than you realise."

"Thank you. That's a nice thing to say," I replied, relishing her appreciation.

Bruce closed the fridge door without a drink in his hand.

Pam nodded at him and turned to me. "There's soft drink if you would like. Coke, lemonade?"

"Actually, I wouldn't mind a glass of lemonade," I said, watching Bruce return to the fridge.

"You too, Jill?" Bruce asked.

Jill nodded. Bruce retrieved a bottle of lemonade and some glasses and walked to the table.

I smiled at Jill. "You a good cook, Jill?"

"Watch out, Jills," Pam said. "He's checking your credentials."

Pam must have noticed my blush. "Just joking, Quinn. Bruce does most of our cooking. He seems to enjoy it."

"Yes, Quinn," Jill added, "I'm a good cook." She gave the biggest smile, making my blush deepen further.

"There ya go, mate," Bruce joked.

In an effort to shift the focus away from me, I asked Pam, "Where did you and Bruce meet?"

"On a school bus. Doesn't that have a romantic feel to it?" Pam laughed.

Jill spooned some veggies on her plate and gestured to me, as if to ask whether I'd like some. I nodded and moved the tray of meat closer to us to add that to our plates as well.

"School," Bruce said. "When our school closed down." He paused and looked at me. "Did you know the school closed the year after you left?"

"Yep, Jill told me," I replied.

Bruce continued, "Well, we started going to another school. They organised a small bus to take us there and back. Pam lived on a property near the new school, and she was picked up as part of the route. She saw me and that was it."

"You believe that, Quinn?" Pam asked.

"Hmm, I'd say it was the other way around."

"Right you are," Pam agreed. "Now get stuck into that food."

Bruce lifted his glass. "Well, here's to life, and it's so good to see you again, Quinn." We all raised our glasses and toasted.

Silence came over the table except for the sound of cutlery, appreciative murmurs, and utterances of "Mmm". Conversation kicked in again partway into the meal.

"Bruce often talked about you, Quinn, when I first met him," Pam said. "He would often say he was puzzled about why you just vanished."

"When we first met Quinn," Jill said, "I told the others at school that he was an alien. So, when he vanished, it was really quite simple: the mothership had returned."

There were chuckles around the table.

"You know, there's an element of truth to that," Bruce added, one side of his mouth chewing. "There were UFO sightings around that time."

"Oh, I've been exposed." I reached for my side. "My laser gun…I left it back in the ship."

Jill shook her head. "He ain't no alien, but he's lost and trying to find his way home."

"That's pretty deep, Jill. We have some openings at the centre," Pam suggested.

"You mean work wise, not checking me in?" Jill queried.

Pam shrugged to keep her response neutral.

"A job, Jill—you're a talented lady," Bruce said.

"She is," I agreed and laughed at her blush.

I noticed several family pictures on the wall, each frame capturing a moment of warmth and togetherness.

"You know, looking at your family photos," I began, "it makes me realise that really, out of our school class, Bruce was the only one who came from a solid family. You had an idea of what healthy relationships looked like."

"I suppose you're right there," Bruce said. "Mum and Dad were pretty solid. Don't remember any real dramas."

"Funny," Jill joined in, "I can remember those days so clearly. You remember Charlie and the twins? Their dad was hardly around and then one day he just vanished from their lives completely. He decided not to come home after one of his business trips. Rumour had it he ran off with another lady. Kids didn't want anything to do with him after that."

I winced. Back then, I'd been oblivious to these things going on around me, so caught up in my own little world. But then, a ten-year-old would've been focusing on the here-and-now, and maybe survival. Still, a pang of something akin to envy twisted in my gut at the thought of Bruce's family life.

Jill continued, "One of my girlfriends ended up in a relationship with one of the twins, Greg. He turned out to be not a nice person. Had no idea how to treat my friend. Bit of a control freak. Saw how his dad treated his mum, and he ended up doing the same thing. All a bit crazy. I don't understand why they don't see that their behaviour is wrong. He started getting violent towards the end of the relationship and the police got called."

"Like you said, he had learned values from his dad," Pam said. "He probably didn't see anything wrong with the way he treated your friend."

"That's sad," Jill said.

"It is, but it's quite common," Pam replied.

"That's even sadder." Jill sighed. "Then Rose and me, Quinn—we had no dad, and the male models we came across were terrible. Some people are more resilient than others. But things eventually come to the surface."

"They do," I agreed, "and as Pam mentioned, we need coping mechanisms for when they resurface."

"Positive ones, not like kicking a cat," Pam joked. "Like exercise. Things like that."

"To change the subject a bit, Jamie mentioned a funny farm. Is that how locals see the rehab centre?" I asked, curious.

"Unfortunately, that's right, Quinn," Pam answered. "They think only lunatics go there."

"Some of the rumours about the place are downright frightening, if not funny," Bruce added. "Men running around with chopped heads under their arms."

"Thanks for the detail, love," Pam said, shaking her head at her husband.

After dessert, we settled in the lounge area and enjoyed some coffee and light chatter. It turned out to be a lovely evening, the best I'd had for a long time. The warmth of genuine connection was a balm to my soul.

Bruce and Pam walked us to my car. As we passed Jamie's motel room, music thrummed from within, punctuated by the acrid smell of smoke wafting through the cracks in the doorway. Bruce gave a helpless shrug.

"I take it you're staying at your mum's?" Pam asked.

Jill nodded.

"Well, make sure you come visit next time you're here." Pam turned to me. "And I'll see you when you check-out tomorrow."

Hugs were exchanged all around.

As we drove off, Jill leaned forward. “Remember, city boy,” she said with a slight grin, “the night life around here is dangerous. Roos like jumping on cars.”

I took it easy on the unfamiliar roads and pulled in near the store.

“Thanks for a lovely day, Quinn.” She leaned over and gave me a kiss on the cheek. “Looking forward to tomorrow.”

She was out of the car and heading to the front door of the store before I could say anything. She looked back, flashed a smile, and waved. A pleasant warmth remained in my chest.

I chuckled. It had been a lovely day.

On the way back to the motel, a shadow flickered near a tree in the park as I drove past. My heart stuttered for a moment. Was it a yowie or a loonie or just the bushman? But it was only a group of teenagers, hanging around in the park, drinking, smoking and who knew what else.

I drove back on towards the motel with a sigh. The world was a bit of a mess, but genuine connection and moments of happiness were still possible.

54 Encounter with Jamie

I pulled into the spacious gravel car park. The leaves on the plants glistened, reflecting the starry night. At first, I thought a brief shower must have passed, but then noticed the garden hose and sprinkler, both glimmering with lingering droplets, that caught the starlight.

I'd forgotten how dark it got in the country at night. Without city lights polluting the sky, the stars seemed closer, sharper. A single light flickered near the entrance, casting long shadows. A few path lights struggled against the darkness, their glow muted by blotches of dead insects trapped inside the covers.

Up the path and onto the deck, the darkness enveloped the rooms, save for one. A door stood ajar, dim light spilling onto the deck. I could see the outline of Jamie sitting on the plastic chair outside his room. His cigarette was aglow in the semi-darkness.

The only way to my room was past him. As I drew closer, he removed his baseball cap, revealing a full head of hair, tousled and unruly. He scratched his head and replaced the cap.

"Jill give you th' flick?" he slurred with a wide, manic grin. "Pity…she's cute."

I didn't respond.

"Why'd ya take th' gold?" he barked, his voice laced with anger. "Was it payback? Cause my old man could be a nasty piece?" His face, etched with a weariness beyond his years, seemed to mirror the turmoil within him.

I met his gaze steadily. "We didn't take the gold."

He took a swig from a can, beer dripping down the side of his mouth. A trail of empty Foster's cans littered the floor from his room to the chair—testament to a night of contemplation, or perhaps oblivion. Part of me wanted to walk past, to escape to the safety of my room and avoid any more comments. But another, more insistent part of me felt a strange sense of obligation.

"Can I sit and chat with you?" The question hung in the air, a surprise even to myself.

He leaned back in his chair, a plume of smoke curling from the cigarette between his lips. Ash flaked down, landing unnoticed on his leg.

"As long as you tell me wher' the gold is..."

I nodded and pulled another chair over. The stench of alcohol hung heavily in the air, mixing with the smoke. Despite his hostility, a profound loneliness radiated from him.

"How do you know your dad doesn't have the gold if you never see him?" I asked.

"You bein' smart or somethin'?" he mumbled, his head lolling back towards the motel wall.

"No, just wondering," I said gently. His eyelids drooped, heavy with fatigue or intoxication. I decided to change the topic.

"You remember when you all took me for a walk up to the big rock and you tried to scare me with that yowie story? And then some mate of yours came running out of the bushes."

He sat up straighter, the story seeming to jolt him awake. "Yeah, it was Gavin—Jill's brother." He thought for a moment. "Haven't seen him in years. I think he's an engineer or somethin', working out west. We went to the same tech school. Parents wanted to make tradies out of us."

His gaze turned distant, moisture welling up in his eyes. Had this brief trip down memory lane stirred up a well of hidden sadness?

"I'm sick of my life," he blurted out unexpectedly. "Sorry for having a go at ya." Tears welled up, and he started to cry.

A memory from the drink-driving course surfaced: *Alcohol amplifies emotions.*

The words came out, messy but more coherent than before, a mix of frustration and raw emotion. "I'm sad…and depressed. Stevie's the same. Our dad…he screwed us up bad. And I think Mum just made it worse, runnin' away." He let out a heavy sigh. "I've always felt there's somethin' unfinished with my dad. But Mum would kill us if we reconnected with him…she hates the man."

Something about Jamie's story resonated with me. The regret he expressed about his dad was familiar.

"I think you should reconnect," I suggested, my voice tentative.

He looked at me, wiping his face with a grimy sleeve. His gaze held a newfound seriousness. He nodded. "I agree."

***

As I drifted off to sleep, Jamie's face lingered in my mind. Would our conversation leave a lasting impression on him? Would he even remember it in the morning?

Upon waking, thoughts of Jill filled me with anticipation for our journey back to Willward.

Exiting my room, I breathed in the crisp morning air. At the rear of the motel, Bruce and Pam had converted an old shearing shed into a dining room. While guests could make their own breakfasts, Bruce had promised he was going to make me the best scrambled eggs I'd ever tasted. Eagerly, I made my way there.

The dining room was a spacious area with a few tables and chairs. Rusted artefacts hung from timber posts, and the surrounding walls were made of corrugated iron. A few strip heaters took the chill out of the air. Bruce was busy beating eggs in a bowl. "There's juice in the fridge. Help yourself," he said, running his eyes over the place. "It's not crowded today, but weekends are a different story—even the locals drop in then."

As footsteps approached, I turned to see Jamie entering the room, and I gave him a nod. Despite looking a bit worse for wear, he managed a genuine smile. He went straight to the fridge and poured himself some orange juice.

"Good morning, Jamie," Bruce greeted him.

Jamie returned the greeting, then gestured with the jug. I nodded, and he poured some juice into a glass.

"Thanks for last night," Jamie said, his smile widening. "I remember our conversation, surprisingly enough. I usually don't retain much after heavy drinking." His eyebrows shot up. "I've decided I'm going to visit my dad, and I'll take Stevie with me. We all need healing. I can't let this bitterness inside me continue to ruin my life."

Bruce came over, placing a reassuring hand on Jamie's shoulder. "That's a good decision, mate. And I'm here to support you every step of the way."

Bruce gestured towards a nearby table. "Sit, and I'll bring you the best scrambled eggs you've ever tasted."

As I joined Jamie, I wondered if Bruce said that to all the guests.

Seated across from Jamie, I caught his gaze, and he spoke up. "I reckon you were sent here to tell me to go see my dad. Like an angel-type thing."

I laughed. "Well, that's a first. I've never been called an angel before."

As it turned out, they *were* the best scrambled eggs I'd ever tasted.

55 Two Sides to a Feather

It was Friday, and we spent most of the morning hiking in the bush, and it was exactly what I needed—a respite in the company of Jill and nature. That had a nice ring to it. Towards late morning, we rested on a bench under a canopy of tall tree-ferns. Jill whispered, "If we're quiet, we may encounter some lyrebirds."

I whispered back, "I've seen them before, doing a mating dance beside the road. I was in Mr Warhurst's car when he stopped, and we watched them. That was one good memory of Lance."

Jill nodded, putting her finger to her lips. "Shh."

Bird calls filled the air, interrupted by a sound that resembled a chainsaw. Jill laughed. "That could be a lyrebird."

"Sounded like a chainsaw," I remarked.

"They can even mimic dogs barking," Jill said, her voice still low.

We sat in silence for a while longer, the gentle rustle of leaves in the breeze the only sound. With birdsong fading into the background, I closed my eyes, feeling a deep sense of peace. When I opened them again, the world seemed sharper, more vivid somehow. I blinked, realising my eyes had watered.

I was brought out of my trance by a tap on my knee. "It's best we go; you may have to start your journey homeward soon," Jill said with a sad expression, "and we need to squeeze in lunch with my mum." We walked on, and suddenly Jill threw her arm out in front of me, pointing to the track ahead.

"It's not!" she exclaimed in a whisper, creeping forward. "It *is*." She pumped her fist. "It's a lyrebird feather. What a treasure. What a find. Maybe we *should* take up gold prospecting."

A long and slender feather lay partially covered by bush litter. Jill picked it up, beaming. The feather was brown and broad, with a curved shape. As she swirled it in the air, the underside displayed hues of blue, green, and purple. It was stunning.

She held it against her chest. "Thanks, Quinn, you've made my day."

I'd done nothing. Mother Nature had stepped in.

We walked on.

Jill waved the feather in front of her face like a fan. "You okay about taking my sister back to Melbourne with you? She can talk, you know."

I thought back to the early morning tea with Jill's family. Rose had shared she was going to visit Katrina in Melbourne. I had offered to drive her.

"No worries, should be fine. Good company." I gave Jill a genuine smile. "Nothing better than a chatty companion."

"Yeah, it will stop you picking up hitch-hikers," she said with a wink. "There are strange people out there." She paused and her voice turned serious. "You make sure you don't pick up any hitch-hikers with my sister in your car, okay?"

"Cross my heart."

As we drew closer to the car park, Jill slipped her hand into mine. It felt so natural, as if her hand belonged there. She glanced at me with a warm smile that sent butterflies fluttering in my stomach.

On the drive back to the shop, we passed a narrow entrance to a property. A "Peace" sign, as large as a road sign, was nailed to a tree trunk—the only indication of what lay beyond.

"Does that road take you to a hippy retreat?" I asked.

"Close," Jill replied. "It takes you to the rehab centre. The funny farm, as some call it, which is really not nice because it makes fun of people who might be struggling."

"These centres seem to be cropping up more and more. Some are even called health farms," I mused. "Replacing the word 'funny' with 'health' is probably a positive shift, though the 'farm' part still feels a bit off."

Jill nodded. "My mum was one of the first to be admitted to the centre," she said, her voice tinged with sadness. "She needed to be weaned off medication that was meant to help her. They were doing some crazy things to her head."

She glanced at me.

I felt out of my depth. "Do you think most of us turn a blind eye to what's going on out there? The hurt, the confusion." I shook my head. "I do feel like an alien, as you suggested."

"Hmm," she murmured, noncommittal.

"With all the things I'm starting to see, I do think I've been transported to another planet," I said.

"But we female aliens are cute, aren't we?" She raised her eyebrows.

"You're funny, yes…and cute." A seriousness crept into my voice. "We're all searching for meaning on this planet. Maybe we're just sojourners, passing through. But that's part of the purpose—learning, adapting."

"Maybe," she said thoughtfully. "But you should know, Quinn, when we talk about toxic relationships, it's not only the men who can be abusive. My mum treated my dad pretty badly."

Her words hung in the air, a sledgehammer blow to my previous assumptions.

"What, women beat up men?" I said, confused.

"Not quite, but just think about it," Jill challenged me. "Imagine telling your mates that your wife beats you up." She paused, her expression hardening. "They would laugh at you because of the 'manly' culture you've grown up in."

"I long for the simple life." I sighed. "How do I contact the mothership?"

"I'm coming with you," Jill joked, though her voice was firm. "It wasn't a physical thing with Mum. She was verbally abusive. Dad copped it from all angles. He was 'useless', 'good-for-nothing', and other hurtful things. We didn't see it directly, although there were inklings. We were confused when he left, until Mum finally got up the courage to tell us why."

Jill took a deep breath, her eyes watery. "They got back together a few years back."

"That's lovely," I said.

"It is, and it's a pity you missed him. He's back next week from a work assignment," she said. "But I just wanted you to know that abuse isn't limited to one gender. I sensed that you're really struggling with how bad men are—but not all men are bad. And not all women are good."

Jill was right. My eyes had been opened and it seemed my past experiences had created a skewed perception. "Can I ask, why do you think your mum was like that?"

After a brief moment of silence, Jill said, "A doctor put her on medication because of anxiety issues, which I'm sure were related to the family business and raising three kids. The doctor didn't tell her—maybe he didn't know—that they could be addictive and lead to psychosis."

"Oh dear…that's tough." I sensed her inner turmoil. "Do you mean she lost touch with reality?"

Her chuckle was tinged with sadness. "Yep, seeing, hearing, believing things that weren't real. Mum has apparently seen a few yowies and, if we are going by her descriptions, real yowies are not homeless, bushman types."

I didn't laugh. A knot of frustration tightened in my stomach. This wasn't how things were supposed to be. Relationships were about wedding vows, promises of love and forever, built on trust and respect. No one should have to endure mistreatment, man or woman. Something was out of kilter.

56 Revelations on a Long Trip

We managed to squeeze in lunch and then the three of us departed Edithburra shortly after.

We left Jill standing at her front door in Willward, waving us off. My heart felt heavy, weighed down by various emotions: sadness to be leaving Jill, excitement about the things unearthed at Edithburra, and a flicker of apprehension at what lay ahead.

"My sister's cute, hey?" Rose said with a smug expression, glancing over at me.

I managed a small nod, still grappling with the strange emotions swirling inside me. I cleared my throat. "She is." My voice was barely a whisper.

"You must come back and visit us all again," Rose said warmly. "Your visit reminded me how much you belong here in the country. You slotted right in."

"Yes, I did feel connected. It's been a wonderful time."

Rose gave me directions to the freeway. I glanced over the rolling hillside, not wanting to leave. My chest tightened at the thought of returning to the Big Smoke and the mixed emotions of seeing Katrina again.

Realisation dawned. The secrets I'd uncovered in Edithburra were minuscule compared to the layers upon layers of the unknowns that lurked within a large metropolitan city. In some ways, now older and wiser, I understood why people escaped to the country. They yearn for a simpler life, a refuge from the complexities and problems that festered in the urban jungle.

"Living in the city, Rose," I began, needing to voice my thoughts, "I would often hear of people escaping to the country. The fresh air, rolling hills, relaxed lifestyle—it all seemed so appealing."

"Yes, and there's less people," Rose responded. "But most bring their problems with them." She paused, her gaze fixed on the road ahead. "Sometimes, the problems lurk beneath the surface—they come as extra baggage, unwanted souvenirs."

"And they're often running away from something." I added.

"But sometimes people have to move," Rose said, "to find a new job, more affordable housing. They have a different mindset and a job that allows movement."

"Like teachers," I quipped, then realised my mistake. An awkward silence descended between us, thick enough to cut with a knife.

"Do you hate Hecat?" Rose whispered.

I'd expected that question. "Not sure. I was young and didn't fully understand things then." A flicker of a forgotten image surfaced—a dark figure towering over me as I lay fearfully on the floor. "But I've noticed that I have problems relating to people in authority. I tend to freeze up in the presence of bosses and the like. Maybe that's a consequence of his actions."

"I know we touched on some of this before. I get muddled when talking about the past sometimes. We were young and vulnerable." Rose's voice was thick with emotion. "And he took advantage of that." She took a deep breath. "I tried to escape the hurt he inflicted on me by drinking and using whatever else I could find to numb the pain."

I wasn't sure how to tackle what had happened to Rose in that classroom. My journey had been about sorting myself out, but healing was needed for others too, some of whom were more damaged than I was.

Rose continued, "I realised those events had a significant impact on my life. Memories that had been suppressed started to surface, painful memories. That's when I ran to alcohol."

"Yes, the dreaded drink," I acknowledged. "Rose, you don't have to chat about these things if it's hard for you."

"It's good to share with someone who genuinely cares and knows what I'm talking about. It continues the healing process."

She was right. "Yes, I do know, and I do care."

"So, I'll continue." She gave me a weak smile. "I reached a low point—a recurring nightmare forced me to face the truth. I couldn't live with the secret anymore. So, when I truly believed that Hecat was incapacitated, I told Mum." Her chuckle was strained. "And boy, did I need to calm her down. She was so full of guilt. But it really helped me knowing Mum knew. We worked through it together; we grieved together. We confronted Hecat. He had been moved to a rehabilitative facility in Willward."

"That's brave. How did he react?" I asked.

"He…he seemed remorseful," Rose said, sounding uncertain. "But in very bad shape health-wise. It would be easy to say he got what he deserved with the car accident, but the Lord has given me a forgiving heart."

I shook my head. "Forgiveness is such an amazing thing. But hard—that must've been a big challenge for you."

"Yes, it is. An amazing thing. The good Lord gave us strength. As Mum mentioned, we reported him to the authorities to protect others, but it felt like hitting a brick wall. There's a huge shortage of teachers in rural areas, so problem teachers were shuffled into country schools. The issue was swept under the carpet."

"I often thought that," I admitted. "Hecat was a problem that had been moved to Edithburra. We suffered the consequences."

Rose nodded. "There are some investigations currently underway. We can only hope that they result in progress."

I sighed inwardly. I craved peace and clarity, a yearning that was magnified by the open road stretching endlessly before us. I thought of Jill. Her quiet strength comforted me.

Rose continued, more softly, "But that's behind us now, Quinn. We're better people because of what we've experienced and what we've found. In our case, Mum and I, we found peace and healing through the church. For others, it comes in different forms."

A sign loomed ahead, advising Melbourne was 100 kilometres away.

"No bullet holes in the signs as we get close to the Big Smoke," I said, trying to lighten the conversation.

Rose chuckled. "Yeah, it's mainly on the country roads the signs get used for target practice." The chuckle faded, and I detected the weight of her gaze. "Quinn, I'm sorry for the heavy stuff, but I need to tell you one more thing. Then no more heavy stuff, I promise."

A prickle of unease ran down my spine. What could she possibly have left to tell me? "All good, Rose. All part of my journey. Shoot."

"You know, contrary to what we were saying before, country folk sometimes have to move to the city for work and they can be quite vulnerable to the pace and pressure of city life."

That wasn't too heavy, but I sensed something more was coming. The mixed emotions remained.

My thoughts went to Katrina.

57 Locked in

"Jealousy is a funny and dangerous thing, Quinn," Rose said, her voice laced with concern. "Me sitting in a car alone with you could set some men off. But not my Davey. We have complete trust in each other."

I wasn't sure where she was going with this line of conversation.

"Katrina couldn't do what we're doing now," Rose went on. "Her partner wouldn't allow it. He's…well, not a very pleasant person. My Davey, he's easy-going, not the jealous type. But Katrina's? He's at the other end of the scale. Possessive, jealous. Very jealous."

"How come she hasn't walked away?" I asked.

"It's complex." Rose sighed, sadness flickering across her face. "It's been three years and her previous relationship was much the same. He ended up in prison."

"What for?"

"He was violent. Got in a pub fight, bashed a cop who was trying to calm things down. At the time, we thought it was a blessing that he went to prison, but before we knew it, Katrina had hooked up with one of his mates."

"Why would she do that?"

"It's complex," Rose repeated, her gaze riveted on the road ahead. "It seems most things are, when it comes to relationships."

I nodded.

Rose continued, "Her self-esteem is shot. I can't believe some of the past conversations I've had with her. It's like she's been brainwashed. It all started with the mindset that she could change a man—maybe a subconscious connection to her dad there. Some men take advantage of that. It gives them power. They take control and shut the doors of escape. No money, no car. All a form of abuse, and then the violence eventually starts."

"What's going on with this world?" Images of a young Katrina flashed through my mind, and a wave of anger churned in my gut. Through watery eyes, I glimpsed a sign for a rest area up ahead. "Might just pull in and have a little break."

"Good idea."

Once parked at the rest area, we headed off to the restrooms. I returned and settled at a picnic table. There were just a few cars in the parking lot, including a minibus loaded with elderly ladies clad in white—perhaps a lawn bowling team—and a van. Love and peace signs splattered the van, with a large peace sign overlaying the VW logo. A remnant of the anti-war hippy movement.

I felt a pang of irony. We were in another war. Not nation against nation, but people against people.

"Phew," Rose interrupted my downward spiral. "You should get a whiff of whatever they're smoking in that van."

I looked over at the van. Plumes of smoke drifted into the clear blue sky and in the direction of the ladies' toilet block.

"I might look into getting one of those when I get home and then take off around Australia," I mused aloud.

"Just don't smoke what they're smoking, or you'll end up in a ditch," Rose joked, her tone turning darker. "I've seen too many people go that route with drinking and drugs."

She was right.

"And you might have to pick up Jill for company on the way," Rose added, a twinkle in her eye.

I blushed.

Rose chuckled. "She could work in different hotels and bring in some income."

"Good idea, and I could pick fruit," I said, joining in the fun.

Rose glanced at my car. "Well, let's keep the rest of the trip light-hearted. No heavy stuff."

"Sounds good to me."

"But there's one last thing—and I'm sorry, but it's about Katrina." Rose's tone shifted, turning serious. "You won't be able to visit her. You can't even give her a call."

I was puzzled. I'd assumed I'd be seeing her again, had been letting myself believe it. My emotions had been working with that assumption.

"I know you could look her number up, though I doubt she'd be listed. But if you called and her boyfriend answered...Katrina could be in big trouble."

My thoughts shot off in all directions, but one stood out: jealousy. It was at play here, and in a big way. But I wanted to know more. "Why?"

"Because he'll think she gave you the number and told you to ring her. You have no idea, Quinn, how these people work. He'll follow her on shopping trips. He would spy on her at her job. If she spoke to men, even for directions, he'd accuse her of flirting, so, she doesn't work. Just sits at home, waiting for him to come home from work. He has total control over her life."

"That's crazy."

"It is, but it's real," Rose said heavily.

"Why doesn't she escape?" I felt responsible for Katrina, though I couldn't quite explain why.

"I'm sure there would be some threat hanging over her, like Hecat had over us," Rose said. "He might threaten to kill himself, which wouldn't be a bad thing, but she wouldn't want to be responsible for his death. And then there's her own family—he could threaten them."

"If I told her dad about this, he'd probably come and shoot the fellow."

"Best you don't, then," Rose advised. "It would only make things worse for Katrina."

"Well, is there anything we can do?"

"I'm not sure. Many of her friends have tried to help. She pushes us away and fits into his world to avoid any pain. If she was to escape, he'd come looking."

"There must be something we can do."

"Now, don't go getting any ideas of being a knight in shining armour," Rose warned me. "I'm serious—you don't want to trigger a reaction from her boyfriend."

The word *boyfriend* didn't sit right here. "I feel so sad, Rose. I've had this image of Katrina in my head, full of life and laughter, the way she was when I first met her. My first love," I confessed.

"I know, I was your second, right?"

"Yes, you were, my first loves." I tried to sound light-hearted but my heart was heavy. "Okay, I just hope things work out for her."

"I hope so, too. I'll keep praying for her. Maybe God will intervene at some point."

For the rest of the trip, conversation was sporadic. I felt emotionally wrung out.

I dropped Rose off a few streets away from where Katrina lived. I gave her my phone number and asked her to ring me before catching the train back home. In return, she handed me a slip of paper with her and Jill's phone numbers. She winked at me, a glint of mischief in her eyes. I placed the paper in my jeans pocket.

I watched her walk off and turn right into a street. I was tempted to follow. But that was a foolish thought—the man Katrina was involved with was dangerous.

I drove on past the street Rose had walked down. She hadn't walked far and stood waiting for me to pass. She was making sure I didn't follow. This was serious stuff.

58 Phone Calls

After dropping off Rose, I stopped to grab some groceries and then returned to my unit. The silence pressed in on me. I'd been living alone for some time now. Counsellor Lee suggested I stay out of a relationship for a while, giving myself some space and time for self-discovery and reflection. Well, my visit to Edithburra had certainly helped with the whole self-discovery thing.

Lee's words echoed in my mind. "Take some time for yourself. You need to heal." I was looking forward to catching up with her, to share what I'd learned after she returned from her holiday.

As I unpacked groceries, an unsettling realisation struck me. My unit was not far from Katrina's. For all I knew, I could have walked past her at the local shopping centre.

I made myself a late lunch: an egg sandwich and a cup of coffee, then sat down to enjoy it. I had grabbed a newspaper from the store, which I placed on the coffee table. As always, I flipped the paper over to the sports pages. The weekend was coming up, with some good games of footy. I considered going to a game, but that decision could wait. I skimmed through the rest of the paper but couldn't concentrate. My mind was on Katrina and her situation.

I looked around the unit. The bare essentials—a couch, coffee table, stereo and TV—provided a living space, but not much warmth. A small dining area with table and chairs. A poster of Charlie Chaplin adorned the wall. There was just something about his expression, a mix of defiance and humour in the face of adversity, that resonated with me. Perhaps it reflected how I felt—a bit battered but not defeated.

A letter sat on the coffee table, confirming a job interview in the city on Monday. While I wasn't in a rush to secure a job since the redundancy payout would cover expenses for several weeks, I needed to at least get the wheels in motion. I smiled at the thought of wheels and the colourful hippy van. Travelling was a tempting idea, along with some gold prospecting.

Glancing over at the small table and chair set up for the phone, I noticed the directory resting beneath it. I hesitated, considering whether to look up Katrina's number—it felt like a potential trigger for trouble.

Before I could move, the phone rang, sending a jolt through my body. I rushed over, banging my shin on a nearby chair, and grabbed the receiver.

"Hello?" I said, remaining standing.

"Quinn? It's Rose."

My heart leaped into my throat. "Everything okay?"

"Yes, it's fine. Katrina wanted to say hi." I swallowed hard as Rose handed over the phone. A beat of silence. Then her voice. My legs felt weak, so I sat down.

"Hello, Quinn." The voice was scratchy and deep. She coughed. "It's been a long time."

"It has." I was nervous and unsure of what to say. "You live not far from me."

"That's nice to know." Her voice lacked emotion. "I'd love to see you, but it's not the right time at the moment. Rose was telling me all about you, so I thought I'd like to say hello. I have fond memories of you from our short time together. Is life being good to you?"

"Getting better."

"That's nice to hear. Childhood was such a good time. A pity we had to leave it behind."

Were our childhoods really a good time? "Yes, there are fun memories. Got a bit complicated at times, though."

"Yes, it did," she said, a hint of sadness creeping into her voice. "I'm sorry about the situation my family put you and your mum through. Hope you can forgive us."

"All good. How are you going?"

"I'm okay. Battling on." Her voice softened, but then a sense of urgency crept in. I could hear Rose's faint voice in the background, a hushed plea.

"I have to go now, Quinn," Katrina said abruptly. "Maybe we can speak again sometime. Look after Rose for me, and from what I hear, her darling sister. You take care."

The line went dead. I leaned forward and let out a deep sigh. A funny thought dropped into my head—could phone calls be traced? I laughed inwardly, realising it was just fear speaking. I'd watched too many spy movies.

I sat there, staring at the phone, replaying the brief conversation with Katrina. The reference to Jill brought a faint smile to my face, and I felt a flutter in my chest. I already missed her. Was she working today? I remembered the piece of paper in my pocket.

I pulled the paper from my pocket and dialled Jill's number. It rang for what felt like forever before I concluded there was no one at home. The urge to hear her voice was strong. My emotions were all over the place. I dialled again, but still no response.

Disappointment gnawed at me. My emotions seemed to be running the show—confusion, a yearning for connection. I was surprised by the strength of the emotions. Some chemicals in my brain had gone into overdrive and I was struggling to control them. The drink used to help with that. It allowed me to block out strong emotions instead of dealing with them. Well, those days were past, and I had to deal with whatever was going on in my head.

I phoned directory assistance to find the phone number for the Willward Hotel. I grabbed a pencil near the phone and wrote the number they gave me on the same piece of paper that held Jill's home number.

Still battling strong emotions, I called the number. It rang for a short time and then a sweet voice said, "Willward Hotel."

"Hello, Jill," I said. "You sound the same on the phone."

She giggled. "You're so sweet, but you shouldn't be calling me at work. I'll ring you back on my break. Maybe in an hour. So, behave till then."

"I will. Look forward to it." A sense of ease gradually settled over me. "Do you have my number there?"

"Yep, in my little black book."

She hung up, leaving me feeling lighter, though a small twinge of jealousy lingered at the mention of a black book. I leaned back in the chair, trying to recall if I'd given her my number. Maybe I had, maybe Rose had. It didn't really matter.

Talking to Jill, even briefly, had a calming effect. Emotions could be so hard to control at times. Connection to a like-minded person was so important. I thought of Katrina and her boyfriend, of the darkness that seemed to drive him. The rest of us, at least, were trying to keep our emotions in check. It wasn't easy, but we were trying.

That evening, Jill and I had a long, easy chat, and I was surprised by how much I'd missed her. We talked about her workday, and I filled her in on mine, though I avoided mentioning Katrina's situation. The conversation flowed easily, filled with laughter and a comfortable familiarity. She accepted, although jokingly, the invitation to join me on the trip in a hippy van.

After our chat, I felt a pleasant kind of tired. The brain must work overtime to process the emotions we throw at it. No wonder it leaves us so weary.

I thought of my drinking days. I'd smoked when I drank, and I'd gambled when I smoked and drank. All these things were connected, a destructive cycle fuelled by a desire for some feel-good chemical hits in the brain.

There were some feel-good chemicals kicking around in my head now, but they had nothing to do with my former habits. This was different. This was a connection, a spark in the midst of confusion. What did it mean, and where would it lead?

59 Back Under the Clocks

It was a lazy Sunday. The clear blue sky and gentle breeze coaxed me outside for a run—a habit I'd fallen out of but missed. After pounding the footpath for a few miles, I settled on the balcony, letting the afterglow wash over me. The familiar rush reminded me that exercise, too, could unleash feel-good chemicals. I was lost in thought, content, when the shrill ring of the phone jolted me back to reality. Phone calls, in my experience, rarely brought good news.

Returning inside, I answered with a wary, "Hello."

"Hi, Quinn, it's Rose."

I felt relief. "Hi, Rose, how's your Sunday?"

"Good," she said in a low voice. "Katrina was so happy to speak to you and that you've come back into the picture. She'd love to catch up with you one day."

"Yes, that would be nice," I replied cautiously. "Are things okay there?"

"Yes, at the moment they're sitting out in the backyard, getting some sunshine." Rose's voice dropped to a whisper. "Her boyfriend's being polite and nice for now."

It sounded like walking on thin ice.

"I'll be going home tomorrow," Rose said. "I'm not far from the railway station and there's a café there if you want to catch up before I leave. Have a cuppa or something."

"That's a great idea. I'm still in holiday mode, although I have a job interview tomorrow in the city."

"That's exciting." The line went quiet for a moment and then she continued, "You know, I wouldn't mind going into the city. This country girl likes the occasional trip to the big city." Her voice softened with a playful warmth.

"Let's accommodate that, then," I suggested. "My interview's at 10:30. I'll be getting a train into the city. Maybe we could meet under the clocks at Flinders Street Station at noon?"

"Under the clocks." She sounded unsure. "Is that easy to find?"

"Have you been to Flinders Street Station before?"

"I have, but only a few trips. Oh, I get it, on the stairs under all those timetable clocks."

"Yep, a famous meeting spot." I wondered if Jill had accompanied her sister on those trips. Thoughts of Jill came easily to mind.

"That should be good. There's a train leaving early afternoon so I can catch that back to Willward."

"Tell you what, seeing as I'm still on holiday, why don't I drive you home?"

"Nah, you don't have to do that."

"I'd like to."

"I get a feeling that there's an ulterior motive behind this offer," Rose said, a cheekiness in her tone.

"And what would that be?"

"You like the food at the Willward Hotel."

"Got it!" I laughed. "We can grab a bite to eat in the city, hop on a train back to my unit to get the car, and then I'll drive you back to Willward."

"That sounds really great, Quinn. You don't have to, but I do appreciate you doing it."

"Not a problem. I look forward to it," I said truthfully. "All I ask is, don't let the Willward Hotel know I'm coming."

"Oh yes, I understand. Big surprise."

"See ya under the clocks tomorrow."

***

It had been a while since I'd worn anything but jeans and a T-shirt. Today, the sensation of an ironed, button-down shirt felt foreign under the unfamiliar weight of a suit jacket—anything but my trusty denim jacket. The tie could wait until closer to the interview.

The phone had rung when I'd closed the door to head to the station. In my panic to answer, I'd fumbled and dropped my keys. By the time I got back through the door, the ringing had stopped.

Who could that have been? I had no time to ponder as I needed to get to the station. Besides, if it was important, they'd call again, hopefully when I was home. But the missed call gnawed at me. It could have been important. It could have been Jill. I could see why answering machines were growing in popularity.

With the rhythmic rattle of the train calming my nerves, I glanced around the mostly empty carriage. A young boy knelt on the seat next to his mum, his face pressed against the train window, pointing. "Look, Mum! The MCG!"

I followed his gaze and saw the iconic Melbourne Cricket Ground shrink into the distance. A wave of nostalgia washed over me. I'd been there many times myself, and grand finals provided the fondest memories. A hundred thousand people screaming, roaring as one with the first bounce of the ball. A sensory overload I wasn't sure I could handle anymore.

The sight of the young boy, now engrossed in a comic book, intensified the memories. I recalled the train trips with Mum, the ones to Willward seeming the longest. Although, there was that one interstate trip to Sydney on the Southern Aurora, an adventure that felt like it stretched on for days.

More and more rail tracks converged as we approached Flinders Street Station, the steel lines multiplying and interweaving like tributaries joining a mighty river. I hadn't set foot in Flinders Street Station in years. Back then, 'under the clocks' was a gateway of potential adventures, including meeting Jimmy and his mates and that weird memory of Katrina and her mum walking down busy Flinders Street—me tailing them like Sherlock Holmes. I smiled at the recollection.

This train trip had become quite sentimental, dredging up nostalgic memories from my younger days.

I stepped off the train, walked out of the station, adjusting to the sudden rush of noise that hit my senses. Standing under the clocks, I tried to remember the last time I'd been here. It must have been a few years ago—work had kept me mostly confined to the suburbs. I gazed up at the clocks. With time to kill, I decided to head towards my appointment, planning to browse a few shops and soak in the city's vibrant atmosphere.

As I strolled down Swanston Street, a brightly lit newsagency caught my eye. Seeking some mindless distraction, I wandered in and went searching for the comic section. The encounter with the boy on the train had rekindled my interest in comics, making me curious about what kids read these days.

A prickling sensation of being watched made me pause. Glancing around, I spotted a man behind the counter watching me. He was roughly my age but with a demeanour more suited to the underworld. I quickly averted my gaze to the magazines, noticing the *MAD* magazines on the rack. I'd read a few in the past, enjoying their crazy humour. However, the uneasy feeling persisted as I sensed the man's eyes still on me, sending a shiver down my spine.

Turning my attention back to the rack, I noticed *Playboy* magazines and others with adult content sealed in plastic. I felt oddly uncomfortable, as if I were being judged. The man's continued scrutiny only heightened my unease. Suddenly, he stepped out from behind the counter and strode towards me, triggering my flight instinct. But before I could react, a booming voice shattered the tense silence.

"Getcha 'erald!" he bellowed, his voice surprisingly jovial and familiar.

My senses went into overdrive. The voice and the words stirred up memories.

"Jimmy?" I ventured hesitantly, battling disbelief.

A wide grin split the man's face, crinkling the corners of his eyes. "You got it, Quinn!" He swept me into a crushing hug. "Knew our paths would cross again."

"How…how did you know that?" I asked, bewildered.

He tapped his chest. "Brotherly love. We connected back in the past. We had a bond. I can't explain. But look at you…you're looking great."

Fragmented memories of Jimmy dropped into my mind, and those words he'd yelled were well-etched in the memory banks.

"I remember your dimpled chin and high forehead. I'm a man who remembers features, but those clothes you're wearing threw me off a bit," he said with a warm smile. "My scar might throw you off, but otherwise, I'm still the good paperboy from the past." He turned to look back at the counter where a few people were lining up. "Look, I have to go serve those people. Can you hang around?"

I dreaded to think about where Jimmy had gotten that scar. "I've got an interview at 10:30, but after that I could drop back before I meet someone at noon."

"You do that. We can reminisce when we catch up. Be good to chat. Doesn't sound like you'll have much time, but we'll work something out."

I had always hoped to reestablish contact with Jimmy; I'd just never thought it would happen like this. I remembered him as a streetwise kid, sharp and a bit untouchable. Now, he looked like a man who had carried those same instincts into adulthood. I wondered what that entailed.

60 The Paper Man

I gazed up at the city skyline, towering buildings obscuring the sunlight and casting long shadows over the bustling streets. Memories of my earlier explorations of the city, back when we stayed at the People's Palace, filled my mind. These skyscrapers dwarfed the modest structures of the Palace days—a jungle of concrete, glass, and steel, pulsating with life.

My interview was on the 37th floor of one of these modern giants. The role of elevators in urban development couldn't be overstated; there was no way I'd be climbing thirty-seven flights of stairs. With a mix of nervousness and determination, I pressed the button marked 37.

As I approached the receptionist's desk, a warm smile greeted me. "Hello, sir, how may I help you?"

"Hi, my name's Quinn Davies, and I've an interview at 10:30."

She looked down at her desk and then returned her gaze to me, a sombre expression crossing her face. "I'm so sorry, Mr Davies, but we had to reschedule your interview. The office has been hit by a nasty bug, and several of our staff are off sick, including members of the interview team. We tried to call but got no answer. We tried several times."

So, that was the missed call. I nodded, forcing a reflexive smile, though I was disappointed.

"We have you scheduled for the same time next week. Is that okay?"

I had plenty of free time. "That should be fine. Glad you're okay."

"I'm out here on my own little island." She chuckled. "I just run for it when I see anyone coming."

She had the right personality for her job. "Okay then, I'll be off. See you next week."

"Thanks for your understanding," she said sincerely.

I nodded, smiling before making my way back to the elevator lobby. As I waited for the elevator, a curious sensation crept over me. Maybe this entire ordeal was part of a mysterious plan to bring me to the city. I chuckled at the absurd thought, but the feeling lingered.

Back out in the busy street, earlier than I expected, I decided to see if Jimmy was free. A tram rattled past, its clattering wheels blending into the city's rhythm. Standing on the bustling street, I peered into the newsagency and Jimmy caught sight of me, exchanged a few words with a girl behind the counter, and made his way out to meet me.

"That was quick. One look at you and they offered you the job?" he teased.

I shook my head. "Nope, interview got rescheduled. People are sick."

Jimmy nodded knowingly. "Yeah, those tall buildings are breeding grounds for germs." He gestured to a café next door. "You have to try the best coffee in Melbourne." Wrapping a friendly arm around my shoulders, he led the way.

"G'day, Jimmy," voices called out from various corners of the café—coffee makers, cup washers, and waiters acknowledging his presence.

Jimmy gave my shoulder a friendly squeeze. "Hello, everyone. Meet my good friend, Quinn."

A flush of warmth spread across my cheeks as some customers looked up, their curiosity piqued by Jimmy's introduction. The café workers responded with smiles and nods.

Jimmy guided me to a booth. I noticed a miniature jukebox centred and attached to the wall at the table. All the tables had them. I had fond memories of these relics from the past.

Jimmy motioned for me to sit down while he wandered over to the counter, bypassing it entirely and opting instead to embrace the person behind it—a man with the widest moustache I'd ever seen.

Across the room, a man lit a cigarette. He placed his lighter on top of a packet of Winfield Reds. Memories of cigarette ads flashed through my mind—tough, sophisticated men, rugged and burly, selling an image of strength. It was all part of the allure, that concept of toughness that had ensnared me too. A wry laugh bubbled up inside me.

I flicked through the jukebox, noting lots of rock and roll classics—Elvis, the Beatles. The wall-mounted mini jukeboxes were connected to a main system. I remembered how the songs played in the order they were selected—sometimes, you'd finish your meal before hearing your chosen song.

"You want to play some music?" Jimmy asked, returning.

"No need. I'm sure the airwaves will continue to be filled with popular tunes selected by others."

"Sounds like you've done this before."

"A couple of times. It gives the cafés a great feel, a uniqueness."

Jimmy settled into his seat, lighting a cigarette. "You want one?"

"Nah, gave it up a while back."

He gave me a respectful nod. "Well done." Taking a drag, he exhaled slowly. "So, tell me what you've been up to for the last…what is it, fifteen years?"

I smiled. "Something like that—maybe closer to seventeen years." It was a daunting question, and I wasn't sure where to start. "We met just before I moved to a small country town called Edithburra. I was only there a short time and had a few good years after I left, but things went downhill fast once I discovered alcohol."

"Sounds like a bit of a rough ride."

"It was. I felt like a pinball bouncing from side to side, completely controlled by the drink. But I'm happy to say I'm on a better path now."

"I understand," Jimmy said. "I think you met some of my friends back then—Ginger, Jack, and Eric. We're still good mates, except Ginger's no longer with us. Grog got the best of him and he's dead now. At the time we knew you, the boys were running away from their abusive and drunk dads. Escaping to the city. My dad was okay, I just wanted to make money."

"I've learned a lot about dads over the years."

"Imagine you have," Jimmy agreed. "But, you're lucky you gave up the grog, Quinn. It can do nasty things to people, completely screw up their lives."

I nodded at Jimmy. He seemed tough, yet beneath his exterior, I sensed gentleness. Still, I felt the need to stay on his good side.

"Me? I'm lucky, not the addictive type," Jimmy remarked, glancing at his cigarette before laughing and tapping his chest. "Ah, I'm a hypocrite."

I smiled at his self-awareness.

"He's weak," the moustached man announced, setting coffee cups down in front of us. "He's been telling me for years that he's going to give up those cancer sticks." He shot Jimmy a playful, scolding glance before breaking into a smile.

Jimmy looked up at the man. "He's a mad Italian but he makes the best coffee and cake."

"Be back in a sec. I'll get the cakes." The Italian ducked back to the kitchen, then returned and placed plates of cake next to our coffees. "Enjoy," he said with a wink, nodding towards Jimmy. "Jimmy's okay." He wandered off.

"It's good to see you, Quinn," Jimmy said warmly, taking a bite of his cake. "Hmm. Eat," he encouraged, gesturing towards my plate.

The cake was delicious and we chatted like old friends as time slipped away unnoticed. But as I glanced at the clock on the wall, a sense of urgency crept over me.

"Jimmy, I'm meeting someone at midday, so I'll have to go soon," I explained.

"Yep, so ya said. Who you meeting?"

"A friend I made from my days at Edithburra."

"That's sweet. So, you've got some old friends, too. Bring him back here for lunch."

"It's a 'she'," I corrected with a smile.

"Bring your girlfriend back here, then."

"Not my girlfriend, just a friend."

"Still, you bring…what's her name?" Jimmy asked.

"Rose."

"You bring Rose back here for lunch."

Before I could protest, Jimmy yelled out to the mad Italian behind the counter. "My mate Quinn and his friend are coming back for lunch. Just after twelve. Could you reserve a table?"

Our Italian friend smiled and nodded.

I finished up the last bite of cake and washed it down with the remainder of my coffee. "All very nice," I commented.

"You wait until lunch. Best sandwiches, and if you're really hungry, a hamburger or a mixed grill." Jimmy's enthusiasm was infectious.

I mentioned that I needed to go and we both stood.

"Quinn, call me superstitious, but us meeting again after such a long time…I think the gods are at work," Jimmy mused. "I might join you for lunch…if that's okay."

"That'll be good. Give Rose a feel for the Melbourne City culture. She'd like that."

As I left, I wondered which gods Jimmy was referring to. I had always believed there was only one.

61 Welcome to the Underworld

Rose stood out from the crowd, wrapped in a black coat, her head turning from side to side as she scanned her surroundings. Her posture was stiff, conveying a sense of being out of place. A travel bag sat at her side, and although some men stood close by, gawking at her, she probably found comfort in the police officer stationed at the bottom of the steps.

Across the road, I waited for the traffic light to change. Though her eyes looked in my direction a couple of times, my waving failed to catch her attention.

It wasn't until I was practically within arm's reach that she finally noticed me, her expression shifting to shock. "You scrub up nicely."

"Thanks, Rose, I'll take that as a compliment." I flashed a mischievous grin.

"It was." She shivered slightly, pulling the coat tighter around her. "I'm already missing the sun. Katrina told me to keep the coat handy, saying the city was like stepping into a dark forest."

"That's a good description," I agreed. A sudden coldness crept over me. Talking about missing sunlight seemed to heighten my senses.

"How did the interview go?"

"Cancelled. The interviewers were sick, but it's okay, it's been rescheduled for next week." I glanced over at the crossing. There was no need to rush off yet. "Here's some nostalgia for you. I lived in the city for a few weeks in the 1960s, met a few boys here under the clocks. Paperboys who screamed out '*Getcha 'erald!*' continually."

"I think I remember hearing that chant," Rose said.

"Well, I sort of connected with one of them. His name was Jimmy. You know how sometimes you just connect with people?"

"I know what you mean. I've got that connection with Katrina."

"Yeah, I sense that. Well, you wouldn't believe this. I just bumped into Jimmy again after seventeen years and had coffee with him."

Rose's eyes widened. "Wow, that's crazy."

"It is, but I suppose it's realistic when you think about it. He runs a newspaper shop now."

Rose smiled. "That makes perfect sense."

"I think he has a bit of a profile. You know, working the streets of Melbourne all his life, one can't help but be well-known."

"Is he a gangster?" Rose asked, a hint of worry in her tone.

I laughed. "Close. But you might meet him because we have a table reserved at his friend's café for lunch." The traffic lights were about to change. "Let's fly."

Rose and I stayed close as we wove through the thick throng of pedestrians crossing the road.

"So many people," Rose mumbled as we crossed the road. "I don't think I'd ever get used to this."

"It takes some adjusting." I called out, sidestepping a large man.

We battled on and soon entered the café. I spotted Jimmy leaning on the counter, engaged in conversation with the Italian proprietor. They turned to us as we approached.

"Ah, Quinn and Rose," Jimmy greeted us warmly, extending his arms in welcome. He took Rose's hand and gently kissed the back of it, causing her cheeks to flush.

Rose chuckled. "That had a *Godfather* feel about it."

Jimmy grinned. "I think it's a respectful way for a gentleman to greet a lady. Don't you agree, Quinn?"

Caught off guard, I scrambled for a response.

Jimmy looked at Rose. "Looks like we may have to teach Quinn how to respect a woman, then?" he teased.

"No, he's okay. He respects us ladies, don't you, Quinn?"

Clearing my throat, I affirmed, "I do indeed."

"Let's sit," Jimmy suggested, gesturing to a reserved booth. "You okay with coffee, Rose? Just for starters, to get settled."

Rose nodded and Jimmy relayed a silent message to his Italian friend behind the counter.

As we settled in our seats, a group of burly men in dark suits entered the café. They paused by our booth, exchanging handshakes with Jimmy before disappearing through a door at the rear.

"This is real *Godfather* stuff," Rose whispered.

Jimmy grinned. "Just the Italian culture. There's a gambling den out the back. But shhh, I didn't tell you that, okay?"

Rose laughed. "This is fun."

Jimmy raised an eyebrow. "Quinn, is this the girl from the country you followed down busy Flinders Street many years ago?" A mischievous glint lit his eye. "I remembered thinking at the time it all felt very romantic."

"What a memory you have, Jimmy. Anyway, I was only ten at the time and it was another girl I was chasing after."

"It's called puppy love," Rose advised.

"So, did you ever connect with her?" Jimmy asked. "And none of this 'I was only ten' stuff. My missus and I met when we were in kindergarten."

"That's so sweet," Rose said.

"I don't know when to believe this guy, Rose," I joked, finding Jimmy's antics endearing.

"I believe him," Rose said. "The country girl you're referring to is Katrina, Katrina Warhurst, and she's settled in a suburb close to the city."

I felt a tinge of discomfort at the mention of Katrina's surname.

"Really?" Jimmy was excited. "Well, there ya go, Quinn. Go get her."

"She's taken," Rose said, putting a dampener on Jimmy's enthusiasm.

"Well, give me the details and I'll remove the obstacle for you."

I had no doubt he would.

"He's not an obstacle," Rose cut in. "Just some control freak. Maybe we should loop him in on the details, Quinn."

Rose had slipped into serious mode.

"I know I'm being a bit intense," Rose continued. "I've just been staying with her for a few days, and I'm feeling a bit tightly wound."

The Italian, who had just arrived with a tray of coffees, raised his bushy eyebrows. "Whoa, there!" he boomed. "Need something stronger than coffee?"

Rose chuckled. "No, I'm fine, but thank you for the offer."

After setting down the coffee cups, the Italian gestured to the menus. "Let me know when you're ready to order."

Jimmy nodded his thanks to his Italian friend before turning back to Rose. "Sorry to hear that, Rose. Did her boyfriend come and visit while you were there?"

"Not exactly, they live together," Rose said.

Jimmy shook his head. "So, they're living a life of sin—living together but not married. Not good for a woman." He smiled. "I'm old school. There's a lot of merit in that way of thinking. We men need to protect our wives and children. I'm sensing that Katrina needs some help."

Jimmy's old way of thinking was certainly under challenge. There was a real push to buck the trend by living together before marriage. I had given little thought to it, but now wondered if it was contributing to the breakdown of the family unit. Rose's voice brought me back.

"She does. Her boyfriend isn't a very nice person," Rose said.

"Maybe you can go deal with it, Quinn," Jimmy suggested.

"No, he couldn't do that, Jimmy," Rose countered. "It would be worse for Katrina."

"What? Does her boyfriend hurt her?" Jimmy asked.

"Afraid so."

"Do you want to tell me his name?"

"His name is Zac Hike," Rose blurted before I could say anything. I glanced at Rose, uncertain if she should have disclosed that information.

Jimmy noticed my reaction. "No worries, Quinn. I promise no harm will come to your friend."

With a notebook and pen in hand, Jimmy confirmed, "Katrina Warhurst and Zac Hike, that correct?"

Rose nodded.

Jimmy was good with names. Strangely, a sense of peace settled over me. Was this part of the mysterious plan that Jimmy had mentioned?

"I'll have some friends look into it for you. Might have a chat with this Zac person. You don't treat ladies the way it sounds like he's treating Katrina."

Rose sat up straight, paling. "Oh dear, I've said too much. Please forget those names. It will only result in harm coming to Katrina."

Jimmy placed his hand on Rose's. "Believe me, Rose, no harm will come to Katrina."

"But I don't want you to do bad things to Zac," Rose protested, her worry evident.

Jimmy patted her hand gently. "Rose, we're not thugs. We'll just have a word to him about how a woman should be treated. We'll use what we call a standover tactic. This man will not harm Katrina anymore."

I detected contradiction in those words and felt uneasy about Jimmy's suggested method. I thought of Katrina's dad and how much he would want to protect his daughter. Sometimes wrong actions could be justified. As my mum would say, the Lord moves in mysterious ways.

Jimmy continued, "We also have some high-ranking police officers who enjoy the food here—we help each other out sometimes when they're short on resources. We might also have a word with them. Katrina is safe, believe me."

I believed Jimmy.

62 Thoughts of Kidnapping

"Trains have a way of drawing you into their world. The rhythm and changing scenery are so soothing," I remarked to Rose as we sat in comfortable silence, gazing out the window. The train made stops at regular intervals, passengers boarding and disembarking. What awaited them at their destination?

I reflected on our recent encounter with the underworld. There was a saying that life resembled a train journey—people came and went, in and out of your life. Some stayed longer than others, and there were some you wished you'd never encountered. Others just jumped on when needed and jumped off when their job was done. Jimmy was the intermittent traveller.

I informed Rose our stop was next. She nodded.

"It's a five-minute walk to my unit. We can refresh ourselves, then set out."

"I'm happy to get the train home, Quinn."

"I know you are—"

"But I think the car trip will be quicker and we can chat about life and the underworld," she joked.

"Looking forward to that chat." That world intrigued me.

***

The car wove deftly through the city streets, and I managed to have us on the outskirts before the peak hour crush descended. Civilisation thinned out, replaced by open fields and storehouses bathed in a glorious sunset. Stealing a glance at Rose, I saw the tension drain from her shoulders. A faint smile played on her lips.

"Life, hey?" I mused, pushing back into my seat and sighing. "So many bends and twists, not a straight path like the road ahead."

Rose nodded, her expression troubled. "Just when I thought I'd seen it all."

"You referring to Jimmy?"

"Yes and no," she replied. "Thinking more of Katrina. Sadly, even if your friend Jimmy and his connections were able to do anything, I'm not sure Katrina would benefit."

"Why's that?" I pressed, genuinely wanting to understand.

"She would soon get into another relationship with the same type. She's in a pattern, a cycle that's hard to break free from."

A sudden spike of frustration hit me, quickly followed by a wave of shame. "I should know better," I said, my voice barely above a whisper. "I've been there myself. It's never as simple as just walking away, is it? Something has a grip on you. The fear, the hope that things will change, the manipulation...it's all so complex."

"Yes, it's complex," Rose said gently. "You're right, there are many reasons why someone might stay in an abusive relationship. Fear, manipulation, a twisted sense of hope…sometimes it feels safer to stay with the devil you know."

"But the pain…."

"Normally, people avoid pain," Rose stated. "But Katrina's situation is complex. Her upbringing likely shaped her desire to help others, but it's also left her vulnerable. She attracts men who exploit her kindness, and once they do, their controlling behaviour isolates her. Fear and financial insecurity trap her in a harmful cycle."

"So, in some ways, she's sacrificing her own life for others."

"Self-sacrifice can be noble," Rose said. "But Katrina is on the path to destruction. She's desperately low on self-esteem and hesitant to reach out for help. It's a perfect storm."

"Hmm, complex and sad," I murmured, staring ahead at the long stretch of road. We had passed a few hitch-hikers, more common on the outskirts of towns.

A weary-looking hitch-hiker appeared up ahead. I was tempted to slow and offer them a lift, but Jill's words echoed in my mind—a firm instruction not to pick up any hitch-hikers with Rose in the car. That brought a warm smile to my lips. The thought of seeing Jill again, with her infectious laugh and bright spirit, was a welcome counterpoint to the heaviness of our conversation about Katrina. But the conversation continued.

"She needs to escape not only from him but from her toxic environment," Rose explained. "The circle of people that surround them are like-minded people."

I gave Rose a quick glance, then focused back on the road. "But didn't you say earlier that she'd just go right back? That abusers are everywhere, not just in Katrina's circle?"

Rose sighed, shifting in her seat. "You're right. It's not as simple as just leaving. The problem is deeper than just her current situation or circle. It's about breaking the cycle, changing patterns...." Rose's voice trailed off, and I detected frustration and sadness.

I nodded slowly, processing the information as I drove. The hum of the car engine filled the silence between us.

"We need to get her back to Edithburra," I blurted out.

"You know, Quinn," Rose replied with a contemplative sigh, "I think you're right, but how we make that happen, I've no idea."

"Maybe kidnap her?" I joked.

Rose's eyes widened, then a flicker of a smile played on her lips. "I know that was said in jest, but maybe that's what we need to do. Maybe not kidnap her, exactly, but if circumstances prevail, bring her back somehow."

The muscles in my forehead tightened. "On reflection, Edithburra holds bad memories that may open old wounds for her."

"Yes, but also good ones," Rose said, "And I think dealing with those memories, both good and bad, might be part of the healing process." She paused. "But there's no way she would even consider coming back or go anywhere else if her partner's still around."

"Well, let's hope Jimmy can intervene somehow."

"And in a nice way."

I laughed.

"What are you laughing at?"

"Just that we don't have the right temperament to be part of the underworld."

She glanced at me. "Maybe we've never really been tested."

A thoughtful silence settled between us. My thoughts drifted back to the life-train analogy. Life, unlike a train journey, was far more complex and unpredictable, the tracks not predetermined. We could change directions, many times. A train took us to a predetermined destination. Life was different, though. We needed to work out what our destination was, and that involved searching for meaning. Which was what I was doing.

Rose interrupted my thoughts. "Yes, we need to get Katrina home."

63 Checking on Mum

Jill's eyes lit up from behind the bar as we walked in. She set a tea towel down and said something to her coworker, who nodded. Stepping out from behind the counter, she walked over and hugged Rose and then turned to me.

"I missed you, Quinn. You back for another tour?" She pulled me into the warmest hug. I felt so comfortable and connected to Jill, like I'd never left.

But then responsibilities kicked in. "I'd love to go for another tour, but I need to be back home tomorrow to catch up with Mum."

She gave me the saddest look, but before I could reconsider, she said, "Mums are important. I love a man who cares for his mum."

I really wanted to stay here.

"Sis, Mum's coming into Willward tomorrow," Jill said. "She suggested you stay the night here, and she'll pick you up in the morning.'

"Sounds fine to me. I can bring you up-to-date on Katrina."

"I'd like that."

Jill looked towards a vacant table. "You want some food?"

Rose looked at me. "I think our lunch with the underworld has kept the hunger pains at bay.'

Jill looked confused.

"I'll tell you all about it later," I said. "What time do you finish?"

"Thirty minutes."

We waited, then gave Jill a lift home.

Jill and I sat on her comfy couch and spoke for hours. Rose left the conversation early, claiming fatigue. I suspect she just wanted to give us some privacy.

***

After returning from Willward in the early morning hours of Tuesday, I slept in. In the afternoon, I stopped by my mum's unit with a big surprise in tow. Unfortunately, she didn't answer her door. Standing on spare paver bricks, I peered through the window. Her bedroom door was slightly ajar and I could see her lying on her bed. It was past lunchtime, so she was either unwell or taking a nap. Usually, she reserved the latter for her favourite lounge chair. Nap time had increased since she gave up her job some weeks back.

My sister had called over the weekend, expressing concern about Mum. I'd been harbouring similar worries lately but had pushed them aside, not wanting to confront the possibility that Mum's health might be declining.

I'd been making an effort to see her weekly, late morning, sometimes more frequently when she had trouble with the TV. Remote controls could be evil things for the elderly.

Going around to the back porch, I found everything locked up. However, I noticed a large crack in the bottom corner of one window. I had no idea what could've caused that, but it worried me.

I headed to the centre management unit to express my concerns. They promptly came and opened Mum's unit, then waited while I checked on Mum. She woke up looking disoriented but seemed okay. Satisfied, I gave the person at the door a nod and they wandered off.

"Oh, Quinn." Mum looked confused as she sat up against the bed-head. "Why are you here? Shouldn't you be home in bed?"

I offered her a comforting smile. "No, Mum, it's early afternoon. You must have had a long sleep-in."

Her bedroom carried a pungent smell and I glanced up at the drawn curtains, wondering when the window had last been opened.

As Mum pushed the blankets off, she mentioned needing to use the toilet. The scent of body odour lingered in the air as she placed her feet on the floor and forced a smile. I nodded and moved to the living room. As I passed by her wardrobe, a mothball-like aroma escaped through a slightly ajar door.

I tried not to feel pity. It was difficult watching Mum age. I had briefly discussed this with Lee. She'd advised me to reframe it as empathy, not pity—to appreciate who she was and try to see past Mum's aging exterior.

My headspace had improved significantly since I'd stopped drinking. It felt as if wisdom was emerging from the darkness of my past, leading me to grasp the importance of respecting and being there for my mum. Some people distanced themselves from their parents once those parents settled in nursing homes or similar facilities, but I knew I had to be present, even when it was emotionally challenging.

The toilet flushed, and Mum emerged wrapped in her dressing gown. "You wanna make me a cup of tea, Harold?" she asked.

Hearing Dad's name, a lump formed in my throat. Her eyes were glassy and distant. Mum had never asked me to make her tea before, but I had seen her do it often enough in her unit, so I knew where everything was.

I guided her outside and settled her into the small outdoor setting with her cup of tea, perfectly positioned to catch the afternoon sun. She sighed contentedly as she basked in the warmth. "Ah, that will get the chill out of the old bones."

The phone rang and I told Mum I'd go in and answer it.

"Glad you're there, Quinn. Is she okay?" It was my sister.

I glanced out at Mum, who was sipping her tea and chatting to a sparrow that had appeared.

"Not sure. She was still in bed when I arrived here. She seems a bit muddled," I replied.

"She's had a urinary tract infection; it can play tricks on the mind. The doctor has her on antibiotics. She should be okay in a day or so."

"I've got her outside in the sun drinking a cup of tea. Did you want to talk to her?"

"No need, you've given me the update. Tell her I called. You'd best get back to her, so she doesn't get muddled about the phone call. See ya, love," she said before hanging up.

I returned to Mum, who was now engaging in conversation with a man. He looked like a gardener, and he seemed amused.

"Hi there," he said to me. "I'm the maintenance man. I wanted to check out the broken window that was reported." He headed over to the window.

"I've seen him before. He's a flasher," Mum remarked, pointing towards my groin. "A flasher," she repeated, gesturing towards the man. "I told him he better not flash me, or I'll deck him."

I chuckled, imagining that was what the man had found amusing. But I couldn't help wondering if Mum had summoned a memory from the past.

"I'd say a stone shot up from a mower and cracked the glass," said the man. "I'll get it fixed."

"Thanks for that." I lowered my voice. "Hope my mum didn't say anything to offend you."

"Nah, they're all lovely ladies around here. Keep me amused and on my toes." He winked and left.

"Good riddance," Mum remarked. "He's gone."

I had Mum's surprise in the small matchbox in my pocket. I went to take it out but hesitated. In Mum's current state of mind, she might not comprehend what it was. I'd wait until this infection passed.

Mum looked at me and smiled. "I remember now, you went chasing ghosts. How was the trip?"

"It was good, Mum." Any further details would likely be lost on her at the moment. But there was one thing I was curious about. "Do you have faith, Mum?"

She smiled, as if she'd anticipated the question. "I do, and I'm looking forward to reuniting with my loved ones when this train journey's over."

I chuckled inwardly at the mention of the train. "Faith seems so important. On my trip, someone said that faith is more important than gold."

"Did a ghost tell you that?"

"No, just a wise old man." Oh, how things had changed. Mum would be shocked to know the identity of that wise old man.

Mum smiled. "That's nice, but I do like gold. Did you find yourself a nice wee lassie up there in those hills?"

"Maybe," I replied, thinking of Jill. She was part of the reason for my delayed visit to Mum. I hadn't gotten home from Willward until after three in the morning.

"Well, it's about time. I look forward to the wedding." Mum's gaze drifted past me to something unseen. "Quinn, before you go, could you get rid of the cat from my bedroom? It climbs up the walls and sits on top of my wardrobe. Its yellow eyes look down at me during the night. I don't like it."

Mum didn't have a cat and I doubted she was referring to a stray. How could an infection cause such strange hallucinations? I wouldn't be surprised if Mum had seen some ghosts in her current state.

I made a mental note to return her gold nugget to her when her mind was sound. It would mean more to her then.

***

I woke Wednesday morning with Jill on my mind. Such thoughts had been constant lately. But there was another thought vying for space in my head: Mum's gold nugget.

There was an urgency to take it to Mum. A sense of impending loss gnawed at me, a fear of losing her, of time slipping away. I needed to get the nugget to her—now.

It was just after ten when I pulled into the unit complex car park. I made my way to Mum's unit. As I got closer, I could hear her TV blaring. Good, she was up and about.

She was out by the front door, watering the plants. When she saw me, she jumped, her hand flying to her chest, eyes wide with surprise.

"Thought you were a ghost," she said with a smile. "What brings you back? I could've sworn you were here just yesterday."

"I was. You feeling better?'

She nodded. "Much better. Think I've shaken off that little infection. Come inside—it's a bit chilly out here."

I followed her in. "TV a bit loud?"

"Huh?"

I wasn't sure if she was joking or not, but she turned it down.

She sat in her favourite chair, a cup resting on the table beside it. She picked it up and had a sip. "Still warm," she said, then took another sip.

"Sorry, I didn't mean to scare you out there."

"Nah, I was just pretending. So why the visit? You a bringer of good news?"

"Actually I am."

Her eyebrows shot up. "You getting married?"

I laughed. "Not yet, Mum."

"Must be something to do with your trip, then. Chasing ghosts. Did you encounter one who told you good things?"

I was starting to wonder if Mum had fully recovered. "Country towns have real ghosts," I said, half joking. "They live in the old hotels."

"I thought so, but I think it has something to do with the spirits consumed."

I gave a gentle laugh and reached into my pocket. "Do you remember much about Edithburra?"

Mum's chest rose, and her eyes softened. "I try to remember the good things. The neighbour was a good man. The countryside was lovely. Big trees. Lots of birds."

"I visited the farm." It felt blunt, but I needed to get it out.

Mum was silent.

"I went and saw Mr Warhurst."

She looked at her cup. "Was that the farm owner? Why would you do that? He wasn't a very nice man."

"Just chasing ghosts, Mum. He gave me something." I pulled the box out of my pocket.

"A box of matches?"

"No, Mum, Mr Warhurst was full of remorse and handed me this."

I pushed the matchbox open, revealing what was inside, and showed it to her.

She let out a gasp. "Oh, Quinn."

Spring 1981
Melbourne

My dearest Martha,

This letter took a long time to write, since arthritis is getting worse in my hand. But I plug away as I do with my crocheting, hoping that movement will help.

I write this letter full of joy. Recently, I had to deal with a urinary tract infection—the delights of old age. My, they're not pleasant. Besides wanting to wee all the time and fever and chills, the confusion and funny thoughts in my head worried me. But away from these negative things and back to the joy bit.

My boy Quinn came to visit me. He came last week but I think it was a confusing time for us both. Well, he has returned from chasing ghosts and they're real, he advised me, especially in the old hotels. He was told stories. I can't help but wonder if what they serve behind the bar might have something to do with the tales.

But let me cut to the chase. The boy found my nugget, the nugget that is so dear to me. He got it back, I don't fully understand how, but he said that evil man was so sorry for the pain he had caused and he handed it back to Quinn. Can you believe that? The Lord indeed works in mysterious ways.

Quinn spoke of ghosts jokingly, but sometimes I think his dad comes and sits on my bed. I feel a pressure on the mattress next to me. Oh, how I miss Harold, more so as the years go by. Can't hold back the feelings anymore.

Between you and me, besides the UTI, I've been having some health issues of late. I can see my daughter knows and around her, I try and bluff my way through things.

I sometimes drift in and out of reality and am getting very forgetful; the UTI just magnified the struggle. Sometimes I wonder if Quinn really did bring back the gold. He did, for I hold it in my hand. I sometimes think of the old man's nugget. He had one too, and it was very dear to him. I thought I knew who had it, but now I'm not sure. Maybe Quinn will find that nugget as well.

But back to my health issues, they're now talking of a nursing home. To be honest, I'm beyond fighting. I'll go to please them for I sense my time is drawing near. It may take time to get it organised. I think I would be a low priority unless these UTIs come back to visit.

My wee boy seems to have even more of a spring in his step now, if that was possible. I think he has found a lassie, and that, added to the return of the gold nugget, fills my heart with joy.

Will keep you posted.

All my love,

Elizabeth

64 Planning the Getaway

Pockets of warm days had been appearing as spring settled in. I'd gone to the rescheduled interview, but I think the panel sensed my lack of enthusiasm about jumping back into the workforce, so no job offer came. I caught up with Jimmy again and spent an afternoon with his family. His twin boys enjoyed kicking a football around.

Jill and I were cruising along, our relationship slowly taking root, nourished by frequent phone calls. We chatted most nights, so when my phone rang, I naturally assumed it was her. But this night, to my surprise, an unfamiliar voice came through the receiver.

"Quinn?" Katrina asked.

"Hey, Katrina." A lump formed in my throat as I anticipated the reason for the call. "How are you?"

"I'm okay, getting better, thanks," she said, her voice strained. "Rose mentioned to me recently that you wanted to kidnap me. That's so sweet. When are you going to do this?" Her tone shifted, a note of seriousness creeping in.

I chuckled. "Well, that was supposed to be a secret mission. She wasn't meant to tell you. The person who is to be kidnapped shouldn't know they're going to be kidnapped."

She snickered. “I’ll keep that in mind for next time.” Her tone remained serious. “On a more sombre note, not long after Rose visited, my boyfriend vanished. I’m losing track of time, but I think it’s been more than a week.”

I felt a chill. It wasn’t long after our chat with Jimmy, too. Maybe a week or so. I had mixed feelings—concern for Katrina, but also a nagging suspicion about the timing.

Katrina’s voice quavered as she continued. “I’ve tried to find him but can’t. I’ve thought of going to the police, but I don’t know what to do.”

I felt a surge of concern. “That doesn’t sound good, Katrina. How are you holding up?”

“Not too good,” she admitted. “A voice in my head keeps telling me to run, but I don’t know where to go. I feel so lost.”

I didn’t know how to respond.

Katrina continued, “But you coming into the picture has given me hope, Quinn. I’ve had no one to turn to. Could you help me escape the mess I’ve gotten myself into?” Her tone softened. “Rose mentioned a return to Edithburra. Do you think I could manage that?”

I hesitated, then reluctantly replied, “I’ve seen your dad.” Instantly, I regretted the mention.

Katrina burst into tears. Annoyed with myself for causing her more distress, I waited for the sobs to subside.

Once she was calm, she asked, “How is he?”

“He’s a changed man. I know what you must have gone through with him. Mum and I only experienced a small snippet of it, but it was enough to understand what you went through. Visiting was difficult, but strangely, it brought a sense of healing—for both of us.”

"I understand," Katrina said, her voice steadier now. "Unforgiveness can have a powerful grip on you. I've been grappling with that myself. I find it so hard to let go."

"Your dad…well, he was affected by the war and alcohol. You don't know the man he is now after being set free from that bondage."

"Please, Quinn, let's not talk about this anymore," Katrina interjected. "I hear what you're saying and I know these things. But forgiveness is a difficult road." She paused, taking a deep breath. "As for Zac, I'm not sure what has happened to him. He wasn't nice to me, but I still care. However, I doubt he'll change."

"So, are you just waiting for him to return?" I asked.

"Yes and no. Some of his mates came and checked on me last night. One made advances, but his mate intervened. I didn't like the look in his eyes. They're like waves on a shore. One recedes, but another's always coming. That's what frightens me the most. I think I need to save myself this time—before the tide takes me out."

"I agree," I said, "but you have friends to support you, too."

"Not really. I should've called you earlier, but I was too scared. Though I think he really is gone." Katrina paused, her voice heavy with uncertainty. "A stranger came with a parcel of food last week. That seemed peculiar, so I asked if he knew Zac. He said he was just a delivery boy and knew of no Zac."

Had Katrina's partner kept her living in a prison where she couldn't even fend for herself? Whoever had organised the parcel seemed to understand her situation. Recalling Jimmy's words about caring for women, I realised Jimmy must be behind all this.

Katrina continued, "There was a note with the package. It said they—whoever they are—understood my circumstances and weren't sure if my partner would be returning. How confusing is that?"

I tried not to dwell on the implications of those words. "He's probably on the run. His past has caught up with him."

"I thought so too. But waiting for him to return presents a problem. I have no money and need to pay rent soon, or I'll be evicted. Can you lend me some money?"

Her request caught me off guard. Initially, I'd thought she wanted to escape and had briefly considered inviting her to stay with me. I could make do on the couch for a while. But having her stay in such close quarters, despite my good intentions, could actually make her feel even more vulnerable.

I needed to redirect her focus towards the idea of leaving. "Do you think it's wise to stay there? What you said about his friends concerns me."

Katrina released a heavy sigh. "My mind is going around in circles. You're right, staying here wouldn't be the best option, but what can I do?"

"Aren't there safe houses or crisis centres that could help you?"

"I struggle with that concept, Quinn. What will people think of me?"

"They'll think you're strong, seeking your freedom."

"He would hunt me down."

"Not if he doesn't know where you are. Besides, he may well be interstate." I avoided mentioning the possibility of him being dead or in jail. I might be wrong there.

"There are only so many places to run to. He would find me." Her tone lightened. "Safe house, crisis centres—they're probably like funny farms. Crazy people running around."

A spark went off in my head. She had found the solution. The rehab centre in Edithburra. "You remember Bruce from Edithburra?"

"Yes, Bruce. Rose would call him her tower of strength."

"He runs a motel in Edithburra."

"That's right, Rose told me that. Are you suggesting I should go stay at his motel? Good thinking." She let out a sardonic laugh. "I'd be in the middle of nowhere, hard to find, and with no money."

Her financial dependence on her partner was clear. "We can worry about money later. I'd be happy to help you out."

There was a pause on the other end of the line, but I continued gently, "I'm going back to Edithburra tomorrow anyway. Why don't you come for a drive with me? We'll stay well away from your dad." The idea hadn't even crossed my mind until that moment. I hadn't planned to go but wanted to help Katrina, and I believed Bruce's wife could also be of help.

Katrina hesitated. "Oh. I'm not sure."

"I'd love to see you again and catch up on old times. Maybe we could go for a hike or something."

"Hmm."

I needed to push. "Okay, I'll be there at ten tomorrow morning."

"Um…do you know where I live?"

"Nope." I grabbed the pad and pencil near the phone.

"Um…it's Twelve Lavender Street…unit seven."

"Got it. I'll ring Rose to tell her about our visit. So, I'll see you at ten, okay?"

"Okay, then." She was still hesitant, but there was a hint of something else—a flicker of hope, perhaps?

"Pack your bags, as we may stay a while," I said, hoping to nudge her towards a decision.

"Not sure about that."

"Up to you. Pack whatever you need. Be ready at ten."

"Oh, alright." She sounded more excited. "A trip could be a good thing."

"Lovely, see you in the morning." I hung up, hoping——praying that she would take this step.

65 Breaking Free

Katrina's street was lined with mature trees, forming a thick canopy of branches and leaves overhead. It reminded me of Edithburra, of my journeys to school along the bush tracks and roads shaded by towering trees. Naturally, Edithburra was heavy on my mind, as we'd soon be heading that way.

Turning into Katrina's street, I half expected to see her waiting outside, a suitcase beside her.

There was no Katrina.

I pulled over and stepped out of the car. The quiet was almost unsettling. Most residents had headed off to work. The unit block had a façade of red bricks, with wrought-iron balconies facing the street. It had charm and character. Yet, the saying "Little did we know what went on behind closed doors" echoed in my mind.

Walking past the letterboxes, I noticed the building's main door ajar. Katrina was in unit seven. Climbing the stairs, I found the door to unit seven was open. A sense of unease prickled my skin. I took a cautious step inside and peered into the dimly lit living room. Katrina was sitting on a couch, her suitcase beside her. She jumped in surprise when she saw me.

She was dressed for the cooler weather in a denim skirt

with black leggings and a thick brown cardigan. She was lean and gave off an aura of vulnerability.

"Oh, Quinn, you're no longer the boy I remember." Her eyes were red-rimmed and puffy. She looked utterly drained. "Letting go is so hard. I don't understand. It feels like I'm trapped."

A lump formed in my throat as I walked over to her and offered her my hand. "It's okay, Katrina, we're just going on a trip. As they say, a change is as good as a holiday."

She forced a weak smile and reached for my hand. I helped her up, and for a moment she clung to me, her body wracked by sobs. Holding her until she calmed, I felt a pang in my chest. She looked me in the eyes and I saw a flicker of the young Katrina I'd once known.

She stepped back. Taking a deep, shaky breath, she reached down for her suitcase. I gestured that I'd take it. I was encouraged to see that she had packed up her things. I looked around the sparsely furnished unit. Bare walls and minimal belongings painted a picture of hardship. She was struggling. She needed to escape.

We drove off through the suburbs. As we chatted about our lives since we'd last seen each other, I could sense her nervousness. "Oh, to be young and free again." She sighed.

Exhaustion finally overtook her, and she drifted off to sleep. I stole a glance at her, wondering how much sleep she'd gotten recently. We were just outside Willward when her eyes fluttered open.

I smiled at her.

"Feel like a cuppa?" I asked.

She yawned and nodded. "Coffee would be great."

"Perfect. We're going to stop at a café and Jill's going to join us. Is that okay?"

"Jills! I'd love to see Jills." Her mood was already lifting.

***

After a refreshing coffee break, we continued our journey towards Edithburra, with Jill joining us. She sat next to me in the front, while Katrina quietly moved to the back seat. It might have been better for them both to be in the back seat, as they hadn't stopped talking since we'd started driving, and Jill might end up with a stiff neck from all the turning around.

Pulling into Bruce and Pam's motel's parking lot, I was surprised to find it deserted. Perhaps it was a combination of the off-season and it being a weekday. I followed Jill and Katrina up the path leading to the motel. I wondered if Jamie might be staying here again, and whether it would be good or bad for Katrina to see her brother. His desire to reconnect with their dad complicated things.

Bruce was most welcoming to Katrina and led us through the office and out to their living area. Pam greeted us warmly, giving Katrina an extra-long hug.

"Not long, and I'll soon have met the whole school," Pam said.

Bruce chuckled. "Actually, love, Katrina went to another school."

Pam waved her hand dismissively. "Oh, well. Nice to see old friends get together." She glanced at Katrina. "I think I may have seen you on our school bus. Long time ago, though." She gestured to the large couch. "Go sit."

While Pam went to prepare lunch, Bruce took Katrina for a walk around the motel. She seemed relaxed when they returned. "Lovely place," she said. "It's like a holiday. My secret hiding place."

Pam soon reappeared with a platter of fresh sandwiches and a steaming pot of tea. An easy conversation flowed between Pam and Katrina, punctuated by laughter. But then tears suddenly welled up in Katrina's eyes. Jill and I exchanged a worried glance. Pam gave us a gentle, knowing nod.

Jill and I excused ourselves. Bruce joined us as we wandered outside and settled into a covered picnic area overlooking a peaceful valley. Jill had slipped her arm through mine as we walked down. I gave it a reassuring squeeze, grateful for her support of Katrina.

A pang of jealousy had shot through me as I observed Jill and Katrina's effortless connection. I felt myself slipping into the background, but then I reminded myself of their close bond. It was an experience that made me more aware of the internal battles we all face within our minds.

"There's a vacant caretaker lodge at the rehab centre," Bruce said. "I think we could get Katrina settled there for the short term. I understand what she needs now is safe accommodation, not rehab, although there would also be access to counselling."

"Makes perfect sense to me," Jill said. "She may bump into her brothers who I'm sure will add that extra bit of protection."

"Healing for the whole family," I said.

Jill smiled, her usual optimism shining through. "I see a family reunion coming."

"What about their mum?" I asked, curious.

"In another relationship," Bruce said. "I understand why she left with the kids, though I wonder if her motives were more self-centred. But I know those circumstances can get quite complex."

"That's a bit tough, Bruce," Jill said.

"Yeah, probably," Bruce agreed. "Those situations are never easy, and the impact on the kids is always the worst part. Makes you wonder what could have been done differently."

"Hindsight is clear sight," I added.

"If only we had a time machine," Jill suggested playfully. "Imagine if we could see the consequences of our choices before we made them."

I heard voices behind us and we turned to see Pam and Katrina walking towards us, Rose in tow. It felt like a miracle. Katrina's face radiated a newfound glow, and a genuine smile played on her lips.

Rose greeted us all warmly, then turned to me with a mischievous twinkle in her eye. "Well done, Mr Kidnapper!"

Confused expressions surrounded us. Katrina and Rose burst into laughter.

"Just a private joke," Rose explained. "Quinn and I decided we needed to kidnap Katrina to get her here, but thankfully, it didn't come to that."

"What would the ransom have been?" Jill asked.

"Freedom," Katrina announced proudly. "Pam and I had a lovely chat, and jokingly we've decided to rename the rehab centre 'The Warhurst Centre'!"

Pam laughed. "Knowing that family members have been at the centre has given Katrina some much-needed encouragement. I'm already getting the accommodation arranged for tomorrow."

Katrina looked at us all and burst into tears. "Thank you," she said, her voice thick with emotion. "Thank you all for everything."

66 A Move to the Country

Winter drew to a close, although the call for "potbelly" warmth and heavy blankets lingered. I had started the new year working for a technology company but just couldn't get into it. Still restless, craving something different. So, I handed in my notice and embraced uncertainty. I rented a house in Edithburra for six months and made sure it had a potbelly stove. I brought Mum to stay a few times, but the sharp, chilly mountain air was not good for her.

Farm work provided an unexpected source of income as I settled into my new rural life. My generous redundancy payment from my previous long-term employment and savings provided a financial cushion as I contemplated my next move. The lower rent and generally lower cost of living in the country stretched my funds further than I'd expected.

Each day, I woke to the crisp country air and a cheerful chorus of birdsong from various species. I enjoyed the tranquillity of fewer people and less noise. The locals, their faces lined by weather and work but warm with kindness, showed remarkable patience as I fumbled through learning to be handy, their calloused hands guiding mine. Though I was still unsure about my future, there was a growing sense of peace in this simpler existence.

My friend Jimmy and his wife visited a few times. Jimmy, always a city boy, despite his love for country music and his own rendition of "Thank God I'm *Not* a Country Boy", found the wide-open spaces unsettling. "Too much space," he'd mutter, "although I did once pine to escape from the city."

When the conversation turned to more serious matters, Jimmy remained tight-lipped about what had happened to Katrina's ex, offering only a shrug when I asked. Noticing my concern, he tried to ease my dark thoughts. "Nothing bad happened," he assured me, his tone casual. "Just a person coming to his senses."

Jill became a regular visitor during those months in Edithburra.

An old-time reunion was planned for the first day of spring, now just a couple of days away. The Warhurst children were finally reconciling with their dad. My dear mother and their mother, Mrs Warhurst, were the only ones who would be absent—Mum because of the lingering cold, and Mrs Warhurst for reasons unknown.

I'd spent some time with Lance. He grappled with the weight of the past and was overwhelmed by the present. I was too, sometimes. Bringing Katrina back to him had been a gamble, but one that had paid off. She'd been visiting him regularly, a beautiful miracle unfolding before all of our eyes.

Lance's rifles, prominently displayed on the wall in his house, seemed to stand guard whenever I visited. It was a sign of the lengths he was now willing to go to in order to protect his daughter.

***

Reunion day arrived.

The dirt driveway came into view, faded letters on the once-dilapidated sign now gleaming with fresh paint. The sign had been secured; the loose bolt tightened. The towering rocket trees hadn't yet reached the moon. Slowing the car, I turned into the driveway.

The trees now fully obscured the massive shed. As the house came into view, figures emerged from the front door.

Lance was still tall and lanky, but his sons had grown tall too, though they lacked the cowboy moustache. Lance's hat was tilted, a detail that instantly transported me back years.

It was here that I'd first heard my dear mum being called 'Lizzie', though at the time, I thought Tom was calling her a lizard. Thankfully, my hearing—and my listening skills—improved over the years.

Jill and I emerged from the car and were greeted by Mr Warhurst. "Welcome, Mr Davies, Ms Toohey," he boomed, shaking my hand firmly before pulling Jill in for a hug. His children followed suit; their smiles were all genuine.

Katrina looked well. Her face, once drawn, was now full and healthy, her eyes sparkling with newfound life. She ushered us inside.

Stevie grabbed a piece of timber and opened the potbelly stove, throwing the wood in and jabbing at the embers with a long metal rod. I laughed.

He looked at me.

"I was so nervous when I first came here," I explained.

"You had that iron stick in your hand, and I thought you were going to poke me with it." I shrugged. "I don't know why."

"Just a nervous ten-year-old boy," Katrina said, gesturing towards the glass cabinet.

The cabinet, once a source of conflict, still held its collection of rocks and minerals. But something was different. A large gold cross now occupied the central space where the gold nugget used to sit prominently.

A hand touched my shoulder. Mr Warhurst's voice was gentle. "It's okay, Quinn. Remember what I told you? Faith is more important than gold." He winked. "Though, me and the boys still hold a fondness for gold and are getting back into prospecting. I'm sure you've heard the saying, 'There's gold in those hills'."

Chuckles rippled through the room. "And we're going to find it," Jamie said. "Why don't you join us sometime, Quinn?"

Jill's eyes lit up. "Great idea! Can I come too?"

"Of course," Jamie replied.

A framed photo on the shelf drew my attention. A smiling Lance held the gold nugget, the image made famous in the local paper. Finding that missing piece suddenly felt like completing a puzzle, a thought that had lingered in the back of my mind for years.

A clatter from the kitchen drew my attention. Bruce and Pam emerged, Pam carrying a tray piled high with fresh sandwiches. "Howdy, folks," Bruce said. "Eat up! But go easy as I hear a walk up to the big rock is happening later."

The big rock. A wave of nostalgia washed over me, memories of the time when we did the walk together as children. A mischievous thought surfaced: wouldn't it be something if the yowie appeared, nugget in hand? I quickly pushed the fantastical notion away, realising my mind might be a little too eager to solve the puzzle.

After lunch, we set out on the single-file track. As the track widened, Jill slipped her hand into mine. I squeezed it. "The sounds of the bush are no longer a mystery to me," I said. "Movement in thick shrubbery usually means rabbits or roos, not yowies."

"That's no fun, Quinn," Jill teased. "I still want to go yowie hunting with you one day."

The track steepened, and I gulped the fresh, cool air. Smaller boulders soon appeared, and we rested on the cool granite rocks like we did as kids so long ago.

"You remember me telling you the story of the yowie right here, Quinn?" Jamie asked.

"I'll never forget it, Jamie. Especially when Gavin made his grand 'yowie' entrance."

Jamie cupped his hands around his mouth and shouted, "Cooee!" He looked at us. "I just love the echo from that call."

Suddenly, a flurry of activity erupted near the bushes. Branches snapped, followed by a howling noise. My body tensed, then I laughed.

"It's not Gavin this time, Quinn," Jamie said. "He's away, working."

As my mind searched for a logical explanation, a dark shape emerged from the shadows, tall and imposing. A figure in a black, hooded cloak stepped past the bushes. We all stood.

"Relax, everyone," Jamie called out. "It's just the bushman."

The figure removed his hood, revealing a weathered, lined face with a mop of grey hair. He approached the smaller boulders and settled himself onto a nearby rock. "Did I scare ya?" he asked, his voice gruff but kind.

Jamie laughed, "Perfectly."

The bushman surveyed us all. "Lived most of my life out here," he said, his voice seasoned by time and experience. "Self-sufficient, with a bit of help from the kind folk at the farms nearby."

The air seemed to crackle. Everything felt surreal. This man, once shrouded in mystery—the yowie—now sat among us.

"Met this young fella years back," he continued, gesturing to Jamie. "Shared a love for the rocks, you see. We go prospecting together sometimes. Got a little hut, keeps me comfortable. Never quite fit back into society after the war and I've never found a gold nugget, but I'll keep looking." He laughed deeply.

A beat of silence followed. Was he implying that he didn't have Lance's nugget?

"Heard about the missing nugget from Jamie," the bushman continued, as if he'd read my mind. "Seems I was the prime suspect for a while. Not me, though. Never one to enter where I'm not welcome."

He stood and stretched, his movements slow and deliberate. "These old bones are complaining," he said before settling down again. "When he visited, Jamie would talk to me about life. We looked out for each other. As it was a special day today, we wanted to have some fun, and hopefully we did." He raised his eyebrows at all of us, as if looking for a response.

Jill clapped her hands. "We did!" She turned to us with a smile, gesturing for applause. We joined in with a few scattered claps. "A great performance," she said.

"And I believe that for this performance, I'll be fed." He grinned.

I warmed to the fellow.

The bushman looked up towards the hill. "I'll stay here while you wander up to the big rock. Pick me up on the way back."

Together with the others, I climbed the big rock. I sat down to take in the breathtaking view before me. Katrina settled beside me.

"Thank you, Quinn, for what you've done."

"What have I done?"

"You brought our family together."

Had I? My inner critic struggled with compliments. I knew it was tied in with my self-worth, but I was learning to accept them, just like I was adjusting to hugging. We are worthy of love and affection, Lee said.

When we returned from our walk, Mr Warhurst was sitting on the front porch, a picture of peaceful contentment. The absence of a rifle in his grasp suggested a familiarity with the bushman accompanying us.

I sat next to Lance while the others disappeared into the house. Katrina paused for a moment, then continued on, as if sensing the unspoken need for a private conversation. We sat in comfortable silence for a few moments.

"That's where my wife used to sit, Quinn," he said, his voice thick. "It would've been nice for her to be here, but I understand." He turned to me. "How is your mum?"

"She seems quite settled, though I think her memory might be fading."

"Could be a blessing—forgetting the bad memories and all that." There was a flicker of hurt in his eyes, barely concealed.

"Yeah. I think Mum just takes things in her stride, accepts them as 'such is life'."

"You ever read the book?" Lance asked.

"Huh?"

"*Such is Life*," he said. "An old Australian classic, stories of country folk from the old days. I think it also has something to do with Ned Kelly, his last words before they hanged him."

I reflected on the phrase. "I suppose it's a good way to put it. Helps you to accept things you can't change. I just use it offhand, never really thinking about it."

"Thank you for what you've done, Quinn," echoing Katrina's words, his voice catching on a sob. "There's a lot of healing happening here—mostly in my head. Sometimes it's hard to forgive myself. The memories, the guilt of it all. But you've helped. You've helped some of that heal."

"I've had my own battles too, Lance. We all have. It's like we're fighting an unseen war."

"Aye, I agree. That's why faith is important. We can't fight this battle alone."

I stood up and placed a hand on his shoulder, a silent gesture of understanding. "We will soldier on."

As if on cue, Lance added, "And faith is more important than gold."

Epilogue

The years have passed by. Jill's and my wedding, held at Edithburra, was a blissful event. Jimmy did well as the Best Man, and his rendition of "Thank God I'm *Not* a Country Boy" added a touch of humour to the celebration. I laughed softly, thinking about the kinds of events where he might have provided such entertainment.

A few local residents attended, including Bruce and Pam. Sadly, due to Mum's fading memory and the years without contact, she didn't recognise Tom, though I'm sure she would've been overjoyed to reconnect with him. It was the same for Mr Warhurst. Although he sat and talked with her for a while, she remained polite, though I thought I detected some flickers of past recognition there in her demeanour.

Meanwhile, Katrina was thriving, having found her own path. She was now living with her dad, which seemed to bring comfort and peace for both of them. Her new partner, a quiet pillar of strength, provided a sense of security.

As for Katrina's ex, Jimmy remained tight-lipped about the man's fate. What kind of deterrent had found him in the end remained a mystery, one that I knew still haunted Katrina's mind, though its sharp edges had softened with time.

Mum defied expectations and lived another ten years. Though her mind often wandered, confusion mingling with brief, joyful moments, she remained largely pain-free. Her sense of humour never faded. In the years leading up to her death, I visited her daily, a routine that became a comforting anchor for me as well.

One day, a compassionate nurse suggested I take a break, gently confiding that Mum might be holding on for my sake. I did as she suggested. Sadly, that was the day she slipped away.

The nurse said that some souls found solace in the embrace of loved ones in their final moments, while others, fiercely independent until the end, departed in solitude. As it turned out, Mum belonged to the latter category.

In the weeks after her death, I shifted into cleaning mode. Trips to the Salvos became a way to deal with years of accumulated objects. Each trip with bags of her clothing felt like a journey into the depths of her world. And hoarding, I realised, might run in the family.

Returning to Mum's unit after another Salvos run, I found Bella, one of Mum's many grandchildren, vigorously scrubbing down the kitchen cupboards. In the bedroom, Jill sat, seemingly overwhelmed by daunting piles of old magazines dragged out from under the bed: *Family Circle*, *New Idea*, *Woman's Day*. I pondered whether or not to ask Jimmy if there was a market for these old magazines.

Bella, who was close in age to Jill and me, wandered in, spotted the piles, and laughed. "No wonder we never saw them. They were all hidden under the bed."

Jill paused in rummaging under the bed and looked up at me, a glint of curiosity in her eyes. "There's a shoebox under here."

There's nothing odd about that, I thought as Jill dragged it out from its hiding place. We dusted off the top, and I slowly lifted the lid. I paused, puzzled by what I saw.

Letters, a testimony to Mum's past and maybe more secrets. But it wasn't the letters that caused my heart to pound with a mixture of disbelief and wonder. No, it was what lay atop them—two gleaming gold nuggets, one in the shape of a heart, the other resembling a blob of gum.

I was overcome by a tidal wave of confusion, grief, and a flicker of something else—I had found the missing piece of the jigsaw and would return it to Mr Warhurst.

Hands trembling, I picked up the first letter and gently unfolded it.

"Dearest Martha," I read aloud, the name unfamiliar to me. "Who's Martha?"

The question hung in the air.

I carefully opened another letter underneath the first, and then another. "Looks like they're all addressed to Martha."

Bella started crying. "Martha is your sister," she whispered, her voice choked with emotion. "She died as an infant. My mum told me about her—a family secret sort of thing. All these years, Nanna's been writing letters to her daughter. It must have been her way of coping with the grief."

Shock swept over me—another secret kept from me—but I pushed that thought away. A deep sadness for this unknown sibling and the pain my mother must have carried all her life curled through me. Layers upon layers of grief, all hidden beneath the surface. Why hadn't she sought help?

Silence descended upon us. A soft breeze rustled through the room, sending shivers down my spine. We gathered around my mother's bed, seeking solace in a shared hug.

But perhaps I'm neglecting to share the good things.

Jill and I wove tales for our children—stories of babies discovered in the cabbage patch or delivered by a stork—whimsical narratives that ignited their imaginations. But amidst these fanciful tales, we also shared stories infused with truth—truth rooted in love and connection.

And we sang lullabies, too. "Twinkle, Twinkle, Little Star" was their favourite.

One night, my youngest asked me, "Are stars people, Daddy? You know, if someone dies, do they become stars?"

I swallowed hard, wondering where he'd gotten such thoughts. "Maybe," I said. "But I know our loved ones who have passed away and believed in God have gone to heaven. And we're told heaven is up there." I nodded towards the ceiling. "So, our loved ones are looking down on us." I hugged all my children close. "Isn't it nice, even comforting, to think there are shiny stars twinkling, reminding us of God watching over us and our loved ones?"

Soft giggles and nods met my words.

They seemed happy with that response. But the truth would never be hidden from them.

There were no more secrets.

I got there in the end, Dad.

The Last Letter

Mum's letters had held a secret—a revelation that came to light at the end of her journey. The weight of this secret saddened me, for it spoke of burdens borne in silence for far too long. But she also carried regrets.

And thus, my story ends with a letter.

My dearest Martha,

Once again, it's been a long time since I put pen to paper. My arthritis has gotten worse, so writing is difficult. This will be a letter of few words and maybe my last.

My one regret remains. My one weakness was revenge, and now it saddens me that I had such a spiteful emotion alive in me. I can see now with the clarity that comes as death draws near that we all need to be set free from our infirmities. That may well be from the Good Book. This world has lost its way and I believe the Good Book tells us that.

Years ago, Quinn asked me if I had faith. I answered yes, but his question has made me dig deeper. Do I really? I needed to answer that in preparation for my journey to the next world.

I feel there are not many days left for me.

I'm not scared. I want death to hurry up and take me to be with you and my dear Harold. You left me at such a young age. A departure that I never recovered from. Your absence has left an ache in my heart that time has failed to heal. In writing these letters all these years, I've refrained from using 'Mum', trying to stay young at heart with you.

Those loved ones that remain will join the family in their time. As they live out their lives, I hope they find solace in the arms of faith. They will discover the gold nuggets that I've kept for all these years—nuggets that taught me faith is a treasure more precious than gold and reminded me of our capacity for both grace and spite, and of our need for forgiveness.

Until we meet again, in that hallowed place beyond the veil.

All my love,
Elizabeth, your dear Mother

Acknowledgements

I would like to extend my heartfelt thanks to the incredible team of editors and proofreaders whose expertise and dedication helped bring this story to life. Special thanks to J. J. Fischer and Kayley Heijnen, whose keen eyes and thoughtful guidance elevated the narrative and strengthened the heart of the book. I am also deeply grateful to Penny Bowden, Rob Filgate, Gareth Evans, and my darling wife (for many, many reads) for ensuring the words flowed seamlessly and the details were flawless.
Your support and meticulous attention to detail have been invaluable throughout this journey.

About the Author

Lacey Cook was born in South Australia and has been heading north via the east coast ever since, collecting life experiences along the way. He lives in Queensland.

Thank You for Reading!

I hope you enjoyed *Mother's Gold* and that it resonated with you in some way. Reviews play a vital role in helping authors like me reach new readers and continue to share stories that matter. If you have a moment, I'd be so grateful if you could leave a review on Amazon. Your thoughts not only make a difference to me but also help others discover this story.

Thank you for your support, and I look forward to sharing more with you in the future!

Visit **www.lacey-cook.com**

Printed in Dunstable, United Kingdom

64693893R00245